Books by Susan Quilty

Novels
The Insistence of Memory
To the Left of Death

The Psychic Traveler Society Series (Young Adult)
Healers and Thieves
Family and Foes

Short Fiction
Audrey and Esther Geekify Greenville
Freely Written Vol. 1

The Psychic Traveler Society
Book 2

Family

and

Foes

Susan Quilty

First printing, 2020

Cover Design: Susan Quilty
Publisher: Bitter Lily Books, LLC

Second edition, 2022

ISBN: 978-1-7379702-6-2
ISBN: 978-1-7379702-7-9

Bitter Lily Books, LLC
Ashburn, Virginia

SusanQuilty.com

Trust with
your heart

Question with
your mind

Chapter 1
A New World, A New Friend

The grass was green in Arcadia. The sky was blue, the clouds were white, and the river was a clear bluish gray. Across the water, needle-thin evergreens intermixed through an autumnal display of crimson, ginger, and amber foliage. Amanda Jones squinted in the direction of the single, yellow sun and smiled at its gentle warmth. If she kept her gaze away from the city skyline, she could almost imagine she was back on Earth.

There were differences, of course.

Despite being at the edge of Arcadia's largest city, the air was filled with floral, earthy scents instead of the faint blend of exhaust fumes and construction dust that lingered throughout Amanda's neighborhood. From every direction, birdsong filtered lightly through the air. It was a thin, silvery backdrop of sound that had gradually become as familiar and unremarkable to Amanda as the perpetual sound of passing traffic back home.

Another difference in Arcadia was the boy who sat beside her. If Amanda were sitting in the small park outside her apartment building, Drew would be by her side. Drew was Amanda's oldest friend. He was the person she turned to with her problems and fears, her thoughts and dreams. But Drew wasn't a psychic traveler. He couldn't follow Amanda to other worlds. He couldn't know how it felt to visit an imaginary house, as if in a daydream, and then be physically transported through one of its many doors.

Mitra wasn't a psychic traveler either, but he knew what it was like to be a child prodigy in a society of adults. He knew how it felt to be watched and evaluated.

They sat quietly on the back edge of an open hover cart and looked out across the flowing river. Their legs dangled above the ground, their shoes barely brushing the longest blades of grass. When the silence had lasted long enough to see two silvery-pink fish break through the surface of the water and splash back into their passing schools, Mitra let out a slow breath.

"This is not an official visit."

It wasn't a question, and Amanda didn't have to respond. If this had been an official visit, she wouldn't have come through the door alone. They both knew that.

"It's a... social visit?"

He sounded less sure, and Amanda's stomach flipped.

"I guess so," she answered vaguely without turning to face him.

"Okay." Mitra nodded, and there was a smile in his voice.

"Did you finish the last book I brought you?"

Amanda changed the subject as a third fish arced through the air. The fish were agitated today, which meant a storm was on its way.

"I did." Mitra frowned. "I left it in my room since I did not know I would be seeing you."

Amanda nodded but was sad to see his face cloud at the mention of the book. She hadn't meant to upset him.

"Your world is…" Mitra hesitated, allowing enough time for his silence to say a lot.

"It's okay," Amanda agreed with a shrug. "I know. And it's not like I made it that way."

Mitra turned to fully face her, and his icy blue eyes pierced deep. Amanda wanted to look away, but her gaze felt trapped by the thrill of feelings that came up when he looked at her like that.

"You couldn't." Mitra's voice was steady, yet soft around the edges. "You are too good, too kind to create the kind of… *discord* I see in your world."

"Discord?" Amanda repeated the word, stuck on an earlier part of the sentence.

"There is so much conflict," Mitra continued hoarsely, as if in physical pain at the thought. "There is so much oppression for the benefit of so few, and for such incomprehensible reasons."

His eyes darkened and Amanda looked away.

"It's no Arcadia," she responded weakly, glancing back toward the city of glass towers.

She could see dark clouds gathering in the distance.

"Arcadia started with an advantage." Mitra's expression softened as he added, "Thanks to you."

"Well, not *me*." Amanda looked down at her hands.

"Your people then," Mitra amended. Though she thought he sounded less reverent, less sure of her people's greatness than he'd been when they first met.

My fault, Amanda thought to herself. *I did that to him. I changed him.*

She wasn't sure she'd done the right thing, but he'd wanted to know. And she'd wanted to give him the truth.

The High Council had sent Amanda to Arcadia to deepen their relationship with the Arcadians, who used a form of psychic energy to interact with some of their technology. The Arcadians were fascinated by Amanda's potential to become a psychic architect—the first psychic architect in nearly 100 years—and seemed to think her mind would show unique abilities. They paired her with Mitra, a teenaged genius who had become the youngest Arcadian scientist in the upper ranks of his field. Yet, after weeks of visits, Amanda hadn't shown progress with even the simplest of their light-based energy games.

Sensing her frustration, their schedule had shifted to include time outside of the lab. Mitra was tasked with showing Amanda the city and answering her questions about their world. Since he was also curious about her people—whom the Arcadians respectfully called the Maiorum—Amanda was given permission to bring Mitra novels from a list approved by Director Alvarsson.

Over time, she became daring, sneaking in historical fiction that offered a grittier view of her world. It had seemed like a small rebellion, a chance to show Mitra a more realistic picture of the world he'd longed to visit.

"Before we became friends, I saw the Maiorum as a venerable culture, richer for its links to an ancient past," Mitra sighed. "And now…"

"I'm sorry I ruined that for you," Amanda kicked at the soft grass, causing the hover cart to rock gently. She hadn't liked the idea of lying to keep up the sanitized image of Earth the Arcadians had been given. But she also felt bad about changing the way Mitra saw her world.

Mitra reached over to rest his hand on top of hers.

"I am not sorry."

She could feel the weight of his gaze without looking up. It felt good to share something secret—something true— between them alone.

Mitra gently squeezed Amanda's hand, drawing her attention back to his clear blue eyes.

"The more I understand your world, the easier it is for me to be your friend." He spoke with an open smile, before letting his lips soften and his eyes sparkle in that deep, promising way. "And I want to be your friend."

"I—" Amanda stuttered, feeling a blush spread over her cheeks.

"Stop! Stop where you are!"

Amanda wrenched her hand from Mitra's grasp. Turning toward the commotion across the river, she saw a woman stumbling out of the forest with uniformed guards close on her heels. She wore tattered clothes, and her curly hair was slipping free from a disheveled braid. She looked wild. Terrified.

The hover cart rocked unevenly as Amanda jumped to her feet and rushed closer to the water. There was no bridge, though she could have easily waded across the short, shallow distance. Her feet were wet before she felt Mitra pulling her back.

"It's okay," he said urgently, leaning close to Amanda's ear. "It's okay."

But it didn't look okay to Amanda.

The woman was nearly at the river's edge when she tripped and fell to her hands and knees. Long grass rose up past her elbows. Her braid fell over her shoulder, hanging alongside her jaw. The guards were right behind her. They reached for her waist as she looked up and reached one hand toward the pair of teenagers. Her eyes locked on Amanda. She reached out with both arms as the guards hauled her to her feet. Mitra tightened his grip on Amanda's upper arms, keeping the two women apart.

"It's okay," Mitra repeated soothingly. "They are here to help her."

"Help her?"

Amanda watched helplessly as one of the guards injected something into the base of the woman's neck. Her eyes widened, dimmed, then closed. Her whole body went limp in the guards' arms. A third guard had appeared in a hover cart, gliding over from somewhere upriver. They gingerly loaded the woman onto the cart, using care to not bump her head or let her arms fall loose. Amanda hoped their gentle touch meant the woman would be okay. That she would wake up.

While two of the guards fussed over the woman's arrangement in the cart, the third turned to face Mitra and Amanda. He studied them blankly.

Mitra tugged at Amanda's arms, urging her back onto the dry grass. Her socks squelched in her soaked shoes. She tried to hold the guard's gaze with the same intensity she'd seen in the eyes of the terrified woman, but he broke their connection with a friendly wave and an easy smile.

"It's okay!" he called over, unknowingly repeating Mitra's words. "We can help her now."

"Thank you." Mitra waved back with a wide smile of his own. "I am glad you found her!"

Amanda looked between them, her mouth dropping open in surprise.

As she watched, the guard joined the others in their hover cart. He waved one more time in parting, and they swiftly drove away.

"This is not your world," Mitra reminded before Amanda could say another word. "People are not taken off to be jailed or tortured. We help people here."

Amanda shook her head, trying to clear away the sight of the scared woman reaching for her help. She looked down at her wet feet and wiggled her toes against the soggy canvas of her shoes. There was a chill in the air, a thin breeze that warned her the storm was drawing closer.

"Do you know her?" Amanda watched Mitra's eyes, not sure what she expected to see in them.

"Yes," he answered sadly. "Well, not personally. But I know who she is. A public alert was issued yesterday. She and her family were in a serious accident and have been in our recovery center. Her treatment has been difficult, and she recently disappeared. Her doctors have been looking for her."

"To help her?"

Mitra's story had brought a tremble of anxiety to Amanda's chest. Or maybe it was the way he'd summed it up so calmly. *But he didn't know them*, Amanda reminded herself. He wasn't personally affected by their accident, and he was confident that the woman was going to be helped. There was no reason for him to feel as unsettled as she did about the experience.

"Does this happen a lot?"

Mitra was about to answer when his attention was caught by an approaching hover cart. Amanda's heart skipped. At first glance, she thought it was the guards returning to round them up, too. But this hover cart was approaching from the city, and it held only one person.

Rory.

Amanda released a shaky breath. Dark clouds were now crowding ominously over the city, lit briefly by a flash of blue lightning.

Rory looked angry and Amanda knew why.

"You are supposed to tell us before traveling off-world," Rory snapped as she slowed to park beside Mitra's hover cart. Amanda shrugged to hide her quaking stomach.

"I told the guards at the checkpoint," she answered flippantly. "They're quick enough to report where I am."

"Amanda," Rory warned with a tilt of her head. There was no need to finish the lecture. Amanda had heard it before, and Rory was tired of giving it. Still, Amanda felt bad for Rory. As her training agent, Rory would be reprimanded for this. Just another thing that wasn't fair about the PTS training program, as far as Amanda was concerned.

"I'm sorry," Amanda mumbled, "for getting you in trouble."

Rory's anger faded as she gave an exasperated shrug.

"Part of this job, apparently."

Amanda bit her lip, annoyed they had sent Rory to fetch her when it was supposed to have been a day off for both of them.

"Hi, Rory." Mitra broke the awkward silence, bringing a reluctant smile to Rory's face.

"Hi, Mitra."

Even Rory had a hard time resisting Mitra's charm.

With the storm building, there was no time to stand around talking. They headed toward the city with Amanda riding in Rory's hover cart and Mitra driving home alone.

Amanda had wanted Mitra to answer her last question, about how often missing people were rounded up by Arcadian guards, but she hadn't wanted to raise the subject in front of Rory. It would only lead to more questions and maybe lead back to the books she'd brought Mitra.

"I know you like him," Rory began, as their cart skimmed the surface of the grass, "but meeting a boy isn't worth all this trouble."

Amanda clenched her lips and gripped the bar at the front of the cart.

"I don't *like* him," she insisted grimly. "We're just friends."

"Uh, huh." Rory shook her head and pressed a button on the control panel to adjust their speed.

"We are!" Amanda pushed back, mostly sure she was telling the truth. "He's one of the few people my age who gets what my life is like now. Drew can't really understand. Trina doesn't even know. And it's not like there are any travelers to talk to."

"You can talk to me." Rory sounded strained, as if making the offer was already asking a lot. Amanda gripped the bar harder, bothered by that reluctant tone more than she wanted to admit.

"No *young* travelers," she clarified. Instead of saying: *But you don't like me.*

"Gee, thanks," Rory retorted.

The distant buildings loomed tall as they neared a smaller, domed structure at the edge of the city. It was the gatehouse where a psychic door would take Amanda and Rory home. Or rather, it contained a *proximity zone* where a door would appear.

Mitra split off toward another part of the city with one last, smiling wave.

"I'm twenty-four," Rory volunteered as she parked the hover cart in an empty bay.

"What?"

"I'm twenty-four," Rory repeated. "Not that you've bothered to ask. And twenty-four is not old."

"It's old to me," Amanda answered automatically, then raised her hands in apology at the look on Rory's face. "I mean, that's like nine years older than me!"

"Uh-huh." Rory punched a button to power down the hover cart. She walked into the building, not waiting to see if Amanda was following.

When they entered the gatehouse, Amanda scanned her surroundings. There was a mix of Arcadian and PTS guards manning the checkpoint at the main entrance. Amanda recognized the PTS guards by sight, though she didn't know their names. Their expressions said they knew all about her. Those stares used to bother her, before she'd gotten used to standing out as the only teenaged traveler.

The main room within the gatehouse was a fairly large, mostly empty space. There were smaller private rooms along the back wall, each with a solid door that had a slit window around eye-height. There was an Arcadian scanner to walk through—which detected any tech that might be concealed—and a table where both Arcadian and PTS guards could inspect items that were being carried through. A thread of guilt twisted through Amanda's gut as she remembered bringing banned books to that table and being pleased when no one had checked whether the covers matched the books inside.

Before they could pass the scanner, Amanda and Rory first had to return their translator discs at the long counter on the other side of the room. They were borrowed Arcadian tech that had to be checked out, and checked back in, during each visit.

"Leaving already?" an Arcadian guard asked Rory as they approached the counter.

"Quick trip," Rory answered shortly, already reaching into her hair to unclip the small device from the left side of her head, just above and behind her ear.

"Will you need anything else?" The guard rushed to ask while she could still be understood.

"No." Rory shook her head, pulled off the disc, and passed it across the smooth white countertop.

"Thank you," Amanda added, turning in her own translator.

The guard smiled and nodded before silently gesturing them toward the scanner. Lke all Arcadians, she had an implanted translator that would let her understand whatever else Amanda and Rory might say, but Arcadians considered it rude to speak to off-world guests when they were not wearing translator discs.

Walking to the scanner, Amanda wished she could bring a translator disc home with her or even have the tech implanted. Being able to automatically understand other languages felt like a superpower. She knew that was the kind of technology PTS wanted from the Arcadians—if she were able to improve their relationship.

"We'll use a private room," Rory told the PTS guard on the far side of the scanner.

He nodded and wished them a good day, but his look said he knew Amanda was in for trouble once she got home from this unauthorized adventure.

If she really wanted to, Amanda could conjure a door in the open space they were crossing, step through to the house, and wake up in her own bedroom before Rory could stop her. But she didn't want to be in *that* much trouble. Whatever talk Rory had in mind was inevitable, so she might as well get on with it.

The private room was empty.

After Rory closed the physical door behind them, a virtual door appeared in the center of the room. Once they walked through that proximal door, their physical bodies would stay in this private room while their minds entered the house—the shared mindspace psychic travelers used to meet and cross into other worlds. As soon as they woke up from the house—or used another door inside it to go to a different world—their bodies would be transported out of Arcadia.

Using a private room wasn't necessary, but it meant their bodies wouldn't be standing frozen in the middle of the gatehouse the whole time they were in the house.

"Wait." Rory turned to Amanda, stopping her from moving toward the door. "You know I'm not here to be your chaperone because of Mitra, right?"

"Uh, yeah." Amanda studied her fingers, scraping at a loose hangnail.

A heavy silence stretched between them.

"Just because he hasn't shown up in months doesn't mean he won't at some point."

"I know."

Amanda knew which *he* Rory meant, even if she'd begun to doubt she'd ever see him again.

Rory frowned.

"Okay," she eventually sighed, letting it go. She then stepped through the hazy door, leaving Amanda to follow behind.

§

"We're taking your mom to brunch in the morning." Judy stood stiffly beside Amanda's bed, where Amanda sat reading a book. Her eyes looked tired behind her black-rimmed glasses, and Amanda regretted making life harder for her aunt.

"For Mother's Day," she added when Amanda didn't respond.

"I know." Amanda closed her book, setting it on the bed beside her. It was the first time she'd been alone with her aunt since returning from Arcadia, and she didn't know what to say.

"Okay, then." Judy clapped her hands together and turned to leave.

"Wait," Amanda called impulsively. She couldn't let Judy just walk away.

When Rory and Amanda has stepped through the door from Arcadia, Judy had been waiting for them in the large Victorian house. Amanda was surprised to see her there. Rory was not.

Judy was more than Amanda's aunt. She was a PTS counselor who transitioned new psychic travelers into a world they'd never suspected before their powers emerged. She had explained the world of psychic travel to Amanda, showing up at a time when Amanda's new powers had her questioning her own sanity. She'd moved Amanda and her mom into her own apartment, and with the help of PTS' vast resources, she'd found Amanda's mom a new job as an office manager at a small web design company.

Amanda knew she owed her aunt better treatment than she'd been giving her.

"I'm waiting," Judy reminded. She stood with her back toward Amanda. Though she'd turned her head just enough to see her niece in her peripheral vision.

Amanda studied Judy's profile. Her dark hair was woven into a thick French braid, making it easier to see the blue streaks that ran through it. She wore multiple earrings and had a small tattoo behind her ear.

Amanda had always looked up to her aunt. She'd wanted to be just like her, with her sarcastic humor and her rock-star style, though she'd never felt cool enough to pull off either. When she'd found out they shared these psychic abilities, Amanda had thought it was finally happening. She was on her way to being just like Aunt Judy. But somehow, over the last several months, it had only gotten harder to talk to her aunt.

Amanda replayed their meeting in the house.

Rory had left them alone, fading out of sight, and Judy had led Amanda out the front door and into the jumbled grounds of the mindspace.

"All of these houses," Judy had said slowly, as their eyes drifted across the crazy patchwork of town and country, desert and jungle, that spread before them. "Each built by psychic architects to create doors to new worlds."

Crossing her arms over her chest, Amanda looked away. The houses no longer impressed her.

When her psychic abilities had first emerged, she'd thought there was only one house: the large Victorian home she'd been daydreaming about for as long as she could remember. Judy had told her it was nicknamed *the birdhouse* but had never said the nickname was to set it apart from other mindspace houses.

When Amanda had finally learned about the others— stunning houses spanning a wide range of cultures and time periods—she had wandered through each one. Room by room. She'd learned their histories and read about the architects who had built them. She'd learned the nicknames travelers had given some of the houses, too. Though those names weren't listed in the official PTS textbooks.

The birdhouse, the castle, the temple, the lair.

"You may build one someday," Judy had continued. Then added more sternly, "but you haven't built one yet."

Their argument had spiraled from there. Judy had called out Amanda's bad attitude. Amanda had said she was being treated like a child.

"You *are* a child!" Judy had exclaimed in frustration.

"A child who created a psychic doorway," Amanda had retorted angrily.

"Accidentally." Judy's reminder had silenced Amanda.

It was true, and Amanda knew it. She may have created a new door from the birdhouse to Terra-V, but she had no idea how she had done it or if she would ever be able to do it again.

Judy had then softened her approach.

"I'm not diminishing your potential or the amazing thing you did last fall. But that wasn't something you intended to do. It wasn't skill. It was a fluke of your developing powers. Something your mind did on its own when you were facing an enormous amount of stress. It's not something you know how to control. Yet."

She had tacked on the *yet* as an afterthought.

Amanda had blinked back hot tears.

"Yeah, but no one is teaching me that. I'm being taught baby stuff. How to send psychic messages, how to carry objects. All that stuff you already taught me before I ever went to Terra-V."

Judy had tried to soothe her, saying that the formal training was important and something Amanda needed to do, just like any other new traveler.

"But I'm not *any other* new traveler," Amanda had insisted. Which had only led to an argument over whether Amanda thought she was above the PTS training program, the experience of Director Alvarsson, and even the wisdom of the High Council.

Here in her room, with Judy waiting by the door, Amanda flushed at the memory of saying that maybe she *was* better than all of them—better than Aunt Judy even—and that they were holding her back because they didn't want a *child* to be better than them.

In the hours since their fight, Amanda had come to regret nearly everything she'd said.

"I'm sorry," she mumbled quietly. The words felt too small to hold all of the feelings welling up inside her, but they were the only words she had to say.

Judy sighed. Her shoulders lifted and drooped. Her chin fell toward her chest. It was as if her whole body was letting go. After a pause, she crossed the room to sit on the end of Amanda's bed.

"Today didn't go very well, did it?"

"Not really," Amanda agreed.

"We're not keeping things from you," Judy repeated. "We're putting you through the normal training process because there's a lot to learn, and we want you to have a strong foundation before we encourage your special skills.

"But you're also doing things that other new travelers aren't allowed to do. Like, working with the Arcadians."

"I know," Amanda muttered. She didn't add that she was only there as a bargaining chip for the High Council, or that she'd already failed the Arcadian's energy games.

"Yet you've been skipping training classes, blowing off assignments, and now traveling to see Mitra without a word to anyone. That's awfully childish behavior for someone who doesn't want to be treated like a child."

Amanda tightened her arms around her ribcage. She'd never been the type to cut classes or break rules, and she wasn't entirely sure why she was doing it now.

"I'm sorry," she repeated weakly.

Judy tilted her head and smiled, perhaps to take away the sting of her next words.

"Don't be sorry, be better."

Amanda pressed her lips together and nodded. Though she didn't know if she *could* be better. And, if she were being honest, she didn't feel all that inclined to change her ways.

CHAPTER 2
CLASSES AFTER CLASSES

Spring in Virginia meant P.E. classes moving outside for track and field events. Most of the students loved it, but Amanda had never seen the appeal. The change of scenery hadn't made her suddenly enjoy running, jumping, and all those other feats of coordination that had eluded her year after year. It was still a P.E. class, even if they were outside.

This spring, however, something was different.

When they'd been indoors all winter, playing volleyball and basketball, Amanda had felt as awkward as ever. She'd served the volleyball backward more often than not, and she never could manage to both dribble and run at the same time. Yet, here on the track, without a ball to worry about, she began to notice some changes. Her legs felt more stable as they carried her forward, her breath flowed without strain, and her core felt lifted and powerful.

Running itself wasn't part of Amanda's PTS training, but physical skills were included at specialized PTS facilities around the world. She'd practiced fencing in France, horse-back riding in Brazil, and archery in China. More recently, she'd traveled to India for lessons on yoga, meditation, and focused breathing techniques.

Now, as her body moved with confidence, Amanda marveled at how much stronger she'd gotten. She won her turn at the 100-meter dash and helped her team come in second during the relay races. Without the stress of remembering the rules to games she didn't like, Amanda found herself actually enjoying a gym class.

She'd never felt this way in middle school. Whenever they'd had to run, Amanda and Trina had lagged behind, alternating walking with short stretches of a shuffling jog. They'd always gotten in trouble for chatting their way around the track. But now, when they lined up to run one mile, Amanda found a place along the front row, curious to see how her legs and lungs would hold up on a longer run.

The starting pistol fired, and the fastest runners darted across the line. Amanda held back, afraid of burning out after a short stretch. Before long, the fast starters slowed, gradually moving Amanda toward the front ranks. She resisted the urge to push faster and focused on the reverberating feel of placing one foot in front of the other, step after step. The continued movement reminded Amanda of riding through Terra-V, and she smiled at the memory of Iveryn, her feathered horse.

As she rounded her third lap, Amanda's steady pace caught her up with those straggling at the end of the pack. Trina was the farthest behind. She walked with one hand resting on her chest and her gaze on the dusty ground.

"Are you okay?" Amanda slowed to a walk, watching other runners pass her by with some annoyance.

"Uh, huh," Trina huffed shortly, her feet barely lifting with each step.

"Hey!" Amanda leaned to peer at Trina's face, worried by her flushed cheeks and pinched expression.

"Stop." Trina shied away from Amanda, staggering to one side. "I'm fine."

But she didn't resist when Amanda steered her off the track and began waving for a teacher.

"Where's your inhaler?"

Trina bent over, pressing her palms against her thighs, and tried to shrug. There was a distinctive wheezing sound as she fought to draw in a deeper breath.

"Trina?" Mr. Meyers trotted beside them and placed one hand lightly on Trina's back. "Where's your inhaler?"

Trina was supposed to carry an inhaler for asthma, but the pockets of her gym shorts looked flat and empty against her thighs.

"Locker," she gasped with effort as kids continued to trudge by, each one staring their way as they passed. "Gym locker."

"Damn," Mr. Meyers muttered, waving toward another teacher for help.

"I'll get it," Amanda volunteered, sprinting away.

"Amanda, wait!"

"It's okay," Amanda called without looking back. "I know her combination!"

She crossed the field at top speed, feeling the strain in her own lungs by the time she'd wrenched open the school door and darted across the gym to the girls' locker room. Her heart thudded in her ears as she spun the dial on Trina's lock, pausing to remember the code she'd helped Trina memorize during their first week of school. She expected to see the inhaler sitting beside Trina's clothes, but it wasn't in sight. A search of her purse came up empty as well.

Amanda unzipped each pocket on Trina's backpack, frantically aware of the time passing. She rifled through odds and ends, then pulled out a stack of loose papers, before finally seeing the familiar red case. She'd just slammed the locker shut with a quick spin of the lock's dial when Maisie Sanders calmly strolled in.

"Meyers sent me to get you." She glanced around dully, oblivious to Amanda's panic.

"Why? Is Trina—"

"She's fine," Maisie shrugged. "I mean, I guess. They called for the nurse and he brought Trina another inhaler. I guess she keeps one there, too, or something."

"Oh." Amanda felt her shoulders drop as a wave of jittery energy flooded her limbs. She knew that. Trina carried an inhaler and kept a back-up in the nurse's office.

Looking down at the inhaler in her hand, Amanda noticed a folded, pink paper lying on the floor.

"Meyers said to bring her inhaler to the nurse's office, then come back outside. Want me to come with?"

"Uh, no thanks." Amanda shook her head, then casually picked up the paper on the floor, tucking it quickly into her pocket.

"Whatever." Maisie shrugged and went back out through the door to the gym.

Once Amanda wound her way to the nurse's office, she was relieved to see Trina sitting up and breathing easily. Their friendship had become strained when Trina started dating Drew and even more complicated after they broke up, though Amanda had tried not to take sides.

"Hey," Amanda greeted from the doorway.

"Hey." Trina offered a weak smile before looking back at the floor.

"Here to check on the patient?" Mr. Woods, the school nurse, asked in his bright, loud voice.

"Yeah, I brought her inhaler." Amanda held out the device for them to see. "I mean, the one from her locker. To, uh, carry."

"Ah, the poor, neglected inhaler that got left behind." Mr. Woods took the inhaler and held it up to his ear. "What's that, little guy? You're sad you missed all the action? I know, you get carried around day after day, ignored, and then when something finally happens you get upstaged by that back-up guy who lives in my clinic. I agree. It's not fair."

He passed the inhaler to Trina with a shake of his head.

"Poor little guy just wants to be a hero when you need it, but instead he gets stashed away in a dark, lonely locker. It's so unfair. Now, he's going to give you another chance, but you've got to promise to keep him with you, okay?"

"Yeah, yeah," Trina smirked, annoyed but trying not to laugh.

Mr. Woods had that effect on people.

"All right, cool. You and that little guy are besties, then. Where you go, he goes." He turned to Amanda, adding, "You are friend number two now. No complaints. Got it?"

"Got it," Amanda agreed, feeling a twist in her gut.

"Great. Sit with her for a bit while I run to the main office, then I'll clear you to head back to class."

Alone in the clinic, Amanda stood awkwardly while Trina stretched out on the narrow patient bed. It was one of those padded, table-like cots with an adjustable back that had been lifted to prop Trina in a seated position. Mr. Woods' talking inhaler schtick had been meant to ease the tension, but the idea of friend rankings troubled Amanda. *Where did she rank among Trina's friends? Where did Trina rank among her friends, now that her world had expanded so unexpectedly?*

"I didn't mean to leave it."

Trina turned the inhaler in her hands, over and over.

"I know." Amanda shrugged, thinking that was obvious.

"I wasn't looking for attention or anything."

"I didn't think you were."

"Yeah, okay."

Trina tucked the inhaler in the pocket of her gym shorts and stared at the poster of a human skeleton hanging on the opposite wall. Smaller posters showed healthy food groups stacked in a pyramid, simple exercises, hygiene tips for changing bodies, and anti-bullying cartoons.

"You can go now," Trina added, without looking at Amanda. "You don't have to wait for me."

"I don't mind," Amanda answered, edging closer to the clinic's second cot. "I mean, I want to wait with you."

"Whatever." Trina leaned to look out the doorway where there was no sign of the nurse returning. "It seemed like you'd rather be out there. Running."

"Oh, uh." Amanda shrugged. "Not really. I just, I don't know, just had some energy to burn today. I guess."

"Yeah, okay."

The awkward silence returned as Trina took a full, slow breath.

Amanda slid her hands into her pockets and felt the forgotten piece of paper.

"Oh, here." She pulled the pink paper out and handed it to Trina. "This fell out of your bag while I was getting your inhaler."

Trina's face flushed.

"And you think it's stupid, right? Especially now?"

Her anger surprised Amanda.

"What? No! I mean, I don't know what it is. I didn't open it."

"Oh." Trina began to stuff the folded paper into her empty pocket, but then pulled it back out. She looked down at the paper for several seconds before holding it out toward Amanda.

"Go ahead." She waved it impatiently. "Tell me how stupid I'm being."

Amanda unfolded the paper, keenly aware of any reaction that might cross her face.

It was a flyer about an interest meeting for cheerleading tryouts. It showed several pictures of the school's current cheerleaders standing together with their arms casually thrown around each other's shoulders or waists. They were laughing and smiling as if they owned all the happiness in the world.

"You want to be a cheerleader?"

Amanda's voice was neutral, but Trina huffed and pulled the paper back.

"It's stupid. I know. I'm not even going. It was just a stupid idea."

"It's not stupid," Amanda cut in. "Why would it be stupid?"

"Well, *you* would think it's stupid."

Amanda pulled back, stung. She saw the challenge in Trina's eyes, but she also saw something else. Fear? She repeated that it wasn't stupid, but Trina went on.

"Not just cheering. You think everything around here is stupid. The whole teenage, high school thing. But not all of us are too cool for this school. Some of us actually *want* to be a part of it."

"I'm not too cool for… cheering… or school… or whatever."

"Please. You rush home every day. You haven't gone to a single dance. You haven't been to a game in months." Trina ticked each item on her fingers. "You had a chance at that writing contest. Did you even try for it? No."

"That's not—" Amanda stumbled, knowing Director Alvarsson and the High Council had made her drop out of the writing contest but unable to explain that to Trina.

"Whatever. It's fine. You just don't have to mock those of us who do want to… to be involved."

"Who's mocking?" Amanda sat on the empty bed beside Trina with a flush of heat spreading across her cheeks and chest. Trina bit her lip and looked down at her perfectly manicured fingernails. Nothing had been the same between them since starting high school.

"Maybe I'll try out with you."

Amanda's words surprised them both, but she kept talking.

"I mean, it's a sport that doesn't involve catching, or throwing, or dribbling a ball. So, it has that going for it, right?"

Trina blinked at Amanda as a mix of emotions played over her face. Confusion, hope, fear.

"Come on, we haven't done anything together like this in ages!"

Amanda spoke with genuine excitement as the idea took root. She could run now. She could ride a horse and shoot an arrow. Why not try cheerleading?

"Remember the karaoke club in fifth grade?" She went on. "The hip-hop dance lessons?"

A wary grin spread across Trina's face.

"We were so bad at that."

"We're older now," Amanda reassured her, as if that made all the difference. "When are try-outs? July? That's plenty of time to practice and be awesome."

Trina sat up straighter, tentatively telling Amanda about a beginner's gymnastics class they could take once school ended. Amanda agreed to the classes, even as her smile slowly froze in place.

A voice inside began questioning whether this was the best time to add *another* commitment to her life. Her PTS teachers would not be happy about working around a cheerleading schedule. They didn't like working around her school schedule already. But they'd figure it out, Amanda decided.

Besides, she didn't have to tell them yet, and, until she did, she would take Aunt Judy's advice and change her attitude. No more missed training. No more skipping off to see Mitra without permission. She would be a model traveler and prove that she could handle it all.

§

The PTS headquarters building in Chicago was an impressive structure. From the outside, its Art Deco construction marked it among the city's oldest skyscrapers. Beyond its spacious public lobby, guarded doors concealed a massive travelers' entry hall that gleamed with white marble and gilded touches. Large, potted trees dotted the open space, while sunlight filtered through opaque windows to cast the polished atrium in a soft, almost enchanting warmth.

On Amanda's first visit, she'd been as awed by the building as she'd been by the many travelers casually arriving and disappearing through a scattered field of proximity doors. Now, she arrived with as little care for her surroundings as the other travelers who had regular business in the building. In the rare moment when she did pause to admire the shine of the carved mahogany doors or a particularly pretty vein of marble, she felt a strange loss for the sense of wonder that had faded into the familiar.

Hurrying through the travelers' entry hall, Amanda walked by two guards into the building's public foyer. The glass entry doors in this much smaller space opened onto a busy sidewalk where passersby had no idea what went on in buildings baring the PTS logo. Even that glimpse of the busy Chicago street had ceased to impress Amanda. It didn't matter if she was at a PTS facility in Chicago, Paris, or Cairo. Her training was largely kept indoors, and the quick trip to get to each place tricked her brain into forgetting her actual distance from home.

Even if Amanda had wanted to pause and mull over how *normal* her strange new life had become, she didn't have the time. She was late for training. Again.

As she stepped off the elevator on the fifth floor, Amanda did hesitate briefly. The left side of this floor led to the training rooms where she'd taken a few self-defense classes. The hall to the right led to the classroom where she was supposed to be working with other new travelers on the art of sending psychic messages through the house. It was a skill Amanda had already mastered, but PTS guidelines required her to complete the classwork under the guidance of an official PTS teacher.

According to Director Alvarsson, Amanda's experiences during her off-world mission to Terra-V did not count toward her official training. The director was responsible for planning her training and he wasn't interested in what she thought of the program he'd designed.

She turned to the right just as a shout from the other direction caught her attention. It was a shout she recognized but hadn't expected to hear today.

Amanda crept toward one of the gyms, where the door had been left ajar, and peeked inside to see Rory battling three men who were larger than her in both height and weight. The brutal sight startled Amanda. She nearly ran in to help, before noticing the padded floor and the trainer standing nearby with a whistle in his mouth and an alert eye following the action.

Rory was smaller than the men, but she was more agile. She wove between them, knocking them off balance with lightning-fast forearm and elbow strikes. Amanda watched Rory disentangle herself from the center of the group, use a powerful kick to shove the closest man sprawling into another, and then jump onto the back of the remaining man, taking him down to his hands and knees with her arm wrapped around his throat. The whistle blew and Rory sprung away, shaking her hands and exhaling in rapid gusts.

"Well done, Lou," the trainer called over, while her opponents helped each other up.

The man she'd had in a chokehold was rubbing his neck but grinning in admiration. Rory nodded with a small smile of her own, then shook her head.

"Took me too long, though. Taylor nearly had me for a minute there."

"Yeah, yeah." One of the men shook his head and grinned. "Humble doesn't suit you, Lou."

Rory rolled her shoulders a few times and stretched her arms overhead.

"So, no rematch?"

The men laughed and the trainer made some notes on his clipboard. Amanda was hoping they'd go again. She'd already suspected Rory was acting as her bodyguard as much as her training agent, but she'd never actually seen Rory in hand-to-hand combat. She'd sort of assumed Rory would use her weapon to protect them if there was ever a threat and hadn't considered her other skills.

"There you are!"

Amanda spun around to see Director Alvarsson standing behind her in the otherwise empty hallway. He did not seem pleased.

"Aren't you supposed to be in class right now?"

"Uh." Amanda edged away from the open door and felt her face flush. She'd never seen the director of PTS on the training floor, but, of course, he would show up today. "I was on my way there now."

"Yet this isn't on the way to your classroom, is it?"

"Well, no." Amanda bit her lip. *So much for being a model traveler,* she thought sourly.

"Amanda?" Rory stepped into the hallway and looked between Amanda and the director with a frown. "Why aren't you in class?"

"Just what I was asking," the director said pointedly. "I take it you did not know your charge was here, watching your training instead of attending her own?"

"No, sir." Rory squared her shoulders before turning toward Amanda ominously. "Care to explain?"

"That won't be necessary." Director Alvarsson waved Rory away. "I think it's time Amanda and I had a little chat. Alone."

"Yes, sir." Rory kept her face blank, but Amanda felt guilty for getting her in trouble. Again. Especially when she hadn't *meant* to skip class. The cheerleading interest meeting had run later than she'd expected, then Trina's sister had been late to pick them up. By the time Amanda had gotten home, Judy was furious and had slowed her down with another lecture on responsibility.

Amanda wanted to explain, but Rory returned to the gym without giving her a chance.

Director Alvarsson led Amanda to an empty classroom on the right side of the elevators. The room was arranged like most of the classrooms on this floor. It had two rows of four-person tables, a desk for a teacher, and a podium. Amanda expected Director Alvarsson to sit at the teacher's desk or stand behind the podium. Instead, he sat at one of the tables, gesturing for Amanda to sit across from him.

"You don't think it's important to attend the classes we've arranged for you?"

Amanda slouched in her seat, irritated by his tone and choice of words.

"I know how to send messages," she muttered while looking at her hands.

She was irritated at herself, too.

"There's nothing else you can learn then? From a teacher who has twenty more years of experience than your own?"

Amanda pressed her lips together and shrugged.

"Why were you late today? I know you only arrived at our building ten minutes ago."

Of course, you do, Amanda thought bitterly. He knew where she was and what she was doing anytime she traveled through the mindspace. *You won't train me, but you'll watch me like a hawk.*

"I had a school meeting," Amanda answered honestly. She hadn't decided whether to admit her cheerleading plans, but he didn't ask about the meeting.

Alvarsson drummed his fingertips on the tabletop and looked into space thoughtfully.

"You're not taking your training with us very seriously, are you?" He turned his gaze back on Amanda and deepened his frown. "You think you're above it? Better than this training because of your *potential* abilities?"

Amanda crossed her arms, remembering her argument with Judy and the way Trina had accused her of thinking she was better than everyone at school, too.

She didn't think she was *better* than anyone else. She just knew she had more responsibilities to manage than other people. *Which he of all people should understand,* she thought bitterly.

"You have nothing to say for yourself?" The director looked down his nose at Amanda and spoke as though she were a child. Which she was, Amanda admitted to herself angrily. Though she felt so much older than other teenagers after everything she'd experienced this year. The resentment swelled in her throat until it burst out in one impulsive question.

"Do you actually *know* how to train me?"

"Excuse me?" A dark cloud settled over the director's stern face.

"I mean, not just as a traveler but as an architect?"

"That is an impertinent question," the director replied icily. "Of course, we have the means to train you."

"Then why won't you?" Amanda forgot her pledge to be a model traveler and let her fears and frustrations break free. "No one will answer my questions or tell me anything about how I created that door. Or tell me how to do it again. And that's just a door. Someday you'll be asking me to create a whole house, and I have no idea how to do that!"

Amanda stood up quickly and paced away from the table.

"There are no psychic architects around to show me how to do any of this," she went on. "I haven't found any books by architects in the library. Are you hiding all that from me? Do you not trust me? Do you think I haven't earned my training yet?"

Director Alvarsson got to his feet and looked down at Amanda imperiously.

She crossed her arms, determined to show she had important questions that needed answers.

"Pull yourself together," he commanded shakily, before running one hand over his perfectly smooth, gray hair. They waited a beat, each taking a breath.

I am together, Amanda thought indignantly. *I have every right to be upset.*

"You *have* demonstrated the potential for architectural skills," the director admitted carefully. "But that does not mean you rank higher than those of us with greater experience and knowledge. You are a new traveler. You are not above your teachers, your training agent, or the High Council. And you certainly are not above me."

"I didn't say that—"

"You have questioned my motives," he insisted curtly. "You have questioned the motives and means of our entire society. Do you genuinely think that you are in a position to do so?"

"Uh." Amanda shrank from his question. There it was again. She hadn't *meant* she was better than anyone else, just that she wanted to know more about their plans for her.

She could feel hot tears flooding her eyes. She was mortified by the way everyone else seemed to see her as a superior, entitled brat, especially when she felt so lost and alone.

The director frowned sternly, uncomfortable with her tears. He wasn't used to dealing with teenagers. Or with emotions in general. He'd rarely bothered to reassure the adults who worked for him, let alone taking special care with a child.

"You're doing fieldwork." His words sounded exasperated as if he shouldn't have to explain the obvious. "We let you go on that quest—that prophecy—in Terra-V."

"I guess…" Her uncertain response seemed to irritate him further.

"Amanda, if we didn't expect great things from you, we never would have pushed you out of the nest that way. And now we have you working on an important project with the Arcadians. That is a sink-or-swim situation and you're in the deep end. What does that tell you?"

Amanda pushed aside his mixed metaphors and answered honestly.

"It tells me you don't care if I drown."

CHAPTER 3
A FAMILIAR FACE

It's hard to live with other people. Amanda wrote the words in her notebook, then read them again. Instead of working on her homework, that was the thought that kept running through her head. *It's hard to live with other people.*

She could hear the evidence of that thought playing out on the other side of her bedroom door.

Her mom and aunt weren't *yelling* at each other. Not exactly. They were speaking very politely—too politely—in voices that were gradually increasing in volume. Amanda didn't have to hear their exact words to know what was happening. They were arguing about the correct way to hang up a damp dishcloth, or load the dishwasher, or use the washer and dryer. It had been like this ever since Amanda and Patty had moved into Judy's apartment, and the tension was wearing on Amanda.

Her pen fanned across the paper, underlining the words she'd written before arcing wider to span the width of the page. It was hard enough to stay focused during the last two weeks of school without the added stress of secret PTS training and arguing adults.

Besides, if they were arguing about dish towels now, Amanda couldn't imagine what it would be like when her mom finally learned about psychic travel and everything Judy had hidden from her all these years.

If it had been up to Amanda, she would have told her mom months ago. After her quest in Terra-V and before they'd made the move to Judy's apartment. Judy had agreed, and they were working on a plan to break the news, until Director Alvarsson had decided against it.

He wanted to wait until they were settled into Judy's apartment. Until Patty's breakup with Chad was permanent. Until Patty was comfortable in her new job. He said they would tell her, eventually, but they shouldn't rush into it. He said it would be healthier, for Patty, to wait.

Amanda had disagreed. There was no right time to share life-altering news, and hiding it longer would only make it worse.

As usual, Director Alvarsson hadn't asked her opinion.

"I'm going to take a walk before dinner," Amanda called into the hush that had fallen between her mom and aunt the moment she'd come out of her bedroom.

"Are you asking or telling?" her mom countered.

"Uh, asking?" Amanda paused at the door.

She'd already texted Drew that she was on her way.

"If it's okay with you?"

Patty glanced between her sister-in-law and her daughter. Judy crossed her arms and looked out across the balcony. Patty could tell something was off between Judy and Amanda lately, but neither would talk about it.

"Fine," Patty answered after a long pause. "Be back before six, please. And don't go too far."

Drew was waiting in the apartment lobby, leaning against the wall near the front door. He was wearing his t-shirt from last summer's basketball camp and a pair of ripped jeans. The jeans seemed out-of-character to Amanda, but he'd changed his style a lot during their first year of high school, so she took it as another evolution to whatever image he was working out. More than the ripped jeans, she noticed that he looked taller today.

"Are you ever going to stop growing?" she asked, leaning back and craning her neck to look all the way up at his smirking face.

"Are you ever going to be on time?" He went out the front door, holding it open just long enough for Amanda to catch it and follow him outside. "Long ride down from the penthouse, I guess."

He'd been making these little digs ever since Amanda and her mom had moved into Judy's large, PTS-owned apartment. Amanda told herself she didn't mind.

Outside, the air was heavy with a sticky humidity that Amanda wasn't ready to endure. She unbuttoned her cotton shirt, thought of the fitted tank she was wearing underneath, and then left her outer shirt on.

"Judy still mad?" Drew set a fast pace but slowed when he felt Amanda lagging a step behind. He wasn't used to his longer limbs either.

"Yeah."

Amanda had already told him about her confrontation with Alvarsson and Judy's disappointment in her. She didn't want to get into it again.

"No travel today?"

Drew kept his eyes forward as he spoke. They walked around the parking lot and toward the small park where Amanda had made her first venture into another world. She hadn't understood what was happening at the time, but Drew had been by her side. As much as he could be.

"No." Amanda crossed her arms.

"They still have you going to Arcadia, though?"

Drew was prodding now, and it made Amanda edgy.

"Do we have to talk about that?"

"No." Drew sounded hurt.

They walked quietly for several minutes.

Amanda regretted snapping at him. Drew knew about her psychic travel adventures because he'd been with her when she was stumbling into that world, but he wasn't a psychic traveler. He couldn't know what it was like to daydream your way into an imaginary house and be transported to an entirely different world. He wanted to understand. He wanted to be the friend who could listen to Amanda's experiences and keep her secrets, but Amanda found it harder and harder to explain. Conversations that had once been a relief had started to feel like a burden.

"I still can't get over it though," Drew said suddenly, breaking the silence.

Amanda waited, wondering what he was thinking.

"The whole Arcadia thing."

"Oh." Amanda nodded. "Yeah, it's kinda weird."

"And it's not the only place like that?"

"I guess not."

Amanda had gotten over her initial surprise at Arcadia's origins, though it *was* pretty amazing.

A psychic architect, way back in the 13th century, had created a door to an uninhabited world that was very much like Earth. A large group of travelers—educated people who were all opposed to the violence of the Crusades—had decided to settle the new world and destroy the only proximal door that connected it to Earth. They named the world Arcadia, for the unspoiled wilderness in Greek mythology, and swore to learn from the mistakes of their ancestors by building a peaceful, science-based community where war would never take root again.

Hundreds of years had passed before another psychic architect connected to Arcadia. By that time, their society had progressed far beyond Earth's technology, but the Arcadian people had evolved away from their psychic travel abilities. Instead, they had created physical travel that spanned their galaxy.

By isolating themselves and starting over, they had surpassed their ancestors.

Amanda had been told there were other worlds with similar origins. Though starting unsanctioned societies had since been banned by the leaders of PTS.

"If they evolved, are they…?"

Drew didn't finish the question.

"They're still human."

Amanda felt her cheeks tingle as Mitra's face flashed through her mind.

"Are they?" Drew pressed. "They've been evolving in a different world, or galaxy, or whatever, for centuries. Even if they *were* human in the beginning, they could have adapted in a lot of different ways. To the new environment."

"It's nearly identical to here," Amanda answered stiffly. She didn't like what Drew was suggesting.

"Still." Drew sighed and let the thought stay open.

Amanda had told Drew about Mitra. To a point. She'd told him about Mitra's genius and interest in their world. She hadn't mentioned the strange, hollow feeling that flooded her stomach when Mitra looked at her in a certain way.

They rounded the last curve into the park and stopped when they saw they weren't alone. A man was sitting on one of the park benches. Though his back was toward them, there was something familiar about him.

Amanda studied his dark hair and broad shoulders. He wore a black, long-sleeved sweater and black pants. Even in this heat. The sweater was relatively fitted but loose enough to conceal a holster and weapon. Amanda's brain finished making the connection.

She gasped and stepped back.

Drew looked between Amanda and the mystery man in confusion. He opened his mouth to ask, but she was shaking her head, silently pleading with Drew to stay quiet.

Before they could retreat, the man stood up and faced Amanda with a knowing smile.

Lucas Flynn.

The ground seemed to drop beneath Amanda's feet as Lucas stepped toward them. His hands were empty. His grin was fixed. Still, Amanda knew he shouldn't be there.

"Amanda Jones." Lucas' lips stretched into a wide smile as a glinting light danced in his eyes.

"Lucas Flynn." Amanda tried not to shrink away. She hadn't seen Lucas since he'd turned up in Terra-V, where he'd been secretly working with the Churukh royalty who had harshly ruled that world.

"Lucas Flynn?" Drew tensed, looked at Amanda for confirmation, then stepped ahead of her, trying to shield her from danger. Drew had heard all about Lucas Flynn.

"Stand down, boyfriend," Lucas said lightly, without taking his eyes from Amanda. "I'm only here to talk."

Amanda believed him. She knew Lucas wasn't there to hurt her, though she couldn't explain how.

"What do you want?" Amanda gently edged ahead of Drew, signaling that he should stay back even as he jostled closer to her side.

"You're a hard girl to find." Lucas smiled. "Despite your celebrity."

"Not that hard," Amanda noted, bringing an appreciative laugh from Lucas.

"I'm glad you aren't afraid of me."

Lucas stepped closer. Amanda pulled back.

"Or not *that* afraid of me."

"What do you want?" Amanda repeated, trying to stop the shaking that trembled through her whole body. She wondered if she could pull off sending a message through the house without Lucas noticing. She could reach out to her aunt. Or Rory. Or Cameron. But she knew she couldn't take the chance with Drew beside her. She needed to keep her focus in the present moment.

Lucas held his distance and lifted his palms up at waist height, subtly showing that his hands were free of weapons.

"What have they told you about me?"

Amanda hesitated, remembering everything she'd been told about Lucas Flynn. His psychic abilities had come on with unusual strength, leading him to be stranded in multiple worlds for months before PTS counselors could catch up and explain what was happening to him. He'd been psychologically traumatized by the experience and had eventually run from PTS, making wild, delusional claims about what was *really* happening in the organization. No one had been willing to tell her what claims he'd actually made about the society, but they said they were dangerous, crazy stories that showed how far his mind had slipped from reality.

"That bad, huh?" Lucas laughed, shrugging off whatever he saw in Amanda's face. "Well, whatever they've told you, I can promise you there's another side to the story. Whether you'll listen to my side is the important question."

He locked eyes with Amanda, searching for something, just as he'd searched her face when they'd met on Terra-V.

"Do you understand your power yet?"

His question felt like a shift in the conversation.

"I, uh…"

Amanda knew she was a psychic architect. She'd proven that on Terra-V when she'd created a new proximal door. Lucas knew that, too. He'd been the first one to step through that door, using it to evade the PTS troops sent to seize him.

Lucas leaned in with soft, encouraging eyes.

"Do *they* understand your power yet?"

Amanda didn't know how to answer. She remembered her accusations toward the director and could tell Lucas saw something in her face that confirmed his suspicions.

"I think you should go now."

Drew stepped more firmly between Amanda and Lucas, trying to stop whatever situation was beginning to unfold. A veil of detachment fell over Lucas' features, cutting off their moment of quiet connection.

"Do you?" Lucas chuckled, assessing Drew with a raised eyebrow. "That's sweet."

Amanda blushed. She wasn't sure if her embarrassment came from Drew's behavior or Lucas' response. She didn't need Drew's protection.

"What do you want?" Amanda asked for a third time, pushing firmly past Drew. This was her situation, her world, and she was capable of handling it herself.

Lucas glanced at the ground, lightly shaking his head, before lifting his gaze with an open plea that chipped away at Amanda's defensive stance.

"Just to tell you I'm not your enemy." He spoke softly, with a level of sincerity that surprised Amanda. "That's enough, for now."

He held her gaze as his body faded away. Disappearing into thin air.

§

They were in the empty party room on the ground floor of their apartment building. Drew paced between the couches. Amanda stood with one arm across her stomach while her other hand covered her mouth. The detour to this room had been Amanda's idea. Once she'd pulled herself together and stopped Drew from leading them straight to Aunt Judy.

"We should have stayed in the park." She was thinking out loud, putting the situation into perspective. "We should have stayed to watch that spot. He could have already come back by now. He could have come back and gone anywhere. On foot."

"What?" Drew stopped pacing and studied Amanda's pale face. "What do you…?" He trailed off, starting to understand.

"He had to use a proximal door to get back to Earth." Amanda spelled it out, for Drew and for herself. "Unless he had kept his origin point somewhere on Earth all this time, but that's highly unlikely. If he came through a door, he'd have passed through one of the PTS buildings. Which means there are guards somewhere who let him through. Guards working with him?"

"Slow down." Drew looked toward the closed glass doors as if making sure Lucas hadn't followed them into the building.

"However he got here," Amanda continued, "he just went back through the house without using a proximal door…"

"Which reset his origin point," Drew realized. "So, no matter where he went…"

"He can wake up in the park. From anywhere," Amanda confirmed.

"It doesn't matter how many doors you travel through, or how many worlds you visit, your origin point stays the same until you daydream into the house from a new location."

They stood with that knowledge, piecing together what it could mean for Lucas to have an origin point just outside of Amanda's apartment building. It would put him within easy reach of her and her family anytime.

But it didn't make sense for him to travel through the mindspace in front of Amanda. All she had to do was tell PTS and they'd have guards stationed in the park around the clock.

Why go to a house from the park? Amanda wondered. *And in front of us? Why risk it?*

Amanda's eyes stung and her ribs prickled. They shouldn't have left the park. If Lucas had already come back and left on foot, he could have picked up a bus at the nearby stop. He could be anywhere by now, setting a new, secret origin point wherever he wanted.

She'd let him get away.

Amanda bit her lip, feeling the force of her mistake wash over her.

"You need to report it." Drew shook Amanda's arm, trying to revive her sense of urgency.

Amanda knew he was right, but she was still stuck on Lucas' motive. *Why go to the mindspace in front of us?*

"Now," Drew urged. "Before any more time passes."

"Uh-huh." Amanda barely heard him. She was trying to pin down the shadow of an idea.

"Amanda!" Drew shook her arm again. "We don't know if he's come back through the park yet. You could still get PTS here in time."

"I guess." Amanda stared into the distance.

The nearest proximal door was in New York, over 300 miles away. PTS did have a satellite office in Arlington, about forty-five minutes by car, and a smaller team had recently set up in an office park only ten minutes from Amanda's apartment building. They could have someone here in minutes and a more specialized team here in a few hours.

Maybe sooner.

For all Amanda knew, there could be an emergency strike team living in her building. That was the kind of thing PTS would do.

"Are you still here?" Drew shifted into her line of sight, trying to tell whether her mind had already disappeared into the house.

Amanda's eyes snapped back to attention. She hadn't been able to draw out whatever thought was teasing at the back of her mind. She let go of the effort with a sigh.

"I'll tell Aunt Judy." Amanda settled into an armchair in a corner of the room that couldn't be seen from the door. "But not in front of my mom."

Leaving Drew to watch the door and alert her if anyone should come in, Amanda closed her eyes and let herself drift into the large, Victorian house she'd once thought was only a daydream.

The attic was cool and dusty.

Amanda was mildly surprised to find herself in the attic alcove, standing in front of a familiar set of doors. She'd planned to enter the living room, where doors connected to the three main PTS offices located in the United States, but her mind had managed a detour.

Her focus was drawn to the seventh door in the attic alcove. The door she had created last fall. The door that had confirmed her psychic architect abilities, even if she had no idea how she had created it.

Tracing her fingers lightly over the rough, silvery wood, Amanda sighed and began to conjure up the image of her aunt. She had to send a psychic call to draw Judy to the house, and that required steady focus. Amanda pictured her aunt's face. Her thick, dark glasses. The blue streaks in her hair. All the details that would help her connect telepathically.

And then she stopped.

No one could see her in the house unless she wanted them to see her. She couldn't see anyone else in the house unless they wanted to be seen. It was how the house functioned as a shared mindspace. There could be multiple travelers standing in this very spot, at this very moment, without ever being aware of each other. Until their minds decided to allow a connection.

The thought that had been teasing earlier broke through.

Lucas Flynn stood beside Amanda in the attic.

"Thanks for seeing me," he quipped drily.

They were both facing the door Amanda had created.

This was why Lucas let me see him enter the house, Amanda realized with a satisfying click. It was an invitation. She ran over their brief conversation in the park and wondered how much more he would have said if Drew hadn't been with her.

"What do you want?"

It was the same question Amanda had asked him three times in the park.

Lucas turned his head to study her.

They were standing just a few feet apart. Except they weren't *actually* in the house at all.

He can't touch me here, Amanda reminded herself. *We can only talk here.*

A fluttery feeling told her that talking to Lucas Flynn might be dangerous enough.

"I answered that question." Lucas smiled. "I want you to know that I'm not your enemy."

"Okay." Amanda kept her eyes forward. "Good to know."

Lucas laughed.

"You're a tough one," he commented lightly.

Amanda shrugged. She didn't feel tough. Her mind was swirling, and she felt like jelly inside.

"Can I confess something?" Lucas pivoted his whole body to face Amanda. She could see his relaxed posture in her peripheral vision, but she kept up her guard.

Lucas sighed gently.

"I do want something more," he continued with a smile in his voice. "I want you to see me as your friend. Eventually."

Amanda swallowed, trying not to react.

Lucas laughed again.

"You find that hard to believe?" He sounded genuinely curious. Amanda considered.

"That you want me to *see* you as my friend, or that you actually *could* be my friend?"

The laughter came again, this time with more feeling.

"Oh, I knew I'd like you!" Lucas leaned against the narrow wall space between two doors and regarded Amanda with amusement. "Clever response. But I already knew you were clever."

Amanda felt a twitch at the left corner of her mouth and tried not to smile.

"Do you know what they would do to me?" he asked. "If they caught me?"

His serious tone caught Amanda off guard. She looked directly at him and felt curiosity playing across her face.

"Do you know what they do with *any* travelers who defy them?" he asked steadily. "The ones who don't accept their almighty rules? The ones they label as mental or social defectives?"

Amanda's confused mind flashed back to the woman in Arcadia who had collapsed helplessly into the arms of a guard and been carted away. But that had had nothing to do with PTS.

"There's a hospital…" Amanda remembered Judy telling her that Lucas had spent time in a special PTS hospital after those months of being lost in strange worlds.

"Yes…" Lucas drew the word out, turning it into a prompt for more information, but Amanda had nothing else she wanted to say. She hadn't meant to say anything at all.

Time stretched between them. Amanda's shoulders softened into the silence. She'd spent hours imagining what that early experience had been like for Lucas. There were very few travelers who had developed strong enough powers to step through a door without training.

Lucas had.

Amanda had.

She remembered the shock of finding herself in Terra-V when she'd thought she'd only been having a vivid daydream. She also remembered the doubt when she'd returned home and the persistent thoughts that she might actually be losing her mind.

How much worse had it been for Lucas to bounce from world to world for almost nine months? To have no idea what was happening or how to get home?

"Do you know what they call that hospital?" Lucas sounded bitter.

Amanda could only shake her head.

"Psychic Trauma Social Detention. Or PTSD."

The laugh that followed was different than any she'd heard before. Uglier. Full of pain.

Amanda blinked at Lucas, trying to understand. She'd heard the term PTSD before but didn't know how to connect it to Lucas' laughter.

"PTSD? Like Post-Traumatic Stress Disorder," Lucas clarified with a shake of his head. "They call their damn psych hospital PTSD and don't even see the irony.

"Or maybe they do and call it that anyway. Which do you think is worse?"

Amanda shifted back a step, distancing herself from the pain contorting Lucas' face.

In the next moment, he brushed away the thought—and his maniacal grin—slowly exhaling his face into the confident smile he usually wore.

"If you're not my enemy," Amanda started slowly and then broke off, second-guessing what she should say.

"It's okay," Lucas encouraged. "Ask. I want you to ask. Anything."

He sounded eager beneath his relaxed slouch.

"You want me to not think of you as an enemy," Amanda tried again. "Does that mean you want me to see the rest of PTS as an enemy?"

"No," Lucas answered breezily. Then added, "Not all of them. But, well, some of them."

Amanda considered that. She thought about her aunt, Rory, and Cameron. Then Director Alvarsson and the High Council. She wanted to ask who he considered his enemy, but she wasn't sure she wanted to hear the answer.

"No. No, wait. That's not right." Lucas swiped his hands in the air as if wiping his previous answer away. "I don't want you to think of anyone as the enemy. At least, not because I see them that way.

"I want you to see them however *you* want to see them. I want you to have all the information and make your own decisions. You should be able to do that. Everyone should be able to do that."

Amanda found herself nodding.

Whatever else Lucas might say, she agreed with him on that.

Chapter 4
Secrets and Lies

"Do you have homework?"

Aunt Judy had waited for Amanda to come home from school, just like she had every day since she and Patty had moved in. Amanda used to look forward to their afternoon time together. Back when Judy would teach her about psychic travel or chat about her day at school. Now, Judy was often distracted and distant. She either focused on managing Amanda's schedule or improving her attitude.

"I have some." Amanda shrugged.

She closed and locked the front door, wondering what conversation they'd be having if she'd told her aunt about Lucas' visit last week. She had planned on telling Judy that afternoon, until she'd come home to find her mom and Judy laughing while making dinner together. They were getting along so well she hadn't wanted to disrupt the mood.

Later, she had to finish the homework she'd neglected before dinner. And every day since, she hadn't found the right time to mention that Lucas Flynn had dropped by for a friendly chat.

"Hopefully, it's not too much. We had to reschedule your Off-World Botany session to this afternoon, and it starts in forty-five minutes..."

"Yeah, okay." Amanda dropped her backpack and went to the kitchen for a glass of iced tea.

An Off-World Botany class wasn't that bad. She liked learning about different worlds and how to safely explore them. But if they knew Lucas Flynn had made contact, would she still be going? Would even training facilities become off-limits? What if they made her stay home from school with a tutor and an armed guard stationed in the apartment lobby?

"This is important stuff for travelers," Judy reminded, misreading Amanda's pensive expression. "At least for those who plan to spend time off-world."

"Uh, huh." Amanda drank half her iced tea in two large gulps, only half listening.

"Off-world travel will be a big part of your life someday, given your unique skills. I know that's important to you."

Of course, you know that, Amanda sulked silently.

Just two weeks ago, after Amanda's outburst with the director, Judy had sat her down for a lecture on patience. She'd said Amanda had to learn to crawl before she could run. Amanda thought of those words whenever she visited her attic door. The door she'd created between two worlds, without expert training or help from anyone else.

On the scale of crawling to running, where did Lucas Flynn fit in?

Would news of his visit hold her back or be a reason to speed up her training?

Amanda topped off her glass before returning the iced tea to the fridge. The cold pitcher had left a watery ring on the counter. Amanda quietly watched her damp glass add to the puddle.

"Once you master these basic skills, we *will* move forward with more specialized training," Judy reassured. "If we rush into more complex skills, we risk leaving gaps, and that could be dangerous. In the long-term."

"I know," Amanda muttered.

"We all want what's best for you."

"Uh-huh."

Judy studied Amanda. The glare on her glasses hid her eyes. The cross of her arms hid most of the design on her tee-shirt. Amanda could see part of the Union Jack flag and the tops of four heads peeking over her aunt's arms. It looked like Judy wanted to say more, but she held her tongue.

Amanda took her glass to her room. She couldn't explain what she was thinking without admitting she'd seen Lucas and kept his visit quiet for a whole week.

In her room, Amanda could breathe in peace.

Everywhere else, someone wanted something from her. In her PTS classes, she had to participate without seeming superior to the other new travelers. At school, she had to reconnect with Trina over cheerleading tryouts without letting on that she was having second thoughts about them. With Drew, she had to assure him she wasn't in danger without admitting she hadn't reported Lucas' visit.

It was all horribly exhausting.

Setting her iced tea on her desk, Amanda looked at the rows of windows along the L-shape of her apartment building. She could still see Drew's bedroom window, only now from a steeper angle than when she'd lived on the seventh floor. This time of day, the sun made his window a reflective panel, but she knew he was home and probably in his room now.

They'd just ridden the bus home together. Instead of talking about Lucas, Drew had said it would be cool if Amanda made the cheerleading squad. They could ride the bus together for away games during basketball season, and he might go out for JV football next year, too.

More bus time, he'd joked. *We're destined to an eternity of bus rides together.*

She'd laughed with him, though it wasn't all that funny. It was just easier to talk about anything other than PTS and Lucas Flynn.

Amanda pictured that future now. She imagined herself on the sidelines, cheering for Drew with Trina clapping by her side. They could meet up wherever the cool kids hung out after the games. Be a real part of the school.

Maybe that wouldn't be so bad.

Maybe her life as a psychic traveler could wait.

Amanda knew she should start her homework, but an urge was growing in the pit of her stomach. It itched at her brain until she locked her door and stretched out on her bed. The sun was low, shining across her face, chest, and arms. She took a slow breath, enjoying the warmth of the sun and the moment to be still. She let her eyes go out of focus and surrendered to the call of a large Victorian house.

Amanda stood in front of the newest door to Terra-V. *Her* door. She wondered if Lucas was in the attic, waiting for her. She could call him to the house with a psychic message, but she didn't dare.

Studying her door, Amanda thought of the Vherahna and Churukh in Terra-V. Last she knew, they were moving forward, creating a new social order after the fall of the Churukh royalty. It would take time, even with a legion of PTS knights to help. But they were making progress.

I did that, Amanda thought wistfully.

She'd been a key part in saving the Vherahna and restoring balance to their world. Was that the kind of work she would someday do on other worlds as well? Was it fair to delay that so she could jump around on the sidelines of high school games, trying to be *normal*?

On the other hand, it wasn't like Director Alvarsson was ready to let her do anything important. He was content to teach her traveler basics and only let her visit a safe world like Arcadia.

And then Amanda remembered something Director Alvarsson had said about her Arcadia assignment.

He'd described it as being *thrown into the deep end*. A *sink-or-swim situation*. That seemed dramatic when she'd only been sent to play light-based games with a teenage scientist and talk up the bright future their worlds could share together.

A memory of Lucas standing across from her in the park floated through her mind.

"Do you understand your power yet?"

Amanda closed her eyes.

When she opened them, she was surprised to see she'd moved to the small den on the first floor. Her subconscious had led her to the place it wanted to visit the most.

Ignoring the trouble she'd be in, Amanda opened the pale door and stepped over its threshold. Back in her bedroom, her physical body faded into the sunlight.

§

Mitra's lab was clean and white. It was sterile yet inviting with its polished surfaces and floor-to-ceiling windows. There were unidentifiable pieces of equipment neatly lined up along one countertop and something that looked very similar to a microscope sitting on a tall cart. Three small tables were set for the different games Mitra had been teaching her to play.

"I only have fifteen minutes," Amanda said when Mitra opened the door. He stepped aside to let her in, checking the hall and realizing she was alone.

"Are you all right?"

"Why am I here?" Amanda asked, instead of answering his question. "I mean, not right now, but in Arcadia at all. Why do your people want me here?"

Mitra led Amanda to a set of white leather chairs by the windows, letting his hand rest lightly on her low back as they walked. Amanda scarcely noticed his touch but felt encouraged by the warmth in his eyes. *It's always his eyes,* she noticed.

"Why do you think you are here?" he asked evasively. Or maybe, she told herself, he was just confused by her surprise visit.

"Well, I know what they told me," Amanda answered. "I'm here to be part of your study of psychic abilities. I'm supposed to help you understand our world and maybe help your leaders see how our people could share technology, and knowledge, and stuff."

"Yes." Mitra held her gaze. "Arcadians have a cautious relationship with the Maiorum and a wish to strengthen that bond."

As the quiet stretched, Amanda felt a prickling in her chest and cheeks. She'd never once seen Mitra agitated or out of control, as she felt now. Looking out the windows, she watched a flock of birds swirl out of the distant forest and skim along the curve of the sparkling river.

"I don't know why they sent me now," she admitted, before rushing to explain. "I mean, I guess I *will* be a psychic architect someday. But I'm not there yet. And instead of training me, they send me here to… what? Measure my potential abilities?

"You've seen how bad I am at those games of yours. I don't know what I'm doing here. Or why it even matters to your people. If I'm better at those games than other travelers, will that change anything? Make your leaders more willing to share technology? Why would that matter? And if it does, why not train me more before sending me here?"

Mitra looked down with a heavy sigh.

Amanda bit her lower lip.

"Never mind." She waved away her earlier words and forced a shaky laugh. "I'm apparently just having some kind of… I don't know… identity crisis or something. It's not your problem…"

Swallowing her embarrassment, Amanda ran her hands through her hair and jumped up to leave.

"I should get back."

Mitra swiftly followed, easing into her path before she could get far.

They stood still, looking into each other's eyes.

"I am glad you came to see me." Mitra spoke seriously. "I do understand what you mean, about being unsure of your abilities and your place here."

He turned back toward the windows. A small aircraft was passing in the distance and the sky was a clear, crisp blue. The birds continued their graceful journey, unbothered by the quiet plane passing over their heads. Though the glass blocked the birdsong, Amanda could hear it in her mind. She remembered how it felt to walk through this sparkling, glass city amid people who offered genuine smiles at every turn. The Arcadians had come so far since cutting ties with their ancestors.

"There are things you do not know," Mitra continued, still looking out the pristine glass. "Things I think you should know."

They moved toward the windows where Amanda sat on the edge of a white chair and folded her hands in her lap. Something in Mitra's voice said he was about to share something important.

"You know our people descended from your people, from your psychic travelers, a long time ago, and then cut their connection to your world."

Amanda nodded, remembering the Arcadian history she'd learned in her PTS training.

"And you lost your psychic travel abilities," she added, with a measure of uncertainty.

Her PTS history books had glossed over the details, and her had teachers discouraged questions. Exiled worlds were a sensitive subject. If it weren't for the Arcadians' advanced technology, Amanda doubted the High Council would have allowed an alliance with them at all.

"Yes, we lost those abilities." Mitra smiled lightly. "In fact, our people once believed psychic travel was an ancient myth. When your world made contact again, we learned the legends about our ancestors were true."

Amanda leaned forward, unsure what this history had to do with her assignment in Arcadia.

"Since then, our neuroscientists have diligently worked to reestablish our own psychic abilities."

"Okay…" Amanda turned over that idea. "You mean, the way you use psychic skills in your technology?"

"Yes, but also in our own psychic *social* abilities."

Amanda puzzled over his words. Was there a social element in the energy games they'd played? They were mostly about mentally moving lights across glass boards or dimming a light's energy at will. But maybe those games worked by combining the players' psychic energy?

"Many of us can now access a shared mindspace," Mitra continued smoothly, causing Amanda to blink in surprise.

"Wait, you can…? What?"

Psychic energy was one thing, Amanda thought, but Arcadians accessing the mindspace…? Why had no one told her about that? Could the Arcadians find a way back to Earth? Would Mitra?

"Our mindspace is an empty place," Mitra hurried to explain. "It seems to have no connection to your own. We can meet and communicate, but we have no knowledge of how to create a structure in that space, let alone doors to other worlds."

Amanda stood up and twisted her fingers, unconsciously backing away. She'd heard Mitra's words, but her mind struggled to make sense of them.

Arcadians have their own mindspace? No one had told her that. Not Director Alvarsson, Rory, Judy, or any of her teachers. They'd talked about the wonder of the Arcadians' translator discs, the importance of their interspace travel, and their connections to people living on planets beyond their own. They'd hinted at other amazing technology that powered their cities and sustained their farms. But they'd never said a thing to her about their mindspace or hopes of psychic travel.

Did they know? Of course, they know. They must. But why didn't they tell me…?

Amanda's eyes widened as the pieces slipped together.

The Arcadians have technology we need, and we finally have a psychic architect to help them develop a house in their own mindspace.

Mitra nodded solemnly, reading her thoughts.

"That is why you are here."

§

Despite being twenty minutes late, Amanda walked into her Off-World Botany class without being stopped by the director or questioned by her teacher. She slipped into her chair with a mumbled apology, tuned out the lecture, and let her mind wander over what she'd just learned.

The Arcadians weren't sure if Amanda would be able to help them. The High Council wasn't sure either, yet they'd promised any help she might be able to provide. According to Mitra.

"Why haven't they told *me* any of this?"

Amanda had asked without expecting an answer, but Mitra had responded matter-of-factly.

"Your leadership, and my own, thought it would be best to start slow, to not put undue pressure on you. Given your early stage of training."

Amanda seethed at the memory of Mitra's words. She felt dismissed. Left out and betrayed. Mostly by everyone at PTS, but by Mitra, too. They'd all known. They'd pinned their hopes on her but hadn't thought she was strong enough to know about it.

"The games you taught me," she'd said suspiciously. "Do they measure my psychic ability? Or my *potential* psychic ability?"

"They are not measurement tools," Mitra had answered carefully, easing in to close the distance she'd put between them. "They clear the mind, calm emotions, and stimulate the psychic connection needed to control the vibrational forces behind much of our technology.

"We also have a theory that they may be used to adjust a Maiorum's psychic wavelengths to allow access to our Arcadian mindspace."

"So, wait. You were trying to change the *energy* in my mind? Without telling me? What if it worked? Would I have still been able to get home through *my* mindspace? Could I have been trapped in Arcadia?"

Amanda's heart had raced just thinking about being stranded in Arcadia. But Mitra had quickly corrected her, saying, "No, it is perfectly safe. We've tried with other Maiorum before you. We have not been successful yet, but we have seen changes to the psychic wavelengths that are encouraging. And those changes faded without causing any difficultly in accessing the Maiorum mindspace."

"But you were messing with my mind," Amanda had insisted, "and you didn't tell me!"

By the time she'd left Mitra's lab, Amanda had been shaking with rage. She'd sat in a private room at the gatehouse and stared at the proximal door she'd conjured, not sure whether to go home and confront her aunt or go into the house and send an urgent message to Rory.

She'd even considered messaging Lucas, but she wasn't ready to take that step.

In the end, she'd gone to the training facility in Chicago and joined her Off-World Botany class as if nothing unusual had happened.

Pushing her thoughts aside, Amanda tried to catch pace with the botany lesson. They were studying root systems. Their teacher, Molly Fitzpatrick, had begun explaining how trees negotiate space for their roots to grow.

"Don't they just spread out? Wherever they can?"

The question came from a man at the table to Amanda's right. She'd had two classes with him before but could never remember if his name was Justin or Jason. He was old to be a new traveler. Nearly thirty. And he was married. Amanda didn't remember anything else about him, but she liked the way he took notes with different colored pens.

"No, they *talk* to each other!" A younger woman in the front row turned around with wide eyes and an excited grin. "I just read about this. Trees talk to each other underground. Some scientist guy recently figured it out." She turned back to the teacher. "They talk through their roots, right?"

"Not exactly," Molly answered with a smile, "but you're close."

"Wait, do you mean *real* trees or crazy, *alien* trees?" Another man at Jason/Justin's table joined in with a cynical shake of his head. Like many novice travelers, he hadn't entirely accepted his new reality.

"Both." Molly moved around her podium to lean against the front edge of her desk. "It's something we've observed for some time on other worlds and have only recently been able to relate to the trees here on Earth."

"So, was that scientist in the article I read a traveler? The one who *discovered* trees here on Earth can talk to each other? Did he really learn that on another world?"

"They don't exactly talk through their roots," Molly explained, ignoring the last question. "At least, not on Earth. In our world, there is a much more complex network of fungus that grows throughout the soil, creating a symbiotic relationship with the trees. This network essentially passes chemical and electrical messages from tree to tree.

"That's an over-simplification, of course, but we'll get into that more deeply in our next class. First, we'll look at some of the trees on other worlds, where many do have more direct ways of speaking with each other."

Molly smoothed her skirt and adjusted the notes she had propped on her podium. The other students settled back over their notebooks, but Amanda shifted in her seat. She watched the teacher skim her lesson plan, looking for where she'd left off.

"Um, the trees from other worlds…" Amanda hesitated until Molly nodded encouragingly. "The ones that talk to each other. Does that include tuntum trees?"

"Excellent question!" Molly placed both hands flat on the podium and smiled widely. "The tuntum trees of Terra-V most certainly talk to each other. And not only through their roots.

"As you may know, tuntum trees create an energy barrier that limits who is allowed to pass into the area beneath their boughs and within their groves."

Molly turned to the whiteboard behind her and began sketching a series of simple trees with twisted trunks. The other students quickly copied her drawing into their notebooks, but Amanda simply sat and watched.

"This barrier is invisible," Molly clarified, as she drew a jagged circle around the trees. "But our scientists have measured its energy fluctuations and found distinct signals being sent between the trees. Even more fascinating, these signals are also passed to the Vherahna, who have a mutually symbiotic relationship with the tuntum trees."

Molly drew a series of stick figures and zigzag lines connecting them to the trees' jagged barrier.

"While we have not deciphered the specific messages the trees send, the Vherahna have confirmed that they *can* communicate with the tuntum trees. We believe this communication is how the Vherahna let the tuntum trees know who is allowed to pass the barrier. Although, the Vherahna have suggested the trees have some part in that decision themselves."

As Molly shifted the discussion toward similar trees in other worlds, Amanda continued to stare at her sketch of the twisted trees. When she had been in Terra-V, the Vherahna had trusted her completely. She was the *waking dreamer*, the girl who had been prophesied to lead them to a sacred treasure. That was all the Vherahna had needed to believe in Amanda.

Amanda chewed on her bottom lip as she remembered the uncertainty she'd felt during her quest in Terra-V. Was her assignment in Arcadia any different?

Yes, she decided firmly. In Terra-V, she'd been told the prophecy, even if she hadn't been told *how* to fulfill it. In Arcadia, they hadn't even told her why she was there.

They'd all lied to her.

§

When she went home that evening, Amanda only picked at her dinner. She was caught up in thoughts of Mitra and the Arcadians when a heavy silence fell over the table. Patty said her name in a way that told Amanda it wasn't the first time she'd said it.

"Are you going home from school with Trina on Thursday? Or will you need a ride there later?"

"Thursday?" Amanda saw her mom's impatience, and the concern on her aunt's face, before she realized what they were talking about.

"Oh, right. Last day of school. Big party. Uh, I'll go home with Trina from school. And spend the night. I mean, if that's okay?"

"Sure," her mom laughed, "you asked weeks ago."

"Right, I knew that."

"Okay, then." Patty tilted her head to one side and studied Amanda carefully. After a long pause, she took Amanda's plate into the kitchen with her own.

Judy leaned close the moment they were alone.

"Are you okay?"

Amanda glared at her.

"Yeah, I'm fine."

Judy opened her mouth to respond, but Amanda quickly got to her feet and went to help her mom with the dishes. For once, she didn't care whether her aunt believed her or not.

CHAPTER 5

THE LAST DAY OF SCHOOL

"Surprise!"

Amanda blinked her eyes open and propped herself up on her elbows. Her mom was standing beside her bed with a breakfast tray bearing pancakes and bowls of fruit. In her groggy state, Amanda squinted at the clock on her nightstand, then blinked a few more times.

"It's not my birthday," she mumbled, while scooting back to make room for the tray.

"Well, no, but it's the last day of your first year of high school," Patty explained with a laugh. "I wanted to mark the occasion."

"Well, thanks," Amanda laughed and handed over the second fork.

It was one of their special occasion traditions. Patty would bring in a tray of their favorite foods, then sit cross-legged on Amanda's bed while they shared breakfast and talked. Amanda hadn't expected a breakfast-in-bed morning. After a restless night of thinking about her situation in Arcadia, the surprise of syrup-soaked pancakes brought a sudden swell of emotion.

"Hey." Patty put down her fork and reached for her daughter with concern. "What is it? What's wrong?"

"Nothing," Amanda laughed, even as she swiped the gathering tears. "Nothing's wrong at all. I just… I don't know. It's nice. And… unexpected."

Patty beamed as she leaned over the tray to kiss Amanda's forehead.

"Careful! You'll spill the juice!"

They laughed together in the joy of the moment until a thread of sadness crept into Amanda's heart. As beautiful as the moment was, it felt fragile. Like a bubble floating in sunlight. Simple, happy moments like this couldn't last. Not with this secret expanding between them.

Sitting in bed, with syrup still sticky on her lips, Amanda wondered if her dad had felt like this when he was home from PTS missions. Had he carried around this edge of sadness even in their happiest family moments? Amanda didn't like hiding a huge part of her life from her mom and couldn't imagine keeping it up for the rest of her life.

Patty was still chatting lightly about parties she'd gone to in her own high school years when Amanda couldn't hold back her thoughts any longer.

"Where do you think Dad went when he was away?"

Patty's story choked to a halt and her hand began to shake. A chunk of strawberry slipped off her fork and onto Amanda's bedspread, making her curse in annoyance as she picked up the fruit.

"He was traveling for work," she answered in a tight voice, while using a napkin to dab at a pale pink splotch on the bed. "You know that."

"Yeah, but *where* was he traveling?" Amanda kept her voice even, despite the quiver she felt inside.

"I don't know." Patty smiled sadly. "He worked as a diplomat, and his trips to foreign countries were classified. But you know that, too."

Amanda nodded, considering how much more she should say. Was it better to plant some seeds for a later talk or rip off the band-aid with the full truth now? Were Director Alvarsson and Aunt Judy right about waiting?

"He could have traveled anywhere, then?"

"Yes," Patty agreed uneasily as she arranged the silverware and napkins more neatly on the tray. "He could have traveled anywhere. He didn't talk about where he went."

"He talked to me," Amanda ventured, then stopped when her mom looked up sharply.

"He told you stories. Fantasy, made-up stories." Patty took another slow breath, holding her eyes closed for just a moment. "Are you done eating?"

She stood up and reached for the tray, but Amanda held it in place.

"What if they weren't made-up?"

"Amanda." Patty abandoned the tray and crossed her arms over her chest. "They were stories about purple forests, and glittering mountains, and mystical creatures in mist-filled caves. Of course, they were made-up."

"But what if they weren't?" Amanda scooted her legs from beneath the tray and sat up on the edge of her bed.

"We don't know where he went! What if there *are* places that are hidden from most people? What if there are ways to travel to those places, but they're kept secret for some reason? I mean, do you really think we're the only planet with life in the *entire* universe?"

Patty half-turned away and covered her face with her hands. Amanda watched her shoulders lift and fall with the depth of her breath. When she turned back, Patty knelt beside the bed, taking Amanda's hands into her own.

"Honey, those stories… Your dad had an incredible imagination, and he also had some *issues* when it came to separating his imagination from reality. Mental issues, like a sickness that affected his brain. He also had excellent doctors who got those issues under control… mostly.

"But I think, maybe, the stories were an outlet for all that. Maybe that's why they seemed so vivid and real. I don't know. But they were just stories. No matter what he might have said about them or how real they may have seemed. You know that, right?"

"Yeah, but…" Amanda saw the worry in her mom's face and tried to keep her own frustration in check. "But what if *that* wasn't true? The part about the mental issues? What if that was part of his cover story?"

Patty let go of Amanda's hands, stood up, and ran her fingers through her hair. Amanda suddenly wondered where Aunt Judy was during all of this and whether she might be listening outside the partially open door. Patty dropped her arms and pasted on a sad smile.

"Amanda, I know you miss your dad, and I know how much that hurts, but this isn't the time to talk about this."

She stepped closer and stroked Amanda's hair gently. "You have school. I have work. And then you're going to Trina's for your big party. Let's make time to talk about dad another day, okay?"

"Yeah." Amanda swallowed back her disappointment, and noticed she felt a sense of relief as well.

§

Trina's parents loved throwing parties. Birthday parties, holiday parties, parties for their friends, parties for their kids' friends. Their house was designed for socializing. It had an open main floor featuring large rooms that spilled from one to the next. There were couches for chatting, tables for snacking, and large spaces for mingling or dancing.

Sliding glass doors along the back of the house looked out on an amazing yard with an outdoor kitchen, a fire pit, and an in-ground swimming pool. Amber sconces filled the stone patio with a golden glow, while white pool lights cast an eerie shimmer from below the clear, blue water.

The rest of the yard was dark by comparison but gently lit by strings of party lights that stretched overhead from wooden beams at the sides of the yard.

Though Amanda had been to big parties at Trina's house before, she'd underestimated how many kids would be at their end-of-the-school-year party. Trina had invited their main group of friends from middle school and some new friends they'd made this year, including Drew and his circle. That would have been a big enough crowd for Amanda's taste. She hadn't expected all the kids invited by Trina's sister, too.

Looking around the packed living room, Amanda saw mostly Izzy's friends, which was an impressive mix. Izzy was a junior and floated with just about every clique at school. The brains, the jocks, the good-ats, the emos, the fine arts, even some loners. They crowded into the sprawling house, while Trina's parents hid out upstairs.

Amanda could imagine a cultural studies class at PTS learning about cliques like this, if they were teens from another world. A textbook would outline their identifying greetings, slang, and fashion choices. On second thought, she wondered if there already was a PTS class like that, since many travelers seemed to think teenagers were an entirely different species.

At the beginning of the party, Amanda and the other freshmen had gone straight to the pool, leaving the older crowd to gather in the kitchen and living room. But as the night went on, the groups mingled more freely.

The younger group ventured inside for food, and Izzy's friends made their way out to jump in the pool or sit on the edge with their feet dipping in. Speakers played music inside and out, leading to makeshift dance floors forming wherever the mood struck.

By ten-thirty, the throng of people was starting to get to Amanda. She'd gone inside to dry off and change out of her swimsuit. When she came back downstairs, the living room had filled with kids she didn't know. Some were dancing. Some were talking. Some were making out at the edges of the room.

Threading her way to the kitchen, Amanda saw Trina hovering near a group of varsity cheerleaders, laughing at their jokes while they barely acknowledged her existence. It embarrassed Amanda to watch, so she headed into the backyard instead. Scanning the area, looking for Drew, she felt a pang of dread when she recognized someone else standing on the far side of the pool.

It can't be, she told herself, even as she slowly made her way around the pool. Her palms felt clammy and her heartbeat echoed in her throat.

Not here. He can't be here.

Their eyes met, and she knew, without a doubt, that it was Lucas Flynn.

By the time she'd skirted the pool, Lucas had moved deeper into the backyard to stand under the very last string of overhead lights. Ten feet beyond those lights, the grass gave way to a patch of woods. Amanda knew the trees were thin here, with a winding golf course on the other side, but at this time of night, the wooded area felt threatening.

"What are you doing here?" Amanda hissed, checking to see how the other kids were reacting to his presence. Surprisingly, no one else seemed bothered by him.

"You aren't happy to see me? I'm hurt!" Lucas grinned and winked before swigging from a red plastic cup. He scanned casually across the backyard as if looking for someone else.

"You can't be here!" Amanda sputtered, unable to act as cool.

"Why not?" Lucas shrugged. "Mike invited me."

"Mike?" Amanda glanced around them. "Which Mike?"

"Exactly." Lucas smirked at his own cleverness before adding, "Relax. I'm an expert at blending in."

"Blending in?" Amanda tried for a neutral expression as she looked over his *disguise* more carefully. Instead of his tactical gear, Lucas was wearing tan board shorts and an unbuttoned, brightly patterned, short-sleeve shirt over a white tank top. His hair was hanging loose across his forehead, and he'd shaved off his scruffy, stubbly beard.

"You are way too old for… *this*." Amanda gestured toward his outfit with both hands. Glancing down, she caught sight of his chunky, leather flip-flops and rolled her eyes theatrically.

"Old? I'm twenty-five," Lucas insisted. "Plenty young enough to look like a friend visiting from college."

"You sound like Rory," Amanda muttered, praying no one would come over to them.

"Rory Beck?" Lucas perked up. "When do I get to meet her?"

"Um, never." Amanda threw up her hands. "Why are you even here?"

"To see you," Lucas answered with a laugh. Then added an exaggerated, "Duh!"

Amanda ran her hands over her jaw and down her neck, rolling her eyes again.

One normal night, she thought to herself. *I just wanted one normal night. One normal party.*

"Come on, Amanda." Lucas nudged her arm. "Aren't you flattered that I'd go to so much trouble to see you?"

Amanda spun to face him.

"Flattered? No! Not flattered! It is not flattering to have you show up here—at my friend's house! How did you even know I'd be here? Are you following me?"

A group of older boys looked their way. One of them raised an eyebrow in a show of concern, the others smirked, and they all moved away with uneasy chuckles. Lucas took Amanda's arm and pulled her deeper into the shadows near the edge of the woods.

"Let's not make a scene," he warned, dropping his cavalier smile.

Amanda's chest pounded and she wondered if she should yell for help, either from the kids at the party or with a psychic message that would bring real backup.

"I still have friends in PTS," Lucas answered plainly, serious for once, and Amanda forgot about calling out for help. "More than you might think. They clued me in on where you'd be tonight."

"But…?" Amanda blinked, trying to settle on what to ask first. "But why would anyone at PTS know I'm at Trina's party tonight? Or even care?"

PTS worked with Judy to arrange her training schedule. And PTS agents had orders to report her for showing up off-world without Rory. But Amanda had never thought about PTS tracking her movements when she was home. Or with her friends. Did Judy report where she would be? She thought of the smartphone Judy had bought her for Christmas. Was that how they tracked her?

"You're surprised?" Lucas shrugged. "You haven't exactly been playing by their rules, have you? Sneaking off to Arcadia? Showing up late to classes?"

"Well, I…" Amanda's face flushed. "Okay, so…? They're just tracking me everywhere now? And you're checking up on me? You think that's okay?"

"Hey, don't get mad at me because they don't trust you." Lucas held up his hands and Amanda sighed, feeling her anger toward him fade. It was PTS who was tracking her, and she wouldn't know that if Lucas hadn't told her.

"Not like I have a reason to trust *them*," Amanda mumbled, thinking of how much Director Alvarsson had hidden from her about their plans with the Arcadians.

Lucas watched her with a sad understanding.

"You know, don't you?"

Amanda crossed her arms over her chest again, hating that her voice sounded so small and hurt. She hated that everyone at PTS had kept secrets from her. Secrets like the ones they'd kept from her mom for decades.

"Talk to me." Lucas spoke simply, without his mocking cynicism.

Amanda hesitated, reminding herself that he was supposed to be the enemy, no matter what he said.

But then she considered how Lucas had gotten lost off-world before anyone could explain what was happening to him. She remembered what Aunt Judy had once told her about him: *He has some disturbed ideas… He wouldn't have hurt you though.*

Were Lucas' ideas really disturbed? Or did he know disturbing things about PTS?

Since he probably knew about it anyway, Amanda told him the highlights of her conversation with Mitra. She admitted that no one had told her the truth about the Arcadian's full psychic abilities, and she shared that PTS hadn't been teaching her any kind of specialized psychic architect skills.

"Maybe they don't even know how to train me," she finished with her deepest fear.

"It's been like a hundred years since they've had a psychic architect, and I haven't found any books on how an architect's powers actually work. Maybe they don't even know."

"Psychic engineers are the closest they have now," Lucas agreed, before noticing Amanda's confusion. "Psychic engineers? The ones who work with psychic architects to maintain the connections. You haven't met with any yet? Wait, you haven't been told about them?"

Amanda forced her mouth shut and tightened her arms around her ribcage. Her head was spinning with questions she didn't want to ask.

"It's not that surprising, I guess," Lucas continued thoughtfully. "They have so few engineers these days, and they keep the ones they do have hidden away."

Remembering what he'd told her before about the PTS detention center, Amanda shuddered. Could the High Council have these psychic engineers held against their will? Were they locked away *for their own safety*? Was that their plan for her, once her powers developed?

Before she could ask, Amanda saw Lucas' eyes gleam in the glow of the nearby lights.

"It doesn't matter," he assured with a sly grin. "Most of the psychic engineers are with me now."

"With you?"

"Yes, you might be surprised at how many travelers are with me, and our numbers are growing." Lucas brushed the subject away. "But we'll get back to that later."

"Later?" Amanda felt like she was falling behind the conversation just as Lucas was regaining his reckless confidence.

"First, we need to talk more about the Arcadians and this deal PTS has with them."

"Deal? You mean, for me to create a house in their mindspace?"

"A-plus!" Lucas nodded with pride. "Do you think Alvarsson or the High Council would offer something like that without getting something in return?"

"I guess not." Amanda considered what little Director Alvarsson had told her. "They want Arcadian technology. The Arcadians have some kind of vibration-based power, and hover carts, and translator discs…"

"Think bigger." Lucas leaned closer, narrowing his eyes and dropping his voice to a near whisper.

Intrigued, Amanda forgot that Lucas was supposed to be a dangerous enemy. She instinctively stepped closer to him, lowering her own voice so they could talk without being overheard. Three juniors ran by, chasing a freshman who was laughing and waving someone's shoes over his head. Amanda and Lucas ignored them.

"What's bigger than their technology?"

"You remember the hypnagogic drug PTS planned to use on me in Terra-V? Psylo4C?"

Amanda nodded uneasily.

Lucas had told her about the drug during their standoff at the Churukh's hidden fortress. PTS scientists had created Psylo4C to put travelers into a dreamlike state. It was supposed to be a medicine used in special cases, but Lucas claimed it could keep a traveler from escaping through the mindspace and even be used to plant false ideas in a traveler's mind.

"The High Council isn't going to stop at mentally and physically controlling travelers," Lucas continued gravely. "They want to control who can—and, more importantly, who can not—have psychic travel abilities at all."

"They can't do that," Amanda protested. "It's genetic. People are born with psychic abilities or they aren't."

"For now," Lucas agreed. "But the Arcadians have methods for manipulating genetics. With their help, PTS scientists could create a gene therapy that would let them turn psychic travel genes on or off at will. They could take away the abilities of travelers who don't fall in line with their plans. Travelers like me… and others."

Amanda felt sick as she thought over the possibilities. The High Council had rules to regulate psychic travel, but travelers could still use their abilities to escape PTS and hide out wherever they wanted… If they really wanted to leave. Like Lucas had…

"Wait!" Amanda hit on a flaw in Lucas' theory. "The Arcadian's ancestors used their free will to leave PTS and start a new society on a completely different world. They know they left for good reasons, and they don't really trust us. They must know it's not a good idea to give PTS that much control over people."

"Unless they stand to gain something that's more important to them," Lucas countered. "Like their own psychic gatehouse in their own separate mindspace… Oh, damn!"

Amanda saw Lucas frowning deeply as he stared over her head at something across the lawn.

"Here comes the boyfriend."

Amanda turned to see Drew walking toward them.

"He's not my boyfriend," she responded automatically, annoyed that Drew was interrupting their discussion just as it was getting interesting.

"Whatever." Lucas shook Amanda's arm lightly, drawing her attention. "We need a more private place to talk. Meet me in the attic in thirty minutes. I have a safe place and some people you need to meet."

"What? No!" Amanda shook her head, pulling away. "I'm not traveling with you."

"Amanda, please." Lucas bent toward her, peering through the dim light to meet her worried eyes. "I promise you'll be safe. And it's important."

"I…"

Drew was getting closer, squinting to get a better look at them, and then speeding up his pace.

"Amanda," he called to her, still struggling to see who was with her in the shadows.

"Thirty minutes!"

Lucas disappeared as Drew reached Amanda's side.

"Was that…? Were you talking to Lucas Flynn? Amanda? Come back here!"

Amanda had pushed past him, walking toward the house. She needed time to think over what Lucas had said, and she wasn't ready to share those thoughts with Drew.

"Hey!" Drew closed the distance between them quickly. "What the hell was Lucas Flynn doing here?"

Stopping short, Amanda saw curious stares all around them. Several groups had gone quiet, watching whatever drama was unfolding. A softer, teasing voice spoke up from behind Amanda.

"Who's Lucas Flynn?"

Amanda turned to see some cheerleaders standing a few feet away. One of the juniors on the squad, Chelsea Simmons, smiled broadly while the others watched with detached amusement.

Trina stood on Chelsea's left. Frowning deeply.

"Boyfriend from another school?" Chelsea smirked.

"Ugh, no," Amanda responded angrily.

"Oh, come on," Chelsea laughed. "You can tell me. Who was he?"

"He's none of your business."

"Amanda!" Trina jumped in. "Don't be rude."

"Rude? Me?" Amanda shook her head and threw up her arms.

"Amanda, come on." Drew spoke urgently, trying to lead her away, but Amanda shook off his hand and glared pointedly at everyone gathered around her.

Their stares reminded her of the first time Judy had taken her to the PTS building in Chicago. The other travelers had gawked at her like she was a freak.

"No." She pulled back from Drew, scanned the crowd with a scathing look, and shouted, "Don't you have your own lives to live? Leave me alone!"

She stormed past Trina and the cheerleaders, leaving Drew in her wake, but she didn't get far before another unexpected adult was suddenly standing in front of her.

"Seriously?" Amanda sighed, causing both Trina and Drew to look at her with confusion.

"Do you know her?" Trina asked, while Drew's face tensed with concern.

"Hi, I'm Amanda's cousin!" Rory waved, using a bouncy voice that was entirely out-of-character.

Amanda stretched her own lips into a brittle smile and tried to act like it wasn't odd at all for her no-nonsense training agent to be here. At her friend's party. Minutes after Lucas Flynn had left.

"Judy has a daughter?" Trina shot Amanda a questioning look.

"Other side of the family," Drew answered, before he stuck out his hand and introduced himself. "Drew Turner. Amanda told me you might be coming to town."

"Yeah, I'm Rory." She shook his hand, playing along. "Just here for a visit."

"Why are you here?" Amanda had stopped smiling, annoyed at the way Drew had jumped in to cover for Rory, no questions asked.

"I'm picking you up," Rory explained. "Aunt Patty asked me to get you."

"But I'm spending the night." Amanda frowned and crossed her arms, determined not to help her.

"Right." Rory glanced toward Trina apologetically. "Unfortunately, we have a family emergency and Amanda will need to come home with me."

"Don't worry," she reassured Amanda quickly. "Your mom and Aunt Judy are fine! But grandpa isn't doing well, and we need to go see him. Tonight."

"Oh, no! I'm so sorry!" Trina reached for Amanda's hand, caught up in her *family emergency*.

Amanda looked past her to lock eyes with Drew. He knew both of Amanda's grandfathers had died years ago, even if Trina didn't.

"We should go," Rory said gently, guiding Amanda forward by the shoulder. She glanced toward Trina, "You'll explain to your parents?"

"Of course!" Trina pulled Amanda into an impulsive hug, shifting into *supportive friend* mode.

Five minutes later, Amanda was riding in the front seat of Rory's rental car with a dull headache and a growing sense of anger.

CHAPTER 6

DR. AGNES WEBB

Rory was all business the moment they got in the car. "Your location was compromised," she explained before Amanda could ask.

"Compromised." Amanda began ticking items off on her fingers. "You showed up at my friend's party. You lied to my friends. Badly. You pulled me out of there without even asking if I wanted to go. You embarrassed me."

"You met with Lucas Flynn," Rory responded coldly.

They listened to the sound of tires on pavement.

Amanda didn't know what to say.

"Were you going to tell me?" Rory asked, after a full minute had passed.

"Does it matter?" Amanda swallowed her guilt and focused on her anger. She'd been tracked and lied to by the people who were supposed to understand her the most. "You found out anyway. What did you do? Plant cameras around Trina's yard? Bug my clothes?"

"I asked Drew if he'd seen anyone suspicious," Rory answered simply. "When you went upstairs to get your bag. He said he'd found you talking to Lucas Flynn. Alone."

"Drew," Amanda murmured darkly.

"Don't be mad at your friend for wanting you to be safe." Rory used a neutral tone, but her words cut deep.

"Fine!" Amanda snapped. "You're right. *Drew* does want me to be safe. The rest of you? I don't know what you want! You say one thing, but that isn't always true, is it?

"So, what am I supposed to think when you hide things, and lie to me, and track me, and treat me like a… a pawn in your secret schemes?"

They drove past the turn for Amanda's apartment.

Amanda didn't bother to ask where they were going.

She crossed her forearms over her chest. Her fingers dug into the tops of her shoulders, and the edge of her seatbelt pressed into her neck. She was fed up with everyone, including herself.

Rory released a deep breath, and Amanda began to tremble. She'd said too much. Her body shook in fear as she realized what she'd shouted and wondered what would happen next.

But Rory didn't say anything at all.

Rory kept driving, letting Amanda gradually take control of her emotions.

As they made another right turn, Amanda realized they'd made a large loop around her apartment building. Rory drove to the end of the block and turned again, starting another loop.

"What did he say to you?" Rory asked at last.

Amanda knew Rory was asking about Lucas, but she shook her head in small jerks, not wanting to talk about it. She wanted time to process it on her own before being questioned. She'd felt that way about a lot of things lately and there was never enough time to work it all out. The problems just felt bigger each day, growing until Amanda didn't know where to begin thinking about them, let alone *talking* about them.

Rory's eyes tracked the road ahead. Her hands guided the steering wheel lightly. Slight bumps in the road sent vibrations through their bodies, and the lights of passing cars broke up the darkness of the narrow streets. They moved steadily, minutes passing in silence. Amanda knew she would have to speak eventually.

"It isn't what he said," she answered at last. "It's what the rest of you *haven't* said."

Rory flipped on her turn signal and began navigating a wider loop around Amanda's building.

"What haven't we said?"

Amanda glanced at Rory, weighing what she should and shouldn't reveal.

"That the Arcadians have their own mindspace," she began bluntly. "And they need an architect to build a house for them. And PTS is creating drugs to control travelers' minds. And Lucas has a bunch of travelers working with him, so he's not some kind of lone psycho. And—oh, yeah— those energy games mess with my brain waves."

She tried to sound indifferent, as if she were above anything PTS said or did, but she could hear the increasing anger in her cascade of revelations.

Without saying a word, Rory pulled the car to the side of the road and cut the engine. Amanda swallowed hard, alarmed by Rory's death-grip on the steering wheel.

A car passed by with a flash of headlights that soon left them in the shadows again. The car's taillights were fading into the distance when Rory finally turned to Amanda and spoke in a slow, serious tone.

"I need you to start at the beginning, and, Amanda," Rory paused, her gaze boring into Amanda's startled eyes. "I need you to tell me everything."

§

Amanda tried to settle into her first weekend of summer break as if her life was normal. Patty wanted to spend some family time together before returning to work on Monday. They explored their favorite museums in D.C., watched movies, and browsed sales at the outlet mall. Sometimes Judy came with them. Sometimes, she had to work.

Each time Judy went to work, Amanda expected her to come home with a punishment from Director Alvarsson. She knew he wouldn't take her meeting with Lucas Flynn lightly. But the days passed without consequences.

During one brief meeting in the birdhouse, Rory and Judy had told Amanda it was better to keep what she knew quiet for the time being. They'd sworn that the Arcadian energy games were perfectly safe and convinced her to continue training as if nothing had changed.

Amanda still had a million questions. Judy and Rory promised they would answer when they could but said it wasn't the right time.

When Monday arrived, Patty went back to work, and Amanda went back to Arcadia.

She sat across from Mitra at a glass-topped table where flashes of pale blue light zoomed in seemingly random directions. Amanda's hands rested on a suspended ledge beneath the table, palms down. She studied the lights with a soft gaze, seeing rippling patterns emerge.

Mitra's coaching replayed in her mind, *"Slow down, feel a rhythm, let your mind flow with the lights."*

He'd once told her this game was used with Arcadian children to calm the mind and strengthen emotional control. Now that Amanda knew what else the games were doing, her stomach quaked with a new nervousness.

Focusing on her breath, Amanda closed her eyes and remembered what Judy and Rory had told her. The table wasn't *changing* her brain. It was training her to shift the rhythms of her own energy. It was visual feedback of the same energy changes she created anytime she meditated. The only difference was that she was meant to be matching her energy to the Arcadian mindspace.

Amanda felt air flowing in and out of her lungs. She imagined waves of light flowing inside her skull, like the tide rolling in and out, like the lights waving across the glass table. Once she felt confident, she peeked beneath her lashes to see that she had actually changed the movement of the pale blue streaks of light.

In response to her mind, the lights had arranged themselves into a pattern of curving lines, like the radio waves Amanda had once studied in science class. This part of the game did help Amanda feel calm.

It hadn't taken long for her to learn how to manage the light in this way, syncing it to the energy flow within her own body. It was the next part of the process where she always failed.

Amanda tried not to tense up or take her eyes from the waves of blue light. After her slight nod, she sensed Mitra place his hands on an identical shelf below his side of the table. Pale green lights streaked across the glass surface, rippling through the crests of Amanda's blue lines like darts. Mitra quickly took control of his green lights and pulled them into smooth, flowing waves of his own.

The two sets of light waves, blue and green, were similar in appearance but varied in size and speed. Mitra's green lines moved more quickly with oscillations that were taller and tighter than Amanda's sloping blue waves. If he were with another Arcadian, Amanda knew the green and blue waves would easily shift into a synchronous rhythm. That was the purpose. She was meant to not only control her own lights but match them to Mitra's pattern.

Instead, the competing waves stuttered and jerked each time they came in contact—just as they had in all of Amanda's previous attempts. It was almost as if the lights were repelled by each other. Like magnets flipped the wrong way. Amanda could feel beads of sweat prickling her temples and upper lip. Her eyes squinted with her effort to control her flowing lights. She tried to breathe steadily, but her chest felt tight and there was a buzzing rapidly building in the back of her mind.

With an involuntary jerk, Amanda's upper body pulled away from the table. Her hands fell to her lap and the glass surface went dark. Mitra stood, his eyes glinting with worry, while Rory caught Amanda's shoulder for support.

She'd pushed herself and had still failed.

"I'm fine." Amanda waved them away and rubbed both fists against her watering eyes. "I just suck at this."

"No, you do not," Mitra quickly corrected her, having learned what it meant to *suck at something* from one of their previous sessions. "We were closer this time."

Amanda looked away, not believing him.

"Really," he insisted before tapping on the tabletop to bring up some complicated statistics. "Our waves may not have matched yet, but if you measure the time you were able to maintain the frequency of your—"

Mitra stopped talking when the door to his lab opened. Three scientists entered the room, led by an older Arcadian woman. She had pure white hair, cut to her chin, and wore a deep blue jumpsuit that looked like fine silk.

Agnes Webb. Amanda recognized her from a picture in the lobby of the science building. She hadn't seen her in person until now.

"Dr. Webb," Mitra greeted with a friendly smile. "We are honored by your visit."

He'd stood up as a sign of respect. Rory had stood as well, but Amanda guessed her movement was more for security than diplomacy. Realizing she was the only one still seated, Amanda began to rise.

"No, please." Dr. Webb gestured toward Amanda's chair. "Stay seated."

She moved to an adjacent table and pulled out a chair for herself. Mitra returned to his seat uncertainly, following

Amanda's lead, though Rory and the scientists remained standing.

"I thought it was time we should meet," Dr. Webb announced with a lift of one eyebrow. "I suppose I might have arranged a more official meeting, but what's the point of being in charge if I can't do what I like within my own institute?"

Her voice was low and smooth, with a gravelly edge that added weight to her words. Her arrogant expression was at odds with the flippant tone of her question.

Amanda couldn't tell whether Dr. Webb was making a joke or asserting her dominance. *Probably both,* she decided, trying to size up Dr. Webb before giving an answer.

Rory watched the exchange with an expression that suggested she wasn't inclined to like Dr. Webb.

"There is nothing to worry about," Dr. Webb smiled thinly, as if well aware of the impression she was making. "This is an informal meeting to simply see how you are getting on here."

"Very well," Mitra interjected brightly. "I was just explaining the results of our latest trial…" He turned back to the statistics displayed on the glass table, but Dr. Webb wasn't interested.

"Later, Mitra. I want to hear from Amanda now. How do you like our world?"

"I, uh," Amanda hesitated. "It's very beautiful."

"You feel welcome here?"

"Yes, Mitra has been very friendly."

"Yes." Dr. Webb looked from Amanda to Mitra with a knowing expression.

"I mean, he's very smart," Amanda corrected, feeling heat in her face. "As a scientist."

She fixed her eyes on the swirling brooch pinned near Dr. Webb's collar, avoiding her eyes. The shape of the jewelry seemed familiar, though Amanda couldn't place where she'd seen the symbol before.

"Amanda." Dr. Webb shifted to a more serious tone. "I understand you have some questions about your purpose here, and Mitra has tried to clarify the situation."

Amanda looked toward the trio of PTS scientists who were watching and listening closely. They came to all of Amanda's training sessions, along with the two Arcadian scientists who were assigned to Mitra's project.

The scientists typically stood back and took notes, often staying to work together after Amanda and Rory had left for the day. She'd gotten along with them well enough but kept her distance, knowing they reported back to Director Alvarsson.

Dr. Webb's eyes followed Amanda's gaze before resuming carefully.

"I want you to feel comfortable with our technology and your part in our project. Nothing we do here will harm you. Our energy tables are safe for Maiorum use and have been used by many of your people with no ill effects."

Amanda nodded, hoping Dr. Webb wouldn't say anything more direct.

"I have some matters that I do need to discuss with your High Council," she continued in a voice that signaled both regret and a warning. "Before I do, I would like to ascertain your feelings on a proposition I am considering."

"All right," Amanda answered uncertainly, after shooting Rory a questioning look.

"I understand the schooling in your world has stopped for a seasonal break," Dr. Webb went on, "which gives you more time to spend here in Arcadia. How would you like to live in our world during this season, allowing for a more immersive training experience?"

"Live? Here?" Amanda looked to Rory for support, but Rory was focused on Dr. Webb with narrowed eyes and a tight frown. "I couldn't. I mean, it's a really nice offer, but I couldn't leave my home… or my mom."

"Your mother is welcome to join us here as well." Dr. Webb smiled graciously.

"No, my mom isn't—"

"Dr. Webb." Rory gave the impression of stepping forward though she'd only shifted her stance. "This is not an appropriate offer to discuss with Amanda directly."

"Appropriate?" Dr. Webb's eyebrows lifted, and she spoke with exaggerated disbelief. "What is inappropriate about conveying a desire to further our relationship with this intelligent young woman? Seeking her opinion is a sign of respect."

Rory pressed her lips together, considering her response, while Dr. Webb slid her chair toward Amanda and leaned in to speak urgently.

"You would be given the freedom to explore our world, learn from our scientists, and live in a sanctuary, protected from the crime and violence of your world."

"Dr. Webb." Rory shook her head and reached for Amanda's arm, guiding her to her feet.

"Wait." Dr. Webb stood as well, putting her hand on Amanda's free arm. "There will be a discussion with your leaders about the condition of your world, such as it has become. However, we do not want that to interfere with our relationship with you, Amanda. We are dedicated to the good we can foster from our common ancestry."

They stood in place, Amanda positioned between Rory and Dr. Webb, who each had a hand on one of her arms. Dr. Webb's words echoed in Amanda's mind. *The condition of your world… The crime and violence of your world… There will be a discussion with your leaders.*

Amanda's stomach dropped to her feet.

"We're done here." Rory pulled Amanda toward the door, breaking Dr. Webb's gentle grip.

"Fine," Dr. Webb agreed lightly, before adding, "You may want to bring your books home."

Amanda cringed, wishing the floor would swallow her whole. One of Dr. Webb's assistants held out two of the books Amanda had brought to Mitra on an earlier visit.

Rory seemed puzzled by the innocent-looking books, though she clearly saw the sick fear on Amanda's face.

"Thanks." Rory accepted the books without further comment and marched Amanda toward the door.

§

"What were you thinking?"

Amanda sat cross-legged on a couch in the party room while Drew paced in front of her. She'd been asked to leave the apartment so Rory and Judy could have a deeper discussion about the books she'd smuggled into

Arcadia, and Amanda had thought Drew would be the one person who would understand and be on her side. Instead, he'd reacted with the same shocked disappointment she'd just escaped upstairs.

"It was only a few novels," Amanda muttered, feeling less righteous by the minute.

"A few novels?" Drew stopped pacing and faced Amanda with wide eyes and an open mouth. "Amanda, you were visiting a different planet! You were meeting with a group of humans who splintered from our species centuries ago and have only been in contact with us for a hundred years or so. Didn't you realize there was a reason you could only bring pre-approved books? Didn't they make you take a whole class on what *not* to talk about in Arcadia?"

"You know they did."

Amanda slumped deeper into the cushions.

"But you brought Mitra those books anyway? You snuck them in under different book jackets?"

Drew raised his arms and shook his head. He went back to pacing, punctuating his steps with short huffs and sneers of disbelief.

"Are you *that* into Mitra?" he asked after a minute of grumpy stomping. "He's so hot that you'd risk interplanetary diplomacy to impress him?"

Amanda sat up in anger. Her lips parted, but her mind went blank.

Drew stopped pacing and they stared at each other wordlessly. Fists clenched. Eyes flashing.

"Bite me," Amanda snapped as she leaped up and stamped toward the door.

"Amanda, wait!" Drew followed but stopped himself from reaching out to physically restrain her. When she stopped walking, he spoke with more control. "I just don't understand how you could have been so..."

"Stupid?" Amanda spun around with tears spilling down her cheeks. Her face was red, and her voice shook as she launched into a tirade.

"I *am* stupid. I don't even know why I did it! It just didn't seem that bad at the time... Mitra kept acting like I was some perfect angel visiting from paradise, when their world is so much better than ours."

She lifted her forearms with bent elbows, mindlessly flexing and clenching her outspread hands.

"They don't have crime, or poverty, or war, or anything like that. Their whole society is built around peace, and love, and reasoning. Arcadia is the paradise! But the High Council has them convinced that our world is just as great in its own way, and that we also evolved away from the war and violence that drove their ancestors to leave all those centuries ago. It's all lies!"

"And you wanted Mitra to know the truth?" Drew asked, reluctantly releasing his anger.

"I don't know." Amanda wiped her eyes and hung her head. "I didn't want to be part of the lie, I guess. And I was mad at Director Alvarsson for sending me to all those basic classes and for holding me back..."

She trailed off, wondering if he really had been holding her back or whether she'd been too impatient to learn more after her experience in Terra-V.

"You're not stupid," Drew said softly.

Amanda looked up and saw something gentle and familiar in his face. It felt like she was finally seeing Drew in a way she hadn't seen him in a long time.

She saw the Drew of her childhood who had welcomed her to the building, let her ride his bike, and grown up with her for the past eight years. He was the Drew she'd lost for a while during middle school but found again at the bus stop last fall.

She thought he'd been here all along, but it was suddenly clear that she'd lost him again, somewhere during the last few months. Or maybe he'd lost her.

"This year has been…" Amanda choked up, feeling tears rush back into her eyes.

"Come on." Drew led Amanda back to the couch and sat beside her, holding her hand. They watched the way their fingers intertwined. His dark hand dwarfed hers. Her pale fingers nestled into the crevices between his knuckles. His fingers gripped hers gently, and she softly squeezed back.

"This year has been crazy," Drew agreed.

Amanda thought of everything that had happened since the fall. They'd started high school, she'd developed psychic travel abilities, he'd dated her best friend…

"You're my best friend," Amanda said suddenly, just realizing it for herself.

Drew leaned his head against hers and chuckled.

"You're my best friend, too."

An ache grew inside Amanda's ribs. She couldn't tell if it held more pleasure or pain, but whatever she was feeling was more than she could handle. It was *all* more than she could handle.

She'd screwed up in Arcadia because she wasn't ready to be there. She'd screwed up with Drew this year because she wasn't ready to see him date anyone else. But she didn't know what that meant. It was all happening too fast.

"I can't do it."

Amanda pulled her hand away and shifted to the edge of the couch, ready to stand up.

"Can't do what?" Drew sat up beside her.

His hand lightly touched her back and Amanda jumped to her feet.

"I can't do any of it!" she insisted sharply. "I can't be a psychic architect. I can't be a psychic traveler. I can't even… I just can't. That's all."

She faced Drew with a fear that made her body tremble.

He sighed and smiled gently.

"Then don't."

Chapter 7

Back in the Shelter of the Tuntum Trees

For two weeks, Amanda lived her life as a normal, 15-year-old girl.

She hadn't been exiled from the Psychic Traveler Society or even been officially reprimanded. But the High Council now knew about her smuggled books. Director Alvarsson had told her not to visit Arcadia until they had reevaluated her position there, though she could continue the rest of her PTS training while waiting for their decision. Instead, Amanda had quit.

It wasn't an official resignation. She wasn't even sure Director Alvarsson and the High Council knew she had quit, but she had told both Judy and Rory that she was done with the Psychic Traveler Society. She wasn't going back for a long time. Maybe not until she was eighteen and out of high school. Or maybe not until she finished college.

She'd thought they would argue, saying her future as the next psychic architect was too important. But they hadn't.

They'd heard her out and agreed that some time away from her training would be a good idea.

So, Amanda lived her life as a normal, 15-year-old.

She went to gymnastics classes and practiced cheers in Trina's backyard. She passed the test for her learner's permit and started driving lessons with Patty. When it was too hot to be outside, she and Drew lounged around the party room, playing card games or just talking. They could go long stretches without mentioning psychic travel or her future with PTS. But psychic travel was never far from Amanda's thoughts.

Without regular visits, the pull of the house became overwhelming. There were days when it physically hurt to stay away. On those days, Amanda wanted it all back, exactly as it had been. But then, she would remember how everyone had kept the truth about the Arcadians from her. Her anger would rush back, along with her resolve to stay away until they appreciated her. She would stay away for years if that's what it took.

Rory decided two weeks was long enough.

One morning, soon after Patty had left for work, Rory showed up at the apartment and told Amanda to put on some warm clothes.

"Jeans and a sweater will do."

Rory's determined face stopped Amanda's protests.

Within minutes, Rory had led Amanda back to the attic. As they stood in front of the seventh door, the door she had created, Amanda shivered in anticipation.

"Terra-V?" She lightly touched the silvery wood.

"It's been too long," Rory answered. "For both of us."

When they stepped through the door, Amanda was amazed by the transformation since her last visit. The proximal zone she'd created was centered in what had once been the paved courtyard of a dismal fortress hidden within an unnerving forest of stone spires. In that fortress, the Churukh royalty had imprisoned a small tribe of Vherahna healers around a single, sickly tuntum tree, forcing them to produce life-giving *vhe* for the royals alone.

Now, as the proximal door faded from sight, Amanda scarcely recognized the courtyard around her. Lemon yellow sunlight reflected off the fortress' stone walls, which were a pale gray after being scrubbed clean from their years of accumulated dirt and grime. The paved floor had been torn up, allowing the island of purple grass at its center to spread throughout the courtyard. Most importantly, the once spindly tuntum tree now flourished, displaying a bower of lavender leaves and iridescent flowers amid its graceful branches.

Amanda moved quickly toward the tree, smiling at the increased width of its twin trunks, then leaned close to feel the reassuring thrum of its sap flowing in a steady rhythm. *Tuntum. Tuntum.* It was midday in Terra-V. The tree had stretched to its fullest height, towering several feet above the fortress walls. Though she was delighted by the tree's rapid growth, Amanda longed to be here at twilight when its twin trunks would twist down to the cozy crouch of its nighttime shelter.

Beyond the tuntum tree, Amanda was more surprised to see lilac-hued saplings now spaced throughout the open area. Wooden stakes and pale blue twine supported each thin tree, and it looked like they were thriving under the glistening sun.

"How…?" Amanda wandered toward the nearest sapling. She studied its unmistakable twin trunks, thin as they were, then reached out to brush the back of her hand against its soft leaves.

"With love," a mellifluous voice whispered over her shoulder.

Amanda's heart lifted and her gaze followed, scanning the landscape until she spotted Alira at the far edge of the courtyard. Though she stood at a distance, Alira's mystical voice had carried clearly. They crossed the expanse, meeting amid the widely spaced saplings.

"It's good to see you, our waking dreamer," Alira greeted warmly.

"You, too," Amanda managed, feeling too many emotions filling her throat.

"Shhh," Alira crooned, sensing Amanda's troubles. "Be calm with me now."

Alira's slender hands delicately enveloped Amanda's upper arms. A familiar tone filled the air, sending a vibration trembling through Amanda's body. She closed her eyes and leaned into the sensations. With each breath, she felt her body both soften and fill with energy as the transfer of *vhe* spread its gentle, healing warmth.

When the chant faded away, Amanda opened her eyes. Alira withdrew her hands and nodded with a tender smile. Her bright, purple eyes blinked in their double rhythm. *Blink-blink. Blink-blink.* Her opalescent skin shimmered in the sunlight, and her deep blue hair swung just above her thin shoulders. Amanda had missed Alira more than she had realized.

"The healing will help," Alira offered cautiously, "but it will not last long on its own. You have questions, doubts, that are in need of a deeper settling."

"Yes." Amanda swallowed, longing to tell Alira everything but not sure where to begin.

"In time," Alira assured her with a gentle wave. "For now, come see what has grown from the fruits of our shared journey."

Amanda gladly let Alira lead her around the changed courtyard. The Vherahna had made great strides with the help of both Churukh workers and traveler knights. The south wall of the fortress was being dismantled, creating open space for a waving row of tuntum saplings to stretch into the stone forest beyond. Over time, Alira hoped to bridge the divide between the tuntum trees here and their sacred Vherahna Forest. Until then, many Vherahna had taken up residency within the fortress so they could tend the trees and nurture the recovering soil.

Those who had once been held captive had relocated to the larger Vherahna community where they could heal and become acclimated to their ancestral home.

"But how did you do it? I thought it wasn't possible to transplant tuntum trees outside of your forest."

"It has been difficult," Alira agreed tentatively. "As we've healed this lone tree, it has grown strong enough to foster new life. We've also had unforeseen help which has provided new methods for enriching the earth."

"Help from…?"

Before Amanda could finish the question, a commotion behind Alira caught her attention. It was a group of knights welcoming Rory's return with laughs, embraces, and hearty slaps on the back. Amanda smiled to see how the other travelers had clearly missed her, but her mind went blank at the sight of an older knight stepping from the center of the group.

Cameron.

Cameron was the first person Amanda had seen in the mindspace. He'd been in the attic, coming out of a door from Terra-V and wearing the same knight's armor he wore now. She'd hid from him that day and run from him on her first trip to Terra-V. Yet, he'd been the one to show up at her hearing and demand the High Council let her come to Terra-V to fulfill their most sacred prophecy.

Cameron had been the one to begin Amanda's field training and prepare her for travel, both physically and psychically, in only a few short weeks.

Cameron told me about my dad, Amanda thought sadly. He'd also been the first to tell her about psychic architects and the abilities he'd suspected in her. He'd taught her to ride a horse, fence, fight, and trust her instincts.

He had believed in her.

And then he'd walked away.

Seeing him now, Amanda's heart ached. Her feet were ready to run toward him and her arms itched to wrap around his waist. But just as fast as the joy flooded her body, a cold river of detachment washed it away.

She studied Cameron with a critical eye. His blue tunic was bright against the aged metal of his chainmail.

He moved with the same confidence that had carried him along their journey through the foreign countryside. Yet, he looked older. Amanda saw the strain under his smile and suspected he might not be happy to see her.

Four months ago, Amanda had expected Cameron to formally take over her field training and accompany her to Arcadia. Instead, he'd said Rory was a better choice. He'd stayed in Terra-V to help Alira and hadn't contacted Amanda since. Now, he was walking toward her with hard eyes and a tight smile.

"It's good to see you, Amanda," he said smoothly.

"Uh, huh." Amanda returned his nod, reining in her emotions.

They stood uneasily, sizing each other up. Rory had separated herself from her friends and joined them, choosing a place by Cameron's side. Amanda crossed her arms and looked away, ignoring them both, until Cameron turned to address Alira deferentially.

"Please excuse us. I would like some time alone with Amanda."

"No!" Amanda reached for Alira's arm impulsively, surprised at her own anger. "I came here to see Alira, and we haven't had time to talk yet."

Rory's lips pressed together in a tight, thin line.

"You came here because I brought you here."

They glared at each other, neither noticing Cameron's exasperated sigh.

"There will be time for us to talk later," Alira reassured, gently releasing Amanda's grip on her forearm. "First, you must go where you are bid."

"I *must*," Amanda scoffed under her breath. "I don't have a say anywhere else, so why would it be any different here?"

"Watch your tone when you speak to Alira." Cameron spoke evenly, but his words were fuel on the fire.

"Watch *my* tone?" Amanda felt a familiar rage building in her chest. "Because *I'm* the only one with the problem, right? I'm the unruly teenager who needs to be ordered around and controlled." She jerked her head toward Rory. "Let me guess, *she* thinks you're the only one who can get through to me?"

"I don't know what Rory thinks," Cameron said, meeting Amanda's fiery gaze with his own cool calm. "*I* thought you might like to go for a ride."

"A ride?"

Amanda followed his gaze toward the open fortress wall, where two feathered horses were being led toward them.

"Iveryn!"

Amanda sprinted across the distance, forgetting everyone and everything else. Her heart raced as she buried her face in the soft down on Iveryn's pink neck, experiencing happiness so sharp it nearly felt like pain. "Oh, you beautiful, beautiful boy!"

Horses on Terra-V were scarcely similar to horses on Earth. Yet Amanda had come to adore the pink-and-red feathered animal that had carried her throughout her first off-world journey. Iveryn stamped his front foot and shook the gold-tipped, red plume at the crest of his head, happy to be back with his young rider.

"Here." A knight handed Amanda a sack of pineapple that she quickly fed to the grateful horse.

Cameron joined them, taking the reins of Ynhara, his own purple-feathered horse.

"I take it you're up for a ride?" he asked lightly.

"Always!" Amanda's lips stretched into an irrepressible smile as Iveryn gracefully lowered his body to the ground, making it easier for Amanda to climb onto his short, leather saddle.

They left the fortress, the horses carefully picking their way through the gloom of the stone forest. Even in the middle of the day, its rock monoliths cast long, eerie shadows. The sunlight that filtered in was jagged and dimmed. It created a haze of melancholy that gradually curbed the excitement of Amanda's reunion with her beloved horse.

Cameron and Amanda rode without speaking, though the horses kept an even, side-by-side pace. Amanda gently stroked the silken feathers in Iveryn's mane. As the shadows pressed in, she mentally replayed her earlier outburst. With each repetition, she felt more foolish for being so angry with Cameron. She didn't know what to say now that they were alone together.

"I'm sorry."

Cameron's apology took Amanda by surprise.

"I'm sorry I haven't stayed in touch," he went on. "I'm sorry I let my work here keep me from checking in on you, and I'm sorry I let myself believe you wouldn't need me if you had Rory by your side."

"Oh, well," Amanda hesitated. "You've been doing important things here."

Iveryn tossed his head with a soft nicker, glancing at Ynhara. They were making good progress through the stone forest, and the horses were impatient to reach the warm sunshine and open desert beyond its reach.

"You're important, too." Cameron spoke so softly Amanda half-wondered if she'd imagined his words. She shifted closer and he continued more forcefully, "Your future is important to me. I want you to do well, develop your abilities, and be an asset to our society. It's what your father would want, and I owe him that much."

"My father," Amanda sighed and centered herself in the saddle.

In the first few weeks after their journey in Terra-V, Cameron and Amanda had met several times. He'd asked about the progress of her training and told Amanda stories about working with her father. Being a few years younger, Cameron had looked up to Gabe. They'd met during one of Cameron's first assignments as a field agent and crossed paths on several other occasions. When Gabe eventually decided to take a permanent position on Terra-V, he'd requested Cameron as a knight on his team, and they'd worked together until Gabe's death.

While she'd loved hearing stories about her father, Amanda didn't want to think about him now. It brought up too many questions about how he'd felt about his own secrets and lies. *Did he want me to know? Were his stories a way to ease me into the truth? Would he have told me about PTS if I hadn't developed psychic abilities?*

"Your father would be proud of you," Cameron told her, unaware of her feelings.

Amanda stayed silent, uneasily wondering if that was true. She could see a space between the towering monoliths widening as they neared the edge of the stone forest.

"He'd also be worried about some of the decisions you've been making lately."

Amanda frowned. It was one thing to have her own doubts but another to hear them out loud. She clenched her lips to keep from blurting out, *"You don't know what he'd think!"*

"*I'm* worried about some of the decisions you've been making lately," Cameron added meaningfully. He was trying to show he cared. Amanda knew that. Part of her even appreciated his concern. But mostly, she didn't want to hear it.

Amanda kicked her heels against Iveryn's sides, urging him forward. They were close enough to the edge of the stone forest that Iveryn required very little prodding to burst into action. Her small nudge was enough to send him sprinting past the last tower of stone and racing headlong into the open expanse of rocky desert.

The sandy soil beneath Iveryn's feet was hard-packed and cracked by the unrelenting sun. There were no trees to get in their way, only a few boulders that were easy for Iveryn to avoid. Knights now stationed at the fortress, often turned their horses out to exercise in this wide expanse, and Iveryn had come to love the freedom of dashing over this gritty, uneven ground. Usually, he galloped around without a rider, but he seemed to trust Amanda would hold fast as he gamboled in sharp zigzags and sent gravelly sand flying with the speed of his tight turns.

Amanda had never been on a runaway horse, of either the equine or feathered variety, but Iveryn's wild stampede was exactly what she needed to clear her troubled mind. She clung to the reins with her body curled against his warm neck. Soft down tickled her nose, while the longer feathers of his red-and-gold mane lashed her face. She felt the thunder of his strong feet against the ground and moved with the twisting, arching undulations of his supple back beneath the short saddle.

As she caught the pace of his rhythm, Amanda felt more confident in her seat. She kept a close crouch but lifted her head enough to feel the warm wind whistling across her face. Though she wanted to open her eyes, Amanda knew that would be a bad idea. Between Iveryn's flying feathers and the clouds of grit kicked up in his wake, it was safer to squeeze her eyes and mouth shut. Instead, she focused on feeling her hair streaming behind her, and her heart pounding with excitement.

After a short time, Amanda's arms began to shake with the effort of holding on. Her legs trembled and her back tightened. The excitement of their mad dash shifted toward fear as Amanda felt the thin, leather reins slipping in her sweaty palms.

I can't hold on, her mind shouted, even as she tightened her grip. Her heart pounded in her ears. She felt one foot come loose from its stirrup.

Iveryn, sensing the shift in her body, slowed his pace to a loping trot. Amanda cautiously blinked her eyes open. The desert was bright after the gloom of the stone forest. The sun was hot on her back.

Amanda heard Cameron before she saw him.

His shouts grew louder as Ynhara cantered toward them. Iveryn pivoted to face Cameron. Sensing the knight's anger, he spread his massive tail feathers like the fan of a strutting peacock. The tall feathers threw shade across Amanda's back as she released one hand from the reins and gingerly wiped some of the grime from her face.

"Down," Cameron ordered between gritted teeth.

Amanda looked up and saw Ynhara's purple and gold tail feathers now on display as well. The horses were old friends, but they were responding to Cameron's hostile energy. Posturing to gain dominance.

Amanda patted Iveryn's neck, encouraging him to settle down, before realizing that Cameron's order had been directed to her, not to her horse.

With murmurs of encouragement, Amanda coaxed the horse into the crouch that would let her slide easily to the ground. Iveryn's tail drooped over the rocky desert floor, and Amanda fed him a large chunk of pineapple from the sack belted to her waist.

"What were you thinking?" Cameron seethed, now standing beside her. "You could have been killed!"

"I'm fine." Amanda shrugged, hiding her quivering nerves. She leaned past Cameron and fed Ynhara a piece of pineapple, despite Iveryn's protesting whinny.

"You're not fine," Cameron answered decidedly. "You're out of control. And you can't go on like this for long without being seriously hurt."

Amanda patted Iveryn absently, then dropped the pineapple sack and clutched her arms across her stomach.

Amanda hadn't been travel sick in months, but the intense nausea that gripped her now felt exactly like her first dizzy trip through the house. Her head spun and flashes of white crossed her vision. Remembering how she'd fainted during her first visit to the High Council, Amanda dropped to her knees and brought her head below her heart. It wasn't enough to stop the churning in her stomach, and Amanda was sure she would lose her breakfast.

Cameron rubbed her back in slow, steady circles.

"Breathe," he urged softly. "Breathe."

The waves of nausea gradually receded.

Instead of throwing up, Amanda burst into a torrent of hot, heavy tears.

§

The sun lowered over the fortress and the deep hum of the descending trees vibrated through Amanda's weary body. *Tuntum. Tuntum.* Alira and Amanda sat beneath the central tree, as they had on the memorable night Amanda's mind had created a new doorway between their worlds.

Looking into the serene purple of Alira's eyes, Amanda wondered why she hadn't been sent back to Terra-V to further her training. Alira had been by her side when she'd created the door. Alira's steady focus had held her presence in the fortress courtyard until her conscious mind had seemed to split itself between both worlds, creating a permanent bridge.

Do they not want me to be a psychic architect?

Amanda puzzled over Director Alvarsson's motives, knowing that she would need these abilities if she were to ever build a house in the Arcadian mindspace. *Or does he not want a Vherahna to help with my training?*

"Where is your mind?"

Alira's gentle question made Amanda jump.

"Sorry," she murmured lightly, embarrassed at how easy it was for her thoughts to wander off.

"Don't be sorry," Alira encouraged, still holding Amanda's gaze. *Blink-blink. Blink-blink.* "Your mind is thinking, as it has been designed and taught to do. Now, we must train it to release thought and focus on the present moment. The breath. The sensations in the body and the sensations of the surrounding world. Nothing more."

Amanda nodded and inhaled deeply. The tuntum tree above them gently lowered. Its twin trunks creaked slightly as they coiled into place. The sound of its swirling sap grew louder. *Tuntum. Tuntum.* Amanda could feel the gentle force of the tree's protective enclosure and was grateful to have earned a place within the circle of grass beneath its arcing limbs.

With each breath, in and out, Amanda settled her gaze more deeply into Alira's violet eyes. The sounds of Churukh and travelers mingling in the courtyard began to fade. The chirping of night creatures grew louder. The tree's rhythmic pulse grew louder. *Tuntum. Tuntum.* The light of the torches on the fortress walls paled. The shine of the tree's luminous flowers brightened. Amanda's breath began to flow in time with the lowering tree. *Inhale. Tuntum. Exhale. Tuntum.*

The whole world softened around Amanda, leaving a shimmering aura that made her feel as though she were encased in a soap bubble. She could almost touch the surface of the bubble. Not with her fingers, but with the reach of her mind. She could feel its gentle resistance and the urge to press deeper.

"That's enough." Alira called Amanda back to the purple grass and torch-lit world with her simple words.

For a moment, Amanda's mind resisted. Her eyes shifted around, searching for the filmy bubble and blinking against the harshness of the true world. But then a calm came over her. The vivid pull of that translucent casing softly faded away.

"Do you think I can do it?" Amanda asked tentatively. "Change my energy enough to connect with the Arcadian mindspace?"

Alira peered into Amanda's eyes. *Blink-blink. Blink-blink.* Amanda had already told her about her assignment in Arcadia and Mitra's theory.

"It is possible," Alira nodded decisively. "It is similar to how we communicate with our sacred trees. We alter our energy to become like the trees themselves. Though that is a mystery I can not explain."

Later, Amanda sat beside Iveryn near the open wall of the fortress. She fed him pineapple while idly trailing her hand over his feathery flank. He was no longer wearing his saddle and was content to lounge in the grass after their earlier adventure.

"That horse shouldn't be rewarded after his behavior this afternoon."

Amanda heard the irritation in Cameron's voice but knew he had forgiven Iveryn.

Mostly.

Cameron sat beside Amanda, and they watched Rory and Alira exchanging their goodbyes. The women were too far away to be heard, but their body language made Amanda realize that leaving Terra-V, and Alira in particular, had been a difficult choice for Rory. She thought of the fight she'd watched Rory win at the training facility and wondered what plans she may have made for herself before Amanda had stumbled into the picture.

"You're ready for the High Council?" Cameron's question interrupted Amanda's reverie.

"Um, yeah, I guess."

After her breakdown in the desert, they had settled in the shade of a large rock formation for a serious talk. Cameron had confirmed that he'd been caught up on her recent behavior, and he suggested Amanda had gotten off track since they were last together. He hadn't lectured but instead let Amanda tell him how she'd been feeling pushed around and left out of planning her own life.

"It's hard to be fifteen," Cameron had said knowingly, irritating Amanda to no end. She told him the problem was with her future at PTS, not with being a teenager, but Cameron had disagreed.

"You think PTS is the problem because it's the problem you see. But your friends aren't travelers, and I'd bet good money they have a lot of the same frustrations about things going on in their lives. Parents and teachers making plans and pushing them into futures they haven't even had time to imagine for themselves yet. It was like that when I was fifteen and that was nearly ten years before my psychic abilities kicked in."

Amanda had shrugged that off, thinking it wasn't worth arguing about, but the idea stayed tucked in the back of her mind where it was sure to come out in the future. Cameron let it go as well, changing the subject to tell her the High Council had scheduled a hearing to discuss her smuggled books. He wouldn't be able to attend, but he'd offered his sound advice.

"You understand why it's best if you don't mention anything Lucas told you?"

"Yes." Amanda bit her lip. "But, Cameron, what do you think about him? And about all of that? Drugging travelers? Changing their genes?"

Cameron ran one hand over his chin. "It's too soon for me to say. Change comes to all societies at some point, if they intend to flourish. Still, those are serious charges, and we all need to be cautious until we understand the full truth. For now, keep your distance and alert Rory—*immediately*—if Lucas shows up again. Understood?"

"Yes," Amanda agreed hesitantly, not sure what Rory would do if she caught up to Lucas.

They saw Rory and Alira embrace, and Amanda knew it was time for them to leave.

"And you'll show Rory more respect?" Cameron pressed, as they got to their feet.

Amanda knew why he was asking the question, but it bothered her. She'd been so wrapped up in her own ideas lately that she hadn't considered how disrespectful she'd been to Rory—who didn't deserve to be treated that way. She nodded tightly, embarrassed to say more on that subject, then turned to say one last goodbye to Iveryn.

When Rory called the proximal door, Amanda impulsively ran back to Cameron.

"My mom," she said in a rush. "I don't want to keep
lying to my mom."

Cameron looked down at her with more sadness than
she'd expected. He looked off into the distance, swallowed
harshly, then turned back with resolve.

"I'll do what I can."

Amanda didn't know what that meant, but in a fit
of relief, she hugged Cameron close before pivoting and
stepping through the door.

CHAPTER 8

A Hearing, A Meeting, and A New Resolve

Amanda's hearing with the High Council was not held in the conference room where she'd met with them before. Judy, Rory, and Amanda were on their way to that simple room when Director Alvarsson's assistant redirected them to the 24th floor.

"The courtroom?" Judy and Rory exchanged a meaningful look.

"Courtroom?" Amanda echoed, picking up on their concern. "Am I…?" She didn't know how to finish the question. *Under arrest? On trial? In trouble?*

They were silent in the elevator, and as they walked down a glass-walled hallway on the 24th floor. The outside wall of the building offered an impressive view of the city. The interior glass wall showed another hallway lined with large, ornately framed portraits.

Amanda thought they might turn into the interior hallway at some point, following some sort of maze into the heart of the building. Instead, their path turned down a short, wide corridor that ended before a pair of massive wooden doors. The doors were deep, glossy mahogany, carved with intricate symbols and patterns. A brass scroll above the door read: *Acta deos numquam mortalia fallunt.* Armed guards stood on either side of the doors.

Amanda stopped walking.

"Give us a moment," Rory told the assistant, who nodded and went inside without them.

"It's still a hearing, not a trial," Judy told Amanda in an urgent whisper. "It's the same council, the same situation, they're just seeing us in a different room."

"They're trying to intimidate you," Rory interjected, and Amanda nodded uneasily.

"It's working."

"Don't let them." Rory leaned close so the guards wouldn't hear. "It's a cheap tactic to take away your power, which means *they know you have power.* Yes, you made a mistake, and we're here to address that. But they need you, and they know it. And we are right here with you, just like we practiced. You are not alone."

"Yeah, okay."

Amanda looked into Rory's steely blue eyes, feeling a little steadier. *I'm the next psychic architect,* she told herself. *I'm important to them, and I have power, whether they like it or not.*

"Okay." Judy nudged her way into Amanda's line of sight, glancing toward the waiting doors. "Confidence, yes. Very good. But let's keep it simple. Apologize for bringing the books, and don't let the future of your training be complicated by shadowy figures and conspiracy theories. Agreed?"

"Agreed."

If Director Alvarsson and the High Council knew about Lucas visiting Amanda, they had kept it to themselves, saying the hearing was about Amanda's book smuggling and subsequent future in Arcadia. No one had mentioned Lucas Flynn. As they entered the hearing, avoiding the topic seemed like Amanda's best option.

Madame Ellis' first question dashed that hope.

"Did you bring contraband books to Arcadia on the orders of Lucas Flynn?"

Amanda sat upright, surprised into a quick response.

"What? No." She frowned at the question, adding, "Why would Lucas Flynn want me to…"

Judy nudged her foot under the table, and Amanda stopped talking. Judy, Rory, and Cameron had all told her to keep her answers short and direct, without adding questions or extra information.

"I mean, no. No one told me to bring them."

"But you have met with Lucas Flynn?" Madame Ellis persisted, looking down from her seat at the center of the raised bench.

Amanda paused to gather her thoughts. Cameron had advised her not to lie to the High Council, saying, *"If they ask you a direct question, there's a good chance they already know the answer. But they'll also fish for information, and you can try to sidestep that."*

Amanda settled on a carefully worded answer. "I met Lucas Flynn in Terra-V, last November."

Madame Ellis scanned her papers while the rest of the council murmured softly to each other. Amanda couldn't hear them as easily as she had in the conference room. But their agitated whispers suggested they didn't think much of her answer.

"We are aware of that."

Amanda waited to be asked if she had met with Lucas Flynn since then. Instead, Madame Ellis frowned and shuffled her papers.

Amanda glanced around the room to take her mind off the uncomfortable silence.

The courtroom was designed to be imposing. The seven-person council sat on a raised dais behind a long bench. It reminded Amanda of her fifth-grade field trip to the Supreme Court. Yet here, the High Council's bench sat before a series of carved wooden arches, much like the double doors leading into the courtroom. The flat panels between the arches were engraved with symbols Amanda did not recognize. The front panel of the bench displayed the Psychic Traveler Society insignia—the partial silhouette of a face in profile—emblazoned on a white marble disc shot through with veins of inky black. It was centered on the bench, just beneath Madame Ellis' seat.

Two tables faced the bench. Amanda, Judy, and Rory sat at one. Director Alvarsson and his assistant sat at the other. Guards flanked the council, and a stenographer sat at a small desk on the right side of the room. She wore a neutral expression and continued to type, even in the silence, making Amanda wonder what observations she was adding to their spoken words.

"Amanda," Madame Ellis resumed at last. "Lucas Flynn is a dangerous individual. It is important that we monitor his interactions with you—and any *attempted* interactions with you—for your own protection. Are you aware that Mr. Flynn obtained information about your whereabouts on the night of Thursday, June 14? When you were attending a party at the home of Trina Rivera?"

"Yes." Amanda felt Judy tense up beside her.

"While it is highly unlikely Mr. Flynn could *physically* enter our world without our knowledge, this security breach suggests he has an interest in contacting you. Has Lucas Flynn appeared to you in the mindspace?"

Amanda remembered Cameron's advice not to lie, but not to offer information either.

"Yes."

Another murmur rippled through the council, growing louder until Madame Ellis rapped the side of her fist on the bench. The others straightened up in their seats, chastised, while the stenographer's fingers flew over her keyboard. Amanda was keenly aware of Rory's presence and how she might be implicated by this confession.

"When was this meeting?" Madame Ellis spoke with her lips pinched in a tight frown.

"Um," Amanda tried, but couldn't remember the date. "About a month ago, I guess. On a Sunday, a week or so before school let out."

"And what did you discuss during this meeting?"

"It's hard to say," Amanda answered slowly. "He was vague, I guess. Kinda cryptic. So, it's hard to know what he meant exactly."

"Leave the interpretation to us," Madame Ellis instructed. "Just tell us what he said."

Amanda saw some of the other council members lean forward eagerly. Madame Ellis kept her face partially lowered and studied Amanda over the rims of her small glasses. From his neighboring table, Director Alvarsson scowled heavily.

"He said he's not my enemy."

The stenographer typed rapidly.

"I see." Madame Ellis' lips stretched in a knowing smile, ignoring the whispers around her. "It's hardly surprising he would say that. Given his attempts to manufacture a rebellion."

"Well, if Lucas Flynn *says* he's not the enemy…" Director Alvarsson added sarcastically, eliciting a ripple of laughter along the bench.

"But he didn't call you my enemy either," Amanda added quickly. "I don't mean *you* specifically, Madame Ellis—or *you*, Director Alvarsson—but anyone at PTS. He said I should learn more and make up my own mind."

The council quieted. Many smiles faded into uncomfortable frowns. Scanning their reactions, Amanda saw one council member at the end of the bench who sat with crossed arms and a neutral expression.

"I see," Madame Ellis answered more coolly. "What else did Mr. Flynn tell you during this illicit meeting?"

"That was about it." Amanda looked off to one side, reviewing their conversation, and caught a subtle nod of encouragement from Rory. Madame Ellis caught the nod as well.

"Did you report this meeting to your training agent?"

"No." Amanda looked at her hands.

"Did you report this meeting to your aunt? Or to any of your teachers within our society?"

"No," Amanda repeated without looking up. She could hear the stenographer's clicking keys.

"Did you report this meeting to Director Alvarsson?"

"No," Amanda answered with an instinctive laugh that brought another kick from Judy.

"Is that a funny question?" Madame Ellis asked with a raised eyebrow. "Director Alvarsson is in charge of your training program. Why is it funny that you would report a concern to him?"

"Oh, I, uh…" Amanda flushed, glancing toward Director Alvarsson, who wore a stern frown and kept his eyes forward. "It's just that I don't really see Director Alvarsson much and we don't exactly… I mean, if I was going to tell anyone, it would have been my aunt. Or Rory."

"I see."

Madame Ellis made a note, then paused to give the stenographer time to catch up.

"And this was your only meeting with Mr. Flynn in the mindspace."

"Yes." Amanda kept her eyes down, hoping Madame Ellis wouldn't realize her mistake and ask if there had been any other meetings. In person.

Instead, Madame Ellis shifted the conversation.

"If Mr. Flynn did not instruct you to bring contraband into Arcadia, who orchestrated this act of political sabotage?"

Political sabotage? Amanda repeated the phrase to herself, realizing the seriousness of what she had done.

"No one…" Her throat felt raw as she forced out the words. "It was just me."

She wanted to hold her head held high and apologize for her mistake the way she had practiced. She wanted to explain how she hadn't realized the potential consequences and had just been trying to bring Mitra some books he would like to read. Instead, her eyes stuck to the marble PTS insignia on the front of the bench. Her shoulders slumped with the weight of her mistake.

"You wanted to impress your friend?"

Madame Ellis' question was asked with an unexpected tenderness. She searched Amanda's face and then nodded, satisfied by whatever she had seen.

"You then pressured Mitra to confirm the Arcadians' interest in psychic travel?" Madame Ellis pressed on, in a gentle but insistent tone. "Having suspected as much during your time with them?"

She was giving Amanda more credit than she deserved. But Amanda hastily agreed, realizing this version of events took some of the blame off Mitra for telling her why she was there. The thin man at the end of the bench smirked in a way that suggested he had a better idea of what had happened. Amanda ignored him.

Madame Ellis shuffled her papers again and conferred quietly with the council member on her left. Amanda watched the stenographer continue to record each moment, then chanced a quick glance to her right. Rory wore a proud smile. Judy's expression was guarded.

Amanda made a point of not looking toward Director Alvarsson's table.

Madame Ellis cleared her throat, bringing Amanda's attention back to the bench.

"Amanda Jones, you have disregarded our rules and compromised a diplomatic relationship by transporting unapproved information into a foreign environment. You have undermined our security by failing to report a meeting with an exiled traveler to your training agent. You have traveled off-world without permission and neglected to take your training seriously."

Amanda shrank into her seat, feeling the sting of Director Alvarsson's disapproving stare.

She then realized that she'd been so busy answering questions, she'd never actually apologized for her mistakes. It was the one thing she'd practiced repeatedly, yet there hadn't been an opportunity to simply say, *I was wrong, and I'm sorry for my mistakes.*

Amanda lifted her head, ready to admit her guilt and accept full responsibility for her actions.

Before she could speak, Madame Ellis held up a hand to stop her.

"However." The word rang out in the silence, leaving everyone hanging on her next sentence. "We believe your rebelliousness and your defiant attitude are both age-appropriate."

"What?" Director Alvarsson stood up in surprise. He scanned the bench, looking for dissent, but the council seemed already resigned to Madame Ellis' judgment.

Amanda tilted her head in confusion.

"What does that mean?" she asked Judy and Rory, who looked equally unsure.

"It means," Madame Ellis resumed disdainfully, "that we accept some blame for underestimating the need to adjust our approach when dealing with a teenager.

"You are new to the world of psychic travel. You are young. And you do not yet grasp the magnitude of our responsibility, not only to our own select society but to all of humanity."

Amanda's face flamed.

Surprisingly, the councilwoman shifted to a softer tone before going on.

"Your actions were misguided but an understandable response to both the sudden changes in your life and the high expectations placed on your future, given your extraordinary abilities. Mr. Flynn's interference has exacerbated the situation—as he had hoped it would—but we believe you are not to be blamed for that alone. A young girl like yourself is no match for a disturbed, manipulative man like Lucas Flynn."

"Well, I don't think—"

Madame Ellis held up one hand, cutting Amanda off mid-sentence.

"We also regret not keeping in mind the old adage: *idle hands are the devil's workshop.* In the past, you've asked to be taught at a more accelerated pace, and perhaps it's best we give you what you want."

A cold sweat prickled Amanda's ribcage and her throat went dry. *What do I want?* She wondered wildly. *What do they think I want?*

"Now, hold on!" Director Alvarsson raised both hands, still standing behind his table. "Don't you think this is something we should discuss first? In private?"

Madame Ellis regarded him archly before saying, "We will be having a private meeting after this hearing concludes. Yet, it is the decision of this council that Amanda will move forward with her next stages of training, correcting the errors you have made so far."

"The errors *I* have made?" Director Alvarsson flushed.

"Yes," Madame Ellis confirmed coldly. "You have mishandled Amanda's training by failing to recognize the exceptional needs of this situation. Given the unique circumstance, we are willing to overlook your missteps, provided you not interfere as we take more direct control of Amanda's training. Now, please, take your seat."

"I—" Director Alvarsson spluttered and fumed, then glared at Amanda before finally dropping to his seat like a chastened puppy.

Amanda watched him with sympathy. She hadn't agreed with some of his decisions, but it wasn't fair for the High Council to blame him for her mistakes. It wasn't his fault she'd skipped classes, and he had tried to talk to her about it in his own awkward way. It wasn't his fault that she'd brought Mitra banned books, either. He'd been painfully clear about his approved book list.

As she turned back toward the bench, the stenographer caught Amanda's eye.

She was still typing, despite the silence, painting a picture of the hearing with her observations.

An idea clicked in Amanda's mind.

It's a show! She glanced toward Judy and Rory, wondering if they'd realized it, too. The hearing was a show being put on by Madame Ellis and the High Council.

They wanted it on record that Lucas Flynn was a troublemaker who was using Amanda to *manufacture a rebellion.* They wanted it to paint Amanda as an emotional teenager running wild to impress a boy. And they wanted Director Alvarsson to take the blame for mishandling the whole thing.

But who's the audience? Amanda wondered angrily. *All psychic travelers? Are these transcripts public for anyone in the Psychic Traveler Society?*

She tried to remember everything that had been said and how it might be used to influence public opinion about Lucas Flynn and his accusations. She was still piecing her ideas together when Madame Ellis' words broke in.

"Your new training schedule will be daunting. We will trust you to tell us when you feel overwhelmed by the knowledge you will be required to learn. Will that satisfy your need to be more involved with your future?"

"Uh, I—"

Amanda tried to focus on Madame Ellis' question. She remembered the complaints she'd made to Director Alvarsson in the past. But so much had changed since then. An image of her fingers twined inside Drew's hand flashed behind her eyes. She could feel the comfort of sinking into the couch beside him and deciding to let all of this go. She remembered last week's gymnastics classes with Trina and their plans for cheerleading tryouts. That world felt far away, and she could feel it slipping further out of reach.

"Dr. Webb has voiced her concerns over the material in those contraband books," Madame Ellis continued relentlessly, "but I believe we have smoothed that over well enough. I trust that you will be careful not to upset that relationship again, now that we are all in agreement about our ultimate goal in that assignment."

"Hold on. Do we understand the '*ultimate goal*' with the Arcadians?" Judy spoke up at last. "We haven't clearly addressed those expectations or any kind of timeline for reaching them."

"We understand your concerns," Madame Ellis said primly. "This is a long-term prospect, and it may take quite some time, years in fact, for Amanda to develop the requisite skills…"

She and Judy continued their discussion while Amanda retreated to her own thoughts. Two weeks ago, she had been prepared to take an extended break from psychic travel and let herself be a normal teenager. She wanted to get her driver's license, go to school dances, and hang out with her friends. She wanted to go to parties without exiled secret agents tracking her down, and she didn't want to live with the fear of screwing up interplanetary alliances.

But then… the echo of the tuntum trees was fresh in her head. The feel of touching that shimmering film at the edge of her consciousness teased with the promise of something larger than herself. Amanda thought of Edmund Robinson and the other psychic architects who had come before her. She pictured the door she had already created, linking two distant worlds and bridging realities in a way few travelers would ever be able to do.

"Amanda?"

With a start, Amanda saw that every eye in the courtroom had turned to her.

"We will need your assurance that you understand and accept the seriousness of this commitment. Unless that's not what you want…?"

Madame Ellis offered a patronizing smile that sparked a flame of anger in Amanda's heart. She sat up taller in her seat and lifted her chin.

"It's exactly what I want."

§

Back home, Amanda flopped onto the bright blue couch and hugged a striped pillow to her chest. Rory dropped onto the adjacent loveseat, and Judy offered to make tea.

"I'm glad that's over."

Amanda kicked off her shoes, propped her feet on the coffee table, and watched her toes wiggle.

"Yep," Rory agreed. "Though we're going to have a lot more work to do."

"Is it too much for you?" Amanda frowned, realizing she hadn't considered Rory in her decision.

"It's all part of the job." Rory shrugged. "But it won't leave you much free time…"

"Yeah…" Amanda hesitated. "About that…"

Before she could say more, the front door opened, and Patty breezed in with a happy laugh.

"Surprise!" She kicked off her shoes and dropped her purse on the side table. "Training finished early today, so we all—"

She caught sight of Rory and hurried over with an outstretched hand.

"Oh! Hello, I'm Patty."

"Uh, hi, I'm Rory."

They shook hands over the back of the couch with Rory standing to lean awkwardly over the furniture. Judy rushed over, leaving the tea steaming on the counter.

"Patty, this is my… Well, Rory and I work together."

"Oh, I see."

Patty's eyes widened slightly. She glanced toward Amanda before welcoming Rory more warmly.

As far as Patty knew, Judy was a specialized counselor who worked with young adults who needed help adjusting to adult life. Judy had always been evasive about the kind of counseling she provided. But, knowing that she often moved around the country to work with her clients long-term, Patty had assumed they were from wealthy families and had extensive challenges.

"I hope it's okay that I invited Rory over."

"Of course," Patty agreed kindly, before turning her attention back to Rory. "So, you live in the area then?"

"I do," Rory answered simply, surprising Amanda. She didn't know where Rory had lived before her time in Terra-V, and she hadn't considered where Rory was living now. She'd assumed PTS was putting her up in a hotel somewhere, but Rory could have an apartment in their building for all Amanda had been told.

"Are you joining us for dinner?" Patty went on, setting down a stack of mail on the kitchen counter and flipping through some papers that she'd left there earlier.

Rory looked at Judy for direction, but Patty changed the subject before either could respond.

"Oh, Amanda, I forgot to fill out this permission slip." She waved a sheet of paper in the air, making Amanda's heart flip. "When do you need it?"

"Not for a few weeks." Amanda jumped up to take the paper from her hand.

"Weeks? But your gymnastics class was last week," Patty frowned. "I thought cheerleading tryouts were after that."

"They are, but not until the end of July." Amanda took the paper and felt heat spreading across her face.

"Cheerleading tryouts?" Judy asked with surprise.

"Yes," Patty answered lightly as she took the paper back. "If I don't fill it out now, I'll never remember in a few weeks."

"You're trying out for cheerleading?" Rory's voice was neutral, friendly even, but Amanda couldn't look at her.

"You never said you were trying out," Judy added.

Amanda avoided her eyes, too.

"You've helped carpool her and Trina to a Gymnastics for Cheerleaders class," Patty pointed out as she bent over the form with a ball-point pen. "Why did you think she was going?"

"You said that was to keep Trina company." Judy tried to catch Amanda's eye. "You said Trina was trying out and gymnastics would be a good skill for... fitness."

"Gymnastics is a good skill..." Rory spoke softly, but Judy ignored her as she moved closer to sit beside Amanda on the couch.

"Are you trying out for cheerleading?" Judy persisted. "Do you think that's wise?"

Amanda shrugged, glancing at her mom. She couldn't explain that she'd made plans to try out before the hearing, and she was annoyed that Judy hadn't put that together herself.

"What's wrong with cheerleading?" Patty asked as she finished signing the form. "Extracurriculars are good for kids, right?"

"Yes…" Judy stood up, gathered her long hair in a low ponytail, then let it go with a sigh. "But not if it overextends her."

"Overextends her?" Patty laughed. "I don't think *one* activity is going to overextend her."

"Right, but…" Judy sighed, "If she *wants* to take on other things, this would be a pretty big complication."

"What other things?"

Patty stood beside the kitchen table, signed permission slip in hand, as an awkward silence filled the living room.

"It's just tryouts," Rory offered gently. "There's no harm in seeing if she makes the team."

"Exactly!" Patty agreed brightly. "Tryouts first and we'll talk about it later. Right, Amanda?"

"Yeah, sure," Amanda mumbled, but she was already halfway to her room.

§

That night, Amanda went back to the attic alone. She stood in front of the door she'd created and studied the patterns in the silvery wood. She wanted some time by herself, to process the day, but a heavy presence hung over the space.

With a sigh, Amanda crossed her arms over her chest and watched the dark-clad figure step out of the shadows.

"Lucas," she greeted.

"Amanda," he mimicked her stern tone, then added a grin. "You had a good day."

"Did I?" Amanda frowned. She was starting to get a headache, which was a strange realization, knowing her head was physically back in her bedroom with the rest of her body.

"*I* didn't come off as well." Lucas stretched his arms behind his back and strolled around some covered furniture, stopping a few feet from Amanda.

"Though, I'll have you know none of my friends think I'm a *disturbed, manipulative man.*"

Amanda recognized the phrase Madame Ellis had used during the hearing.

"You read the transcript?"

"I have friends in high places." Lucas winked. His stubbled beard had grown back since his disguised visit to Trina's party.

"Great," Amanda sighed. "Then you know I'm not supposed to be talking to you."

"But you are." Lucas smiled.

"It's the last time." Amanda frowned. "I don't know if what you're saying is true, or what I can do about it if it is. But I already have enough to manage on my own, so I want you to leave me alone."

The attic felt cold as dust motes drifted through a shaft of light between them. There was a creak as Amanda shifted her weight on the aged wooden floor. Lucas clasped his hands in front of his waist, rubbing the base of one thumb with the other.

"I understand." He nodded thoughtfully. "You'll be reporting this meeting to your training agent? As you promised?"

"Yes," Amanda agreed uncertainly, having not thought that far ahead.

"Wonderful," Lucas encouraged with a hearty smile.

"Great," Amanda responded with less conviction and waved a half-hearted goodbye.

She was reluctant to leave, despite what she'd said. She wanted to tell him her suspicions about the hearing, especially now that she knew he'd read the transcript. She wondered if that access had really come from friends in high places or if High Council transcripts were public record.

"Is there something else?" Lucas asked with a tilt of his head, trying to break Amanda's distant gaze.

"Uh, no," she answered slowly. "I guess not."

"Okay. Then do me one favor?" Lucas asked lightly. "When you report this to Rory, tell her to ask 4212 about the chance of rain, okay? Thanks!"

He faded out of the attic before Amanda could say another word.

Chapter 9

The Psychic Engineers

"It will be fine," Drew reassured from his side of the table. "I know," Amanda replied unconvincingly.

They were playing gin rummy in the party room while rain poured down the arched windows. Several rounds had passed quietly as they took turns picking up cards and quickly discarding them. Amanda rearranged the sets in her hand, frowning over a run of cards with a missing five at its center.

"You can do anything you set your mind to," Drew went on, drawing a card and grinning as he tucked it into his hand. "I know you can."

"Uh-huh." Amanda waited for his discard and groaned when it was another six.

She pulled the queen of hearts from the deck, then looked up abruptly.

"Wait, what?"

Drew looked up from his cards in confusion.

"What *what*?" he asked gamely. "I believe in you."

"Yeah, I get *that*." Amanda folded her cards. "But what are we talking about?"

"Oh." Drew brought his cards close to his chest as he studied Amanda's puzzled expression. "Uh, your training today? Or tryouts? Or… well, all of it, I guess? Whatever you're worried about."

He sounded sheepish, despite his attempt to play it cool, and Amanda laughed.

"Well, as long as you believe in me," she sighed, wishing she felt half as confident.

Drew set down his cards.

"Okay, back it up then. What are you worried about? Right now?"

"Right now?" Amanda fanned her cards and scanned their faces. "Right now, I'm worried that this deck is missing its five of hearts."

"Amanda…"

"Seriously." Amanda frowned. "Did it come up in the last game?"

"Yes," Drew sighed. "It was in the last game, and it's in this one, too."

"Shoot. You have it?"

Amanda rearranged her cards, planning a new strategy.

"Amanda, come on." Drew put his hand over her cards. "Forget the game. What's going on with you?"

Amanda brushed his hand away, focusing on whether she could fit the queen of hearts she'd drawn into a meld with her other cards. After a moment, she discarded the queen and prompted Drew to take his turn.

"Are you still going to tryouts next week?" Drew picked up the queen, moved some cards, and discarded a ten.

"Yeah." Amanda drew a card, keeping her eyes on her hand. "Trina would kill me if I backed out now. And I already went to that gymnastics thing."

"And if you make it…?" Drew sounded hesitant.

Amanda shrugged.

She hadn't given tryouts much thought. In the last ten days, she'd had meditation sessions with both Alira and her PTS teacher in India, as well as daily training sessions with Mitra, riding lessons at the PTS stables in Brazil, and her usual classes at headquarters. She'd also started private lessons with Edwina Finch, a historian who specialized in mindspace houses and their architects.

"Still nothing about 4212?" Drew changed the subject after Amanda took her turn, and he'd drawn a new card.

"No," Amanda sighed and watched rain run down the nearest window. "Rory hasn't found anything yet, and it's driving her crazy—though she says it isn't."

"Hmm…" Drew tapped a card on the table. "*Ask 4212 about the chance of rain.* Could that be a radio station? An address? Or an amount of something? Could he have meant *four-thousand-twelve* instead of *forty-two-twelve*?"

"An amount of what?" Amanda squinted skeptically. "He definitely said *forty-two-twelve*."

"Maybe coordinates?" Drew brightened. "You know, latitude and longitude? Or a combination lock?"

"A lock on what?" Amanda shook her head, and Drew slumped back in his seat. "Rory's all over it. She'll figure it out when she figures it out."

Amanda sounded resigned to waiting, though the riddle was bothering her, too. Lucas had clearly given her a coded message, and no one knew what to do with it.

"Maybe he just wants you to talk to him again," Drew suggested. "He gives you some nonsense you can't solve and then you—or Rory—finally go see him to ask what it meant. When it never actually meant anything."

Amanda shrugged. She didn't think Lucas would do that. Besides, he accepted that she didn't want him to contact her anymore. It hadn't even bothered him. She pushed that thought away and chewed her lower lip.

The conversation was putting her in a bad mood.

"It doesn't matter," Amanda snapped, her cards blurring under her intense focus. "It's just one more thing I don't know about this stupid *society*."

"There's a lot to learn. And you're new to this."

"Yeah, but I'm—" Amanda stopped talking and shook her head.

"A psychic architect?" Drew guessed.

Amanda bit her lip and rearranged her cards.

Drew waited, surprised when she actually answered.

"Sometimes they act like being the next architent is such a big deal—but then they keep me on the outside. They don't tell me the truth about Arcadia. Or Lucas. Even with this new training, it's like they're just keeping me busy. Like, too busy to ask questions or cause trouble, but not like they're really letting me in on… I don't know… whatever has everyone so bothered lately."

"You're meeting with psychic engineers today."

Amanda's stomach flipped.

"Yeah, and that's progress, I guess… but…" Amanda trailed off, thinking deeply before meeting Drew's eyes. "There's something *different* lately. I don't know how to describe it. It's not just Aunt Judy, or Rory, or my teachers. Something *feels* different. Like everyone is on edge. Waiting for something to happen. I used to think other travelers were just edgy around me. You know, being the youngest traveler and then the whole psychic architect thing…"

"But you think there's something else going on?"

"I don't know." Amanda looked at her cards. "Maybe it's about Lucas and whatever he's planning. Maybe people are starting to believe what he says about PTS scientists and the High Council. I hear whispers sometimes, but they stop when I'm around. It's like everyone else knows something I don't, and they don't want me to know."

Drew looked at Amanda over his cards.

"Maybe you shouldn't know then."

Amanda's eyes flashed and he rushed on.

"Look, I get that you want to know what's going on, and it *is* important that you're going to be the next psychic architect, but… Amanda, you are only fifteen, and you aren't the psychic architect yet."

"But I will be!" Amanda clamped her lips over her teeth to keep from saying more.

"And maybe that's why they want to keep you out of things. To keep you safe."

Amanda fumed as thoughts raced through her mind. Drew might be right, but that was still upsetting. She didn't want anyone hiding things to protect her. Besides, she thought it was less about keeping her safe and more about keeping her from choosing a side. Cameron had said all societies change, which had sounded like he might think it was time for something to change about PTS. But he'd also said Lucas was making serious charges without enough proof. Was that what had everyone on edge? Were more travelers hearing about Lucas' claims?

"What are you thinking?"

Amanda shook away her thoughts.

"Nothing. I don't want to talk about this anymore."

"Are you mad at me?"

"No," Amanda sighed.

"Really?"

"Can we just play the game?"

"Sure." Drew glanced at his cards, then fanned them out, face-up on the table. "Gin!"

Amanda studied his cards and dropped her own on the table, crossing her arms sulkily.

"Look, you may not want to hear this," Drew began slowly, "but maybe you were on the right track before the hearing. You feel like people are keeping you on the outside, like you don't fit in, and maybe that's because you're there too soon."

Amanda looked at the table, listening as Drew built his case.

"Other travelers get their abilities in their early twenties, not at fifteen. Maybe you'd be happier if you pulled back on your training until after high school. Be a teenager with me… and Trina. Go to tryouts, join the debate team, or the Spanish club or whatever you want. PTS will still be there in a few years. Until then, let the travelers figure out whatever they're trying to figure out. Come be with people your own age."

Amanda nodded slowly but kept her eyes down. She didn't want to tell Drew that she didn't fit in with him and Trina either.

§

Amanda's meeting with the psychic engineers was in the castle. It was an older house in the mindspace, but not the oldest. It had been nicknamed by travelers, just as the Victorian house had been nicknamed the birdhouse.

Officially, PTS records listed the castle as Martio House, for the architect who had primarily built it. Just as the birdhouse was listed as Robinson House for its architect, Edmund Robinson. But no one actually used those names, except for teachers like Ms. Finch.

It was easy to see why Martio House was called the castle. Built in the late 13th century, it looked like a smaller version of the stone castles Amanda had seen in European history books. There were enclosing walls, crenelated towers, a fortified gate, and a central keep. Amanda assumed those architectural defenses were added for style. They meant nothing in the mindspace, where travelers could simply appear within any room at will.

She didn't remember much about the architect who had designed the castle. He had a single name, Martio, though some PTS historians now called him Martio de Léon. Edwina Finch was not one of them.

When they arrived in the castle, Amanda and Rory were greeted by a tall, thin man who introduced himself as

Ben Hastings. He wore a dark gray suit with a dark green tie, wire-rimmed glasses, and a watch that was too big for his wrist. After studying his pinched expression, Amanda recognized him as a member of the High Council.

He was the member who had sat at the right end of the bench at her last hearing. The one who hadn't joined into whispered conversations with the other council members. He gestured for them to take a seat.

There were upholstered chairs in the large room, likely added well after the house was built. Otherwise, the gray walls were as rough as the stone floors, and the few tapestries did little to warm up the chilly space. Weak light from the windows left shadows in every corner, and Amanda didn't see any electric lights. The castle had the hushed feel of a rarely visited museum, dusty and unused. Amanda longed to be back in the cozy warmth of the birdhouse.

"Is Ms. Finch coming?" Amanda asked, more to fill the uncomfortable silence than out of any genuine curiosity.

Ben looked up sharply.

"Why would Edwina Finch be joining us?"

Amanda glanced at Rory, who rolled her eyes and looked away. "I just thought… because she's the historian teaching me about psychic architects and engineers…"

"I see." Ben's lips pinched tighter. "Ms. Finch will not be needed at this meeting."

Amanda crossed her hands on her lap and decided not to say anything else until the engineers arrived. After a minute or two, Ben cleared his throat and spoke again.

"While I am not an official historian, I have been chosen to monitor your training with our psychic engineers. This monitoring is for your own benefit. There are concerns about the pace of your training and your ability to manage your responsibilities in a safe and effective manner. If this training appears to be too taxing for you, that will be noted in my official report. Your future training may be adjusted accordingly."

Amanda bit her lip to keep from telling him what she thought of his official report.

"Your input is encouraged as well," he added uncomfortably before bending his thin lips into a brief hint of a smile. The expression was so awkward, Amanda felt her own lips stretch into a grin as she tried not to laugh.

Clearing his throat again, Ben made a beckoning gesture with his left hand. Three older travelers appeared in the empty space beside their group of chairs.

The oldest was a man with salt-and-pepper hair and a snow-white beard. He wore jeans, a striped polo shirt under a cardigan sweater, thick gray glasses, and black sneakers. The two women seemed relatively close to his age, though it was hard for Amanda to tell. The taller woman had chin-length hair that was dyed a striking shade of pale peach. She wore a long white sweater over a pair of black, Capri-length leggings. Gold earrings hung halfway down her neck. The shorter woman wore red-and-black checkered pants with a black t-shirt. Her wispy, silver-blonde hair was pulled into a low ponytail and tied with a short black scarf.

Amanda didn't know what she had expected, but it wasn't a trio who looked like they were off to play bingo or stroll around a mall.

"You're psychic engineers?" she asked in surprise.

The sweater-clad woman looked Amanda up and down with pursed lips.

"You're a psychic architect?"

"Uh, I'm…" Amanda felt Rory tense beside her. Until the woman winked.

"It's about time you showed up!" She laughed loudly, and the others joined in without reserve.

"If only we'd get some more engineers around here, too!" The bearded man shrugged and shook his head. "Not many of us left."

"Hush!" The other woman slapped his arm with mild annoyance. "You'll scare Ben into increasing our guard!"

"Guard?" Amanda glanced behind them, now noticing the burly travelers who stood at the back of the room. They were armed with some kind of compact weapon that looked like a dart gun. Amanda wondered if it was loaded with tranquilizer darts or maybe injections of Psylo4C, the drug Lucas had warned her about.

"The guards are for your protection," Ben insisted.

"Ha!" The older man turned his back on Ben. "You're Amanda, then?"

"Uh, yes?" Amanda didn't know why her answer had come out like a question, when she did know her own name, but the older man let it go.

"I'm Gerald," he introduced himself gruffly. "This is Elaine, and this is Dot."

"Dorothy," the tall woman corrected. "Only Gerald calls me Dot, and who knows why I let *him* get away with it!"

"We're happy to meet you," Elaine added, tugging on the hem of her t-shirt. "And you must be the training agent?"

"Rory," Rory supplied, without offering her hand.

"I guess we should get started then." Gerald brushed his hands together briskly. "Bye, Ben. Bye, Rory."

"What?" Rory bristled with a sharp look toward Ben. "I'm not going anywhere."

"Neither of us is leaving," Ben responded firmly. "That is the arrangement."

"Well, that arrangement isn't going to work." Gerald planted his feet and crossed his arms over his thick belly.

"We are sworn to keep our work secret from the uninitiated," Dorothy added with a toss of her peach hair.

"That means you," Elaine told Ben, pointing at him with one waggling finger, before turning toward the guards. "And them."

"That's how this works," Dorothy insisted, crossing her arms beside Gerald's firm stance.

"That's how it *used* to work," Ben corrected primly. "The High Council has decided that this training will be monitored by myself, as a representative of the council, and by Amanda's training agent. You've already been told about those stipulations."

"But we didn't agree to—"

"Enough!" Ben stopped Dorothy with a tense frown.

He looked at each of the engineers, assessing their resolve, then made his final offer.

"The guards will be dismissed to the next room. Rory and I will observe your session from a distance."

Dorothy, Gerald, and Elaine eyed each other in a thoughtful way that made Amanda's skin tingle. After a moment, Dorothy nodded curtly.

"You stay across the room, though," Gerald conceded, pointing to a set of couches on the far wall.

"Rory?" Amanda looked back in confusion, but Rory nodded her assent, saying that she would be close by if Amanda needed anything.

"You must have so many questions!" Elaine chirped, while leading Amanda to the other side of the room.

Dorothy and Gerald followed, then stepped past them to peer intently at an iron-banded, wooden door. Amanda watched them lean toward the door, then lean back, then step close to hover their hands above the door as they traced its edges.

"Um." Amanda watched Dorothy close her eyes and turn one ear to the door. "I have a few."

"They're checking the door," Elaine explained succinctly. "It's due for maintenance soon. But not quite yet."

"Maintenance?"

"Yes, maintenance." Gerald narrowed his eyes. "Haven't they taught you anything? Architects make the connections, but these doors don't stay open forever. At least not without our help. Same with the houses. If we weren't here to take care of them, they'd fade out of existence."

Amanda pictured the door she'd made from the attic to Terra-V. The idea of it simply fading away sent a shiver down her spine.

"The council wants us to teach you about our work." Dorothy turned away from the door, seemingly satisfied with whatever she'd felt during her inspection. "We're happy to help, but it won't be easy. Psychic engineering requires dedication and meticulous training. We've spent decades honing our abilities, and there are many complex skills you will have to develop to create a strong foundation. It is not an easy calling."

"But she's an architect," Elaine reminded Dorothy with wide eyes. "This won't be like training the others. Her innate abilities will make all of this so much easier for her!"

"You don't know that!" Dorothy fired back, but Amanda's attention was caught on something else Elaine had said.

"Others?" she asked, glancing among the three of them. "You've trained other psychic engineers?"

"Of course," Dorothy sighed dismissively. "We've worked with all the younger engineers."

"How many—?"

"We should probably assess her established abilities before we do anything else." Elaine interrupted Amanda's question. Dorothy agreed that testing Amanda's abilities would be the best way to begin, but Gerald shook his head decisively.

"We have a training plan that works. There's no reason to change it."

"But she's an architect!" Elaine repeated emphatically, triggering an intense debate where each began talking over the others. No one was listening to anyone else. Then, they stopped talking and stared at each other. The way they studied each other—as their eyes seemed to continue the debate—gave Amanda's skin the same twitching, prickling feeling she'd had during their earlier silence.

Amanda looked over her shoulder and saw Rory watching blankly. She raised one eyebrow and gestured for

Amanda to do something. Or maybe it was a gesture to ask if she needed help. Amanda wasn't sure, but she wanted to handle the situation herself.

"Hello!" Amanda waved both hands, reminding the engineers of her presence.

They turned their eyes on Amanda intently, clearly expecting her to have something more to say.

"Um, I don't mind starting at the beginning," Amanda said nervously. "I mean, I know there's a lot I have to learn, and I'm ready to trust you… No one else has really taught me that much about psychic architects yet. I've never even met anyone who's known one before…"

"You still haven't," Dorothy interrupted with an exasperated glance toward Elaine.

"Edmund Robinson died in 1926," Gerald reminded. "More than a decade before any of us were born."

"More than *two* decades before some of us were born," Elaine added stiffly.

"Well, I didn't mean…" Amanda blushed.

"It's been a long time since there's been a psychic architect," Dorothy conceded. "Let's leave that at that. But it's a good point. None of us ever met a psychic architect or worked with one directly. We've heard stories. And we have an understanding of how engineers worked with architects in the past. But this will be a new experience for all of us. To some degree."

"Where are we?" Gerald asked Amanda abruptly. "That's the place to start."

"What?" Amanda studied the intricate web of creases around his eyes.

"Where are we? Right now."

Amanda glanced around, wondering if it was a trick question. "We're in the castle. One of the houses in the mindspace. Uh, it was built by—"

"That's enough." Gerald frowned. "This isn't a history lesson."

He turned toward the others, again engaging in some kind of quiet exchange. Amanda watched them, letting her eyes flick from one to another until Dorothy returned her gaze with a startling intensity. The rest of the room dimmed around them, fading to shadow.

"Keep looking at me." Dorothy spoke in a near whisper. "You can blink, but don't lose contact."

"What's happening?"

Amanda's heart raced as the floor disappeared. There was blackness all around them, but they stood together—Dorothy and Amanda—as if alone in some kind of endless void. Amanda's mind reeled at the sensation of standing firmly despite having no solid ground beneath her feet. A cold sweat broke out under her arms. Prickling sensations traveled along her collar bones and behind her eyes. Her skin itched and twitched.

Dorothy smiled encouragingly.

"I knew she could do it!" Elaine's voice drifted into the void. Amanda could sense her presence just off to the right, exactly where she had been standing when they were still in the castle.

Amanda nearly shifted her gaze toward Elaine, when Gerald's voice broke in loudly.

"Keep looking at Dorothy!"

Amanda's eyes watered with the effort to keep her attention trained on Dorothy's face.

She could sense Gerald to the left, as well as Elaine to the right, but she couldn't fully see either of them. Her focus tightened in on Dorothy's eyes, even as the pounding of her heart spread into her mind. The pounding grew faster. Her breath was fast and hard. The darkness that had once been a room began to shift and spin around them. Then, just as Amanda stumbled forward, the castle came rushing back into existence.

Swallowing hard, Amanda felt her flushed cheek against Dorothy's soft chest. A moment later, her body was pulled backward, held up by Rory's strong hands.

"What the hell was that?" Rory shouted toward the trio of engineers before peering into Amanda's bleary eyes. "Amanda? Are you okay?"

"Yeah, yeah." Amanda stood upright and closed her eyes. She took a deep breath, but the darkness behind her eyes was too much like the black void she'd found herself in a moment before.

Her eyes flew open, and her gaze darted around the room, orienting herself to the space. It wasn't a physical place either, but it felt like one to her muddled brain.

She heard a murmured conversation between Rory and the engineers, then glanced away to see Ben watching them all with disapproval. *It's part of her training.* Amanda heard the words but couldn't tell whether they came from Dorothy or Elaine.

"I'm fine," Amanda insisted, shaking free of Rory's grip and meeting her concern with determination. "Really."

Rory reluctantly agreed to go back to her place beside Ben, who was rapidly scribbling notes. Once she was gone, Amanda turned back to the engineers.

"What was that?"

"It was too soon." Gerald frowned.

"It was your idea!" Dorothy scoffed.

"You wanted to assess her."

"It went well!" Elaine chimed in with a smile. "She joined us before we could even explain!"

"Can you explain now?" Amanda rubbed her temples, still feeling the aftereffects of whatever had just happened. It was one of those times when she mildly wondered what effect all this psychic travel might be having on her actual brain.

"We met in the *pure* mindspace," Dorothy answered reverently. "It's something we can do, as psychic engineers… and psychic architect. The pure mindspace is not discussed with other travelers, even if they ask." She paused, making sure Amanda understood its secrecy. "The pure mindspace is a void that exists without the framework of a fabricated house."

"Like in Arcadia," Amanda muttered, trying to make sense of this new experience.

"No." Gerald shook his head tightly. "The Arcadians meet in a void because they have no one able to create an interactive world—houses and doors—that would give their connection substance. We access the pure mindspace— outside of our houses—to maintain our created world."

"And to have conversations without being overheard," Dorothy added with a wink.

"It will get easier." Elaine patted Amanda's arm kindly. "With practice."

"How's your head?" Gerald asked, but didn't wait for an answer. "That will get better, too. For now, that was a good start. You can rest and we'll meet again soon."

"Wait, what?" Amanda looked among them frantically. "The session is over? But we just started!"

"You said you didn't mind starting at the beginning," Dorothy reminded. "You said you would trust us to teach you."

"Right," Amanda sighed and rubbed the base of her skull with one hand.

In the shock of experiencing the pure mindspace, she'd forgotten all about the High Council's plans for her. She'd forgotten about her friends and family back home and about Lucas and his revolution. She'd forgotten everything beyond the surreal feeling of slipping out of this created mindspace and into the void that existed beneath it all, separating her from the physical world in a way that had felt both terrifying and intensely comforting.

Amanda felt weak from the experience but eager to return. As disorienting as the pure mindspace had been, it had also felt like home.

CHAPTER 10
A CHANCE OF RAIN

The darkness swallowed Amanda. There was nothing to see and nothing to touch. Fighting the unnerving sensation of being untethered, Amanda focused on the techniques she'd practiced with the engineers. She slowed her breath, imagining a pale light building inside her body with every inhale. She could feel the light, warm and soft, glowing inside her chest. With every breath in, the light traveled down her spine. With every breath out, the light pooled around her heart, gathering strength.

After several breaths, the orb of light grew too large to contain. With her next inhale, Amanda put all of her focus on that shimmering light. With her next exhale, she let the light pour out into the darkness around her.

Softening the tension in her jaw and forehead, Amanda peered at the dim light she'd created. *The light is here,* she muttered to herself. *The light is real.* She narrowed her gaze on the light and gave it freedom to shift and grow.

Lead me, she whispered to the light. *Show me the way.*

Amanda had been in this dark before. Alone with the light. Each time, the light had been a bit brighter, but it had never moved or grown after it was created. It had never illuminated anything else in the void. Until today.

Off to the left, Amanda gradually became aware of… *something.* Her mind saw it as a shadow, yet there couldn't be a shadow in a sea of endless black. After a moment, she realized the shadow was lighter than the darkness around it. It was a gray haze, tinged with an aura of the white light she'd created. Resisting the urge to move quickly, Amanda shifted her eyes—then her head, her shoulders, and her body—to face the pale shimmer.

The image held her full attention. Amanda forgot to control her breath, easing into a natural, mindless rhythm, as she watched the glowing haze with fascination. With every moment, the haze brightened, revealing the form of a darker *something* at its center.

Leaning forward, Amanda watched the shadow within the light take the shape of a human. A head. A body. Arms and legs. The form brightened and it became Mitra.

"Mitra!" Amanda spontaneously called his name but didn't hear a sound leave her lips.

He stood in the glow of light, entirely unaware of her existence beside him.

Amanda shifted her attention from her friend to the light around him, noticing a familiar quality in its enveloping shape. The glow was more than a ray of light. It had a filmy shimmer, like a surface she could touch. Like the iridescent shine of a soap bubble. It was the barrier she'd seen before, during her meditation sessions with Alira. It felt close but just out of reach.

Mitra slowly looked around whatever space he was in, maybe searching for Amanda. She wanted to call out again but knew he wouldn't hear her. There was no sound here. Except for the buzz that was growing behind Amanda's eyes. It was a high-pitched whine that grated on her focus and interrupted the steady flow of her breath. *Not yet,* her mind cried out, but the sound began to hurt, and she struggled to catch her breath. *Not yet! Mitra! I'm here!*

And the darkness was gone.

Amanda collapsed forward, slumping over her crossed legs with her hands braced against the ground. Rory ran one hand soothingly over her rounded back.

In a moment, Amanda's awareness returned, and she looked around the room carefully.

They were in Mitra's lab. Mitra sat across from her on a low cushion identical to her own. Rory crouched beside her. A small team of scientists—some travelers and some Arcadians—took notes from one side of the room. Agnes Webb was not among them.

Mitra opened his eyes and gazed at Amanda with concern.

"Nothing?" he asked gently, surprising Amanda.

"There was—" She stopped, glancing at the hopeful scientists and then back at Rory. "There was something, I think. A larger glow…" She trailed off, running her hands over her face. "I'm not sure. I need a minute."

The room was quiet, waiting, but Amanda felt the pressure of everyone's focus.

"Let's give her some space," Rory said, shooing everyone out the door. They allowed a 30-minute break, leaving Amanda and Mitra alone in the lab. Rory had offered to stay, then agreed to wait just outside the door.

After standing to stretch and drink a glass of water, Amanda joined Mitra in the armchairs by the window. It was the seating area where he'd first told her about the Arcadian mindspace, the place they used to rest and talk during work breaks. It felt different now.

Amanda wanted to tell Mitra that she had seen him in the void. That she now knew, without a doubt, that she was connecting to the Arcadian mindspace. In a way. But something stopped her.

Their relationship had changed over the last few weeks, though Amanda didn't know what was different. Mitra treated her the same. He hadn't gotten in trouble over the contraband books or for telling her the truth. In fact, the other scientists seemed to respect him even more.

There were still moments when he looked at her with his deep, liquid eyes, but it didn't have the same effect. There was a slight twinge when Amanda saw that expression, like her stomach twisting over, but it didn't bring the curious heat she'd felt before. If anything, it felt sad now. Like a missed opportunity.

"What did you see in there?" Mitra's eyes were soft, and his voice was encouraging.

Amanda didn't want to talk about it. Not yet.

"What happened to that woman?" she asked instead. "The one we saw the guards take away when we were down by the river."

"The woman?" Mitra frowned and shook his head before his face brightened in recognition. "Oh, the woman who had run away and needed help. I don't know. I suppose they helped her, and she now has a better life. I never heard anything else about her."

"Can you find out?"

"Maybe." Mitra shrugged. "Are you worried about her?"

"Yes."

"There's no reason to be concerned." Mitra reached for her hand. "I told you before, this is not your world. We help people who are hurting here."

Amanda's fingers were limp in his hand, but she didn't pull away.

"How do you help them?"

"Lots of ways. Medical treatment, various psychological modalities, *nescientia*, energy renewal…"

"Wait!" Amanda tapped the translator disc behind her ear and asked Mitra to repeat what he had just said. When he had, she tried to repeat the strange term. "*Nay-shen-sha*? I don't think that's an English word."

"Oh, huh." Mitra tilted his head to one side, puzzled. "It is an Arcadian word. Perhaps there is not an English equivalent."

"What does it mean?"

Amanda's palms itched, and her throat went dry.

Mitra pursed his lips, thinking deeply. "It is a treatment of healing, I am not sure I can describe exactly how the procedure works, but essentially it—"

The door opened, and two Arcadian scientists entered with Rory close on their heels.

"Apologies for our interruption." The lead scientist bowed his head toward Amanda. "Mitra, you're needed in the neurogenetics lab. We'll have you back shortly."

Amanda stood as Mitra prepared to leave.

"You need him right now?"

She shot Rory a puzzled look, wondering whether their timing was a coincidence or an intentional break in their conversation.

"Actually," Rory said to the scientists smoothly. "This would be a good time for us to leave, as well. We have a tight schedule today, and it would be better if we could pick up where we left off at our next session."

Amanda barely had time to say goodbye before they were on their way to the gatehouse.

Rory walked in stony silence, and Amanda followed her lead. Glass buildings towered on either side of them, though the sidewalks were wide, and the streets between them were even wider. Lush parks nestled between the buildings, large sculptures dotted the walkways, and birdsong filled the air. The pedestrians they passed offered pleasant smiles, and an assortment of vehicles zipped along the streets, either on the ground or hovering in the layers of space above.

Being human, Arcadians looked like any other people Amanda had met on Earth. She could see familiar ethnic features in some of their faces, though most showed elements of several different cultures.

Arcadians didn't have the kind of racial divisions Amanda was used to hearing about back home. Their skin included the same diverse shades, but it was treated no differently than eye or hair color.

What stood out to Amanda were the alien visitors mingling among the Arcadians. The Arcadians were capable of space travel and had allies on several planets. The city had landing bays that welcomed space travelers, just as the gatehouse allowed passage to psychic travelers. Most alien visitors were decidedly non-human. Some had skin in shades of blue, green, yellow, or purple, or animal-like features, including scales, feathers or tails. Their clothing and hairstyles could be elaborate or simple.

Those who walked among the Arcadians were allies who had been trusted to visit the city, and Amanda did her best to walk by them without staring or nudging Rory. Sometimes that was easier said than done.

There were fewer pedestrians as they neared the edge of the city, which bordered a vast meadow with the river at its far end and a forest just beyond the water. Squinting across the grass, Amanda thought about the day she and Mitra had sat beside the river and the woman they were just discussing.

What was that treatment Mitra mentioned? Amanda tried to remember the strange word, but it had been lost in their interruption and abrupt departure.

Once they were off the city streets and crossing a long stretch of pavement toward the gatehouse, Rory slowed her steps and sighed.

"Something wasn't right back there." She frowned. "What happened during your session?"

Pushing aside her memories, Amanda reminded herself that she was in Arcadia for another purpose. Her attempts to connect through the Arcadian mindspace were what mattered more than anything else.

She bit her lip and puzzled over an answer. Rory had been by her side through her enhanced training. She'd watched Amanda's lessons with the psychic engineers and had even taken part in some of her meditation training. She'd watched each time Amanda had tried—and failed—to mentally connect with Mitra.

Amanda had grown to trust Rory, but she still wasn't sure how to explain what she had seen in the Arcadian mindspace today. She wasn't entirely sure she hadn't imagined the whole thing.

"I think I saw him," she admitted warily. "I think I saw Mitra in their mindspace."

Rory slowed her pace and listened intently while Amanda described what she had seen.

"Mitra didn't see you?" Rory's eyebrows lowered in thought. "You didn't tell him any of this?"

Rory looked back at the city pensively before setting aside whatever idea was bothering her.

In the gatehouse, they approached the Arcadian counter together and quietly began to remove their translator discs. Rory's fingers were behind her ear when she stopped and left the disc in place.

"Have we met before?" she asked the Arcadian man behind the counter with a twist of her lips and a show of friendly curiosity.

Though Amanda hastily reattached her translator, she missed the man's response. He was smiling pleasantly, but his eyes both brightened and narrowed at Rory's next question.

"What are the chances of rain today?"

Amanda sucked in her breath. Rory leaned casually on the counter, twiddling her fingers. The man held her gaze intently, as if they were the only two people in the room, but his voice remained casually pleasant.

"If you are interested in tracking our weather, I can offer you an information packet designed for visitors to our world."

He reached under the counter, shifting some items around before handing Rory a thick blue envelope. She accepted it gratefully, and no one else seemed to take note of the exchange.

Rory removed her translator disc and handed it over before stepping aside for Amanda to do the same. Though questions were flying through her mind, Amanda smiled and passed her translator disc to the Arcadian man. That's when she noticed the badge on his chest included the same swirling design that she had seen on Dr. Webb's brooch. Below the badge, a flat metal bar showed his identification number: 4212.

§

Amanda's feet dangled a full three inches above the clean stone floor. Her chair, built for the elongated limbs of the Vherahna, was made of the silver-blue wood she'd seen in other structures around Terra-V. The matching table in front of her was decorated with a simple glass bowl holding a selection of small pineapples.

Cameron and Rory sat at the table with Amanda, along with Brendan, an older knight who had accompanied them on Amanda's first journey through this world.

As Cameron and Brendan studied the contents of the blue envelope, Amanda let her eyes drift around the domed, stone hut. Alira had kindly let them meet in her own home, and Amanda had been mildly surprised by its simplicity. There was only one room, and it was just large enough to hold a table with six chairs, a narrow bed, an armoire, and a cushioned seat near the home's only window. Silky blue curtains hung beside the window, and decorative glass vials were scattered on stone ledges built into the walls. Amanda knew the forest had communal bathhouses and kitchens. But she had expected the leader of the Vherahna would have a more impressive home.

"These are the names of doctors and scientists in the society, then?" Brendan cradled his chin in one hand as he puzzled over one of the sheets of paper that had been tucked between Arcadian travel brochures.

"Yes." Rory repeated what she'd already told Judy and Amanda before this meeting. "Doctors and scientists with assignments at PTSI."

"Any of them at PTSD?" Brendan's eyes widened and his palm pressed against the table.

There was worry in his voice.

Amanda shifted her attention to Cameron, noticing the tension in his jaw. She remembered what Lucas had told her about the PTS detention hospital and the geneticists who worked there.

"Is it really that bad there?" Amanda asked. "I mean, a hospital is where they help people, right?"

The others looked at each other warily.

Rory started to answer, but Cameron quickly cut in.

"PTSD is one of the hospitals in a larger research facility." He studied Amanda thoughtfully before continuing. "There are risks to traveling off-world. Injuries, illnesses. Many things that doctors in the normal world would not be able to treat. And then, there are the mental risks as well. Traveling to other worlds—or even just accepting the existence of the mindspace—can take a toll on the human mind. Sometimes that requires treatment beyond a normal hospital. The Psychic Trauma Social Detention center is for special cases. Extreme cases."

Amanda nodded along until an idea broke through.

"Is that hospital just for travelers?" She remembered Judy once telling her how risky it could be to tell normals about the psychic world. "Are there normals there? People who found out about us and couldn't handle it?"

Rory looked down at her hands, and Brendan turned toward the fireplace.

Cameron studied her face before answering.

"Yes."

A cold sweat prickled along Amanda's collarbones and down her ribs. She pictured her mom at work, going about her day without any idea of the huge secret waiting to crash into her life.

"PTSI is also where they research new drugs." Rory spoke softly but with weight in her words.

"And new treatment procedures, to be sure," Brendan agreed with a gruff edge in his voice. "Do we know what these all are working on?"

Rory shook her head, scanning over the list that lay on the table between them.

"Not really." She pulled out another sheet of paper. "Here's a copy with my notes. You can see some of their fields, but usually not the specific work they're involved in. The underlined names are the ones I couldn't find in any directories. They may not be at PTSI, or they might be working on projects so classified that their names are kept secret, too."

Cameron and Brendan looked over the list, making suggestions about some of the names, but Amanda was lost in her own thoughts. She had never really considered what might happen if her mom couldn't handle the news. *Would she lose her mind?* The thought brought a shiver of dread.

"Why give you the list this way?" Brendan's question caught Amanda's attention. "Why not give it to us himself? Or give it to Amanda when she saw him?"

"Because he wants us to know he has Arcadians on his side," Rory suggested with irritation. "Because he wanted us to work for it. Chase him down for answers."

"Or because he didn't have a choice."

A voice from the door caught them all off guard.

Amanda didn't have to look to know it was Lucas.

Rory was out of her seat in an instant. She closed the distance between them and had Lucas pressed to the wall by his throat before he could say another word.

"Whoa!" Cameron jumped up to stop her. "Stand down!"

"What are you doing here?" Rory hissed at Lucas, leaning in closer.

"Rory!" Cameron shook her arm, adding, "It's okay. I sent for him."

Rory sharply released her hold and watched Lucas slump into the wall. After taking a moment to catch his breath, Lucas rubbed his neck and grinned up at her.

"You must be Rory Beck. Pleased to meet you."

Once they were settled around the table, Amanda was surprised to learn that Cameron and Brendan had been working with Lucas in Terra-V. Lucas had brought Alira a soil additive that had revived the sickly tuntum tree and made it possible to transplant saplings. He'd also used his connections within the Churukh community to ease the overthrow of their corrupt royalty and support the foundation of a diplomatic leadership council made up of both Churukh and Vherahna elders.

"Where did you find a soil additive for tuntum trees?" Amanda asked in awe.

"There are many, many worlds out there," Lucas began with his usual swagger. "And when you've been to as many of them as I have…"

"Can we stick to this world?" Rory stabbed one finger onto the list of names. "What have you been doing in Arcadia? What's the purpose of this list?"

Lucas winked at Amanda, then faced Rory with a forced expression of professionalism.

"Unfortunately, our esteemed High Council has made it impossible for me, and many of my colleagues, to continue visiting Arcadia. I do, however, have Arcadian connections who share our concerns about the alliance between our worlds. In fact, you might be surprised to see how high up those concerns go among Arcadian leaders. Or maybe you wouldn't be… given their history with our world."

Cameron cleared his throat, bringing Lucas' monologue to an abrupt halt.

"Why the games with getting us this list? You could have given it to me directly."

Lucas' grin faded as he dropped his eyes in genuine discomfort.

"Mm… that was a bit artless," he admitted ruefully. "I didn't have the information yet. I knew it was coming, but I didn't have anyone I could safely send to get it. And I didn't know how long it would be before… Well, that doesn't matter now."

He looked at Amanda solemnly.

"I wanted to respect your decision to not meet with me anymore, but I knew you and Rory might be my best chance to get this intel. Maybe I should have been straight with you, or worked it through Cameron, but, in the moment, a cryptic message seemed like a good option.

"And, yes," he told Rory with a sly smile, "it doesn't hurt to prove I have Arcadian allies."

They were all quiet for a moment.

Though Amanda couldn't tell what the others thought of his explanation, she had to admit his improvised plan had worked. Rory probably would have refused if he had asked for her help directly, but she couldn't resist figuring out his cryptic message.

"And these names…?" Brendan asked leadingly.

"The PTSI scientists and doctors who are working with Arcadians in some capacity," Lucas confirmed.

They all looked back at the list.

"That's a lot of names." Brendan frowned.

"And you think they're working on gene therapy to control the ability for psychic travel?" Cameron asked Lucas, breaking the grim silence that had fallen around the table.

"I do." Lucas nodded solemnly.

Amanda watched intently as Cameron sized up his old companion. She knew they shared a complicated history, and she could see Cameron's inner struggle over whether to trust Lucas now.

"I'm not alone in this," Lucas stated frankly, using the fervent tone Amanda had last heard from him at Trina's party. "The resistance to the High Council is growing, and we're close to having solid evidence to prove our case. But I need more help."

"Cameron." His voice shook slightly. "I need *your* help."

There was a shift from Brendan's side of the table, but Amanda kept her eyes trained on Cameron. She watched as he drew in a deep breath, let his eyes go out of focus for a moment, exhaled slowly, and then focused on Lucas with a new resolve.

"A list of names isn't proof of anything," he said at last.

"No," Lucas agreed, "but it's a start."

Lucas held his right hand toward Cameron, his forearm hovering just above the table.

There was a question in his eyes.

The room was silent as the first, creaking hum of the tuntum trees filtered in through the open door. Cameron nodded, grasped Lucas' hand with his own, clasping his elbow with his free hand. Lucas slumped forward in relief, and Cameron bowed to meet him, their foreheads lightly touching.

With a lump in her throat, Amanda turned away.

Rory sat back in her chair, arms crossed over her chest, and narrowed her eyes.

She wasn't so easily moved.

§

Later, as they were preparing to leave, Lucas proposed another meeting where he could introduce some of the travelers who worked closely with him.

"There's a world where we meet," he explained. "A primitive one that's largely off the PTS radar. No guards there and very few patrols. We even have a camp for those of us who have been officially exiled. Though it's a bit of a hike from the door."

His nonchalant charm was back.

Cameron agreed, after confirming that Brendan could handle their responsibilities in Terra-V on his own. Lucas said there was a meeting already planned in the morning, and he could arrange a guide to bring them to the camp.

"Tomorrow?" Amanda looked to Rory for help.

"We're not available tomorrow," Rory answered calmly.

"Training?" Cameron asked mildly. "Will you be back in Arcadia?"

"No," Amanda responded uneasily, wondering how to change the subject.

"We're taking a personal day," Rory said, while casually adjusting the knife on her belt.

"A personal day?" Cameron raised an eyebrow. "I thought the council had your schedule packed, especially during the times when your mom is at work."

"Amanda has something to do." Rory clapped her hands together and started toward the door. She didn't make it two steps before Cameron had moved closer to Amanda.

"Is everything alright? With you… and with your mom?"

"Yeah, fine," Amanda stammered, knowing her nervous response was only raising his concerns.

Lucas and Brendan watched the exchange with puzzled looks until Rory turned back with an exasperated sigh.

"She has cheerleading tryouts, okay?"

Amanda felt her face burn.

"Cheerleading?" Cameron's face broke into a bemused smile. "You're not serious…"

He stopped talking as he saw a film of mortified tears glinting in Amanda's eyes.

"What's wrong with cheerleading?" Rory snapped with her hands on her hips. "Amanda does have a life outside of PTS, and she has a right to be part of that world when she wants to be."

"Uh, yeah," Cameron faltered and glanced at Lucas for support. "I suppose she does."

Lucas shrugged and shot Amanda a look that seemed caught between admiration and amusement. Her stomach twisted and flipped.

"Cheerleading?" Brendan scratched his chin and asked, "That's the one with the gymnastics, and human pyramids, and such?"

"Yeah," Lucas answered. "It's a bigger deal in America. Though I've heard it's catching on in your neck of the world now, too."

"Really?" Brendan shrugged and walked toward the door. "Huh."

"Well, tryouts…" Cameron coughed and composed his expression. "Good luck, then? Uh, Lucas, I guess we'll still meet up tomorrow. Let's discuss the logistics and agenda."

They said their goodbyes and left Alira's home, while Amanda's eyes stayed glued to her feet.

"Ignore them," Rory advised as soon as they were alone. "Do your best tomorrow. You'll be great, and we'll figure the rest out from there. Okay?"

"Okay," Amanda agreed, though she still felt sick to her stomach.

Chapter 11

Tryouts and Surprises

Amanda passed through the school's double doors and was hit by the humid summer air. Like walking into an invisible wall of heat. Her feet slowed, and her eyes squinted against the glare of sudden sunlight. She wanted to pause, to adjust to the shift from the school's dim, air-conditioned hallways, but she was swept along by an adrenaline-fueled cluster of chattering girls.

The nervous energy coursing through the crowd was as palpable as the wall of heat that closed in on them with every step. Months of dreaming and a week of cheerleading clinics had just ended in a blur of competition. No one knew what they were saying, but that didn't stop anyone from talking. Except Amanda. The others rambled on about the mistakes they'd made, the stress of facing the judges, or the hell of waiting for the emailed list. Some were checking their phones already, hours before the expected results.

Amanda was silent.

Once they'd cleared the doorway, the pack spread out. Amanda moved away from the school, getting distance from the other girls, though Trina stayed close by her side.

"I mean, Varsity would be amazing," Trina rattled on. "But sophomores rarely make Varsity. We do have a chance at JV, though. Don't you think?"

"Uh-huh," Amanda reassured automatically as they peeled away from the crowd.

Tryouts had ended earlier than expected. Those who could drive made their way to their parked cars. Younger girls broke into smaller groups, waiting for their rides to show up. Giggles, groans, and heavy sighs carried across the open space. Amanda saw one girl burst into tears. Most of them weren't going to make either squad. Amanda knew that. Though she didn't know how she *felt* about it.

With a sigh, Amanda looked away and noticed some boys hanging out on the track behind the school. She narrowed her eyes to see if the tall, lanky one was Drew.

"I wish we could have watched each other in there!" Trina complained.

"Uh, huh," Amanda vaguely agreed.

They'd been brought before the judges in small groups for the first round of scoring, then called in one-by-one to show an individual cheer, a series of jumps, and a tumbling combination. Amanda and Trina had both planned on doing a simple cartwheel into a roundoff since neither had much experience with gymnastics. Yet once she was in there, Amanda had instinctively gone into the roundoff back handspring combination she learned from one of her PTS fitness trainers instead.

She hadn't told Trina about the switch.

"What are *they* doing here?" Trina wrinkled her nose as she caught sight of Drew waving and walking toward them. Trey was close on his heels.

Trey and Amanda's last run-in had ended with his head knocked into a locker, his parents called to the school, and a week of detention. Drew had stopped hanging out with Trey after that, but it had been hard to cut him out completely when they had several friends in common.

"How'd it go?" Drew called over, once he was close enough to be heard.

"Fine." Trina shrugged before asking what they were doing at the school.

"Running some laps." Drew smiled at Amanda, noticing her frown. "Some of us are joining cross country this fall. Thought it would be good to start running now."

"You should join, too," Trey told Amanda, stepping up to their group. Drew turned, annoyed that Trey had followed him. "I saw how you ran on track and field day."

"I'm not interested," Amanda answered coldly, hoping he knew she was talking about more than joining the cross country team.

Trina was more direct.

"Why are you talking to us?" She glared at Trey with her hands on her hips. "No one wants you here."

Amanda looked back toward the school, avoiding Trey's flushed face. Drew and Trina had inched together, creating a sort of open shield between her and Trey.

She didn't want their protection, but she didn't want another confrontation with Trey either, so she chose to ignore the whole thing. She heard Drew tell Trey he should head back to the track.

"Fine. I was just being nice, but whatever…"

As Trey walked away, Amanda twisted her fingers nervously. She could still see him towering over her, crowding her into her locker, before she'd used a self-defense move Cameron had taught her to escape and push him away. She hadn't meant to knock his head into the locker, but it had been effective.

"He's gone," Trina said flatly, then turned her back to the track so she wouldn't have to look at him anymore. Or maybe to block Amanda's view.

Drew cleared his throat. "So, tryouts went well?"

"Uh, yeah." Amanda answered uneasily, shaken by the brief encounter with Trey.

Trina jumped in with more enthusiasm. "We're trying for both Varsity and JV, but sophomores almost never make Varsity…"

As Trina calculated the odds, Amanda's mind wandered into the birdhouse. The living room's antique furniture materialized around her. An inlaid floor replaced the grass beneath her feet, and a plaster ceiling shielded her from the blazing sun.

Amanda was alone in the room. She shivered in the cool space as her eyes drifted past glass-fronted bookshelves and carved mahogany doors. The velvet couch beckoned. She felt the energy of the room around her, sensing a subtle vibration she had only recently learned to identify. It was the hum of the pure mindspace existing underneath everything she saw. She could connect to its rhythm, let the objects around her fade away, and be alone in the void below, where it was easier to feel the energy…

Amanda pulled herself out of the house and blinked at the glare of the bright world around her.

"Everything okay?" Drew asked, interrupting Trina's soliloquy.

"Yeah." Amanda brushed off his concern. "I was just thinking I should text Aunt Judy about finishing early, but it's almost four anyway."

"Ah. Can I get a ride home?" Drew asked, then winked, "Since there's no bus in the summer."

"Yeah, of course." Amanda grinned, but her thoughts had wandered to Lucas and Cameron's meeting.

A trio of girls sauntered out of the school, led by Chelsea Simmons. They were cheerleaders who had been on the Varsity squad last year and everyone expected them to make it again this year.

Trina gripped Amanda's upper arm.

"They're headed this way!"

Amanda and Drew turned to see the group stop near the edge of the parking lot, about ten feet away.

"Hey," Chelsea called over. "You need a ride home?"

Trina lived only two blocks from Chelsea, but she'd never been offered a ride before.

"Yeah, that would be great!" she exclaimed, just as Amanda was calling back, "My aunt will be here soon."

Trina and Amanda looked at each other, and Trina widened her eyes emphatically.

"Yeah, but I'm way out of her way," she told Chelsea. "It would be so much easier if I caught a ride with you!"

"Whatever." Chelsea shrugged. "But I have to drop off Kaitlyn and Emma first."

"Fine!" Trina pushed between Drew and Amanda without looking back. "No problem!"

The group walked toward their parked cars with Trina tagging along by Chelsea's side.

"Bye, Trina!" Drew called loudly as he waved one arm over his head.

"Yeah, bye." Trina waved over one shoulder with a look of excited disbelief.

Amanda shook her head.

"I guess that saves us a drive."

"Yeah." Drew cocked his head to one side, watching Trina nearly trip over her own feet while climbing into the backseat of Chelsea's car. "How much do you think she'll regret that?"

"Trina or Chelsea?"

Drew laughed. "Either? Both?"

"Yeah, that won't end well," Amanda smirked, though she hoped it would.

"She really wants this, doesn't she?"

Drew's observation prodded the queasy feeling in Amanda's stomach. Glancing at the time on her phone, Amanda made a decision.

"Keep an eye out for Aunt Judy, okay?" She trotted toward the school, shouting back, "I'll just be a minute!"

The school was quiet.

Amanda didn't see anyone in the hall as she walked to the gym teachers' small office. A reinforced window showed a room crowded with extra sports equipment, an overflowing bookshelf, and a metal file cabinet. Mrs. Martin sat at the cluttered desk with a stack of papers in front of her. The half-sheet scorecards the judges had used during tryouts. Amanda knocked and eased the door open.

"The results will be emailed tonight," the coach said without looking up.

"I know." Amanda shifted her feet, unsure of herself but trusting the impulse that had brought her back inside. "That's not why I'm here. I, uh, shouldn't have tried out."

Mrs. Martin lifted her head.

"I don't want to be a cheerleader anymore," Amanda continued. "I mean, if my scores were even good enough to be considered."

Mrs. Martin invited her to take a seat across from the desk, then tapped the end of her pen against her closed lips before asking what had changed Amanda's mind.

"My life is pretty busy right now," Amanda explained. "It's sort of a family business thing… I thought I could do both, but the more I think about it, I just don't see how it will work out."

"Well, we might be able to—"

Amanda interrupted to add, "Look, I thought this would be a fun thing to do with my friend, but after this week… Well, other people want this a lot more than I do, so I think it would be better if I'm not given a spot."

"I see." Mrs. Martin's face softened. Her eyebrows drew in as she considered Amanda's position. "Why not wait to see if you earn a spot and then make your decision?"

She sounded so much like Rory that Amanda briefly wondered if Mrs. Martin could be a traveler. She wouldn't be the first. Her math teacher had been sent to the school to keep an eye on her. Why not her gym coach, too?

"That was the plan," Amanda answered honestly. "But then someone would know they only made it because I gave up my spot. I don't want that to happen."

"You're thinking of your friend?" Mrs. Martin nodded without waiting for confirmation. "Trina Rivera? She did well today. Better than I expected, actually."

Amanda was glad to hear that, but her face fell when Mrs. Martin went on.

"You were better, though. Is there anything I can say to convince you to stay on? I think you'd be really good for our team, and I'm hoping we'll take Regionals this year."

"No, I…" Amanda stopped and swallowed hard. "Does that mean I made it?"

Mrs. Martin folded her hands over the papers stacked in front of her.

"Does that make a difference?"

Amanda's heart raced. She'd been sure of her decision a moment ago. But images of cheering on the sidelines and winning at competitions flooded her mind. She could be a normal girl with a normal high school experience… Until the pulse of the pure mindspace flickered through her body and swept those images away.

She was sad but sure.

"I finished adding up the scores," Mrs. Martin admitted. "You have a place on the JV squad if you want it. But, Amanda, I would expect you to be at every practice and every game. If you really don't think you can make that commitment, I'd rather know that now."

Amanda felt her phone vibrate in her pocket and knew it meant Aunt Judy was waiting.

"I'm sorry," she said over the lump in her throat. "I wish I could, but I can't."

"I'm sorry, too." Mrs. Martin smiled sadly.

Amanda started to leave, then turned back quickly, before she lost her nerve.

"Did Trina make it?"

Mrs. Martin frowned.

"I think I've said more than enough already. If Trina's name is in my email, will it matter whether she got the spot you gave up or made it on her own?"

"No." Amanda shook her head.

After everything she'd been through in the past year, letting people think she hadn't made the cheerleading squad seemed like a pretty small addition to her growing pile of secrets. Even if Trina made it without her.

§

Amanda didn't tell anyone about her conversation with Mrs. Martin. Not Drew or Judy, and especially not Trina. The email came out that afternoon, and her name was not on the list. Neither was Trina's.

"Sorry," Drew texted, when he heard the news.

"It's okay," Amanda responded, stretched out on her bed where she'd just ended a long phone call with Trina. "I wouldn't have had time for it anyway."

She watched the three little dots dance across the bottom of her screen, waiting for his reply. The longer it took, the more she braced for his questions.

Amanda expected him to ask about her going back into the school. He was so smart, he might even ask if she'd turned down a spot on the squad. If he did, she wasn't sure how she would answer. She didn't like to lie, but she didn't want the truth to get back to Trina.

The dots flickered and faded. Amanda imagined what would happen if Trina did find out. She'd have to deny it, of course. Trina was already devastated about not making the squad. But how would Trina have reacted if she had gotten a spot? Would she be cool about it or make a show of pitying Amanda for not making it, too? Amanda imagined a scene where she was pushed into shouting the truth, then felt bad for enjoying it.

When her phone buzzed, Amanda scrambled for an excuse about going into the school that Drew would believe. But she didn't need it.

Drew's text read, "Yeah, you're pretty busy. Probably for the best."

Amanda dropped her phone on the bed beside her and stared at the ceiling. It was for the best. But she felt like crying and was angry when the tears never came.

$

On Saturday, Rory was invited over for dinner with the family. Patty made Amanda's favorite baked chicken, and the conversation was light and easy. Since she thought Rory was Judy's counseling client, Patty steered clear of questions about their relationship. Instead, they talked about their favorite books and some of the TV shows they'd recently watched.

They'd finished eating and were clearing the table when there was a solid knock on the apartment door.

Rory asked Amanda if she was expecting anyone. Judy said she thought the front desk was supposed to call up when they had visitors.

"Oh, it's probably just Drew," Patty said as she stacked plates, but Amanda told them he was at the movies with his dad.

"Well, there's one way to find out," Patty laughed with her hands full of dishes. The knock came again, three steady thumps. "Somebody, answer the door."

Judy and Rory exchanged a worried look before Judy crossed the short distance. Rory stayed back, and Amanda could tell she was subtly ready for action. It occurred to Amanda that Rory's defensive stance was mainly for Patty's benefit. If someone dangerous came to their door, the three of them could simply disappear through the house. Her mom could not.

The realization worried her.

Oblivious to the tension in the room, Patty hummed lightly while loading the dishwasher.

There were two more knocks.

Judy opened the door.

Amanda's jaw dropped, while Rory's clenched tightly.

Ignoring their surprise, Cameron stepped easily into their small entryway.

He was dressed in slacks and a white button-down shirt, instead of the chainmail and tunic he typically wore in Terra-V. His hair was neatly trimmed, and he wore thin, wire-rimmed glasses that Amanda had never seen him in before. Amanda was so busy studying his casual appearance, she didn't notice her mom walking over to join them.

"Cameron?" Patty sounded confused, but nowhere near as shocked as Amanda felt in that moment. Cameron smiled softly at Amanda before turning his full attention on her mother.

"Patty." He held out both hands, and Patty took them, pressing her cheek briefly against his. "I'm sorry to show up without warning. Especially after so many years."

Patty waved his apology away and nervously tucked a lock of hair behind her ear.

"It's fine. I mean, it's a surprise, but it's fine."

They both wore gentle smiles as they stared into each other's eyes. Judy and Rory eyed each other, but Amanda kept watching her mother and her mentor. Cameron had talked about working with her father, but he'd never once mentioned knowing her mother.

After a long moment of silence, Patty shook her head and let out an awkward little laugh.

She gestured toward Judy, saying, "Let me introduce you to my sister-in-law…"

Cameron quickly interrupted.

"I already know Judy," he stated plainly.

"Oh?" Patty's smile faltered. "You met at Gabe's memorial… or…?"

Judy's lips parted, but no words came out. She clasped her hands together, twisting her fingers side-to-side, as Patty' studied her pale face.

When Judy didn't speak, Patty looked back at Cameron with growing confusion.

"We work together," he clarified. "Well, not together exactly, but for the same organization."

"You… work with Judy? But she's…?" Patty glanced toward Rory and stopped talking.

"We have a lot to talk about." Cameron stepped closer to Patty and tried to retake her hands. This time, she pulled away and crossed her arms over her stomach. The next look she shot Judy was angry, suspicious.

"You don't understand." Cameron held up both hands, pleading. "There's a lot to explain."

"That you *work* with Judy?" Patty blinked rapidly.

"About that," Cameron agreed, "and about Gabe."

They studied at each other again, intensely, shutting out everyone else in the room. It reminded Amanda of the psychic engineers, though she knew *they* hadn't dropped into the pure mindspace. Cameron and her mom were standing in front of her, caught up in a tension that Amanda didn't understand.

She wondered if it was the shock of Cameron showing up years after her dad had died. His appearance had shocked her. She couldn't understand why he would show up without warning.

"Patty…" Judy tried to break the silence, but Cameron waved her away. He then spoke to Patty so softly Amanda had to strain to hear his words.

"Gabe was very important to me." Cameron's words brought tears to Patty's eyes. "You were important to me, too. I told you that at his memorial. I made promises that day, and I'm terribly sorry I wasn't in a position to keep them. But I am now, and I want to live up to my word."

"I…" Patty looked like a lost child as she stared at him with wide eyes.

"I want to keep my promises to you," Cameron repeated, "and to Amanda."

"Oh," Patty gasped lightly. She shifted her attention to Amanda as if just remembering she was still in the room.

"Rory, would you mind taking Amanda out for a while? For ice cream or something? I think Cameron and Judy and I have some things to discuss."

Amanda wanted to protest, but she wasn't given the chance. Rory swiftly agreed and practically pushed Amanda out into the hall. As the door closed, Amanda watched her mom and aunt walking toward the couch with Cameron following closely behind.

She stared at Rory in shock.

"What the hell was that?"

"I don't know," Rory admitted. "But I'm sure Judy will let us know when it's safe to come back."

They stood in the hall uncertainly, until Rory broke into Amanda's racing thoughts with a very Rory suggestion.

"Want to go to the gym and hit things?"

Chapter 12
Evasive Maneuvers

"Faster!"

Amanda blinked and nodded, bouncing on flexed knees and shaking the tension from her arms. Her forehead glistened with sweat and her cheeks were flushed. They'd spent twenty minutes warming up with practice strikes on the training dummy before moving on to one-on-one techniques. Facing off, Rory had given Amanda one simple objective: *Don't let me touch you.*

This was a familiar practice. Amanda was expected to step and pivot out of Rory's line of attack. Yet, time after time, Rory had managed to shove Amanda's shoulder, grab her flailing arm, or knock her to the padded ground.

"You know how to do this," Rory reminded with a clap of her hands. "You're not focusing."

"Uh-huh," Amanda grunted agreement, trying to shake her head clear. Hitting the dummy had been easier. She'd let her mind wander as she hit and kicked however she pleased.

Which, she realized, was why Rory had shifted their practice to something more focused and controlled.

Bracing her forearms on her thighs, Amanda caught her breath and said, "It's faster to run *away* from the attack."

"Is it?" Rory asked. "What if you're in a narrow space? What if you're boxed in?"

Amanda straightened up and shrugged.

"I know this is a tricky move," Rory said in a softer tone, "but it's important. You're likely to be up against someone bigger and stronger. You have to give yourself an advantage. What if you run and you aren't faster? Or they have more endurance? You evade the attack this way so you can avoid a hit, keep them moving in circles, and watch for your best way out."

"But I'm stepping toward you!" Amanda groaned. "Of course, you're going to grab me."

Rory pressed her lips together and exhaled slowly. Amanda could tell she was getting impatient.

"You're stepping toward me but *out* of my line of attack. It's about the pivot and the timing. You come at me to evade my attack. Now, you can do this. Let your gaze relax, don't focus on any single part of me, and watch for any shift of movement. Ready?"

Amanda pulled herself together and nodded.

Rory waited, shifting her weight from foot to foot, as she sized Amanda up. The waiting was what killed Amanda. Her body was tensed, ready to move, but her muscles began to twitch with uncertainty after the first few seconds.

Come on! Her brain screamed, even as her arm jittered with anticipation. She tried to stay loose but alert, keeping her body from locking up. A slight cramping in her shoulder pulled her attention, and Rory chose that exact moment to spring into action. Amanda jerked forward, trying to pivot out of the way, but tripped over her own feet. Rory quickly spun Amanda's back toward her own chest and wrapped her arm around Amanda's throat. The hold wasn't tight, but it was enough for Amanda to know she'd be in danger if she'd been up against an actual attacker.

Amanda knew she should find a way to break free. She could stomp Rory's foot, elbow her stomach, or even dig her nails into Rory's arm, but she didn't have the energy to go on. She tapped out and Rory quickly released her, making sure nothing but Amanda's pride had been hurt.

"I'm okay." Amanda waved Rory off, though she felt anything but okay. She took a few steps toward the end of the room and sank into a seat against a padded wall. Rory joined her. Their backs pressed into the wall as they stared into the open space at the center of the gym.

"It takes practice," Rory said. "You *will* get this, and once you do, you'll see why it's a valuable maneuver."

Amanda wasn't listening.

"Do you think he's telling her?" she asked instead. "Right now? About psychic travel. And about… me?"

"I don't know." Rory sighed but wasn't surprised by the change of subject. "It's hard to get why he'd do it like this."

"He showed up without warning us," Amanda agreed. She was angry but too overcome by the situation to put much fire into her words.

"Ye-es," Rory drew the word out. "That was surprising, but he has a reason."

Amanda felt her stomach turn over.

"You mean, like, something happened? To make him tell her right now. Like, for her own protection?"

"I don't know," Rory repeated. "He met with Lucas and some more of his people today."

"Without us?" Amanda sounded as offended as she felt.

"It's hard for you to get away on weekends," Rory reminded. "When your mom is home from work."

Amanda twisted and flexed her fingers.

"Maybe that's why he wants to tell her? Maybe he's just tired of sneaking around her schedule?"

"Maybe," Rory conceded.

Amanda's mind spun up another thought.

"If my mom knew him, back when he worked with my dad, then did I know him, too? Was he around when I was a baby or a little kid? He never told me that. Just talked about the time he spent with my dad off-world. Why didn't he tell me he knew my mom?"

"I don't know," Rory answered again.

"Do you know anything?" Amanda snapped. She knew Rory was just as blindsided by Cameron's appearance, but there was no one else to take her anger.

Rory inhaled slowly, giving Amanda enough time to regret her outburst, then gently said, "I know a lot of things. But I don't know what's happening at your apartment right now."

"I know." Amanda felt tears prick her eyes and blinked them away. "I'm sorry."

"I know," Rory echoed with a smile in her voice and nudged Amanda with her shoulder.

Amanda nudged back, then let out a long exhale. They sat together, looking at the empty room until the overhead lights, which were controlled by a motion sensor, clicked off. Light spilled in from small windows on the double doors at either side of the gym. Otherwise, Rory and Amanda were left sitting in dense shadow.

Neither made a move to stand up or trigger the lights.

"Are you upset about cheerleading?" Rory asked after a moment of quiet. "About not making the squad?"

"Ha!" Amanda let out a short dry laugh. "No."

Cheerleading was the furthest thing from her mind.

"It's okay if you are," Rory went on. "It would have been hard to work around, and I know Judy didn't want you to do it, but I get it. You had other plans before this psychic travel stuff came up. It sucks to have to give all that up. Especially when you didn't ask for any of this."

Hearing the bitterness in Rory's voice, Amanda forgot about cheerleading and about what was happening back at her apartment.

"What did you give up?"

The dim quiet stretched around them. Amanda's eyes adjusted to the limited light, making it easier to pick out the shape of the human-shaped training dummy in the far corner. The stacked mats and racks of sparring equipment reminded Amanda of Mrs. Martin's cramped office, and she quickly pushed that thought away.

Just when Amanda thought she wasn't going to answer, Rory shifted in her seat and cleared her throat.

"I was a lieutenant in the Army." Rory kept her eyes forward. "I was one of the first women in a combat unit, and I was on track to be one of the first—or maybe even *the* first—woman to graduate Ranger School."

"That sounds… important." Amanda wished she knew more about the Army but grasped the idea that an Army Ranger was an elite soldier.

"It is," Rory confirmed tightly. "I had it all planned, and it was all falling into place. With every step, they said I wouldn't be able to do it. But I did it anyway—with honors. I dedicated everything to that one goal, and then the visions started…"

Amanda didn't ask which *they* had said she would fail. She could guess. She imagined it had felt like everyone, like the whole world, had been stacked against her, but Rory had kept at it anyway. Fighting for her dream. It hurt Amanda's heart to think of Rory accomplishing so much only to have her psychic traveling brain mess it all up.

"I thought I was crazy," Rory admitted. "Like most of us do. I thought I was cracking under the pressure, and I struggled against it for a long time. Even after my PTS counselor showed up to explain what was happening."

"Was it…?"

"Your aunt?" Rory asked when Amanda didn't finish her question. "No, it was someone else. She was very kind and patient, which didn't work with me at all. Eventually, she realized I needed a tougher approach, and she forced me out of a really dark place. I owe her a lot. Everything, really. She pushed me to see psychic travel as a new adventure, and she got me hooked up with the knights on Terra-V."

Amanda took that in. It wasn't hard to imagine Rory as an angry, former military officer who had to readjust to life in a whole different world. Literally. It cast a new light on Rory and Cameron's relationship. One that brought up a vague sense of jealousy, though Amanda didn't like to admit it.

She could easily picture Rory going from her Army combat training to sword fighting and riding a feathered horse. She wished she'd been there to see Rory figuring it all out, and to see how Cameron had gotten her through it. And then, another thought occurred to her.

"How did you leave the Army? Weren't you enlisted with them? Or had a contract or whatever?"

Rory tensed, sitting taller and pressing her palms into her thighs.

"I was discharged." Her strained voice didn't sound like her at all. "PTS worked it out, behind the scenes somehow. The Army… the other soldiers… knew I'd been seeing things. It was hard to hide after a while. There were a few incidences… but that doesn't matter now. Officially, I was given an honorable discharge… a medical discharge…"

Her voice cracked and she stopped talking.

Amanda considered that.

"So, PTS got you out of the Army, but everyone thought…"

"Everyone there thinks I cracked," Rory spit the words. "They think I couldn't take the pressure, so I lost my mind and disappeared somewhere."

Amanda straightened up and turned toward Rory's dark silhouette.

"What about your family? Your friends? Where do they think you are now?"

"That doesn't matter." Rory swiped a hand across her cheek and cleared her throat again.

"But it does!" Amanda insisted. "Does your family even know where you are? I mean, even if they don't know about PTS, you could still tell them…something?"

"Amanda," Rory interrupted wearily. "My family thinks I was discharged after a mental break, and that didn't sit well with them. We… lost touch after that."

"Lost touch?" Amanda felt a tumble of questions building in her mind. But Rory abruptly stood up, squinting as the overhead lights flashed back on. From her place on the floor, Amanda could see a ropy muscle running from Rory's tense jaw to the base of her collar bone. Rory's fingers flexed once, twice, and then hung limply by her side.

"We should head back," she said, glancing at the caged clock on the far wall.

Amanda was about to argue when her phone vibrated in her pocket. There was a text from her mom:

"Come home now. Right NOW."

Within fifteen minutes, they were standing in the hallway outside Amanda's apartment. Amanda started to reach for the door handle when Patty's angry shouting made her stop and look back at Rory in alarm.

"I want you out of my sight! Out of my life! And out of my daughter's life!"

They couldn't hear the response but could guess what had been said by Patty's next words.

"Fine! Then we'll leave! I'm not staying in this… this… This is insane! It is not going to be my daughter's life!"

Amanda backed away from the door.

"They told her," she whispered to Rory while looking at the door with dread.

"Yeah," Rory whispered back. "Sounds like it."

They stood together, staring at the wooden door. The apartment number, 1208, wobbled in front of Amanda's eyes. She remembered how impressed she'd been by Judy's spacious penthouse. She remembered moving in. Leaving their two-bedroom apartment only a few floors below.

Amanda had arranged her bedroom furniture the same way as in her old room and found she had more space here. A comfy reading chair filled in the empty corner, and she loved to curl up in it when she could find time to relax with a good book.

If they left, where would they go? Would her mom really take her out of the apartment? Maybe even out of the state? Away from Judy, and Drew, and Rory, and everyone she knew? Questions flew around Amanda's mind. What could she say to make her mom understand that this new life—that being a psychic traveler—was a good thing? An important thing?

"We can't stay out here all night," Rory said. Before adding with a shrug, "I mean, we could. But it's not a great hiding place. Eventually, someone will open that door."

"Yeah." Amanda's feet felt cemented to the floor.

"Do you want me to go first?" Rory stood beside Amanda, giving her time to consider their options.

"No." Amanda shook her head. She looked at Rory, grateful to see her stoic face.

She had once thought Rory's unsmiling expression was a sign of dislike, or even anger. But lately, she'd realized it was a sign that Rory was ready for anything. After tonight, she had a better understanding of why, and she hoped this wasn't the last day Rory would be standing by her side.

§

Amanda sat on a park bench with the sun warming her skin. A light breeze kept the day from being oppressively hot. Butterflies fluttered around lavender flowers on a cluster of fat bushes, and Drew slouched beside her. Somewhere above, a trilling call reminded Amanda of the birdsong that rang throughout Arcadia. It was a lovely summer day that felt wonderful and entirely wrong.

Back in their apartment, Patty was curled on the couch, under a thick blanket, staring blankly out the balcony's sliding glass door. At least, that was how Amanda had left her. Patty hadn't moved from that spot all morning. She hadn't wanted breakfast, though she had silently sipped a cup of coffee until it was gone—never moving her eyes from the window—and had gripped the empty mug until Amanda took it away.

Amanda had planned to stay with her mom all day, waiting for something to change. But Cameron had shown up just before noon and said it would be good for Amanda to get some fresh air. He'd promised to sit with Patty and do whatever he could to help her. Amanda had resisted, until her mom turned from the window just long enough to ask her to go.

Sitting with Drew now, Amanda didn't know what more she could say. She'd already filled him in on the chaos of the previous night. She'd described coming home to find

Patty in a terrifying state. Her face red and blotchy, her eyes puffy and smudged with pooled mascara. She'd flown at Amanda, wrapping her in a protective hug, before hissing at the others, "Stay away from my daughter."

Amanda remembered how it had felt to wriggle out of her mom's arms, replaying what she had said.

"Mom, I know this is hard, but—"

And she hadn't gotten any further. Patty had pulled back, accusing Judy of twisting her daughter's mind.

"You've manipulated her into believing this insanity!"

They had all talked over each other—Cameron, Judy, and Rory. Each trying a different approach to calm, assure, or sway Patty into accepting her new reality.

It was Amanda who had finally stepped close, placing her hands on her mom's upper arms and whispering, "It's a lot to take in, but it's true."

Patty's eyes had widened, spilling more tears. She'd slumped to the ground, and Amanda went with her, holding her hands as they crouched on the carpet and stared into each other's eyes.

"I'll be right back," Amanda had whispered, hoping she was doing the right thing. Then she'd stepped through a door in the attic. The first door she had ever used in the house.

Amanda had stood in the meadow in Terra-V, knowing her body had just faded from her mom's sight. The meadow had been dark, the tuntum trees spiraled down for the night with their dual trunks coiled tightly and their lush blossoms casting a shimmering glow. The air had been cool, the purple grass damp with dew. Amanda had tipped her head back, taking in the blanket of stars above.

She'd drawn one deep breath. In and out. Then conjured the door that would take her home.

Then she had opened her eyes.

Patty was still angry, still afraid, but she could no longer refuse to believe.

"So, Judy just left?" Drew asked with a shake of his head. "Like, she's moving out?"

Amanda bit her lip.

"I don't think she'll move out," she answered carefully, hoping she was right. "I think she's just giving Mom some space. She's staying with Rory for now. I don't think it will be for long."

"And Cameron never explained why he told her? I mean, why now?"

Amanda watched a butterfly perched on a spear of purple petals. The flowers reminded her of the Vherahna Forest, and she wished there was a way her mom could experience the beauty of that world. Cameron had given her a dose of Vhelox after Judy and Rory had left. It had calmed her nerves, but the synthetic drug was a weak alternative to the actual *vhe* Alira could have offered through her healing touch.

"Amanda." Drew lightly shook her arm, drawing her attention to someone approaching slowly from the far side of the park.

It was Judy.

Amanda jumped up and was wrapped in her aunt's rocking embrace. She closed her eyes, breathing in Judy's spicy vanilla scent, and resisted the urge to dissolve into a puddle of tears. The hug stretched on until Amanda became aware of both her aunt's soft *shushing* and Drew's awkward presence only two paces away.

When they parted and sat on the bench, Drew moved to the grass. He bent his long legs and sat upright, forearms resting on his knees, and he didn't seem much lower than Amanda and Patty.

"How is she?" Judy's voice shook. Amanda noticed how small her eyes looked without their usual shadow and mascara.

She gave a brief update, explaining that Cameron was with Patty now.

"She's in shock," Judy said. "But we'll get her through it. She'll be okay."

She launched into a plan for Patty's transition, talking about stages of acceptance, and how they'd have to give Patty time to adapt gradually. She had a bag of books about psychic travel with her. They were introductory textbooks for new travelers, but she said they could also be used to teach Patty more about psychic abilities.

"Why now?" Amanda cut in with barely concealed anger. "Why did he just show up like this? Without warning? Without a plan? Without even *asking* if we thought it was the right time?"

"Amanda, I…" Judy spread her hands wide, trailing off helplessly.

Amanda looked at Drew, who nodded his quiet encouragement for her to go on.

"I asked for his help," Amanda confessed bitterly. "I wanted him to help me tell her, but not like this."

"I know," Judy agreed. "This was not… ideal."

The word hung between them, entirely inadequate to the situation. Yet something in Judy's tone promised she had more to say. Amanda clung to that hope. She needed answers and was angry she hadn't questioned Cameron herself. But there hadn't been time.

Cameron hadn't stayed long after Judy and Rory were gone. He'd helped Patty breathe in some Vhelox, then given Amanda the vial to offer more as needed. Patty had been exhausted by then, coming down from the adrenaline rush of her initial shock. Surprisingly, she hadn't seemed upset with Cameron. All of Patty's anger had been directed at her sister-in-law, and she'd let that go once Judy had packed a bag and left. Without her anger, Patty had sunk into a silent shell of herself.

And then Cameron had left.

"He didn't have a choice."

Judy's words confused Amanda. She was still stuck in the memory of her mom's speechless withdrawal. *Didn't have a choice about leaving me alone with her?* Amanda tried to pick up the thread of their conversation. *Or didn't have a choice about telling her like this?*

"Or he felt like it was his only choice," Judy corrected, shifting her gaze between Amanda and Drew. "He came over to tell us more last night, after he left her with you."

"To tell you and Rory?" Drew asked, seeing Amanda's confusion.

"Yes," Judy went on haltingly. "He met with Lucas yesterday. They had new information from a contact who works within the inner support staff for the High Council. Apparently, there's growing concern about having to hide your training from your mom. Especially once school starts in the fall."

"So, they want her to know?"

"Not exactly," Judy answered carefully. "It seems they've been discussing other ideas. Like offering you a place in a fake boarding school while actually moving you to Arcadia. But they didn't think you'd willingly stay away from your mom and your friends."

Amanda and Drew glanced at each other.

"I've told you before that normals can have a hard time accepting psychic travel," Judy continued. In some cases, it can lead to a psychotic break."

"Obviously!" Amanda gestured toward their building as she pictured her mom staring at nothing from her place on the couch.

"No," Judy disagreed. "Your mom is shaken, but that's not a psychotic break. It will take some time, but she's going to accept this and be okay."

"Like I did," Drew chimed in from his place on the grass. Amanda smiled at him weakly.

"What was their plan then?" Amanda leaned into the hard, wooden bench, holding back the panicked feeling that was fizzing up from her gut.

"It's not definite that they were ever going to do this, but Lucas' insider said there was a plan on file that outlined the worst ways they could tell your mom. Situations likely to cause a mental break, preferably in a public setting."

Panic broke into Amanda's chest, making it hard to take a breath. For a moment, even her vision seemed to go slightly out of focus.

"But why?" she croaked past the ache in her lungs.

Judy reached for Amanda's hand. There was pain in her eyes when she said, "Because if your mom had a mental break, they would have a reason to take away her custody rights and put your care in the hands of a traveler."

"You mean, you?" Amanda sat up straighter and pulled her hand away.

"It's not my plan!" Judy insisted. "I would never want anything like that to happen to your mom."

"But you're my aunt!" Amanda jumped to her feet and fluttered her hands as if she could shake this conversation out of her body. "You'd be the one they'd put me with if… if…"

Drew rushed to step in with open arms or indignant anger. Whatever Amanda needed. But she held her palms toward him with stiff arms, maintaining her space.

He turned on Judy instead.

"So, these people have a plan to shock Amanda's mom with the truth, and Cameron decides he'll just do it for them?"

Amanda shied away from Drew's raised voice, feeling a need to move. She shook her arms, pacing as Judy and Drew continued to argue.

"It wasn't ideal, but he told her as gently as he could."

"But he had to do it right then? Without warning Amanda? Or any of you?"

"He didn't know when they might decide to use that plan," Judy defended. "It might have been today, or next week, or never. He didn't want to take that chance."

"Who is he to decide?"

Drew's question broke through Amanda's hazy mind, reminding her that her mom had already known Cameron when he'd shown up. She'd been surprised but also happy to see him.

"It's done," Amanda said firmly, putting her hand on Drew's forearm.

"Yes," Judy agreed gratefully. "And now we need to focus on helping your mom accept this. Once she understands and supports your training, there will be no reason for anyone at PTS to see her as a threat."

"Yeah." Drew nodded reluctantly. "But I still don't get why he was in that much of a rush."

Judy chewed her lip, fighting the same frustration.

"He had to get ahead of it," Amanda answered, staring into the distance. "Pivot out from their line of attack."

He was throwing the High Council off balance, she realized. He was evading their attack by lunging forward and off to their side. It was a tricky maneuver, but maybe their best defense.

As long as her mom survived the shock.

Amanda had wandered through the impressive Patel House several times since discovering the wider world of the mindspace. Known as the temple, the structure featured a large central dome covered in gold and topped by a tapering spire. A swooping overhang partially concealed a paved walkway on the ground below. Inside, the temple's grandeur featured soaring ceilings, lavish wall hangings, massive statues, and gilded carvings. Exploring its opulent rooms was like stepping into a TV travel show, but without the other tourists.

During lessons, Ms. Finch had said the Patel House was built by Sonam Patel in the mid-1700s and designed with many of the same elements as an ancient Buddhist temple in Myanmar. Sonam had been influenced by the psychic architect before her, Ryou Nakamura, whose mindspace house reflected a traditional Japanese pagoda. Sonam had also been making a cultural statement with her design, as

Japanese pagodas in the real world had actually been based on ancient Buddhist temples.

Most of that lecture had gone over Amanda's head.

Her takeaway was that previous psychic architects had made meaningful statements with their mindspace houses, and she'd cringed at that idea. There was enough pressure to build a fantastic mindspace of her own someday without adding expectations for a cultural statement, too.

Here, in the blue and gold temple room, Amanda set aside the future so she could focus on her training.

She sat cross-legged on a thick, red cushion with her feet resting on the mosaic floor. The psychic engineers—Gerald, Dorothy, and Elaine—perched on similar cushions. They formed a small ring near a series of carved doors, each set within an ornate archway. Columns paved in blue and gold stones ran the length of the room. A swirling, abstract mural filled the arched ceiling. The room was awash in color and glitz, lit softly by windows of pale-yellow glass.

About fifteen feet away, Rory and Ben Hastings—their High Council observer—sat on plush, blue chairs flanking a large, gold statue. From their perspective, Amanda and the engineers were engaged in silent meditation. In the pure mindspace, the group sat in the same circle but were engrossed in a lively discussion.

"If the house exists there," Amanda puzzled through her idea, "and we're in a layer beneath the house, how can you maintain the house from here?"

"Well, you can't very well maintain it from there!" Elaine laughed, as if Amanda were making the subject more complicated than it needed to be.

Amanda squinted at her, then looked to Dorothy.

"When you told us about creating the door to Terra-V," Dorothy reminded, "you said it was like your mind was both in the birdhouse and in the fortress—at the same time—until your mind eventually split to form a bridge between the two. Right?"

Amanda glanced around the circle, seeing Elaine's encouraging smile and Gerald's wry smirk. "I guess so."

Those moments when she'd created the door to Terra-V were difficult to explain. She didn't remember describing it so succinctly. But it was a pretty good summary.

"Maintaining the house happens with your mind in two places, too," Dorothy continued. "There, as you call it, and here. You're still adapting to being in the pure mindspace, but practice will make it easier to navigate the two layers seamlessly."

"Let's bring up a door!" Gerald proposed with a slap of one knee. "Easier to practice when there's something here to practice on."

Dorothy and Elaine exchanged a look before Dorothy gave a tight nod.

"The Parliament door could use a recharge."

Elaine spoke while looking in the direction of the carved doors, but Amanda only saw darkness surrounding them. Right and left. Top and bottom.

Even the cushions they sat on were nonexistent in Amanda's view of the pure mindspace. And yet… their bodies were stable as if sitting on something instead of floating in actual space.

"The Parliament door?"

"Second from the right," Gerald clarified, though his pointing finger only led to more black nothingness. "Picture it and it will appear."

Amanda stared at the darkness.

"Can't see it?" Dorothy asked sympathetically. "Okay, try shifting back to the house to see the doors, focus on the second from the right for a few seconds, and then shift back here."

Amanda glanced at her skeptically before closing her eyes and willing herself back into the temple. When she reopened her eyes, their circle was again seated in the blue and gold room. The engineers looked at her in a calm, pleasant way, making her unsure if their minds had shifted to this space with her or were still back in the pure mindspace. Or maybe aware in both?

She chanced a quick look at Rory, who winked and tipped her head toward their High Council liaison dozing beside her. Stifling a laugh, Amanda studied what Elaine had called the Parliament door. She tried to memorize its details before blinking her eyes closed.

Feeling her mind back in the pure mindspace, Amanda knew she should open her eyes, but she was worried about what she would see—or wouldn't see—when she did.

"It's right in front of you," Elaine encouraged softly. "Take a look."

Amanda cracked one eye open, then opened both eyes in surprise.

"I see it!"

The door was a little hazy, though it sharpened as Amanda's eyes skimmed its surface.

"What if I walk over to it?" she asked impulsively. "Would Rory and Ben see me get up and move? Wait! Can I walk in the pure mindspace?"

Gerald and Elaine laughed. Dorothy shook her head and smiled.

"Go ahead and try."

Though Dorothy sounded genuinely encouraging, Amanda took one look at the lack of floor around them and lost her nerve.

Glancing down at her own body—which appeared to be sitting on absolutely nothing—made her queasy. *I'm sitting on the floor.* The thought whispered through her mind, reassuring her shaky nervous system. It was a grounding technique she'd practiced in her previous sessions with the engineers, but it only helped so much.

She still felt disoriented and on the verge of startling back into the comfort of the mindspace house.

I'm sitting on the floor. I'm sitting on the floor.

When Amanda still didn't move, Dorothy pressed her hands to the empty space in front of her, rolled to her knees, and stepped lightly to her feet. Instead of sitting in the void, she was now standing.

Panic flooded Amanda's body until she told herself that *standing* in an empty space wasn't any stranger than *sitting* in an empty space. As she came to terms with that thought, Dorothy turned and crossed the empty space to stand beside the wooden door.

Amanda's stomach clenched as she watched Dorothy walk so casually—so firmly—when there was nothing beneath her. Elaine scrambled to her feet as well.

"Let's go then," Gerald muttered as he hoisted himself up to follow. He was older and bigger than both women. As he shifted to his knees, he leaned heavily on one hand—though there was nothing beneath it—and paused for breath. Amanda instinctively reached out to help him, rolling to her own knees in the process. A moment later, they were both upright, and Gerald began laughing.

"Look at that! You can stand up!"

"What? Oh!"

Amanda looked down, felt her head reel, and thought: *It's okay. I'm standing. I'm standing on the floor. I can't see it, but I'm standing on the floor.* She took a few tentative steps, holding her arms out to her sides for balance. She reminded herself that she had stood in the pure mindspace before. The only difference now was moving, and that wasn't so bad—if she didn't look down. Gerald nodded his approval.

"It's easier when you don't think about it," he advised, then held out his bent arm to casually escort Amanda over to the door.

"Do they see us standing here?" Amanda jerked her head toward the area where Rory and Ben were sitting in the house. She was still confused about how they appeared to other travelers in the house when they had shifted into the darkness of the pure mindspace.

"Yes," Dorothy said. "They see us because we are still in the house with them. It's just part of our minds that are visiting this deeper place."

"But they can't hear us talking," Amanda pointed out, drawing an eye roll from Dorothy and a short laugh from Gerald.

"Because we aren't talking," Elaine explained patiently. "We're communicating with the parts of our minds that are outside of the house. It just looks to you like we're talking because that's how your brain processes it."

Amanda felt the fluttering confusion that came over her whenever the engineers explained the details of their abilities. Being in a shared mindspace didn't mean reading each other's minds, she still needed to talk for anyone to hear her. But this sounded like something completely different, and she couldn't figure it out.

"It's like the walking," Gerald winked, "easier when you don't overthink it!"

"Okay…" Amanda turned back to the door, ready to change the subject. "So… the Parliament door goes to England?"

"London, yes," Dorothy answered while Elaine hovered her hands around the surface of the door.

"Literally under Parliament," Gerald added. "Special sub-basement. Very secret."

"All the doors in this room go to government centers in either India or the United Kingdom," Elaine explained absentmindedly. Her focus was on inspecting the door frame.

"All of them?"

"Well, this house was built in the mid-1700s," Gerald reminded, as if that explained everything. "By a psychic architect based in India…?"

"Oh, right." Amanda realized he was prompting her toward something. "There was that whole British and India tea trade thing around then, right?"

Gerald crossed his arms in stern surprise. His white beard twitched as his lips pursed in irritation.

"What are they teaching you in school? Haven't you taken a World History class?"

Amanda's face flushed. "Ninth grade was World History to the 1500s. I won't get to the 1700s until next year."

"Oh, leave her alone, Gerald!" Dorothy chimed in. "Not everyone shares your love of history. Besides, we have more important things to teach her!"

Gerald relaxed his arms and muttered, "Ninth grade. Well… next year, then."

Amanda didn't have the heart to tell him that she had never been all that interested in history and couldn't remember most of what she'd studied last year.

"What are you doing?" she asked, as Elaine pressed her cheek close to the door jamb.

"Come, feel this!" Elaine beckoned excitedly.

Amanda let Elaine guide her hand just above the crack between the door and its frame. She was about to ask what she was supposed to feel when she noticed a pulsing warmth beneath her palm.

"What is that?" Amanda's eyes widened as she caught Elaine's excitement.

"It's the connection. The energy."

Amanda closed her eyes to better feel the sensation. It had a weak, irregular rhythm that unsettled Amanda's already overwrought nerves. She opened her eyes to see Elaine looking at her with gleaming pride.

"You can feel it, can't you? The erratic pulse? Give us a minute and you'll be able to feel the difference."

Amanda made room for Elaine and Dorothy to hover their hands over either side of the door. She couldn't see anything happening, but there was a slight vibration that echoed through her body.

For several moments, Amanda's vision flickered between the darkness of the pure mindspace and the showy grandeur of the blue and gold temple room. The effect was as unsettling as a strobe light. She lifted her hand for balance against the sudden dizziness and Gerald's solid arm slid under her trembling palm.

"They're almost done," he said softly. "They're drawing energy from the pure mindspace into the created door, kind of like caulking a window."

Amanda knew about window caulk. When she was ten, their apartment building had been updated with some energy-efficient features. A maintenance crew had come in to scrape out the old caulk and reseal the windows. She'd been fascinated by the process. One of the workers had even let her squeeze out a bead of the white paste from a plastic tube. He'd used a flat tool to smooth out her globby line, and she'd been surprised to see it dry clear.

After a minute or so, their work was complete. Elaine told Amanda to feel the door again.

"Wow!"

Amanda's smile widened as she felt the steady cadence of the pulse that now thrummed joyfully from the surface of the door. *Dah de-dum. Dah de-dum. Dah de-dum.* The triple-beat rhythm had an entirely different feel than the sap of a tuntum tree, but it reminded Amanda of the purple trees. Like the heartbeat of a living thing.

"What if you hadn't been here to help?" Amanda asked, removing her hand from the door.

Dorothy and Gerald looked at each other. Elaine's eyes dropped to the nonexistent floor.

"It takes a long time for a door to lose its connection," Dorothy began. "But over enough time…"

"It dies?" Amanda felt a pang in her heart.

"It fades away," Dorothy explained sadly.

"And there aren't enough of us to maintain them." Elaine hugged her arms over her chest tightly. "Not with the way things are going."

"But… there are more than just the three of you."

They had said they'd trained younger psychic engineers. And then Amanda remembered Lucas saying that most of the engineers were now with him.

"It's complicated." Dorothy shook her head. "And we've given you enough to think about for one day."

"No, wait!" Amanda looked at each of them, before finally settling her eyes on Gerald. "They've gone with Lucas, haven't they? With the other rebels?"

Gerald ran a hand over his beard.

"Gerald, no." Dorothy touched his free arm with a worried edge to her voice.

Elaine twined her fingers nervously until Dorothy snapped at her to pull herself together.

"Ben can't hear us, but he can see that!".

Elaine dropped her arms with a forced smile.

Gerald was still looking down at Amanda's bright eyes. He muttered something under his breath before turning back to Dorothy.

"Dot, the girl has a right to know," he said somberly. "And it sounds like she already knows a lot."

"We don't have much time," Elaine warned. Her faraway look showed she was peering into the furnished house. "Ben keeps checking his watch. I think Rory is stalling him."

"All right, fine," Dorothy snapped.

Gerald faced the door, his back toward Ben and Rory, then gestured for Amanda to do the same. He confirmed that many young engineers had gone into hiding, adding that things were changing within the society.

"And our numbers were already shrinking."

"Shrinking?" Amanda considered the possibilities. "Because something's happening to them? Or because there aren't as many travelers who are psychic engineers?"

"Both." Gerald paused. "There have been fewer new travelers in each generation—at least, fewer who successfully transition into our society—and fewer psychic travelers in general means fewer psychic engineers. And fewer psychic architects, too."

Amanda's head swam. Part of her wished she had let Dorothy end the lesson, but another part knew this was information she needed to understand.

"There are fewer new travelers now?" She tried to pick her most pressing question from the swirl in her mind. "What do you mean by successfully transition?"

Elaine stepped between them, stopping Gerald from answering.

"I think our time is up!" she said cheerfully, using a bright voice that carried Amanda back into the furnished mindspace house.

Touching her temples lightly, Amanda took in the bright décor swirling around her. She pivoted to see Ben and Rory walking toward them and noticed the look of shielded concern on Rory's face.

"Amanda does have a schedule to keep," Ben reminded curtly. Dorothy raised an eyebrow at him. Elaine frowned. Gerald was the only one to smile at Ben with ease.

"Sorry to hold her up," he said smoothly. "It's just nice to have a young person around."

"Yes, yes," Ben responded with a thin smile. "She's a good student, then?"

They agreed enthusiastically before Gerald added, "They aren't teaching her enough at that high school, though. Edwina needs to firm up her World History along with the architect stuff."

"Noted." Ben jotted something down on his clipboard. "That should be easy to remedy. Though Ms. Finch only teaches a limited number of hours these days."

"Ah, well, If Edwina has too much on her plate, I could lend a hand," Gerald suggested. "I used to teach World History, you know."

"Yes, I know." Ben narrowed his eyes.

"Might be nice to tutor a student again," Gerald added, pretending not to see Ben's wary look. "In history, that is. Haven't had a chance to do that in a long time."

"I suppose that would be all right," Ben answered uncertainly.

"If you need to run it by the High Council first...?" Gerald shrugged, and Amanda shifted her eyes between the two men.

"No, no. I don't need to bother them with something this trivial," Ben affirmed stiffly. "Rory, can you see to the arrangements?"

Amanda barely heard Rory's response. She'd already dipped into the pure mindspace where Gerald was waiting with a pleased grin and a mischievous glint in his eye.

"Really?" Amanda frowned, worried about how this might play into the High Council's plans for her return to public school in the fall. But it was hard to stay mad at Gerald, and there was so much more he could teach her.

"Yes, ma'am." Gerald winked. "We're going to straighten out your fundamentals on history."

"And on the decline of psychic travelers?"

"That, too!"

They blinked back into the temple as if they'd been fully present all along. Amanda said her goodbyes, wondering where Gerald and the others stood on Lucas and his growing rebellion. From what they'd said, the rift within the Psychic Traveler Society might be bigger than she'd thought.

§

"You're late."

Patty sat upright on the couch, glaring at Rory and Amanda as they came out of the apartment's small home office. In the days since Patty had learned about psychic travel, she hadn't gone back to work. She'd mostly stayed on the couch, staring at the TV. Cameron visited every day but wasn't there now. He'd been limiting the length of his visits, giving Patty time to process the shock on her own.

Judy was still living with Rory.

"Sorry," Rory apologized. "Training ran over a little."

"We're ten minutes late." Amanda rolled her eyes.

She wanted to be understanding, but it was getting harder every day. Patty stayed in her pajamas all day and snapped at everyone. She claimed nothing she did would matter anyway since PTS was paying their rent and putting her up in a sham job.

"It was hard to get away," Rory explained, "but we never left the mindspace."

Training in the mindspace was a condition Cameron had suggested while Patty adjusted to the reality of PTS. That way, Patty could look into their small home office anytime and see Amanda was safe, even if her mind was occupied elsewhere. It was a halfway measure before letting Amanda resume her psychic travel.

Amanda didn't like it. It was creepy to know her mom could be checking on her body while her mind was in the house, and the High Council wouldn't allow the limitation much longer. They wanted Amanda back in Arcadia and had given Patty one week to come to terms with the truth of their world. Cameron insisted that would be plenty of time—as long as they gave her some control of the situation. He was sure she was warming up to the idea and accepting it in stages.

Amanda didn't see that progress.

"You can go now," Patty dismissed Rory bluntly.

"Mom!"

"It's okay." Rory shook her head at Amanda before turning back to Patty politely. "Judy asked me to remind you that she wants to talk to you. When you're ready."

Patty waved Rory away and turned her head toward the far wall. On the TV, a couple was dancing on a moonlit balcony. The music of their waltz filtered through the living room, though no one was watching their dance.

Amanda walked Rory to the door, then stomped back to the couch with her fists clenched.

"You don't have to be rude to her."

Patty glared at Amanda. Her eyes were red and puffy.

"Rude?" she asked sarcastically. "I think I'm being pretty tolerant, considering she's been undermining my authority—and lying to me—for months."

"Rory only met you, like, a month ago!"

"Fine!" Patty hugged her arms around her bent knees. "Lying to me for weeks. But she was still part of it. Going along with Judy and the rest, without my permission."

"Whatever." Amanda looked up at the ceiling and exhaled deeply. She was exhausted from training and wanted to go lie down where she could give her brain a rest.

"Watch that attitude, missy. I don't have to let you go anywhere with her!"

"Really?" Amanda shouted, losing her last shred of patience. "You think you can stop me?"

"Excuse me?" Patty released her knees and sat upright. Her face flushed, and her eyes widened.

Amanda didn't care anymore. She grabbed her own hair with both hands, close to the roots, and pulled in frustration before letting go and unleashing the fear and anger she'd been carrying for days.

"You... can't... stop me," she growled, pausing between her words for emphasis.

Patty struggled to her feet. The blanket tangled around her legs and she kicked it aside, nearly falling to the ground in the process.

"I am still your mother!"

"And you *still* can't stop me," Amanda taunted, feeling the heat flooding her cheeks. "This is too important. This is my life! Whether you like it or not!"

Patty opened her mouth to respond, but Amanda was already gone.

She had disappeared from the living room and now stood, shaking and crying, in the fortress at Terra-V. The central tuntum tree stood before her, reaching toward the clouded sky. Workers bustled at the far end of the courtyard, and the tuntum saplings swayed in a cold gust of wind. A familiar friend approached swiftly.

"Amanda?"

Within moments of hearing her gentle voice, Amanda found herself leaning into Caeph's warm embrace.

It had been months since Amanda had seen the young Vherahna, yet they settled into conversation as if no time had passed. Caeph explained that Alira had gone to visit Sage Village, leaving her to oversee the work at the fortress. Amanda explained what had been happening with her mother over the past few days.

Caeph listened quietly, holding space for Amanda's tears, anger, and fears. She said nothing until Amanda finished speaking and sat sniffling in moody silence.

When Caeph did respond, her soft words cut into Amanda's heart.

"Your mother deserves more from you."

Amanda sat on the purple grass and wound a single blade around her finger.

She didn't know what to say.

"Do you remember the night we sat on the balcony in Sage Village?" Caeph asked softly.

Amanda nodded. It was during their journey through Terra-V. They'd sat on the balcony of their bedroom and looked out over a moonlit pineapple grove. Amanda had been sure she'd let Caeph and Alira down that day. Instead, Caeph had apologized to Amanda for not offering enough support.

"You said my fear was holding me back."

"Yes," Caeph agreed. "You were afraid your decision might put me, or Alira, in danger."

"Then you said that if you were in danger, the harm would come from that danger, not from me," Amanda recalled slowly. "You said it wouldn't be my fault."

"And you had a hard time accepting that."

Amanda studied her finger, seeing the tip turn red above the twist of strong, purple grass.

"I felt responsible," she admitted.

Caeph's own hands rested gently in her lap.

"As your mother feels responsible for you now?"

Amanda unwound the blade of grass, being careful not to pull it from the ground.

She knew Caeph was right.

When Amanda slowed down and thought about the situation from her mom's point of view, it hurt to imagine what she must be feeling. It wasn't a new thought, but it was a hard thought to hold onto.

Amanda had trouble looking at it from her mom's perspective when she wanted her to hurry up and accept it already. *But that takes time,* a voice whispered through Amanda's head. She'd had months to come to terms with her psychic travel abilities—and she'd had the experience of visiting Terra-V to drive home the truth. Her mom had only known for four days.

"I need to go home," Amanda whispered. "I need to talk to my mom."

"What will you tell her?" Caeph asked, as they stood up from the purple ground.

Amanda considered her options before offering Caeph a grateful smile.

"I'll tell her about a conversation I had on a balcony in Sage Village."

Chapter 14
The Quiet Zone

The fabric snagged lightly beneath Amanda's fingertips. She moved to the next rack, trailing her hand along the row of shirts without slowing her restless pace. Across the rack, Trina draped another shirt over the growing pile on her left arm. They'd been shopping for over an hour, and Amanda's heart wasn't in it. Eyeing Trina's collection, she picked up a blue shirt to study more closely.

"So, you aren't going out for cross country then?"

"What? Why would I go out for cross country?"

Amanda almost added, *if I didn't have time for cheerleading,* but she stopped herself just in time.

"With Drew and…" Trina paused before adding, "and the others."

Amanda wasn't sure who the others were, but she shook her head anyway.

"No. I don't want to run cross country."

It wasn't entirely true.

Amanda had as much interest in cross country as she'd had in cheerleading, maybe even more, but she didn't have time for anything like that. She barely had time to shop with Trina now.

Amanda hung the blue shirt back on its rack and checked her watch.

"But you *like* running now," Trina persisted, making it sound like an accusation.

Amanda shrugged and moved to another rack. She had forty-five minutes until Judy was picking her up and thought she should find something for the new school year.

Trina changed the subject.

"I'm thinking of switching up my schedule to add a theater class."

"It's too late to change your schedule."

Amanda picked up a pale gray sweatshirt emblazoned with a tabby cat wearing black-rimmed glasses and a beret. She could picture her aunt wearing it, so she draped it over her arm.

"Could you at least *try* to be supportive?"

Trina's irritated wail took Amanda by surprise. She looked up from a sweater display and watched Trina struggle to push a lock of curls out of her face without dropping her armload of clothes.

"I am supportive!" she protested. "I can't help it if it's too late to make schedule changes."

"It might not be," Trina muttered. "My mom is asking, and she usually gets what she wants."

"Oh." Amanda moved toward a rack of jeans, trying not to add a sarcastic *must be nice.*

"I'm trying this stuff on," Trina announced, just as Amanda felt her phone vibrate in her pocket. "Are you coming?"

"Go ahead." Amanda saw the text was from Cameron. "I'll be there in a minute."

Moving into the small clearance area at the back of the store, Amanda puzzled over Cameron's message: *Taking your mom out to lunch.*

Patty had been getting better over the last two weeks. She hadn't stopped Amanda from resuming her PTS training, even when that meant traveling off-world to Arcadia, and she'd listened when Amanda explained why psychic travel was important to her. But she hadn't gone back to work and was still spending a lot of time on the couch.

Going out to lunch seemed like a big step.

Amanda stared at the message. She wanted to feel happy but only felt the headache that had been threatening all morning. She wasn't in the mood for back-to-school shopping. She wasn't in the mood to think about how much time her mom and Cameron had been spending together. And she really wasn't in the mood for a pair of large hands to suddenly slip over her eyes.

"Guess who!"

Amanda didn't guess. She dug her elbow into the body behind her back and felt a whoosh of air as she lurched forward, dropping the cat sweatshirt on the floor.

"Ooof!" Trey doubled over, rubbing his gut. "Geez, Amanda! You're always hitting me."

"You're always invading my space," Amanda countered.

"Wow, you have no sense of humor, do you?"

"Guess not." Amanda scooped up the sweatshirt, keeping one eye on Trey.

"It's okay." Trey smiled. "I forgive you."

"Great."

Looking around the clearance area, Amanda was annoyed to realize a display rack was blocking them from shoppers in the main part of the store. Trey inched closer. Amanda inched back.

"Shopping for school?" Trey asked with a suggestive smile that Amanda didn't understand.

She took a step to the right, edging her way out of the clearance section.

"Come on!" Trey laughed. "You aren't actually afraid of me, are you?"

Amanda blinked. Seeing the disbelief in his eyes, she thought she might be making too much of this. Trey was annoying, but he wasn't dangerous. It wasn't like facing off against the Churukh castle guard. She tried to relax—a little—and act like a normal teenager.

"No," she scoffed and then grinned. "We already know I can take you."

"Ha!" He lifted his arms, lacing his fingers behind his head with his elbows out to the sides, and laughed with an indulgent shake of his head. "Yeah, okay."

Amanda saw he was embarrassed and let it go.

"Yeah," she answered his earlier question instead. "School shopping with Trina."

"Cool."

They stood together awkwardly, not knowing what else to say.

Trey rubbed his palms together. Amanda adjusted the sweatshirt over her arm.

They both spoke at the same time.

"Well, I better—"

"Amanda, I—"

They laughed self-consciously.

"Before you go…" Trey stepped closer when he saw Amanda moving away. "I'm sorry about before. You know, the way I acted last year."

He was standing too close, but Amanda was distracted by the shamed look on his face.

"I was a jerk," he admitted, looking at the floor. "I was putting on this macho, tough guy act, 'cause I thought… I don't know…"

Amanda tried to weigh his sincerity, but it was hard with Trey's gaze glued to the floor.

"The thing is," he continued slowly. "I've liked you for a long time. I just, well, I felt all weird around you and wanted to hide that, so I acted… You know. Like a jerk."

"Oh." Amanda's face felt hot. She'd never seen Trey like this before. He'd always been Drew's loud friend. The one with the crude jokes and the cruel pranks. Now here he was hanging his head and apologizing.

"You're really important to me," he went on, lifting his face until their eyes met. His were sparkling and hopeful. Hers were searching and confused. "I tried to hide it, but it's true."

"Uh…" Amanda backed further away.

"You're the most important person in the world to me," he whispered gently.

Amanda swallowed hard against the queasiness in her stomach and inched away from him until a rack of clothes pressed into her back. She wanted to tell Trey to leave her alone. She wanted to say she didn't like him, not the way he liked her. Not in any way really. But he looked so sad and vulnerable. Pathetic. Like someone with feelings she didn't want to hurt.

She turned her head toward the main part of the store, hoping to see Trina.

And his lips pressed against her mouth.

"Hey!" Amanda shoved Trey away. Hard. She watched him stumble as she wiped the back of her hand over her lips. Her cheeks were on fire and Trey was laughing.

"Aw, come on, Mandy!" He winked. "You know you like me. Deep down."

In an instant, he'd shifted into the jerk she'd known for years, and Amanda felt stunned. *It was an act?* Her mind tried to catch up to the change, struggling to understand his game.

"No," she answered with a shake of her head. "I really don't like you."

He laughed again. There was no trace of the shame he'd shown before.

"You will, though," he promised. "Just give me time. I'm growing on you."

"Like a fungus," Amanda shot back with disgust.

Trey stopped laughing. His face fell and he sighed.

"I meant it, though," he said with a half-smile. "I do like you, Mandy. And, someday, you'll come around to liking me, too."

Amanda clenched her jaw, feeling angry and off-balance. "My name is Amanda."

Trey laughed and blew her a kiss, calling, "Bye, Mandy!"

Amanda gripped the cat sweatshirt as he left the store, knowing she'd never buy it now.

§

Amanda and Mitra strolled the streets of Arcadia. For once, Amanda was glad to have Rory trailing behind. There was nothing threatening about Mitra or the world around her, but she hadn't entirely shaken off her experience with Trey. She felt sick with anger every time she remembered the feel of his lips. She hadn't told Trina about it and hoped no one would ever find out.

"You're quiet today," Mitra observed.

They were wandering the district around his lab during a work break. A storm had swept through that morning, leaving the sky clear and the air crisp. Many Arcadians strolled around them, and the ever-present birdsong had a spritely lilt. A woman with golden skin, magenta hair, and silvery-blue eyes passed by with a fair-haired Arcadian man by her side. A trio of Arcadian children walked behind them, carrying light-up toys that sent trails of small bubbles shimmering through the air.

Amanda smiled at them as they passed, pausing by a large metal sculpture shaped like an angular sphere. A *dodecahedron,* Mitra had told her on a previous walk. It was like a 12-sided die used in role-playing games, except the facets were open and the inside was hollow. A narrow obelisk stood in its direct center.

Amanda peered at the obelisk, noticing something etched into the stone. She paced around the sculpture and saw the same design repeated on each of its four sides. Mitra circled with her, while Rory watched from a stationary point. As they walked, Amanda saw a larger opening on the far side of the dodecahedron, like a doorway spanning two vertical facets.

"Can we go in?"

Amanda waited for Mitra's nod before passing into the sculpture's interior space. There was little separation from the people outside, yet Amanda felt enveloped by the metal framework. It was as if an energy field had made the air heavier. But instead of feeling weighed down, Amanda felt slightly buoyant. Almost like floating in saltwater. She waded toward the obelisk and studied the swirling design up close. There were three spirals branching from a central hub and curling into distinct circles.

"It is a triskele," Mitra explained. "A sacred symbol in our world. I've been told it appears in yours as well."

"It's on Dr. Webb's brooch," Amanda realized. "And I've seen it on other places in Arcadia, too. The guards' badges… On the bronze plaque near the elevators in your buildings…"

"Yes, it's easy to find if you start looking for it."

"What does it mean?"

"In our world, it represents the connection of mind, body, and spirit. Our thoughts are shaped through learning and life experiences. Our physical bodies are created through genetics and modified by our activities. And our spirits transcend both body and mind as our purest form of self. All three make up each individual person."

Amanda considered that carefully. Her mind and body were easy to understand, but she'd always thought words like *spirit* and *soul* were just expressions. They were used to explain emotions and gut-level instincts, but the spirit wasn't an actual part of her existence.

She was about to tell Mitra that when another thought crept in. Amanda had come to accept that reality existed in two places: the physical world and the mindspace. Yet her work with the engineers had revealed another level. There was the *pure mindspace* that somehow existed beneath—or within—the mindspace realm. Most couldn't access it, but Amanda had.

Was that the *spirit* of reality?

"Amanda?"

She looked at Mitra sharply, pulling away from her deep thoughts. His smile was gentle, and his eyes were soft. Amanda felt herself smiling in response. She noticed the thickness of his eyelashes and the slight crinkle at the corner of his left eye. The familiar, melting sensation returned, and she found herself imagining what it would be like to lean closer… and closer…

Until the repulsive memory of Trey's lips prickled across her mouth.

Amanda snapped out of her daze. She brought the back of her hand to her lips, then caught herself and let her arm drop by her side. Fixing her eyes on the triskele, her gut twisted with anger that didn't belong to this moment.

"Amanda?" Mitra tried again, sounding mildly amused. "Were you elsewhere?"

"Just in my thoughts."

"Ah." Mitra paused. "I looked up the woman for you. The one by the river."

Amanda turned to Mitra expectantly.

"I thought it would set your mind at ease to meet her," he continued. "Unfortunately, that will not be possible for some time. She is in the process of nescientia and cannot be bothered."

"Nescientia? You mentioned that before but didn't explain it."

"Yes." Mitra puzzled over an explanation. "Nescientia is a sacred journey that incorporates mind, body, and spirit. It is a rebirth of the whole person."

"Rebirth?" A prickling sensation ran down Amanda's body. "But the person doesn't actually *die*?"

Lucas had told her PTS wanted to control travelers. They'd developed a drug, Psylo4C, to let them manipulate susceptible minds. Was this connected?

"Does it...?" Amanda faltered. "Does nescientia erase memories?"

"In a sense," Mitra answered slowly, "but there is more to it than—"

Amanda had heard enough. She cut him off and flashed a gesture to Rory that would end their meeting and get her out of Arcadia.

§

"Slow down. Take a breath."

Lucas handed Amanda a glass of gold-tinged water, then leaned on the counter behind him. They were in his apartment in the hidden rebel settlement on Pacha-Inti.

Rory sat beside Amanda at the kitchen island. Cameron stood with his arms crossed as he looked out a narrow window.

"We know about nescientia," Lucas told her, after Amanda had taken a sip of the purified water. "It's not what you think."

"Well, what is it then?" Amanda set down her half-full glass, trying not to make a face at its bitter taste. "What does nescientia do?"

Lucas sighed and glanced at Cameron, who continued to stare out the window.

"Okay, guess it's on me," he muttered, before turning back to Amanda.

"Nescientia is trauma therapy. Basically, it puts a person's memories on hold while their bodies go through a healing process. It's rather involved. But the memories go back once the body and spirit are ready to reprocess them. It's effective. When done right."

He pursed his lips and glanced away, lost in serious thought. When he looked back, his characteristic smirk had returned.

"But the High Council doesn't do anything right, so we can't have nice things. The end." He pushed Amanda's glass closer, adding, "Drink up, you had a long walk."

Rory seconded his suggestion with a nod of agreement. Her own glass was empty.

"It doesn't sound like a nice thing," Amanda ventured, after another sip of the beige water. "I mean, if it can erase memories… couldn't they use it on anyone?"

The room was quiet.

Cameron turned from the window, narrowing his eyes at Amanda.

"Why did Mitra tell you about nescientia?"

Amanda glanced at Rory. In her rush to tell them about nescientia, she'd skipped over the story of the woman by the river.

"Mitra swore it was fine," she added, after summing up the story. "He said they were helping her."

Lucas frowned darkly.

"When exactly did that happen?"

Amanda didn't know. It was before school let out but close to the end of the year.

"It was May 12th," Rory answered for her. "The day before Mother's Day."

Amanda took another gulp of the bitter water. She hadn't mentioned the part about going off-world without permission that day.

Cameron looked at Lucas with concern. He nodded tightly, saying, "That fits."

"Are you sure?"

Amanda watched Lucas for an answer before realizing Cameron's question was for Rory.

"Yes," she said solemnly. "It was a memorable day."

"But you didn't report it?"

Rory shifted in her seat. "I didn't see it. Amanda had gone to see Mitra without me."

Amanda felt Cameron's eyes on her as she finished the last of her water.

"I see." His voice was tight, controlled. "And did Mitra's explanation today concern you?"

When she turned toward Rory, Amanda was surprised to see another look of discomfort.

"They were in a quiet zone."

"A quiet zone?" Amanda asked, but no one answered.

Instead, Cameron questioned Rory's attention to her charge, and Rory argued that Amanda deserved some privacy.

Ignoring them both, Amanda considered the energy she'd felt inside the sculpture. She had never heard of a quiet zone, but the more she thought about it, she couldn't remember hearing outside sounds when they were inside the statue. Not traffic passing by or birds singing overhead. She'd been so intent on the triskele, she hadn't noticed that absence until now.

"Is this the woman?"

Lucas thrust his arm between Cameron and Rory, holding his phone to face Amanda. There was a picture of a young woman on the screen. She was wearing different clothes but had the same long, dark braid falling over one shoulder. Amanda recognized her immediately.

She looked up to answer, but Lucas knew from her expression. He set his phone on the island and muttered under his breath. "Okay. Nescientia might explain her absence, but the guards…?"

"You're sure it's her?" Cameron picked up the phone to show Amanda the picture again. "This is the woman you saw by the river?"

Amanda felt her whole glass of water swish in her stomach as she confirmed her answer. She watched the muscles in Lucas' neck tense and his shoulders rise. His lips were still moving, but his whispered possibilities were too quiet to hear.

"She was a… contact?" Amanda asked nervously. "An Arcadian who brought you information?"

Lucas scoffed and turned away.

"Sophie is a traveler," Rory answered. "One exiled by the High Council."

"No," Amanda blurted with a shake of her head. "That doesn't make sense. If she was a traveler, why would she run from the guards? I mean, physically run. She could have just popped into the mindspace and come out here on Pacha-Inti. Or… anywhere."

"She has a family on Arcadia," Lucas answered with his head still turned away. He sounded resigned, deflated by what he'd learned. "She wouldn't leave them."

Amanda remembered what Mitra had told her.

"Mitra said…" She didn't want to go on but knew she had to tell them. "He said the woman and her family were in a serious accident."

Lucas jerked his attention back to Amanda.

"What kind of accident?"

Amanda pulled back, tipping her stool and catching the edge of the island.

"I… He…" All eyes turned on her as she tried to remember exactly what she'd been told. "He just said an accident. They were in the hospital, and she ran away because she was, I don't know, in shock or something. He said the guards were taking her to get help."

Lucas pressed his palms together. His index fingers rested against his mouth while his thumbs pressed the underside of his jaw. His tense stance reminded Amanda that Lucas was a fighter. He'd survived hostile planets, evaded a powerful organization, raised a rebellion, and built a settlement for exiled travelers.

Without the shield of his sarcastic charm, Amanda felt the force of his strength, and it was chilling.

Outside, a peal of laughter rose above the other voices passing by. It was hot in this desert world, even in the shade of the oasis. There were few supplies and limited resources. It was not an easy place to live, yet everyone Amanda had met on Pacha-Inti had seemed comfortable there. She'd guessed Lucas was the heart of that energy. He was a survivor, and Amanda was watching that ability in action as his eyes rapidly shifted under his half-closed lids.

"She would have told me," he muttered, speaking to himself. "Unless it isn't true."

"Lucas, if she is undergoing nescientia…" Cameron let the suggestion hang, and Amanda watched Lucas wave it away. His casual attitude snapped back into place, but Amanda could see a tremor in his hand.

"We don't know that's true," he insisted. "Or that any of it is true."

Lucas pressed his hands into the kitchen island and looked at Amanda confidently.

"Luckily, we have someone who can find out more."

§

On their long walk back to the proximity door, Cameron, Rory, and Amanda trailed several paces behind the exiled travelers who led the way. Twin suns beat down on their backs, making Amanda long for a glass of water, even if it was bitter and beige.

Pacha-Inti was a barren planet with very little animal life or vegetation, and no native inhabitants on par with human development. It had once been used for religious rituals but had since been largely abandoned by psychic travelers. Its sole door connected through an older structure Rory had called the *stone house*. Amanda didn't remember learning about it in her lessons with Ms. Finch, but she was fascinated by its architecture. The walls were built from interlocking blocks of various sizes with space left open for trapezoidal doors and windows. Its simple design was plain but impressive.

Nearing the ridge that concealed the oasis settlement from the proximity zone, Amanda wondered why the psychic engineers maintained the door to Pacha-Inti when the High Council didn't seem to think anyone was there. She was so lost in her own thoughts, minutes passed before she realized Cameron and Rory had begun talking quietly beside her.

"Do you think he…?" Rory asked softly.

"It's likely," Cameron agreed.

Do you think he what? Amanda wanted to ask, but she kept quiet, hoping they'd say more if they didn't know she was listening.

"If so, he's closer with them than we thought."

Cameron agreed but didn't add anything else. Amanda was on the verge of asking her own question when Rory spoke up again.

"Are you worried about this nescientia stuff?"

Cameron glanced at Amanda before answering.

"I think Lucas is right. Nescientia isn't dangerous. At least, not the way the Arcadians do it. I am concerned that PTS scientists could misuse the process—if they were taught them how to do it—but it's hard to prove what someone *might* do."

"Do you need proof?"

Amanda's question slipped out before she could stop it. She hurried on, "I mean, you would need proof for a *formal* accusation, but not if you just wanted to get people worried about the High Council. You'd only need a way to spread the idea quickly. Like, a viral meme. Or a group chat of some kind. Can you do that with psychic messages?"

Rory started to answer, but Amanda rushed on.

"Like in my Off-World Botany class! We learned how trees communicate through their root systems. There are different ways they pass messages. Like when the tuntum trees—"

"Amanda," Cameron interrupted with a slight cough.

The exiled travelers glanced back at them. Amanda realized her voice had gotten louder with each word, and she clamped her mouth shut.

"We already have a way to spread messages quickly," Rory answered quietly. "It's called the internet."

That night, Amanda stretched out on her bed and explored secret PTS sites that formed a shadow internet. She browsed chat rooms and social media sites used exclusively by psychic travelers around the world.

In the hours since Rory had set up her access, Amanda had already connected to Judy, Rory, Cameron, and Gerald.

Friend requests had also started to come in from other travelers—some she knew and some who knew about her by reputation—but she held off on responding.

She was scrolling through the profile of a woman she'd met during a fencing lesson when a text alert appeared at the top of her screen. It was a message from Drew.

"Only 11 days to school. Crazy, right?"

Amanda smiled sadly. His message brought her back to last fall. Before she'd known anything about psychic travel. A second text came in.

"How was your day?"

Her smile faded.

"Don't ask," she typed and hit send with a sigh.

"That bad?" Three dots appeared to show he was typing more. "Tell me about it?"

Images of Mitra, Lucas, and the mysterious Sophie tumbled through her mind before a flash of Trey's invading lips brought a wave of disgust.

"Not now," she texted shortly.

"Okay." Three more dots. "There's a dance the first Friday of school."

Amanda read his text. She knew about the dance. Trina was getting a group of girls to go together and had badgered Amanda about it during their shopping trip.

She started to type, *I know,* but deleted the words. She started typing about her plans with Trina, then stopped. She wasn't sure she was going, or if she even wanted to go.

"Yep," she finally texted, dropping her head back to stare up at the ceiling.

Her phone buzzed.

"I'm going with Mitchell and his girlfriend. He drives now." Three more dots. A pause while the dots disappeared. Then, three more dots. "Want to go with us?"

Amanda sat up. She wasn't sure what he meant. Get a ride with them? Go with him, like… a date? She stared at her phone until the screen dimmed and went black.

She had to say something.

"Not sure if I can," she typed, feeling a lump in her throat. "Have to check with mom and stuff." She hesitated. "But if I can, then yeah. Sounds good."

She reread the message, hating every word, then hit send and flopped back onto her bed.

It had been a very long day.

CHAPTER 15
THE SEAT OF POWER

Amanda's back cracked as she hugged her knees to her chest and rocked from side to side on her yoga mat. The morning sun slanted in beneath the roof of the balcony, falling over Amanda's body with a gentle warmth. Her eyes stayed closed as she rolled onto her right side, paused, then pressed herself up to a cross-legged seat. She brought her palms together in front of her chest and bowed her head. If she were with her yoga teacher, they would chant an *om* to close their practice. Instead, she let the chant echo through her mind. She had hoped to finish her practice before her mom woke up, but before she opened her eyes, the glass door slid open beside her.

Patty stepped onto the balcony with a mug of coffee cradled in her hands.

"Good morning." She moved toward one of the teak chairs, thought better of it, and gestured toward Amanda's mat. "May I join you?"

Amanda scooted back to make space and they sat together. Cross-legged and self-conscious.

"Where did you learn yoga?"

"Were you watching me?" Amanda saw that the glass doors had turned to hazy mirrors in the glare of the sun.

"For a little while," Patty answered. "You seem to know what you're doing. This is part of your… training?"

Amanda nodded, watching for signs of distress. Instead, Patty sipped her coffee, then softly smiled.

Slowly, as if trying out an unfamiliar language, she asked, "You learned at your PTS training center?"

"At one of them." Amanda watched for a reaction as she added, "In India."

"Oh," Patty blinked and held her coffee closer to her chest. "You've been to India."

Her voice was carefully neutral, but Amanda could tell she was bothered.

"Are you mad?"

"No." Patty shook her head sadly. "It's just… Disappointing, I guess. You've done so much, and I wasn't there for any of it."

Amanda thought about that, noticing the lump that had formed under the center of her ribcage.

"You didn't miss much," she said after a pause. "I mean, PTS facilities are pretty much the same everywhere. And I never really got a chance to go anywhere. Outside of the facilities, I mean."

Patty considered that quietly.

"Aunt Judy said she'd maybe take me sightseeing some time, but she wanted to wait until you knew. She said—"

Amanda stopped abruptly, waiting for her mom to snap at the mention of Judy.

"What did she say?" Patty prompted, without any noticeable anger.

Amanda studied her twined fingers. "She said vacation travel had to wait until you knew about everything. And it was bad enough we had to keep training from you."

Patty nodded, then took another sip of her coffee.

"I'm going to work on Monday," she offered, bringing the cup back to her lap.

Amanda perked up. Back to work was a definite improvement. Even better than lunch with Cameron.

"It's time," Patty continued. "I'm not entirely sure how I feel about all of… this…" She swept one hand wide to include more than Amanda's yoga practice. "But I'm starting to accept that it's real. And I can't change that."

"I'm glad," Amanda said happily, then rushed to correct herself. "I mean… glad you're accepting it. Not that you can't change it."

"I know what you meant." Patty laughed.

They sat together, content for the moment.

"School starts soon." Patty observed. "Sophomore year, PTS training. Friends here, and responsibilities on other worlds. You have a lot to juggle these days."

"You have no idea," Amanda sighed, looking toward the park below.

Patty surprised her by saying, "Cameron has been telling me about Lucas and the… unrest. I hope you're being careful and keeping Rory with you. Cameron says you're in very capable hands with her."

Cameron has been telling you a lot, Amanda thought irritably. She wondered if Cameron had told her how Lucas was counting on her to get more information about Sophie. She'd been up half the night wondering if she could get Mitra to show her Sophie's file or help her find out what had happened to Sophie's family.

"Does yoga help?" Patty asked, noticing the shift in Amanda's mood. "With everything you have going on."

"Yeah. Meditation helps, too."

Amanda considered her mom carefully before deciding to share more.

"Actually, I've gotten to the point where my physical yoga practice—the *asana*—feels a lot like meditating. It's like my mind is aware of my body moving—like, really, extra aware of every little thing—while all the other thoughts just kind of disappear. Or maybe they float in the background somewhere. I kind of know the thoughts are there, but it's easy to let them go."

Patty nodded in a knowing way.

"I remember that feeling when I used to practice tai chi. Back in college. It was something your father was into for a while."

They were quiet for a moment. Amanda wondered if tai chi had been part of her dad's PTS training, then wondered if her mom was having the same thought.

"I could use some of that now," Patty mused, and then her eyes lit up. "Could you teach me some meditation?"

The request caught Amanda off guard. She'd been about to ask more about her dad's interest in tai chi, but the moment had passed.

"Yeah, I guess. It's really not that hard. I mean, some of the special stuff I'm working on can be pretty hard, but meditation can be really simple."

"Can we try some now?"

"Uh, sure." Amanda had been taught to sit upright while meditating, elevating her hips on a thin cushion and letting her spine follow its natural curves. Sitting tall without slouching. They didn't have cushions on the balcony, so Amanda helped her mom adjust her legs to find a more natural, upright position.

"Okay, now that you're comfortable, close your eyes. We'll use our breath as a focal point. Breath in," Amanda instructed, "and breathe out."

She walked Patty through a few slow, deep breaths, then said, "Notice how it feels every time you breathe in and every time you breathe out. Let it have a natural, easy rhythm, and stay focused on how it feels. Don't use words to describe it, just *feel* it."

They sat together silently for a minute or two. Amanda closed her eyes and took two more breaths before saying, "Notice if you've started thinking about anything besides your breath. Notice the thoughts, then let them go like clouds passing overhead. You can think about them later. For now, simply feel your breath."

Amanda waited through a longer period of silence. She tried to remember her early meditation sessions at the PTS center in India. Instead, her mind wandered back to Terra-V. She closed her eyes and imagined the cool shade of the tuntum trees. She could almost hear them echoing through her entire body. *Tuntum. Tuntum.*

Pulling herself back to attention, Amanda looked at her mom's calm face. With her eyes closed and her mouth relaxed, she looked younger somehow. Or maybe more fragile. More vulnerable.

"Take a deep breath in," Amanda said gently, "and let it out."

She walked her mom through a few more rounds of breath before saying it was time to open her eyes. Patty blinked a few times, her vision coming back into focus.

"And that's meditation," Amanda said with a shrug. "One kind, at least."

Patty rolled her shoulders and stretched her arms.

"That felt great! Do you want to teach me another style? Maybe we can make it a morning routine? Something new each day?"

Amanda stifled a sigh, wanting to remind her mom that she already had a lot going on. A snarkier part of her almost suggested Cameron teach her, since they were spending so much time together, but then she had a better idea.

"What if I make you a deal?" She asked cautiously. "I teach you some meditation, and you have lunch with Aunt Judy. Or coffee, whatever. Just meet with her and hear her side of things."

Patty looked into her empty coffee cup. Amanda held her breath. They'd been having their first good moment together in weeks, and she was afraid she'd just ruined it. Instead, Patty gave an odd sort of shake of her head and shrugged uneasily.

"I met with her yesterday," she admitted sheepishly.

"What?" Amanda's shriek drew a whispered hush.

Lowering her voice, she asked, "When? How? Why didn't you tell me?"

"You were out all day." Patty shrugged. "And you seemed tired at dinner."

"Not too tired to hear about that!" Amanda lifted her hands, palms up, then dropped them in exasperation. "So, what happened? How did it go?"

Patty made a half-shake, half-nod movement with her head. "We're not totally there yet, but we're working things out. And I… I told her she could move home."

"What? Seriously?" Amanda shook her head, sure she'd misheard something.

"Yes." Patty laughed self-consciously. "I know, I've been… well… I think I was justified in being angry. But I'm open to the idea that she meant well. And it's worth trying to start over, now that the truth is out."

Amanda's smile stretched wide as she clapped her hands together and bounced on the mat in excitement. It was more than she'd dared to hope for. Patty watched her with amusement.

"Does that earn me a meditation lesson?"

"That earns you two or three, at least!"

Amanda beamed, and Patty laughed.

"Cameron said that would make you happy."

Amanda's smile faded. She shifted her seat and watched a flock of birds fly by.

"What's wrong?" Patty studied Amanda's face as she shrugged off the question. "I thought we were going to stop keeping secrets."

Amanda sighed.

"It's nothing. It's just…" Amanda stopped herself from complaining about how much time her mom had been spending with Cameron. "You never told me how you know Cameron. Not from now, but from before."

"Oh." Patty picked up her coffee cup and glanced inside. "Well, he worked with your dad. Cameron said he told you about that."

"Yeah, but he didn't say he knew *you*."

Patty cradled the empty cup in her lap.

"There was a time when I knew Cameron really well. He and your dad were close outside of work, too, so we'd all get together sometimes. Go out to dinner, play board games, that sort of thing."

"I don't remember him."

"You were really little, and it wasn't all that often."

Amanda searched her memory. She was seven when her dad died. She thought she should remember something about her parents having a friend who came over to visit. Even if it wasn't all that often. She remembered being left with Judy while her parents went out some evenings. She remembered her parents and Judy laughing over board games after she was sent to bed. Had Cameron been with them some of those nights?

"But you didn't see him after dad died?"

Patty straightened one leg, easing an ache in her knee, and nearly knocked over her coffee cup. She moved it quickly and shook her head.

"I saw him for a while," she answered slowly, gently bending and straightening her stiff knee. "Judy had moved away, and he came to check on us sometimes. But it was a hard time, and I wasn't… I don't know, I wasn't all that fit to be around people, I guess. We lost touch."

Amanda had no reason *not* to believe her. Yet, it felt like there was more to story. It was the same feeling she had when dealing with most of the travelers in PTS. Maybe Cameron had been right when he said part of that feeling was just being a teenager. Life had once seemed so simple, but now everyone Amanda knew seemed to be carrying whole worlds of thoughts and experiences that they never talked about.

It was like everyone had their own house full of doors that only they could choose to open. And maybe that was okay. Maybe it was better if people were allowed to keep some things to themselves.

§

Judy came back to the apartment that night. Amanda watched her mom and aunt make dinner from her place on the couch. At first, they were stiff and overly polite as they moved around the small kitchen. Then a disagreement over salad dressing shifted from snarky comments to hugs and tears. Amanda stayed out of it, awed by the speed of their emotional journey. By the time dinner was served, they were back to normal. Maybe even better.

The next morning, Patty went back to work, and Amanda went to meet Gerald for a history lesson.

While he was supposed to be tutoring her in World History, Gerald often wove in events that happened within PTS, showing how the shadow organization could shape larger world events. He also explained why the PTS headquarters, and the High Council, had moved from various countries over the years.

The PTS seat of power, as he called it, traditionally moved to the home country of the psychic architect. The last psychic architect, Edmund Robinson, had British parents but was born in New York, making him the first American psychic architect. When he came into his full powers, PTS leadership had transitioned to the United States.

Today, Gerald reminded Amanda of that. He then showed her a timeline of when each psychic architect had worked on each house in the mindspace.

"Wait!" Amanda studied his list of architects with a perplexed frown. "This shows there being more than one architect at a time."

"Yes," Gerald confirmed. "Because there were. Ms. Finch may be focusing on the houses that are still standing, but they aren't the only houses that were built.

"Up until a few hundred years ago, it was common to have psychic architects from different parts of the world at the same time. Some worked together to design houses. Some created their own. Later architects would often recreate connections to some of the same worlds in their new houses. The older, smaller houses would then be left to eventually fade away."

"I guess having fewer houses means less maintenance," Amanda said thoughtfully. "But if there were architects from different countries, at the same time, how did they decide where the High Council would be."

"That's an interesting question." Gerald smiled. "In the earliest days, the seat of power stayed in the country with the eldest living architect. Which, as you can imagine, led to a lot of power shifts. When architects from different countries died close together, High Councils were dissolved and relocated too often to be feasible.

"In the 1200s, they switched to a plan where the country with the eldest architect retained control until his or her death. But then, the seat of power would shift to the country with the youngest known architect. The High Council would stay with that country until their once-youngest architect became the eldest remaining architect, and the process would begin again."

Amanda puzzled over that explanation.

"Eventually," Gerald added, "psychic architects became so few and far between that those rules no longer mattered. When there's only one architect in a generation, the seat of power obviously moves with him or her."

Amanda considered that. Gerald had previously shown her how the number of psychic architects—and psychic engineers—had dropped with each generation. The decrease had been gradual and easy to hide. As Gerald had said, those who wrote the textbooks could teach whatever history they wanted to tell. And—just as it was in the outside world— new psychic travelers often weren't all that interested in studying history.

"I guess that does make it easier."

"It does," Gerald agreed. "Fewer architects also means fewer people for the High Council to keep tabs on. And if you want to stay in power, it helps to keep your most powerful people under control."

Amanda's frown deepened.

She remembered accusing Director Alvarsson of not caring about her success.

"But they'd want there to be an architect now, right? Since they don't have any?"

Gerald pressed his lips together. He appeared to be pondering the question, but Amanda suspected he already had a theory and was only deciding how much of it to share with her. "I would think that depends on their priorities. Most things in life depend on a person's priorities."

"Like, if their priority is to build a new mindspace house and connect to new worlds, then they'd want a psychic architect," Amanda ventured. "But if they'd rather just keep control of what they already have, then they'd be fine without a new architect who might mess things up?"

"Yes," Gerald agreed. "They also might worry about a new psychic architect turning up in another country. Though, even with a psychic architect in the *same* country, they might not be keen on sharing power either. Remember, there would traditionally be a psychic architect sitting on the High Council. That is, an architect who had completed her training."

Amanda took that in slowly. It was hard to imagine being part of the High Council. And she wasn't sure what it would mean for her training to be complete.

"Of course," Gerald added, "they'd have to weigh all of that against whatever they might get from the Arcadians if a psychic architect could help that relationship."

Amanda glanced around the room. They were alone in the living room in the birdhouse. No one else could hear them, but Amanda still felt uneasy.

"Do you think I can do it?" she asked. "Do you think I can change my energy enough to get into the Arcadian mindspace?"

"No," Gerald answered plainly. "The mindspace doesn't work like that. Not as far as I know. It's not like people speaking different languages."

"So, I'm going to fail?"

Amanda's heart sank.

"I wouldn't call it a failure," Gerald said. "I think you're doing exactly what the High Council wants you to do."

"Which is what?"

"Think about it." Gerald leaned in. "The Arcadians are already ahead of us in every way, including space travel. It wouldn't help us if the Arcadians were capable of psychic travel, too. So maybe the High Council doesn't want you to succeed. Maybe they just want you to show enough progress to keep the Arcadians happy and hopeful."

"They want me to string them along?" Amanda felt chilled at the thought. "Let them think we have something valuable to trade? When they know it won't work?"

"I could be wrong." Gerald shrugged. "But if you get too close, do you really think the High Council would let you keep trying?"

CHAPTER 16
SOPHIE STAVROS

By the time she arrived in Arcadia, Gerald's lesson was weighing heavily on Amanda's mind. She was important to the High Council because she was important to the Arcadians. If she couldn't connect to the Arcadian mindspace, she would be useless to the Arcadians. But if she could, would she be dangerous to the High Council?

She performed worse than ever on the energy table and knew it was Gerald's lesson getting in the way. That, and knowing Lucas was counting on her to find out what happened to Sophie. In a flash, she realized she was wasting her time with Mitra when there was someone else who could answer her questions.

"How do I get a meeting with Dr. Webb?"

"Is there a problem?" Mitra looked up from his data with an expression of concern.

"No…" Amanda consciously relaxed her tone. "I just want to talk to her about something."

"Amanda," Rory warned from her seat near the lab's entrance. The other scientists had gone out for a break after Amanda and Mitra's last round on the table.

"What?" Amanda turned to Rory, feigning innocence. "Dr. Webb came to see me when she wanted to talk. Why can't I see her when I want?"

Mitra glanced toward Rory helplessly.

"I'm happy to arrange a meeting, though it may take a few days. Dr. Webb has a very busy schedule."

A tone sounded from a panel on Mitra's desk. He crossed the room to read the incoming message, then laughed lightly. "This is a strange coincidence… Dr. Webb is asking to see you now."

In her office, Agnes Webb invited Amanda and Rory to the sitting area adjacent to her desk. As in Mitra's lab, there were comfortable chairs arranged near floor-to-ceiling windows. Yet Dr. Webb's office was on the top floor of the building, high above the multi-layered traffic, and higher than any other building in sight. From this height, they could see dark clouds gathering far beyond the city.

"You wanted to see me?" Dr. Webb began pleasantly, before noting their uneasy expressions. After a short pause, she added, "No one listens in on my office. Neither Arcadian nor Maiorum. But if it will set your minds at ease…"

She flipped a switch on the small table beside her chair, and Amanda immediately felt a shift in the room. The air thickened, lifting her with a nearly imperceptible buoyancy. Amanda didn't know much about quiet zones, but she knew how it felt to be in one.

"Now, how can I help you?"

Amanda looked to Rory, but she gestured for Amanda to begin with a look that said, *this meeting was your idea.* Amanda nodded and decided on a place to start.

"A few months ago, I saw a woman down by the river."

She watched for any twitch of unease, but Dr. Webb responded mildly.

"We know about your presence by the river, and I am well acquainted with Sophie Stavros. What do you wish to know about her?"

Amanda and Rory exchanged a look.

"Whatever you can tell us," Rory answered.

"Is she all right?" Amanda asked with more concern.

Dr. Webb's eyes softened. "Yes, she is well."

"Is she…?"

"Undergoing nescientia?" Dr. Webb chuckled at Amanda's look of surprise. "We know Mitra accessed her records. I was fairly certain he was not prompted by his own curiosity."

"So, is she?" Amanda pressed, as Rory listened with alert attention.

"No."

Amanda glanced at Rory, who seemed reluctant to add to the conversation.

"But you know Sophie?" Amanda asked uncertainly. "So, you know she—"

Amanda stopped talking at a sharp nudge from Rory's boot.

"That Sophie is Maiorum?" Dr. Webb smiled. "Of course. Do you think one of your people could establish a home in this city without our knowing? Sophie has become a valuable member of our society. As far as I am aware, her friends and neighbors do not suspect her origin."

Amanda had hoped her questions about Sophie might rattle Dr. Webb enough to let something useful slip. Instead, Dr. Webb seemed more than willing to tell them everything.

"Why do you have her in hiding?"

Rory's question hinted at an accusation, but Dr. Webb continued to smile.

"Isn't it obvious? Your people found out about her, and we are keeping her safe."

At their looks of confusion, Dr. Webb began a longer explanation.

"Nearly three years ago, Lucas and Sophie came to Arcadia seeking sanctuary. They had been exiled from your community, and we agreed to take them in. While they were secluded from most Arcadians, they did interact with a small team of scientists and counselors. There came a time when Sophie wanted to marry one of our scientists and make a home here, and we arranged for her to integrate into our city. Lucas left us then, believing he had unfinished work to do in your world."

"Mitra said her family was in an accident. Are they…?" Amanda swallowed, unwilling to finish the question.

"They are fine," Dr. Webb reassured. "That was merely a story to explain their sudden disappearance. Serious accidents are rare here, but when they do happen, it is not unusual for those involved to spend an extended period in a recovery center. You must realize they are all very important to us, especially the child."

"Why?"

Dr. Webb paused, looking to Rory.

"The child is part Arcadian and part traveler."

Amanda wondered how Rory knew that and why no one had told her. Then she put the pieces together.

"Oh, right. Since Sophie married an Arcadian…"

"Sophie is not the child's biological mother," Dr. Webb cut in.

Amanda looked at Rory in confusion, but her stony expression made it hard to tell what she already knew about Sophie's family.

"The scientist Sophie married is a woman and the child's biological mother," Dr. Webb explained patiently. "Lucas is the child's biological father."

Amanda slumped in her chair. She remembered Lucas' anger and fear when she'd blurted out the news that his child had been in a serious accident.

"We have to tell Lucas they're okay."

"We will," Rory agreed, keeping her eyes on Dr. Webb.

"You have questions as well?" Dr. Webb prompted her.

"Can Sophie still visit our mindspace?"

One eyebrow lifted slightly.

"You are a good soldier, Rory, but not much of a diplomat. A diplomat might come to the same conclusion, but she would be more artful in her approach. I would prefer it if you would be yourself and ask directly. You want to know if we have disabled Sophie's traveler genes."

"Did you disable Sophie's traveler genes?"

Amanda studied their faces. Rory wore a neutral expression, while Dr. Webb's eyes looked sad above her smile.

"Perhaps it is better if you ask her yourself."

Dr. Webb typed a short message into a device on her side table. Rory kept her silence, and Amanda followed her example, though her mind was full of questions. *Why would the Arcadians disable Sophie's traveler genes? Was it to show the High Council that they could? But Dr. webb had said they were protecting Sophie from the High Council… Was it to keep Sophie from leaving Arcadia?*

"While we wait," Dr. Webb went on smoothly, "will you answer a question for me?"

Amanda held her breath, afraid to say the wrong thing.

"Do you believe you will be able to connect to our mindspace?"

A flush came over Amanda's cheeks. She could tell Dr. Webb what Gerald had said, but on the other hand, Alira had thought that it was possible. She wasn't sure which of them she believed. And it wouldn't matter if Gerald was right about the High Council not wanting her to actually make a connection.

Dr. Webb watched the debate play over Amanda's face and didn't wait for her to answer.

"I have my doubts as well," she said simply. "Though I have reasons to be hopeful. Do you know much about the genetics of psychic travel?"

"No."

"I do." Dr. Webb smiled. "To put it simply, we know which genes are involved in psychic travel, and both our people possess the same traveler genes. As far as we can tell, there are no genetic differences. No mutations that would explain why we end up in a different mindspace than your own. We also have found no variations in the genetics of a psychic engineer or psychic architect. I suspect this means there are other factors we do not yet understand about psychic travel."

"Like the wavelengths of the energy we use?" Amanda asked, thinking of Mitra's theory.

"Something like that," Dr. Webb responded, avoiding a more complicated explanation. "The energy readings we have captured during your session with Mitra are already promising."

A knock sounded at the door, and Dr. Webb ushered Sophie into the room. Amanda recognized her immediately as the woman from the river, though she was now dressed in clean clothes and wore her hair loose down her back. After making introductions, Dr. Webb nodded to Rory and Amanda kindly.

"While I hope you will come to trust my word, I do not expect it at this point in our relationship. Our guest will answer your questions, and I will return shortly."

Dr. Webb left her office, keeping the quiet zone active. As they settled into their seats, Sophie regarded Amanda and Rory apprehensively.

"You can trust her," Sophie said bluntly, "if you'll take my word for it."

Rory and Amanda exchanged a glance.

"You were running away from them," Amanda pointed out. "When I saw you by the river, you were running. I saw them capture you."

"Ye-es," Sophie drew the word out uneasily. "But that was a… misunderstanding."

"Are you safe here?" Rory leaned forward, forearms on her thighs.

"Yes." Sophie looked down as she clasped her hands in her lap and worried one thumb against the other. Rory dipped her head, trying to catch Sophie's eye.

"Are you still able to travel to our mindspace?"

Tears gathered in the corners of Sophie's eyes. She wiped them away before answering.

"You won't understand."

"Try us." Rory reached for her hands and Sophie nodded, pulling herself together.

"You know that I married an Arcadian scientist," she began. "And that my wife gave birth to Lucas' child?"

She paused for their confirmation.

"Lucas fathered our child as a parting gift, for me and for the care that the Arcadians had shown him. Our child's mixed genetics may provide insight, or he may even be the psychic architect we need."

"Does the High Council know about this?" Amanda asked nervously, remembering what Gerald had told her. "About your child?"

"No." Sophie extricated her hands, freeing them to swipe at the tears in her eyes and tuck her hair behind her ears. "Only Lucas knew."

Rory changed the subject.

"What happened that day by the river?"

Sophie met Amanda's gaze and smiled softly.

"We heard about you before you even arrived in Arcadia. The next psychic architect. A teenager. We heard you would be working with Mitra and knew how our people hoped you'd be the key to creating a mindspace house of our own. Though it wouldn't be *my* own… it would be for the Arcadians."

She dropped her eyes, then stared out the window. The dark clouds were keeping their distance.

"You can't imagine what it's been like for me. I've chosen Arcadia as my home, but I'll never *be* Arcadian. I live in the city, but I can't meet in the Arcadian mindspace."

"There are other Arcadians who can't either," Rory reminded.

"Yes, but it's not the same. They've never been able to access it. Most of them don't even know about it. But I do! I know what it's like!" Sophie's voice shook. "Our mindspace pulls at me. Lucas pulls at me. Always reminding me who I really am. What I *should* be doing."

Amanda leaned forward as an idea clicked into place.

"You asked them to turn off your traveler genes?"

"I tried Mitra's energy tables," Sophie said abruptly, turning from the window to face Amanda. "I tried over and over, every day for months, but it never worked. I never even got close. They say your readings are better. That you may have a chance. I didn't have a chance."

"I understand," Rory told her gently. "You *needed* them to turn off your traveler genes."

Sophie nodded once, blinking back fresh tears.

"They wouldn't have done it if I hadn't asked them." She spoke in a near whisper. "I had to practically beg them and go through weeks of counseling before they agreed it was the best choice."

"But you didn't tell Lucas?"

"No." Sophie bit her lip. "I tried to tell him. So many times. But I knew he wouldn't understand, and he can't get past the PTS guards here anymore. Now that they're watching for him."

"It's okay," Rory reassured her. "We'll tell him for you. Can you tell us what happened that day by the river?"

Sophie hesitated, staring out the window for several seconds before beginning her story.

"Turning off the traveler genes sounds easy, like flipping a switch, but it isn't. It involves a short stay in a clinic and a procedure that can be… disorienting."

The storm clouds crept closer to the building, dimming the light in Dr. Webb's office.

"The clinic is across the street," she gestured vaguely toward the window. "On the day I arrived, one of your scientists was outside, and he recognized me. He reported back to the High Council, which led to a demand for my arrest and return. Of course, I didn't know any of that, and neither did my doctors.

"I was well into the procedure when I overheard someone talking about my family being in an accident. If I'd been in my right mind, I might have asked questions or demanded to see Agnes. Instead, I only remember thinking that I had to get to my family."

"You left the clinic?" Rory prodded, as Sophie was again watching the darkening sky.

"Yes," she answered reluctantly. "I wish I remembered more about where I went and what I did. The procedure was half-finished, and I was still on powerful sedatives. I remember going home and arguing with a neighbor who tried to call for help. I remember running when others tried to detain me—for my own good—and I remember falling asleep in a clearing in the woods.

"When I woke up, I was scared and still very confused. When I saw you with Mitra, by the river, I knew who you must be. I don't think I knew what was happening, but I wanted to talk to you and give you a message for Lucas. I don't even know what that message would have been, but it didn't matter. The guards had already caught up to me. They brought me back to the clinic, where they finished the procedure, and Agnes explained her plan to keep me and my family safe."

Amanda and Rory were quiet, taking in Sophie's story.

"I don't want what I've done to affect your relationship with the Arcadians," Sophie told them nervously. "You have to believe it was my choice. They would never do anything to hurt me."

§

"Do you believe her?" Rory asked, when they were walking back to the gatehouse.

The storm had passed through while they were in Mitra's lab. The sidewalks were damp, and the buildings glistened with the remains of the rain.

"I think so," Amanda hedged, "but didn't she seem a little…? I don't know. Like she was really trying to convince us it was all her fault?"

"Yeah, like the Arcadians can do no wrong," Rory agreed.

They walked quietly for a few minutes.

"I don't know Dr. Webb or any of the Arcadians well enough to trust them," Rory admitted. "And, until today, I only knew Sophie Stavros by name."

"But we know someone who knows her a lot better."

Amanda and Rory agreed that talking to Lucas was their best option.

"We promised to update him anyway," Rory conceded as they passed the hover carts parked at the gatehouse.

Amanda thought about Sophie saying Lucas was not able to travel to Arcadia anymore. She wondered when that had started and why the PTS guards were watching for him now if they hadn't been before.

If Rory and Amanda had concerns about Sophie's story, Lucas didn't. He sat with them in the main hall of the temple and listened to Rory repeat everything Sophie had told them. He kept a neutral expression throughout the story, only nodding when hearing that the family was fine. He stayed very still when learning that Sophie had asked to have her traveler genes suppressed.

"I'm not surprised," he said, after the story was finished. Amanda thought she heard a hint of sadness in his words, but nothing like what she'd expected. "After what we've been through, she was done with PTS. She said it wasn't much of a society. Compared to the Arcadians."

He looked off into space, reminding Amanda of the way Sophie had kept staring dreamily out the window in Dr. Webb's office.

"What had she been through?" Amanda asked, drawing a sharp look from Rory. Though Rory seemed just as interested in Lucas' answer.

"She hadn't been through much of anything before she met me," Lucas said with a touch of regret. "She was fairly new to psychic travel when we met, and I was still trying to have it both ways. Working with Cameron by day, stirring up a rebellion by night.

"Sophie listened to my pitch and jumped in with both feet. We broke into some PTS labs, destroyed research projects, and spread whatever information we could find. Among other things. We raised as many doubts as we could and caused enough trouble that the High Council eventually had to exile us."

"No one told me about her before," Amanda admitted, feeling strangely sad that Sophie had been exiled without a trace.

"Did anyone tell you about me? Before I showed up to meet you?" Lucas challenged with a familiar glint in his eye. "Not many travelers knew about Sophie's exile. It was better for them to paint me as a lone rebel who was mentally disturbed. Besides, she was relatively unknown, and I was already a household name due to my spectacular entry into the world of psychic travel."

"You believe it was her choice?" Rory pressed. "To have her traveler genes turned off?"

Lucas eyed her warily, then turned to assess Amanda's reaction to her question.

"What would be the alternative?" he asked innocently. "You think the Arcadians were trying to keep her there? Or trying to stop her from talking to me?"

Rory stayed quiet, still waiting for him to answer her question.

"Oh, Rory Beck, you are skeptical, just like a good soldier." Lucas laughed. "But no, the Arcadians wouldn't do that. Agnes Webb would never do that. Unlike our dear leaders, the Arcadians believe in respecting the wishes of others and in causing no harm."

Amanda shifted in her seat, sensing their tension.

"Causing no harm," Rory repeated musingly. "That is a moral approach."

"Yes, it is," Lucas agreed, though his eyes narrowed.

Rory smiled at him before asking, "But who decides what counts as harm?"

CHAPTER 17
WELCOME BACK

"Having fun?"

Drew sat forward in his folding chair with his hands clasped between his knees. They had to lean close for Amanda to hear him over the music echoing through the gym. The overhead lights were dim, two columns of party lights flashed from either side of the DJ table, and a banner above the DJ read: *Welcome Back!* Amanda idly wondered how many times the DJ had reused that sign before stringing it up in their gym.

"Yeah." She smiled and nodded, then looked away.

They were sitting alone at a table, sipping soda, and watching couples move in slow circles at the center of the gym. They'd already danced through one fast set, gathering a group of friends as the music played on. But when the DJ switched to a slow song, Drew had suggested a break.

With nothing else to say, Amanda let her thoughts shift back to nescientia.

After their meeting with Dr. Webb, Amanda had taken Mitra to a quiet zone and asked him to explain the process. Rory had joined them, asking questions of her own.

From what Mitra said, the process didn't actually remove memories. It was more like inserting a mental barrier to keep the memories from being accessed. While the memories were caged off, the person would go through weeks—or months—of specialized physical and emotional therapy. According to Arcadian science, memories imprint themselves on a person's physical body and shape their emotional language. Without access to those memories, the body and spirit could heal more easily.

What fascinated Amanda the most was the way the memories were restored after healing.

First, the person would watch pre-recorded videos of themselves telling their most important life stories. Amanda could only imagine how odd it would feel to see a video of herself telling stories about her own life—stories that she couldn't remember for herself. But Mitra said it gave the person a chance to hear about their own life with some emotional distance.

When the time was right, the mental barrier would be removed, and the person would complete the nescientia experience by internally reprocessing their own memories. Of course, a team of specialized therapists would support the person throughout the entire process.

Remembering what Mitra had said about nescientia healing mind, body, and spirit, Amanda had thought it sounded like an amazingly effective treatment. She'd wanted to describe it to Drew in detail, but they'd been busy with the start of school and distracted by other topics. Thinking about it all now, she was about to suggest they find a quiet place out in the hall, where she could give him the full story, when the DJ broke in on his mic.

"All right, all right! Who's ready to take it up? Come on, people! Make some noise!"

A shout went up as the DJ spun up a Latin rock beat. Couples parted, shifting back into a thronging mass.

Drew grinned as he offered Amanda his hand.

"Dance?"

They found a spot with some friends, and Drew twirled Amanda under his arm before breaking into a hip shimmy that got a laugh from the crowd. Amanda jokingly rolled her eyes and matched his simple cha-cha step, content to let Drew get all the attention.

The set continued and their circle of friends grew. People took turns in the center, breaking out their best moves. Drew stayed by Amanda's side, nudging her side with laughing winks, but never pushing her into the spotlight. She shook her head at him, happy to laugh and move—and take a break from the world of psychic travel.

The mix switched to another favorite. Amanda shrieked with the crowd and threw her hands in the air. The circle dissolved back into a formless mass of bodies. They jumped and swayed, bumped hips, and spun in wobbly little circles. Amanda laughed harder as Drew grabbed both of her hands and spun her around in an improvised swing style.

Drew was still holding Amanda's hands when the bass faded away, blending into another slow set. Couples formed around them. Single friends fled the dance floor.

They stood for a long moment, still as statues, waiting for each other to react. Amanda felt her mouth go dry. Drew moved one of his hands to her waist, stepped in close, and began to lightly move with the music. His side-to-side cadence tugged at her balance until Amanda began naturally stepping with the beat. They rocked in time, inching closer. They didn't snuggle up like some of the other couples, but Amanda let the side of her face lightly rest against Drew's upper chest.

It wasn't the first time Amanda had slow danced with a boy. It wasn't even the first time she'd slow danced with Drew. They'd been paired up at school dances often enough. Yet, there was something different about this dance. Amanda felt it in the way Drew's heart raced against her ear and his arm settled across her low back.

She only wished she could feel it in her own body. In her own heart.

Her mind raced as their bodies swayed, and she felt like a fraud. She told herself she was supposed to be feeling something else. Something *more*. But she wasn't sure what. Besides, she liked what she already had with Drew and didn't want it to change.

While Drew's right arm rested across her low back, his left hand clasped her right hand in the space between their chests. The tip of his first finger lightly stroked the back of her hand. Amanda swallowed her anxiety. She *did* like the feel of being close to him.

Maybe that's enough, a voice in her head suggested. *I'm only fifteen.* But she was almost sixteen, and she knew other girls her age who wanted to do more than slow dance with a boy. She worried that there might be something wrong with her if she didn't. She told herself she shouldn't feel pressured like that, not even by her own fears. And all that silent talking started to make her head hurt.

The song stretched on. Amanda smelled the clean, detergent smell of Drew's shirt. She heard him hum lightly before catching himself. She smiled to think he might be self-conscious, too. It was weird to be held close this way. He was still Drew, but it felt... different.

Looking at their intertwined fingers, she remembered the day they'd held hands in the party room. Sitting close on the couch. Nothing more had happened that day, but the memory made her heart flutter. Her heart sped at the idea of lifting her face now, of feeling Drew's lips hover close.

And then she caught sight of Trina.

Dancing with Trey.

"Hey, what's wrong?" Drew held Amanda in place when he felt she was about to bolt away. Following her angry stare, he cursed under his breath. "Well, that's not good."

"No," Amanda agreed through clenched teeth. "It's not."

Drew relaxed his grip, hoping she wasn't about to storm across the gym and cause a scene.

"What is she thinking?"

Drew shook his head helplessly.

"It's just one dance," he offered soothingly.

Amanda stopped moving and let go of him, crossing her arms over her chest. "One dance with *Trey*."

"Yeah, I know, but..." Drew led Amanda back toward the line of tables. "Let's go out in the hall to talk."

"Good idea!"

But Amanda didn't follow him toward the double doors. Instead, she marched right up to Trina and Trey—who were nestled close—and stood where Trina could see her.

"We need to talk."

Trina opened her eyes but stayed in Trey's arms.

"Later," she snapped and turned her other cheek to Trey's chest, looking away. Trey smirked and pulled Trina closer. Drew tried to take Amanda's arm, but she shook him off and moved back into Trina's line of sight.

"Now."

Amanda hadn't yelled, but something in her tone made Trina sigh and free herself from Trey's arms. Amanda glared as Trina apologized to Trey with a kiss on his cheek. They walked away and Drew blocked Trey from following.

The fluorescent hall lights felt harsh after the dimness of the gym. Trina looked at her nails, making a show of not caring about whatever Amanda wanted to say.

"You hate Trey," Amanda reminded bluntly.

"He's not so bad."

"How can you say that?"

Three girls passing from the bathroom looked at them curiously before going back into the gym.

"You're making a scene," Trina complained, but when she looked up, she seemed unusually calm. "And you don't know him. Not really."

Amanda couldn't process this sudden reversal.

"Look," Trina continued, "I know *you* hate him. I did, too. But, Amanda, he's changing. Growing up."

Amanda stared. It had been two weeks since that day at the mall. He couldn't have matured in just two weeks. Then she remembered the way he'd acted that day and she wasn't surprised by Trina's next words.

"He opened up to me this week. He's embarrassed about the way he acted last year and how he sometimes acts still."

"Trina—"

"No, wait!" Trina wouldn't let Amanda speak. "The thing is, he likes me. I mean, like, he *really* likes me, and he has for a long time. He was just shy and—"

"And he felt weird around you, so he acted like a jerk to hide it?" Amanda asked sarcastically.

"Well, yeah." Trina's face hardened. "I know you don't want to believe that, but if you'd seen how sincere he was—"

"I did!" Amanda snapped, seeing the instant confusion on Trina's face. "I saw it when he said the exact same thing to me two weeks ago."

"What are you talking about?" Trina crossed her arms over her chest and glanced back at the gym doors.

"It's an act, Trina!" Amanda spoke loudly, letting her anger at Trey color her words. "He's lying to you to get what he wants."

"I don't believe you." Trina shook her head. "Where would you even see Trey before school started?"

"When we were shopping." Amanda explained how Trey had cornered her while Trina was in the changing room but stopped short of the kiss.

Trina seemed torn as she paced the short width of the hall. When she stopped walking, the look on her face was half-warning and half-pleading.

"You misunderstood him," she insisted with growing confidence. "He knows we're friends. So, he probably just wanted to smooth things over with you before admitting his feelings to me."

"You're making excuses."

"No." Trina shook her head again. "I'm important to Trey. He told me himself."

"Trina, that's his game. It's an act."

Trina glared at Amanda.

"I *am* important to him," she insisted. "I might not be anything special to you, or Drew, or anyone else, but I'm special to Trey. I'm important to him."

They stood together, listening to Trina's words.

"Why does that matter?" Amanda lost her patience. "You wanted to be a cheerleader to feel important. You want Trey to think you're important. Why does that mean so much to you?"

Trina stared as if that were the most ridiculous question she'd ever heard.

"Everyone wants to feel important."

Amanda hesitated, remembering the way she'd acted out when she wasn't getting special treatment at PTS. It had stung when Gerald put her importance in terms of the High Council's priorities. And she'd gone out for cheerleading, too. Why? To be important at school? Or to be important to Trina?

With a rush of emotion, Amanda stepped closer.

Trina stepped back, holding in a rush of tears.

"You're important to me," Amanda said quietly. "You're special to me."

Another group of girls burst through the gym doors, giggling as they walked toward the bathrooms. Pop music filled the hall, fading behind the heavy wood door as it swung shut.

Amanda?

Judy's voice echoed in Amanda's mind.

Not now! Amanda thought, trying to focus on Trina.

Trina narrowed her eyes.

"I'm important when you see me here with Trey," she corrected. "You wouldn't have even noticed me tonight if I wasn't dancing with him."

"That's not true!" Amanda insisted. She'd looked for Trina as soon as they got to the dance but hadn't found her in the crowd.

Amanda. Aunt Judy's message slipped into Amanda's conscious mind. *Have you heard from Rory?*

Amanda split her attention. Rory wouldn't be out of reach unless something was wrong.

"It feels true," Trina responded in a near whine. "It's not that I want to date Drew again—I really don't—and I don't mind if you date him, but you didn't even tell me you were coming here tonight. And then I find out you're on a double date with…"

Amanda tried to listen to Trina while simultaneously forming a message for Judy.

I haven't heard from Rory. Is something wrong?

Having sent her response, Amanda returned her full attention to Trina.

"…and if I were an important person in your life, you would have told me that you and Drew are dating."

"We're not dating."

"You're on a date now."

"Well, we came here together…" Amanda agreed uneasily.

"With another couple," Trina added, before looking at Amanda in surprise. "Wait? You do know that you're on a date, right?"

Okay. Judy's next message broke through. *But if you hear from Rory, let me know.*

Amanda dropped her head into her hands. It was really beginning to ache with the loud music, her split focus, and her worry over why Judy was looking for Rory.

"Oh, wow!" Trina laughed. "You're hopeless!"

Amanda scowled at Trina's smug face.

"I'm hopeless?" she fired back. "You're the one who's so desperate to feel important you'll date the biggest jerk we know."

A driving rap beat burst into the hall as the gym doors opened again. Amanda kept her eyes locked on Trina. She didn't care if the girls going back to the dance overheard them. People were probably already talking about them arguing out here. It was too late to stop the rumors.

"He's not a jerk!" Trina yelled. "You're just jealous that I have a boyfriend and you can't even figure out that you're on a date!"

"Oh, yeah," Amanda scoffed. "I'm so jealous of Trey!"

She tried to form another message for Judy, but Trina kept talking. Ranting about how Amanda didn't want to admit Trey had changed or accept his feelings for her.

"Really?" Amanda gave up on her psychic message. "If Trey is so crazy about you, why did he kiss me?"

Trina's eyes widened and her mouth fell open.

Amanda regretted the words the moment she'd said them. She regretted them even before she heard Drew's voice cut through the silence.

"Everything okay out here?"

§

When Amanda got home from the dance, she stood alone in the hallway outside her apartment. Drew had accepted her explanation about Trey. But they'd shared an uncomfortable ride home and an even more awkward goodbye when he stepped off the elevator at his floor.

As she unlocked the apartment door, Amanda hoped to go to bed unnoticed. Instead, she was surprised to find Rory sitting on her living room couch. Judy stood across from her, near the balcony door, and Patty sat on the loveseat. They all looked upset.

"She just got here," Judy explained, pointing at Rory.

"You're home early," Patty said. "Did something happen at the dance?"

Amanda settled her gaze on Rory. She didn't want to talk about the dance. "What's going on?"

"Come sit down," Judy suggested, ushering Amanda to a seat beside Patty.

As soon as she was settled, Amanda raised an eyebrow at Rory, ready for answers.

"It's Gerald. He's in the hospital."

"Gerald?" Amanda had expected bad news but nothing like that. "No, I just saw him two days ago. He was fine."

"I know," Rory agreed. "Dorothy reached out today to say she hadn't heard from him since after your last meeting.

280

Ben told her Gerald was sick, but she didn't know if she could believe him. She thought…"

Rory didn't have to finish the sentence. Dorothy was afraid the High Council had taken him away. Amanda remembered talking about the connecting door to Pacha-Inti at their last meeting. The conversation had happened in the pure mindspace, outside of the High Council's hearing. Unless they'd found a way to listen in.

"She sent you to check it out?" Amanda asked, guessing why Judy had been worried about Rory's whereabouts.

"Yes. I wasn't in a good position to respond to messages. But I can confirm he's in the hospital at PTSI. He was admitted after a stroke, and he's in stable condition."

"PTSI?" Amanda sat up in alarm. "That's the detention hospital place?"

Judy and Rory exchanged a worried look, while Patty listened silently. Amanda realized how strange it felt to have her mom here for this conversation, but it would feel just as strange to ask her to leave now. It was amazing how much Patty had come to accept in only a month.

"Sort of," Judy hedged. "Gerald is in one of the hospitals at PTSI, which is the society's largest research and treatment facility."

"It's not the detention center," Rory clarified. "He's in a different hospital in the same complex."

"Close enough," Amanda argued. "This hospital is still in the same place where they dope up travelers and lock them away until they fall in line, right? The place where they mess with genetics and are trying to turn off psychic traveler abilities? The place they call PTSD?"

Judy met Amanda's worried eyes.

"I know you've heard a lot of frightening things about the Psychic Trauma Social Detention Center—which is officially shortened to PTS-DC, by the way—but whatever may, or may not, go on in *that* building, PTSI is also the most advanced medical facility in the world. Gerald will have excellent care there."

"If he even had a stroke," Amanda challenged. "What if they found out what he was—" She stopped, not wanting to say what Gerald had been teaching her.

"Amanda." Rory sounded tired. "I checked it out. Gerald is in his seventies. Reliable sources say it was a relatively mild stroke, but that would still put him in the hospital.

"It took some pushing, but Ben said we can visit as soon as the doctors allow it. There's nothing more we can do tonight."

Sinking into the couch cushions, Amanda looked up at the ceiling and let out a long exhale. She could see Gerald's teasing eyes as he frowned at her lack of interest in World History. She could hear his prodding tone when he nudged her toward some new idea. Picturing him, Amanda realized they'd never met in the physical world. Only in the mind-space, which had felt as real as anywhere else.

"Fine," she relented. "I'm going to bed."

Amanda locked her door and entered the birdhouse, reaching out to someone who would tell her the truth.

"You've heard about Gerald?"

"Yes," Amanda confirmed. "Rory says it was a stroke."

"You don't believe her?" Lucas leaned against the attic wall, regarding Amanda skeptically.

"I don't know," she admitted after a pause. "Do you?"

The attic alcove usually calmed Amanda's nerves. Tonight, the sight of its silver-blue doors wasn't enough to settle her anxiety. She wanted to step through one of those doors to find Alira, or Caeph, or—better still—take Iveryn on a long ride through the rocky desert.

"I do, but it's still a problem," Lucas answered darkly, shattering Amanda's daydream.

"Because he's been helping me?"

Lucas closed his eyes briefly, then stepped away from the wall insisting, "No. It has nothing to do with you."

Amanda felt her chest shake. "But Gerald has been teaching me and using the pure mindspace to tell me things they might not want me to know…"

"Bah!" Lucas waved the idea away. "We're meeting in the regular old mindspace now, and they can't hear that either. Look, Amanda, the High Council can't control what any of us say to each other here, so they don't bother with anything like that."

"But you said…"

"It's a problem," Lucas agreed. "And it is, but not because of anything you've done."

"But he's at PTSD! Or PTSI… whatever they call it. It's bad either way, right?"

Lucas scowled, and Amanda regretted mentioning the hospital he hated.

"A few months ago, we met right here, and I said I wasn't your enemy," Lucas responded carefully. "You asked if they were the enemy—the High Council, Alvarsson, and the rest—and do you remember what I told you?"

"You said that I should decide for myself."

"As everyone should." Lucas shrugged. "And here we are. I didn't expect to be here quite so soon, but best-laid plans and all that…"

Amanda shook her head, trying to keep up.

"What does that mean?"

Lucas regarded her thoughtfully. His hands were shoved deep in his pockets and his shoulders slumped, lessening some of the difference in their heights.

"I appreciate what you did for me," he said, ignoring her question. "By meeting with Agnes and bringing me information about Sophie and her family."

"Oh." Amanda was surprised. "Yeah, of course."

They stood together without talking, and Amanda couldn't guess where Lucas' thoughts had gone. He seemed to be juggling a million ideas and Amanda knew how that felt. She waited as long as she could before curiosity got the better of her.

"What did you mean about best-laid plans?"

Lucas sighed, ran his hands through his hair, and gave her a wry smile.

"I'll let you in on a secret," he said with a gleam in his eye. "I don't know what I mean half the time. None of us do. I come up with plans, like anyone else—okay, maybe more elaborate plans than most anyone else—but I don't always know what will set those plans in motion. There's a spark, a timing, in these things. Months can be spent on planning and preparation, but a big change doesn't come without a catalyst. And it's hard to know when a catalyst will appear."

"I don't understand…?"

He waved her unasked questions away.

"Things may be about to change, and more rapidly than you might think. If this is the moment."

"And you're saying I need to decide whose side I'm on?" Amanda asked uncertainly, then added with a shy smile, "Isn't that kinda clear already?"

"If only everyone had your wisdom." Lucas grinned with feigned modesty.

There was a beat as Amanda watched his smile fade.

"I don't know how the next few days, or weeks, will play out," he said seriously. "I hope you aren't involved at all."

"Why not?"

Amanda felt stung by his words before remembering how she'd criticized Trina's need to feel important.

"No, I get it," she told him, stopping whatever he was about to say. "Not everything is about me."

Lucas raised an eyebrow, weighing the intent behind her statement.

"You're a powerful person, Amanda. Never doubt that. But revolutions are messy, and I'd rather bring you in when the dust settles. For your sake. Understand?"

"Yeah, but I—"

"Want to help," Lucas finished her sentence. "I know you do, and I appreciate it. I also appreciate the powers you are developing and don't intend to put you in harm's way. That wouldn't be smart for anyone."

Amanda looked glum, and he chucked her under the chin before going on.

"That doesn't mean I'll keep you in the dark, either. I'll tell you as much as I can, whenever I can. I've told you before that I believe in people making up their own minds about things. They can't do that if they aren't given all the information. Okay?"

"Okay." Amanda nodded, feeling slightly better.

But that night, as she tried to fall asleep, Amanda wondered when Lucas Flynn had become the person who made her feel better.

Chapter 18

The Physiology, Technology, and Science Institute

They were given permission to visit Gerald on Sunday afternoon. Preparing to go, Amanda was surprised to learn that PTSI was not connected to a proximal door. The facility had been built about an hour outside of Chicago. Which meant they would have to use the mindspace to travel to PTS headquarters and then be driven to the hospital from there. As a condition of their visit, Ben Hastings would drive them and be their escort in the facility.

They would also leave their cell phones at home.

Rory explained that the hospital at PTSI provided lockers in the lobby but did not allow phones on patient floors. It was a standard policy at most of the buildings in PTSI. She thought it was safer to leave their phones at home and rely on psychic messages to stay in touch while they were away. Amanda could tell that didn't sit well with her mom, but Judy promised to stay with her and relay any messages that came in.

"We'll check in as often as we can," Rory reassured, earning an impulsive hug from Patty.

When they arrived at PTS headquarters, Ben was waiting for them in the main lobby. He clucked his tongue and eyed his watch—though they were right on time—then hurried them outside where a town car and driver was waiting at the curb. Amanda had expected Ben to drive them in his own car, though the hired driver made sense when she remembered that he was on the High Council, which controlled travelers all over the world.

Amanda's PTS History teacher had explained that their society had local, national, and regional councils spread throughout the world. Above that, the International Council included delegates from each nation. The High Council sat at the very top. Amanda wondered if the High Council were as powerful as the U.S. government. Or maybe more powerful.

She had plenty of time to think about it on the ride to PTSI. Ben spent the drive looking over more paperwork, and Rory wasn't interested in small talk. Amanda watched the scenery roll by and thought about how the High Council and other PTS leaders secretly interacted with governments and institutions in the normal world. It was a topic that no one talked about. At least, no one who talked to Amanda. Except for Gerald.

They'd been on the road for over an hour, passing through suburbs and widely spaced towns, before finally approaching a tall gate connected to an imposing fence. Amanda thought it looked more like a military base than a hospital. Though she'd never been on a military base.

A metal sign on the fence read: *Physiology, Technology, and Science Institute — Private Property — No Trespassing.* Amanda assumed the name was public camouflage, remembering how the society had many public businesses that changed the PTS acronym to fit their needs. The rest of the sign made it clear that public visitors were not expected or allowed.

Despite the barrier, they passed the guardhouse easily. The driver flashed an ID badge, and they were soon passing through a maze of buildings that looked like a small city.

When Ben packed his papers into his briefcase, signaling that they were close to their destination, butterflies woke up in Amanda's stomach.

The building Ben led them into looked like a regular hospital with rows of rooms and nurses bustling through the halls. Except they'd passed through a security checkpoint in the lobby and by two guards when they got off the elevator on Gerald's floor. There was another guard posted outside of Gerald's room.

Amanda hesitated by his door. Rory gave her a nudge.

"He's expecting you. It'll be fine."

Ben said nothing but opened the door and walked in ahead of them. As soon as he did, Amanda heard Gerald's familiar voice ask, "Well, where are they?"

She took a deep breath and walked into the room with a smile pasted on her face.

"There she is!" Gerald laughed. He looked pale and tired, and older than he'd seemed in the mindspace. His words were slightly slurred, but his eyes had their same sparkle. "Did I scare you?"

"A little bit," Amanda admitted, moving closer to his bed. She had brought him a get-well card, a set of markers, and a coloring book of world maps.

When he reached for the gift bag with his right hand, she noticed the left side of his mouth didn't lift quite as high as the right.

"Minor incident," he said dismissively. "Ben here is too under... uh.. under-pro.. no... over-pro..."

"Over-protective?" Rory asked, moving close to the other side of his bed.

"That's the one," Gerard chuckled.

Amanda and Rory's eyes met.

"He's still on some medication," Ben told them, before settling into a chair at the far side of the room.

Rory had warned Amanda about that before their visit. She'd been told Gerald was being mildly sedated to keep his mind at rest and avoid unintentional psychic travel. Amanda was afraid that meant Psylo4C, but Rory explained there were other sedatives that prevented psychic travel more gently and without the hypnagogic effects that caused hallucinations and suggestibility.

"So, you're feeling okay?" Amanda asked gently, trying not to think about drugs the High Council could use to get information Gerald wouldn't otherwise share.

"Yeah, yeah." Gerald shrugged off the question gruffly. "Such a fuss over nothing."

Amanda searched for something else to say.

"Did you do the reading?" Gerald asked fuzzily, as if pulling the words together was a challenge. "The Tennis Court Oath. Did you read it? You need to read it."

"Um, yeah," Amanda soothed him, trying not to obviously check if Ben was listening. "We don't have to talk about that now. Classes can wait."

They'd been studying the French Revolution, with Gerald explaining why some powerful systems needed to be overthrown and replaced with a government that would represent the needs of all the people.

It didn't seem like the best topic to bring up in front of a High Council member.

"It's important!" Gerald grabbed Amanda's wrist and started to sit up from his propped pillows.

Rory put a hand on his left shoulder, easing him back and gently shushing him.

"If this visit is too much…" Ben half-stood, clutching an open folder of notes to his chest. He'd been reviewing some documents and it wasn't clear if he'd been listening to their conversation before Gerald's outburst.

"It's fine," Rory reassured, before picking up a plastic water pitcher from Gerald's bed tray. "Maybe some more water would be good. Amanda, go ask the nurses where you can fill this up."

Amanda looked between Gerald and Ben uncertainly. Rory clearly wanted her out of the room, so she agreed to go without understanding why. Ben settled back into his chair and rearranged the notes on his lap while telling Amanda to be quick and not wander off.

The nurses' station was deserted. Amanda stood with the empty pitcher in hand and looked up and down the hall uncertainly. When a nurse finally returned, she went straight to a computer and began rapidly typing. Amanda caught her eye and was hastily directed to a water fountain around the corner. As she turned from the nurses' station, she almost walked right into Director Alvarsson.

"Visiting the patient?"

"Yeah…" Amanda blinked at him in confusion. "What are you doing here?"

"I have many responsibilities," he answered vaguely.

"Okay…?" Amanda hadn't seen Director Alvarsson or given him much thought since her hearing with the High Council.

"You're fetching water?" The director gestured toward her empty pitcher. "I'll walk with you."

Amanda threw a curious look back at the guard as they moved away from Gerald's room, but he showed no reaction to the situation.

As they neared the end of the short hall, Director Alvarsson cleared his throat.

"There's a problem in Arcadia," he began decisively. "I would like to know what it is."

Amanda stopped walking. The director kept on for a few paces, saw she was no longer by his side, and impatiently returned, closing the distance between them.

"There's no problem," Amanda told him, as calmly as she could manage.

He narrowed his eye skeptically, then gestured for them to resume walking.

Amanda spotted the water fountain as soon as they turned the corner. She quickly moved to fill the pitcher and Director Alvarsson began ticking off points on his fingers, one by one.

"You have left sessions before their appointed end times. You have held back details of your experiences in said sessions. Last week, you conducted an unauthorized appointment with Agnes Webb.

"Before I report to the High Council, I will give you one opportunity to explain yourself."

Amanda's hand shook as she positioned the pitcher under the spout. Once it was in place, she pressed the button and watched the water sputter into a steady stream.

"Because you happened to run into me?"

The director was confused by her question.

"I mean, if you wanted to give me a chance to explain, why didn't you call me into your office? Or did you just decide when you saw me here?"

"This is not the time for your insolence."

"Isn't it?" Amanda watched the waterline rise. "This all seems a little… weird to me. The High Council was pretty clear about my training going directly through them now. Are you the one who tells them what happens in Arcadia? I thought the scientists who travel with us do that."

Amanda leaned forward to check the water's progress and let go of the button. She could sense Director Alvarsson's spluttering rage in her peripheral vision, but she didn't care if she upset him.

Snapping the lid onto the pitcher, she remembered how he'd spoken against her at her High Council hearing and how Madame Ellis had shut him down.

"Actually," she added lightly, "Ben is here with me today. Ben Hastings? You know, from the High Council? We could ask him about that, I guess."

She turned around, seeing his flushed face.

"You think I'm out?" The director's voice sent chills down Amanda's spine. "You think they're on your side? The High Council does what's best for our society, and they hold my opinion in higher regard than you may think."

Clutching the pitcher, Amanda thought over her past interactions with Director Alvarsson. He'd rarely met with her in person. When he had, it had been to intimidate her into blindly following his orders. He'd never respected her enough to have an open conversation or trusted her to form her own opinions. As far as she was concerned, respect had to be earned, and he didn't deserve hers.

"We can ask Ben about that, too."

A muscle twitched near Director Alvarsson's right eye. He towered over Amanda, looking down with a sneer.

"You had a choice today," he said ominously. "You could have worked with me, shown you could be trusted, but you chose to reaffirm your rebelliousness."

Amanda's stomach quaked, but anger won out over fear. She looked the director in the eye and said, "Rebellion can be a good thing."

§

Back in Gerald's room, the rest of the visit went smoothly. Amanda colored one of the maps she'd brought while Gerald told her facts about its various regions. They kept him company until lunch, then left so he could rest.

During their quick lunch in the hospital cafeteria, Ben commented on how good Amanda was with Gerald and how happy her visit had made him. She smiled in response, remembering one of Gerald's lectures on the dangers of idealism where he'd said, *"Ben may be a prig, but he's a realist and a pretty decent guy at heart."*

When she got home, Amanda told Rory and Judy about her run-in with the director. They weren't concerned about it but said they'd mention it at their meeting with Cameron and Lucas that night.

"There's a meeting?"

Amanda offered to go, but they said it wasn't necessary.

"Spend some time with your mom," Rory suggested. "It's been a long day, and you could use a break."

Though she wanted to argue, Amanda was feeling the stress of the day catching up with her. She thought about Lucas' wish to keep her safe until the dust settled and decided it would be a relief to sit this one out.

That night, they stayed in and ordered pizza.

"You never told me about the dance," Patty prodded casually, taking her second slice. "Did you have fun?"

"I guess." Amanda shrugged. She picked some black olives off her third slice of pizza.

Patty waited patiently, but her eyes showed she knew something was up.

"You remember Trey?" Amanda asked warily. "The guy from my locker last year?"

"Yes," Patty answered tightly. "I remember Trey."

Amanda nodded as if that were all she planned to say. Really, she was trying to decide whether to start with what happened at the dance or at the mall.

"Did something happen with Trey?" Patty put down her pizza and wiped her fingers.

"Yeah… or no." Amanda stumbled over her words. "I mean, he was there. Dancing with Trina."

"Oh?"

"Yeah, and he's an absolute jerk!" Amanda insisted. "But she says he's *different* around her."

"Ah." Patty sighed knowingly before taking another bite of her pizza.

"That's a thing, right?" Amanda asked. "Like, a common line some jerks use?"

Patty nodded as she finished chewing.

"Yep. It's pretty standard. A cliché even."

Amanda ate another olive glumly, then moved on to a chunk of green pepper.

"And then you argued with her about it." Patty said, surprising Amanda with her certainty. "What did Drew think about all that?"

Hesitating, Amanda remembered the look on Drew's face when he'd overheard her say that Trey had kissed her. She'd tried to explain, while Trey lied about the whole thing, and Trina had taken his side.

Then Drew and Trey had started arguing. Amanda had pulled them apart and taken Drew outside to cool off.

"It's kind of complicated," Amanda admitted, unsure where to begin or how much to include.

Drew had said he believed her but was edgy the rest of the night. Later, when Mitchell and Sarah wanted to leave early and hang out at a diner with a group of friends, Drew had said he'd rather just get a ride home.

Patty dropped her pizza crust on her plate and eyed Amanda shrewdly.

"This sounds like an ice cream conversation," she said decisively. "Chocolate-dipped cones. No, wait, brownie sundaes. What do you say?"

Amanda smiled.

"I'll get my shoes."

§

They were nearly at their favorite ice cream shop, and halfway into Amanda's story, when blue lights flashed behind them. Patty checked the rearview mirror nervously. A police siren screamed into the night. As they pulled over, Patty muttered that she hadn't been speeding.

"Patty Jones?" The question was asked as the officer approached her window.

"Yes?" Patty and Amanda were both surprised he knew her by name.

The cop bent down to look across the car at Amanda.

"And this is your daughter, Amanda Jones?"

Amanda shrank into her seat, then startled to see another cop on her side of the car. Nothing about this felt right. She bit her lip and her mom refused to answer any questions until he explained why she'd been stopped.

"Ma'am, please get out of the car."

Patty sat with her hands on the wheel and stared at the officer. Amanda's eyes darted between the cop on her side of the car and the one talking to her mom.

She didn't think it would be wise to reach into her pocket for her phone. She tried to send Judy a psychic message, but it was hard to concentrate while her mom was arguing with the police.

"Why did you stop me? I wasn't speeding. I have a right to know why you stopped me!"

Patty's voice shook, growing louder. The officer ignored her questions and kept asking her to step out of the car. Suddenly, the door handle on Amanda's side of the car rattled.

"Ma'am, please unlock your car."

Amanda heard banging on her door as the other cop motioned for her to open it. More blue lights appeared, and a second police car pulled up behind the first.

Patty kept arguing. Amanda covered her ears, trying to block out the noise so she could send a message. She was about to go directly into the mindspace, making it easier to call for help, when she felt a rush of cool air.

Her eyes flew open. Her mom twisted to look back at her, about to get out of the car.

"Stay here. I'll be right back."

But Amanda's car door opened, too. The other officer began asking her name and whether she was all right.

Of course, I'm all right, Amanda thought angrily. She pushed past him, following her mom. The sun had recently gone down and it was dark on this stretch of the road. Patty stood between their cars, shaking her head violently as the first cop listed a series of concerns.

"… erratic behavior at work, paranoia about a secret society, and stories about your daughter being in danger."

"That's not true!" Patty shouted. "None of it is true!"

Amanda felt the second cop tug at her arm, but she swatted him away, moving closer to her mom. There were now three police cars on the side of the road and six cops swarming around them. One of them opened their car trunk and called over to the first officer.

"Two duffel bags, packed to travel."

"Are you going somewhere, Mrs. Jones?" The officer asked as Patty stared at Amanda with wide eyes and an open mouth. "Are you taking your daughter somewhere?"

"No!" Patty insisted, angry tears flooding her eyes. "We're going for ice cream!"

"You need travel bags for ice cream?"

Amanda watched two duffel bags being lifted from the trunk. She recognized the bags but couldn't understand why they were in the car. A black van pulled up. Amanda squinted into its headlights, shielding her eyes with her left hand. Two people got out of the van—a man and a woman—but they weren't police officers.

"Ma'am, there are some special people here who want to talk to you."

Patty backed away from the new arrivals, nearly tripping in her rush to get to Amanda. They met near the back of their car, wrapping their arms tightly around each other. None of it made sense. Not the packed bags, or the police, or the strangers in the black van.

The blue lights flashed, and passing cars slowed. Amanda saw curious faces staring from car windows. The newcomers from the van were getting closer. Patty tried to pull Amanda away from them, but several cops were now closing in from behind.

"It's okay, Patty," the woman from the van said as she held out a laminated card. "We're from Psychiatric Trauma Services, and we're here to help."

"Psychiatric Trauma…" Patty began to repeat the name, but Amanda had already figured it out.

"No, you're not!" she shrieked. "I know who you are, and my mom is fine! There's no reason for this!"

"Miss, you need to calm down," one of the cops warned as he edged closer.

"You don't understand!" she shouted at him before turning back to the woman from PTS. "My mom has accepted everything. Check with the High Council. This isn't supposed to happen!"

"We're here to help your mom, honey," the woman told her gently.

"I don't need your help!" Patty insisted. "This is some kind of misunderstanding! It's—"

But she didn't get a chance to finish her sentence.

Strange hands grabbed at them, trying to pull them apart. Amanda felt her cheek crushed against her mom's chest. Their legs tangled as Patty tried to move them both away. Amanda clung tighter.

She began screaming, "Let go of me!"

It happened fast, but also in slow-motion.

Strong hands wrapped around Amanda's arms and waist. She tightened her grip but still felt the space growing between their bodies. *"No! No! No!"*

Their hands clutched each other's arms, nails scratching thin red lines. Their fingers twined, then broke apart, still scrabbling through the night air. Amanda looked up from their separated hands to see her mom's tear-streaked face being pulled away.

She was still screaming. They were both screaming.

The police dragged Patty to the van while Amanda continued to hit and kick, fighting wildly against the arms holding her back. She stopped screaming, hearing Rory's voice in her head. *Calm down! Breathe! Think!*

The air rasping through her raw throat hurt. She could barely see through her tears. But Amanda forced herself to slow down enough to assess the situation.

Most of the cops had let go once they were separated. Only one set of arms wrapped around Amanda's waist, pinning her arms by her sides. She twisted her hands around his fingers, quickly felt for the bed of his thumbnail, and jabbed her fingernail deep into his cuticle.

"Yeow!" He flinched, loosening his grip just enough for Amanda to break free. Evading the hands that reached for her, she darted toward the black van where the unidentified woman and one of the police officers were forcing her mom into the back seat.

She'd nearly reached them when the man from the van stepped into her path. He was holding something in his hand. Another officer grabbed her from behind.

There was a pinch near the base of her neck.

Everything went black.

Chapter 19

WAKING IN A NIGHTMARE

Gray walls, gray sheets, and a gray ceiling. Flat on her back, Amanda stared at the ceiling through a blurry haze. There were two beds in the room, but the other bed was empty. The door was closed, and she didn't know if it was locked. She still wore her own clothes. She thought it was the next morning, but she couldn't be sure.

From her place in the bed, Amanda's eyes fixated on a thin crack that ran the length of the ceiling. Her mind replayed memories of how she'd gotten here.

The blue flashing lights. The siren. The police closing in. The van. Her mom's arms sliding from her clutching hands. Her mom's face twisted with fear and pain. The pinch at her neck. The darkness. Waking up in the back of a police car. Her mind fuzzy. Her thoughts unable to take her physically away. Waking up in the night. In this bed. Over and over. Creeping out of the room only to be caught and marched back in.

They wouldn't tell her where she was. They wouldn't tell her where her mom was.

Her mind played tricks on her. Fading in and out.

Amanda stared at the crack in the ceiling, feeling her mom's arms slip through her fingers.

The door opened. A voice sounded far away.

"Amanda!"

The back of a cool hand pressed gently against her cheek, then forehead. A mass of blue-streaked hair swished in front of her eyes before being swept away, revealing dark-rimmed glasses and a familiar face. A concerned face.

"Aunt Judy?" Amanda tilted her head, not sure if the face was really there.

"It's okay, Amanda," the tear-filled voice reassured. "We're going home."

§

Bolting upright, Amanda gasped for air, then looked frantically around her room. The blinds were closed, but it was her room. Her closet. Her desk. Her chair. Her aunt sitting quietly in that chair.

Judy's head leaned against the seatback, and her glasses reflected a streak of daylight that slipped past the edge of the blinds. Amanda was on the urge of saying, *I had the most horrible dream…* when a sinking sensation pushed the words away.

"It wasn't a dream," she said instead, knowing it was true but wanting to be contradicted. Her eyes trailed toward the closed door, expecting her mom to walk in with a cup of coffee in her hand.

"It wasn't a dream," Judy confirmed.

"Where's my mom?"

The room swam and Amanda pressed both hands into the bed for support. Her head pounded and her stomach churned. She didn't know what time it was or when she had last eaten anything.

"She's fine," Judy reassured, stepping close to feel Amanda's forehead with the back of her hand.

"Then why do you look so scared?"

Judy removed her hand and offered a glass of water from the end table, urging Amanda to take small sips.

"It's a scary situation," she said, once Amanda had tried some water. "When I heard… when I was trying to get to you… I don't think I've ever been more scared in my life."

Amanda pushed the glass away.

"So, where is she?" Her vision was steadier, and her mind was beginning to clear. "Do they still have her? Is she at PTSD?"

Judy placed the glass on the end table and carefully sat on the edge of Amanda's bed. The room was dim and quiet around them.

"Yes."

Amanda's eyes went out of focus, shifting to stare toward the thin line of sunlight streaking across the floor. A soft knock on her bedroom door startled her.

"Who's here?"

Before Judy could answer, the door cracked open and Rory leaned into the room.

"Oh, good, you're awake," she noted with relief, before adding, "They let him in."

Judy hurried over to her.

"And she's okay?"

"Yes, but I need to back before—"

"Go!" Judy interrupted. "I'll take care of things here."

"Ben wants to have that meeting," Rory glanced toward Amanda, "when she's ready."

"Yes, yes. I'll take care of it. Just go."

Amanda watched the exchange, still feeling as if she were in a dream. *Wake up,* she thought over and over. She ran her hands across her woven blanket. Its soft texture felt very real.

"Your mom's okay," Rory called from the doorway. "Cameron is with her now, so listen to Judy and take care of yourself, okay? Everything's going to be okay."

She left before Amanda could respond.

Judy came back to the bed and tried to hand Amanda the glass of water again.

"How do you feel? Can you eat something?"

"Eat?" Amanda stared blankly, then pushed the water away. "What's going on? Why did they take my mom? Why aren't you telling me anything?"

Her voice rose and cracked. Amanda pushed back her blankets and wobbled on her feet before storming out into the apartment.

"Rory?" She looked around the empty living room, walked toward the kitchen, and peered into the small den. There was no one else in the apartment. Rory was gone. Judy followed her, offering a seat at the dining table. Amanda only glared at her.

"Tell me everything. Now."

Judy pressed her lips together, then sighed.

"I will, but you need to eat something while I do."

Amanda sat grudgingly, and Judy began talking while pulling food out of the refrigerator. From the moment they heard what had happened, Judy, Rory, Lucas, and Cameron had worked tirelessly to locate Amanda and Patty and get them back.

"I don't think Rory has slept more than two hours in the last two days," Judy added, while setting a bowl of fruit salad in front of Amanda.

"Two days?!" Amanda's mouth dropped open. "It's been two days? What day is it?"

"It's Tuesday," Judy replied gently, sitting on the chair beside Amanda and catching the focus of her wandering eyes. "They took you on Sunday night. It's Tuesday morning, so it's been about 35 hours. I'm sorry. I thought you knew, but the drugs they gave you can affect your memory."

"My memory?" Amanda felt her chest moving with short, shallow breaths. "It's Tuesday? What about school? What about…?"

"Shh, it's okay." Judy stood and pulled Amanda into her arms. "I called the school and told them you'd be out sick this week."

Amanda twisted away from her aunt, nodding as she tried to take it all in.

"Okay, so it's been 35 hours…" Her mind spun as she wondered what could have happened to her mom in 35 hours. What could have happened to *her* in 35 hours? What did Drew think when she didn't show up at school?

"Where's my phone?"

Amanda scanned the apartment as if expecting to see it on the coffee table or kitchen counter.

"Don't worry about it," Judy answered smoothly. "We'll get you a new one."

Amanda stared back at her in horror.

"They have my phone?"

Her face burned as she thought of everything she'd kept on that phone. Her pictures, apps, conversations with Drew. Amanda froze, realizing everything she'd texted to Drew from that phone. Information about Lucas, the exiles, the psychic engineers, Mitra, the Arcadians, her mom, all of it. She hadn't been careful at all. She'd talked about whatever had come to mind. Secret things… Private things…

"It's okay," Judy said, but Amanda was on her feet.

"It's not okay!" She paced the room, feeling angrier by the moment. "It's my phone! My privacy! My…" She trailed off as her anger shifted toward her own carelessness.

"Amanda." Judy spoke forcefully. "Your phone doesn't matter. Now sit down and eat something, so I can tell you the rest of this. There's still work to be done. I need you to calm down and not make yourself sick."

Chastised, Amanda sat at the table and picked up her fork. Judy watched her eat a bite of melon, then toasted a bagel. While getting cream cheese and a package of smoked salmon, Judy explained that they didn't know why the High Council decided to take Patty. They thought the High Council was happy with Patty's acceptance of the situation and had put that plan behind them.

"Whatever they were trying to do, it backfired," Judy said, joining Amanda at the table. "Lucas had everything in place in case something like this happened. Not an hour after you were taken, he'd managed to get footage from the police officer's bodycams and use it to spread outrage among travelers all around the world.

"The outcry has been amazing. Protesters have flooded PTS facilities. Travelers who were already suspicious of the High Council have gone on strike. Even some of the scientists and doctors at PTSI have been speaking out and swearing to uncover whatever unethical projects their coworkers might be working on."

"But my mom…?" Amanda couldn't take another bite until she knew more.

"The doctors at PTSI swear she hasn't been harmed. Cameron has been camped out at the hospital, and they've finally let him in to see her."

"When can I see her?"

Judy looked at her hands, clasped on the table. Amanda noticed her left thumb rubbing the one below it. The gesture reminded her of someone else, but she couldn't place it. She took a bite of her bagel, hoping to get her aunt talking, and her stomach grumbled with hunger.

"I don't know," Judy answered honestly. "Apparently, there are concerns about something in her trunk. Some packed duffel bags. One for each of you. Do you know anything about that?"

Blue lights flashed in Amanda's mind as she pictured a cop pulling packed bags out of their trunk. They'd asked her mom about the bags, and she'd said… *something.*

Amanda saw her mom's scared face in that moment, she could even see her mouth moving, but she couldn't remember what she had said. Something about them not going anywhere. But why were the bags there at all?

Shaking her head, Amanda tore into the second half of her bagel. Now that she'd tasted food, she couldn't stop eating. Her mouth was half-full as she told Judy she didn't know anything about the bags.

"Well, they complicated things." Judy sighed. "The High Council is claiming she was running away with you. That her fear of psychic travel had pushed her to run off into the night and keep you away from it all."

"Do you think she was doing that?" Amanda choked on her last bite of bagel. "Like, PTS agents saw her put the bags in the car and did this to keep us from leaving?"

"Maybe." Judy picked a grape out of Amanda's fruit salad, then prompted her to finish eating. "I doubt she was actively planning to take you away. I'd guess the bags were a back-up plan. Just in case. Your mom was always big on being prepared, just in case."

That made sense. Patty loved saying *just in case*. Her purse was stocked with band-aids, hand sanitizer, snacks, and a book. Even had a tiny sewing kit in it. *Just in case.*

"But even if she wasn't planning on going anywhere, do you think the bags are what caused this? If someone saw her with them?"

"Doesn't matter," Judy said firmly. "Their story only made people more sympathetic to you and your mom. Protesters are saying Patty had a right to worry about your safety and it's her choice to keep you out of PTS.

"Remember, a big part of the rebellion is travelers who think the High Council is trying to control them. They aren't about to say the council has more say over your future than your mom does, even if you are the next architect."

Amanda finished her fruit, chewing thoughtfully.

"It's hard to imagine," she admitted with a slight frown. "I mean, this is a huge thing for me and my mom, but it's hard to imagine people who don't even know us getting involved like that."

Judy pulled her phone from her pocket and quickly brought up some secret PTS news sites.

"Here. See for yourself."

The PTS news feed was flooded with headlines about the unfolding events. Photos and videos showed protesters carrying signs that said *Free Patty Jones.* Interviews with prominent travelers condemned the High Council for keeping a traveler's family member held hostage.

Patty was painted as a brave mother, a *mamma bear* protecting her young, while Amanda was an innocent teenager manipulated by evil, would-be dictators.

As Amanda scrolled, she quickly moved from protest pictures to images of herself and her mother being pulled apart. A clip from a cop's bodycam showed the chaos and brutality of that moment. Their hands grasped desperately. Their faces twisted with pain.

Judy took the phone out of Amanda's hands.

"Let's not to watch that right now."

Amanda nodded. The video had sent her breakfast pitching and rolling through her stomach.

"We need to get you cleaned up and ready for a meeting with Ben," Judy said, surprising Amanda. "You know, Ben Hastings from the High Council?"

Amanda nodded numbly. She knew Ben Hastings. She also knew Ben had been in Gerald's hospital room a day before this had happened. Was that related? Had he heard something that spooked the High Council? Amanda worried but didn't mention it to her aunt. She would know what Ben wanted to tell them soon enough.

§

They met in the living room of the birdhouse. Judy and Amanda were sitting on the couch when Ben appeared in an armchair across from them.

When he didn't use the door from PTS headquarters, Amanda remembered pictures of the entry atrium flooded with protesters. They'd filled the space so tightly, there was barely room to summon a single proximal door.

Ben looked tired. His clothes were rumpled, his tie was loose, and his top button was undone. There was something Amanda liked about his less polished appearance.

"I'm glad to see you," he said simply, before a cloud of worry crept over his face. "How are you feeling? I mean, are you okay? Physically?"

Amanda didn't know what to make of his concern. Ben had never been rude or mean to her, but his detachment had made her think he didn't see her as a person. Sincere concern was something new.

"I'm worried about my mom, obviously."

Ben nodded, looking embarrassed, so Amanda added, "But I'm not physically hurt or anything."

"Good." Ben smiled awkwardly. "I see the, uh, sedatives have worn off."

Amanda frowned, her face like stone. They'd had to wait another hour after she'd eaten before Amanda's mind had cleared enough for her to enter the mindspace.

"Can we get on with it?" Judy asked in a tight voice.

"Of course." Ben ran his hands over his hair in a nervous gesture Amanda hadn't seen from him before. "I know this may be hard for you to believe, but we did not order your mother's detainment."

The silence was heavy.

Judy narrowed her eyes and clenched her fists.

"That is hard for us to believe," she said icily. "Are we also supposed to believe that it wasn't the High Council who accused Amanda of global treason?"

"What?" Amanda asked sharply. "When was I accused of that?"

"Yesterday. It was front page in *The Traveler Times.*"

"Which quoted an anonymous source," Ben countered, "who was not authorized to speak to the press. Look, this has been a mess from the beginning, but I want you to know that it wasn't our doing. It wasn't *my* doing."

Ben looked genuinely upset as he leaned forward over his clasped hands.

"Well," Judy relented grudgingly, "are you going to tell us who it was then?"

"Yes." Ben sat up straight and looked Amanda in the eye. "Director Alvarsson."

Amanda blinked. She expected to feel surprised, but she didn't feel anything.

"It was because of the hospital," she said hollowly. "Because of the way I treated him."

"This isn't your fault," Judy insisted.

"I know." Fiery anger washed over Amanda, chasing away the numbness she'd been feeling.

"I didn't cause this," she told them, her eyes glinting. "Director Alvarsson did because he's a petty man who can't stand a teenage girl having more power than him."

She eyed Ben, "What are you going to do about it?"

Ben met her glare with some fire of his own.

"Alvarsson is out."

"Out?" Judy echoed. "What does that mean?"

"It means the High Council is going to make an example of him." He faced Amanda. "Your mother is being released from the hospital now. Alvarsson has been terminated and is being held while the matter is investigated. The High Council will issue a formal statement in a few hours."

"Why are they waiting?" Judy asked shrewdly, while Amanda puzzled over a nagging feeling in her gut.

Ben hesitated, looking between Judy and Amanda, before sinking back in his chair.

"They want Amanda to be at their press conference." Ben held up his hands to fend off their protests. "I know, you don't want to do it. You aren't going to do it. I already told them it was too much to ask, but they insisted I try. So, I tried, you said no, and that's the end of that."

Studying Ben's deflated slump, Amanda realized what had changed about him. He used to be proud of his seat on the High Council. Now, he looked like someone who had woken up to a nightmare. The world had changed around him, and he was struggling to find his footing.

Amanda could relate.

"But my mom is coming home?" Amanda's question brought a soft smile to Ben's face.

"Yes, she'll be traveling the long way, of course, on a plane with Cameron." Ben glanced at his watch and sat upright. "Actually, Cameron should be here by now. He planned to meet us here."

He glanced around the room. Amanda instinctively followed his gaze, though they both knew he wasn't there. As Amanda looked around, she didn't notice Judy watching her carefully.

"While we wait for him," Ben began uneasily. "I should warn you that your mother does have an injury, not exactly from us... It seems she fought the police and PTS agents rather aggressively when she saw them sedate you. She sprained her shoulder in the process, though I'm assured it's minor and will heal quickly."

"I'd count that as being from PTS," Judy said darkly.

"I do, too," Ben agreed. "I said as much to the rest of the council. For whatever that's worth."

He frowned deeply again and loosened his tie even more. Amanda was deciding how to respond when Cameron appeared in the space beside their seating area.

"Amanda!"

Before she knew what was happening, Cameron had rushed to her side and wrapped his arms around her. Instead of pulling away, Amanda's whole body relaxed in his arms. The emotion of the last two days threatened to erupt in a flood of hot tears, but she choked them back, unwilling to cry in front of Ben.

"Your mom sends her love," he told her gently.

He loosened his arms but made no move to end the embrace, giving her time to pull herself together.

Amanda nodded, followed by a large sniff.

"Ben says she was hurt."

"It's nothing!" Cameron laughed proudly. "Did you see the footage yet? Your mom put up a hell of a fight for you. You should see the other guys!"

Amanda leaned away from his chest and looked up at him skeptically.

"Seriously," he promised. "She should take up sparring with you and Rory!"

A laugh bubbled up at the idea of her mom taking on Rory, and Amanda felt the threat of tears pass.

"I'll leave you to catch up," Ben said, standing up from his armchair reluctantly. "I should go tell the council you won't be at their conference."

"Wait a minute." Cameron stood, throwing an arm around Ben's shoulders. "Not until Amanda and Judy know how much you've done for us."

He told them how Ben had fought the council to have Amanda released to Judy's care, Cameron allowed in to see Patty, and Director Alvarsson removed from office.

"He's been on our side through all of it," Cameron said. "Even when it meant putting his neck on the line."

"It was the right thing to do, that's all," Ben said with a dismissive wave. "If I lose my place on the council, it will have been worth it."

He nodded goodbye and disappeared.

"If there's a council for him to go back to," Lucas added, walking in from the hall.

"Wait, what?" Amanda was shocked by his appearance. "You were listening?"

"Relax," he laughed, taking the seat Ben had recently left. "I wouldn't have been able to hear him if he didn't want me to."

Amanda puzzled through that. He was right, of course. Travelers couldn't see or hear each other in the mindspace without permission. When her abilities first brought her to the house, Amanda hadn't known how to mentally give or withhold permission. That's how she'd been spotted by other travelers, and by Cameron in particular.

But Ben would know better than to let his guard down. Unless he'd subconsciously wanted to see Lucas…?

"The press conference will hurt us, you know," Lucas went on smoothly.

"Will it?" Judy was the first to ask, bringing a dramatic sigh from Lucas.

"It will destroy my momentum. Do you know how hard it is to set the stage for a political revolution? They're giving up Alvarsson and releasing Patty in an attempt to save face because the pressure to replace them is mounting. The International Council has called an emergency session for tomorrow afternoon.

"After this press conference, we'll lose some protesters, and we might not get two-thirds of the vote if the outrage dies down."

"But they've called for a vote," Judy countered. "The people have already shown what they want."

"Revolutions are messy," Lucas told her. "Even when they come about by vote instead of violence. Some of the delegates would rather stick their heads in the sand as long as the High Council's dark dealings don't affect them personally."

"I don't see how we can stop it." Cameron sighed.

"And we're not going to!" Amanda cried angrily. "We are not leaving my mom stuck in that place for your stupid politics!"

"Of course not!" Lucas snapped, before taking a breath and replying more calmly. "I'm not suggesting we stop your mom's release. Though it would be better if she'd stay in Chicago and give a statement at tomorrow's meeting. Cameron can take her to a hotel for the night."

They were quiet for a moment, thinking about the situation. As much as Amanda wanted her mom to come home, it did make sense for her to make a statement to the International Council.

Amanda didn't entirely understand the process, but Judy had explained that the International Council was involved in electing the High Council and could use a vote of *no confidence* to have them replaced.

"I'll go to Chicago, too," Amanda decided. "I'll stay at the hotel with you."

"No," Lucas cut in before Cameron could agree. "I need to do something to offset this press conference, and I need your help. In Arcadia."

CHAPTER 20

A MINDSPACE BEYOND REACH

The view from Agnes Webb's office was even more impressive at night. Unlike cities on Earth, Arcadia remained fairly dark. Its buildings were fitted with high-tech glass that could retain most interior light while still allowing clear visibility to the world outside. Yet, there was still a soft gleam to the skyline, highlighted by dots of blue light designed to make buildings visible for passing aircraft, both above and within the city. This scant light etched the outlines of the city while still allowing a field of stars to shine in the night sky.

It was nearing sunrise in Arcadia and late morning on Earth. Off-world visits were typically planned around planetary time variances, so participants from both worlds would be meeting during their own daytime hours. This was not a typical visit.

Despite the early hour, Dr. Webb had greeted her guests graciously. She wore a burgundy silk wrap tunic with matching wide-legged pants. Her triskele brooch was pinned just below her left collar bone, and her hair was arranged in a low, neat bun. She looked as though she'd been in the office for hours, not recently woken by an emergency call from the gatehouse. With PTS in turmoil, Lucas had walked past the traveler guards without concern. A call to Dr. Webb had calmed the Arcadian guards as well.

Settling into their seats, Amanda and Rory had been surprised to see Dr. Webb's professional manner soften as she and Lucas touched foreheads and murmured soft words as if they were reunited family. It did not take long for that tenderness to fade.

"There's more you can do!" Lucas jumped to his feet, irritated by the direction of the conversation.

"We gave you the list of PTSI scientists who have approached us with projects we find ethically questionable," Dr. Webb reminded him. "That is something you can take to your International Council."

"And I appreciate that," Lucas said tightly, "but that isn't enough, and you know it."

He stood beside the seated women. Dressed in the same black tactical gear he'd worn when Amanda had first met him, Lucas radiated the conviction of a soldier dedicated to his cause. Amanda felt intimidated by his aggressive stance until she saw how little impact it had on Dr. Webb. Arcadia's Director of Science merely smiled at him sadly and continued to speak with firm kindness.

"I do not know that," she corrected. "It is not my place to interfere in the politics of your world."

Lucas sneered in disbelief.

"Even when our leaders jeopardize our alliance?"

"Even when your leaders jeopardize our alliance."

"Gah!" Lucas pivoted on one foot and ran his fingers through his hair.

"Maybe we should take it down a notch." Rory cast a disapproving look toward Lucas' tense back. She was about to say more when he spun toward the group.

"Or we should take it *up* a notch," he suggested with a gleam of his typical charisma. "You could strengthen Amanda's position with them."

Dr. Webb's smile froze. She shook her head emphatically.

"You know I cannot do that."

"I do not know that," Lucas countered, retaking his seat and grinning to charm her.

It didn't work.

Dr. Webb stayed seated but straightened her spine and addressed Lucas coldly.

"This meeting is over."

No one moved or barely dared to breathe. Lucas paled, the smile evaporating from his face. Rory's lips parted to speak, but Amanda beat her to it.

"Will someone tell me what's going on here?" She glanced between Dr. Webb and Lucas rapidly, feeling sick to her stomach. "In the last few days, I've been kidnapped, drugged, and taken from my mother—who has been held in some crazy torture hospital. Now, instead of finally going to see her, Lucas made me come here. For what? To sit and listen to you two talk about me like I'm not even here?"

"Amanda." Rory reached a hand toward her, but Amanda swatted it away.

"No! I'm tired of everyone talking *about* me instead of talking *to* me." She turned to Lucas. "I get that you wanted to keep me out of this, and I was okay with that, but it didn't work. So, if you're trying to bring me in now—even more than I already am— then I want to know how."

Amanda looked out the windows and saw the sky gradually lightening. When she turned back, Dr. Webb was regarding her shrewdly.

"You are right," she relented, surprising Amanda and bringing a relieved sigh from Lucas.

Rory watched warily as if assessing how to protect Amanda from whatever was about to come.

"It is all right, Rory," Dr. Webb reassured. "This won't hurt Amanda." She looked at Lucas pointedly, "If we don't try to use it to our political advantage."

Amanda pressed her palms into the arms of her chair. Her outburst had been unplanned, and she hoped she was ready for whatever Dr. Webb was about to tell her.

"There is a reason behind Mitra's theory for adapting your energy to match our mindspace," she began slowly. "He did not come up with the theory on his own. It was my suggestion that urged him in that direction, though the idea did not originate entirely with me either."

She hesitated, as if reconsidering her approach, then went on smoothly.

"Like psychic architects before him, Edmund Robinson connected your people to many worlds. He held societies on some of those worlds in higher regard than others, and he spent time cultivating relationships with the leaders of those worlds. As you will one day do yourself."

Amanda leaned forward intently, too fascinated to notice Lucas closely watching her reactions.

"Edmund Robinson entrusted the leaders of those societies with sealed training documents for the architect who would succeed him.

"Arcadia is one of those societies."

The sky continued to lighten, causing the interior lights to shift accordingly.

The uncomfortable silence was broken by Rory's rush of questions.

"You have psychic architect training documents? Have you read them?" She spun toward Lucas. "And *you* knew about this? Who else knows? Does the High Council?"

"No, we—"

"I only found—"

Dr. Webb and Lucas tried answering at the same time, then stopped, each gesturing for the other to speak first. Before either of them could, Amanda found her voice.

"When can I read them?"

"Agnes?" Lucas raised an eyebrow toward Dr. Webb.

"They are not here," she began uneasily. "We have a responsibility to protect the documents until the appropriate time, and we take that responsibility seriously."

"But you're holding them *for* Amanda," Rory clarified.

"Yes," Dr. Webb agreed haltingly. "With instructions to deliver them when the time is right."

"When is the time right?" Rory sounded as impatient as Amanda felt.

"That is hard to explain." Sensing the reaction to her statement, Dr. Webb added. "The instructions given to me, as the guardian of the document, are both strict and vague. Ultimately, the timing is left to my discretion."

"And if you were to decide now is the right time," Lucas explained, "the International Council would know Amanda was that much closer to completing her training."

"Giving her a stronger voice against the High Council," Rory finished, putting the pieces together. Lucas pointed toward her with a wink and a nod.

"Your political maneuvers do not weigh into my decision," Dr. Webb told him firmly. "I am the guardian of the documents, and I will not release them to Amanda until I know she is ready."

"But you've read them?" Amanda asked. "You said Mitra's theory was based on something in the documents."

Dr. Webb smiled at Amanda softly.

"I have only read the guardian's introduction. The remaining documents are sealed."

"Can you tell us what the introduction says?" Seeing that Dr. Webb was about to refuse, Rory added, "Or tell us why it led you to your theory?"

Dr. Webb chose her words carefully.

"A passage in the introduction references a psychic architect's ability to adapt his or her energy to *traverse the mindspace beyond reach.*" She paused, meeting each pair of eyes in the room. "We believe this implies multiple mindspaces, such as ours and your own, which can only be crossed by a psychic architect."

Rory sat back in her chair heavily. She turned toward Amanda, expecting to see confusion. Instead, Amanda slowly shook her head while holding back laughter.

Lucas leaned forward, looking past Rory to catch Amanda's attention.

"And why is that funny?"

"It's not," Amanda managed, letting out an incredulous laugh. "It's just…"

She trailed off, realizing she couldn't explain how absurd this all was. As soon as she'd heard Dr. Webb's explanation, she knew the document wasn't talking about separate mindspaces. It was describing the *pure mindspace*. Gerald had even told her that the pure mindspace was once called the *mindspace beyond reach*.

The Arcadians' plan was based on a misunderstanding from an ancient text they didn't think she was ready to receive. And she couldn't explain that without revealing a psychic mystery she had to keep secret.

"It just… doesn't mean that," she finished lamely, no longer laughing. "And I can't tell you what it means."

Dr. Webb accepted that with a thoughtful nod.

Lucas was less understanding. Rory stood up to him, literally blocking his way when he tried to move closer. Amanda tuned out their arguing as she thought over the situation. She'd spent so much time trying to shift her mental energy, and it was all for nothing. All those attempts at reaching Mitra's shadowy outline through a barrier she'd never cross.

Amanda's cheeks tingled as her mind followed that thread. If she'd been *outside* his mindspace, where had she actually been? There'd been nothing there with her, only darkness. Had she seen him from the pure mindspace? Was that a connection running between them?

The reality of her situation crept in, dashing Amanda's hopes. Even if there was a connection, she couldn't do anything about it. She couldn't build a house from outside the Arcadian mindspace. She didn't even know how to build a house inside her own mindspace. Or a coffee table. Or a lamp. All she'd ever built was a door…

Amanda sat up suddenly.

"You don't need a house, just a door."

§

Back in the birdhouse, Rory shook her head angrily. "It's the wrong time," she insisted. "It's too rushed, and there are too many unknowns."

"It won't hurt her to try," Lucas argued, waving off Rory's concerns. "And if it works, think how it will influence the delegates!"

"Will it?" Rory crossed her arms, unimpressed by Lucas' swagger.

"The delegates are *this* close to voting no confidence. The Arcadian alliance is their most important off-world focus, and they know Agnes isn't happy. But, then—out of nowhere—Amanda creates a door to connect our mindspaces?" Lucas clasped his hands like two worlds coming together. "That's a game-changer! And they aren't going to trust this High Council with that."

"Or they'll think it's a bad time to be choosing new leadership."

Lucas scoffed, too excited to be brought down by her skepticism, and turned to Amanda eagerly.

"You're ready to give it a try, right?"

"What?" Amanda was nervously biting her fingernail and barely listening. "I, uh, I think so."

"Well, there's the confidence I want to hear." Lucas smirked sarcastically and gave her a pat on the shoulder. "Come on, kid, have a little faith in yourself. You made a door before; you can do it again."

"That was different…"

"Aren't you the one who just finished telling us you could do this?"

"Well, yeah…"

"That you think the mindspaces are connected by a wall? And you can put a door in a wall?"

"Yeah, but…"

"Back off, Lucas," Rory snapped. She stepped between them and held Lucas back with a straight arm across his chest until he willingly stepped away from Amanda, raising both hands in the air.

Amanda felt shaky, remembering the bold claims she'd made in Dr. Webb's office. It was the excitement of the moment. The idea had seemed so simple, so obvious, but she had no idea if she could pull it off.

"I know this is a big ask," Lucas pressed on. "You feel like you're in over your head, but you aren't. Trust yourself. You can do this."

"I know," Amanda lied. "I'm just not really sure about the details…"

"Run it by the psychic engineers." Lucas shrugged. "I have some if yours are stuck behind guards."

"You don't really expect her to do this now?" Rory asked with annoyance.

"Why not? It was her idea, it's brilliant, and it's perfect timing… Speaking of timing," Lucas glanced at his watch, "I have places to go and protesters to rally. Let me know when you're ready, and I'm there!"

Once he was gone, Rory stopped Amanda from saying anything more. They woke up from the mindspace, back in the small office in Amanda's apartment, and Amanda checked the time on the wall clock. The High Council's press conference should be underway. She hoped Cameron had gotten her mom to a safe hotel in Chicago.

Rory was still focused on Arcadia.

"Have you even thought this through?" she asked. "Do you know what you'd be doing if this works?"

"Yeah." Amanda was surprised by the intensity of Rory's concern. "I'd be connecting our mindspaces. Giving the Arcadians access to our houses so they wouldn't need one of their own to…"

Amanda stopped talking as she began to understand the repercussions of her suggestion. If this worked, she'd be throwing open the gates to their own mindspace houses and to every world connected through them.

The Arcadians were far more technologically advanced. If they wanted, they could easily take over most of those connected worlds with very little effort. Maybe even take over Earth.

"You don't trust them?" Amanda realized. "With psychic travel?"

"I don't know," Rory answered honestly. "They seem like a peaceful society—"

"Better than we are."

"Maybe," Rory conceded. "But this isn't something to do on a whim. This is something that takes careful planning and precautions."

Amanda glanced toward the office door, wondering if Judy had gone out.

"Why didn't you say any of this to Lucas?"

Rory sighed. "Amanda, do you really think Lucas would have listened?"

After a short pause, Amanda agreed.

"I guess not. So, you don't think I should do this?"

"I don't think you should do this," Rory confirmed. "Not yet."

Amanda hesitated, remembering all the time she'd spent with Mitra over the last six months.

"What will I say to Dr. Webb?" she asked, feeling her stomach churn. "It's not like I can say, *oh, sorry, I don't actually trust you to come into our mindspace right now, maybe later.*"

"Of course not. You just say you don't feel ready."

But I am ready! Amanda thought, despite her fear.

Rory had made a good point, but the idea of creating this door pulled at her, begging to be tried. Waiting for approval could take weeks or months, or even years.

Gerald had suggested the High Council didn't want the Arcadians to have psychic travel abilities at all. What if they stayed in power and pulled Amanda out of Arcadia before she had a chance to make the connection? Would they end the alliance to keep control? What if the Arcadians could make the universe a better place, but that didn't happen because she didn't try this while she had the chance?

"What if connecting our mindspaces is the right thing to do?" Amanda asked carefully. "The Arcadians can help people in other worlds. And help us. Just think about the technology they might share if we were psychic travelers together. And Dr. Webb would have to give me Edmund's documents if I could make this work."

Rory crossed her arms and shook her head.

"So, that's it? You'll hand over our mindspace—and all the worlds beyond it—to get something you want?"

"That's not what I said!" Hot anger flushed Amanda's cheeks. "You're twisting it around."

"No, I'm not," Rory responded calmly. "You want the documents Dr. Webb *says* she has, and you're rushing into a huge, dangerous plan to get them without any kind of oversight or approval."

"Approval from who?" Amanda raised both arms. "The High Council is about to be tossed out. The International Council will talk about it for months before they decide anything. I'm the psychic architect, and I think this is important, doesn't that count for anything?"

Rory clamped her mouth shut and scowled.

"Look," she said through clenched teeth, "you've been through a lot over the last few days, and you aren't thinking clearly. I know waiting is hard, but there is a right way to do these things.

"How about this? You put together a plan and present it to the International Council tomorrow. That will do everything Lucas wants, and get the ball rolling, while also showing you care about doing this in a safe way."

Amanda relaxed into the idea and Rory smiled.

"Cameron should have your mom in a hotel by now," she reminded. "I'll go check on them. You talk to Dorothy and Elaine about your idea. Then, we'll go stay with your mom until tomorrow's meeting. Sound good?"

"My mom…" Amanda repeated hollowly. She'd been so caught up in her idea she'd almost forgotten about her mom. "Yes, Let's do that."

§

The den on the first floor of the birdhouse was only a little larger than Amanda's home office, but its walls were filled with five white, wooden doors. Amanda prowled the room as if expecting one of the walls to suddenly expand and make space for her plan.

"I'm not sure it would work," Elaine said gently from her place on the green sofa.

"Doors connect to a physical place," Dorothy added.

Amanda stopped pacing.

In Arcadia, she couldn't talk about the pure mindspace, so she'd only said the two mindspaces might be connected, and there might be a way for her to create a door between them. Talking to the psychic engineers, she was free to be more explicit.

"If I can see Mitra's shape through some kind of barrier, then our mindspaces must be touching. If the same pure mindspace runs through them both, then I can use that to connect them."

Dorothy and Elaine exchanged an uneasy look.

Amanda tried another angle. "Do you know of any other mindspaces? Besides ours and the Arcadian one?"

"Not that we know about," Dorothy conceded.

"So, maybe they are same mindspace, but with some kind of wall between them. I can put a door in a wall."

"In the wall of a mindspace house," Elaine corrected.

"Anchored to a physical place," Dorothy added.

Amanda sighed loudly.

"And we don't really know much about the Arcadian mindspace," Elaine reminded.

"Fine. What do you think it is?" Amanda was rapidly losing her patience with them. "How did it show up? How did the Arcadians lose their connection to our mindspace in the first place?"

"Selective breeding."

"What?"

Amanda hadn't expected an actual answer. Her PTS teachers had never been willing to explain the Arcadian's separation, since plotting an unauthorized off-world colony was one of the highest crimes a traveler could commit.

"Selective breeding is the leading theory for how the Arcadians lost their psychic travel abilities," Dorothy explained. "It's obvious when you understand the basics."

Amanda took a seat as Dorothy went on patiently.

"People with *active* traveler genes develop psychic travel abilities. People with *inactive* traveler genes don't but can pass the abilities to their kids. Finally, people with no traveler genes can't do either. It's kind of like dominant and recessive genes for eye color, except more genes are involved, making it much more complicated.

"Now, the theory says the earliest Arcadians stopped traveling through willpower alone. Then, after their first generation was born in Arcadia, only non-travelers were allowed to have children. Eventually, that selective breeding would prevent anyone from being born with active traveler genes. Of course, some would still carry the inactive genes without knowing it. Are you following me?"

"I think so." Amanda puzzled through the explanation. "So, after we reconnected with them, Arcadian scientists figured out how to turn on the inactive traveler genes in people who had them? But why didn't they end up back in our mindspace?"

"Evolution?" Dorothy shrugged.

"No one knows," Elaine added.

Amanda thought about that for a moment, then pressed her hands against her thighs and stood up resolutely.

"Well, no one knows if there can be a door between separated mindspaces either. I might as well try. I did make a door once before."

Dorothy shook her head. Elaine looked at her lap.

"You were in a physical place and made a door back to an existing mindspace house," Dorothy reminded. "Not to take away from your, uh, *achievement,* but that's very different than creating a door from a mindspace house to a place you've never been."

Her cheeks flamed as Amanda picked up on Dorothy's implication. The door she'd made from Terra-V was a lucky accident. She hadn't known what she was doing. She hadn't even been consciously trying to make a door. It had just… happened.

"Fine, then how did other psychic architects connect to new worlds?"

Dorothy and Elaine looked at each other blankly.

"You don't know?" Amanda frowned.

"We aren't psychic architects," Elaine reminded. "We share some abilities above your typical traveler, but when it comes to psychic architect skills, well, that's…"

"A mystery," Amanda finished for her darkly.

She looked at the existing doors.

"Do all of the doors to one world have to be in the same room?"

"No," Elaine said. "There's no *rule* about that."

"But it's more *organized* that way," Dorothy added.

Amanda shook her head. There simply wasn't room for another door in this small room. She ran her hands over her face, considering the other rooms in the birdhouse and in all the other houses.

After a moment, she closed her eyes, deciding to let her subconscious thoughts pick a location.

When she opened her eyes, Amanda was outside in the open mindspace. There were clusters of houses in each direction, except for a large, grassy area off to the right of the birdhouse. She walked to the center of the open lawn, counting her paces. A moment later, Dorothy and Elaine appeared beside her.

"What are you doing out here?" Dorothy asked, wrinkling her nose in distaste.

Elaine squinted at the houses in the distance.

"You aren't thinking of putting a door out here?"

"Why not?" Amanda shrugged. "There's enough space."

"But it's… outside!" Dorothy seemed shocked. "No one comes out here except historians and new travelers."

"You need a *house* for a door," Elaine reminded.

"There won't be a house on the Arcadian end," Amanda said, then scowled at their knowing expressions. "If you don't want to help me, you can go."

"No, no," Dorothy waved the thought away. "We'll do what we can."

"We can't tell you how to make a door," Elaine added more cooperatively, "but, when the time comes, we can help you draw energy from the pure mindspace. Then it won't take so much out of you."

Amanda considered that, remembering Alira's support when she created the door to Terra-V.

"Until then, go see your mom," Dorothy suggested. "We'll vouch for your plan with the International Council tomorrow."

"So, you think it will work?"

"Well…" They exchanged another skeptical look.

"You can try."

CHAPTER 21

THE INTERNATIONAL COUNCIL

Voices from the next room woke Amanda just before midnight. She was alone in her hotel bed, and the space where Patty had been sleeping was still warm.

"Mom?" she asked blearily.

The bathroom light was off, but the door to Cameron's adjoining room was cracked open. Rolling over, she saw the bed Judy and Rory had been sharing was empty and knew something was wrong. As she crept to the door barefoot, she heard the worry in Cameron's deep voice.

"Lucas has clearly lost control."

"Has he?" Rory asked. "Or is this part of his plan?"

Cameron sighed heavily.

"He's always said he wants a vote, not violence."

"And if he can't get the vote?"

Amanda inched the door open. Cameron was fully dressed in slacks and a dark sweater. He leaned against the wide dresser across from the two double beds, which both looked like they hadn't been slept in. Rory, wearing black tactical gear in Lucas' style, stood near the covered windows, while Patty and Judy huddled in their pajamas on the bed closest to the door.

"He never should have associated with the Vertex," Judy said, stifling a yawn.

"If the rest of us hadn't held out so long, he wouldn't have needed the support of extremists," Cameron told her, ignoring the stubborn shake of Rory's head.

"Amanda?"

Listening to their conversation, Amanda hadn't noticed Patty turning her way. She opened the door.

"What's going on?"

"Honey, you should go back to bed," Patty told her gently. But Rory disagreed, saying Amanda needed to know what was happening.

Expecting the worst, Amanda sat on the bed between her mom and aunt. She let Patty put her free arm around her, being careful of her mom's other arm in a sling.

"A fringe group has taken over headquarters," Cameron answered simply. Frustration and exhaustion were written in every line of his face. "They have the International Council—and the High Council—barricaded in their chambers. I think they have Alvarsson in there, too."

"The International Council?" Amanda didn't understand. "They aren't supposed to meet until morning."

"That's the public session," Judy explained. "They had a closed session tonight to review tomorrow's agenda."

"The protestors didn't think they should be meeting privately," Rory added, before peeking around the side of one curtain. They had a view of the PTS building from that window and Amanda wondered what Rory could see.

"They always have a private session the night before," Judy defended. "It's protocol."

"Well, it's usually not in the midst of a rebellion." Rory readjusted the curtain. "The street is quiet. Nothing to tip off the normals yet."

"No one knows?" Amanda had pictured a scene from a movie with a police barricade around the building entrance and a mob watching the action.

"Everyone knows," Rory answered. "It's all over the traveler news, but we're good at keeping these things quiet from the rest of the world."

"Even in a revolution," Cameron added, sounding thoughtful. His eyes shifted toward the curtained windows as a frown darkened his face.

"Where's Lucas?" Amanda felt her mom's arm tighten around her.

"He's there, trying to reason with them," Rory said.

"And we're going to help him," Cameron added. He then clarified, "Not you, Amanda. Rory and I are going to help. You'll stay here with your mom and aunt."

After they left, Judy put on a pot of coffee, and Patty shooed Amanda back to the other room, telling her to get some sleep. Amanda pointed out that they weren't trying to sleep but went back to bed without a fight. Judy had given her a new phone after dinner, and she wanted to read the PTS news sites for herself.

Amanda was deep into an article on the Vertex when she heard her name called from the house.

She glanced toward the adjoining room where she heard the sound of a murmured conversation.

"Amanda Jones!" The call was more urgent.

Laying her phone on the bed, Amanda pulled the covers half over her head, closed her eyes, and met Lucas in the house.

§

"I shouldn't be here," Amanda protested, as she accepted a translator disc from the night guard in the Arcadian gatehouse. Meeting Lucas in the house, while her body appeared to be sleeping, was one thing, but sneaking out to Arcadia was sure to get her in trouble.

"It's fine." Lucas tossed her a forced smile as they clipped their discs in place. "Cameron and Rory are holding down the fort back at HQ, and I need your help here."

She almost asked if they knew Lucas was bringing her here but stopped herself. If Lucas had cleared it with them, Rory would have insisted on coming along.

They left the gatehouse, and Amanda paused in the empty parking lot. When Lucas urged her to follow him onto a hover cart, she held her ground. With a quiet sigh, he jumped off the cart and moved to her side.

Under the glow of a streetlight, Amanda noticed Lucas' ragged appearance. His eyes looked sunken above dark circles. His hair stood in rumpled clumps, and the stubble along his jaw had grown in uneven patches. His body was tense, and she instinctively pulled away from him.

"You said it was an emergency…" Amanda glanced at the sleeping city. "That you'd explain when we got here…"

"I will," Lucas swore, "but we aren't there yet. Just a short ride… We could walk, but the cart will be faster."

Amanda felt trapped as the dark night surrounded her. Lucas took a slow breath and pointed toward a faint light in the open field between the city and the river.

"Mitra is waiting for us."

The hover cart crossed the distance swiftly as Amanda kept silently repeating, *I can go back anytime.* Going back without a door would reset her origin point to Arcadia, but that didn't matter anymore. She'd already reset her origin point to the hotel by coming here and would have to fly home from Chicago with her mom and Cameron.

Nearing the light, Amanda saw two people standing beside a hover cart. She squinted. One looked like Mitra. She released a deep breath, relieved to see that Lucas wasn't lying. She hopped out of the hover cart and let Mitra catch both of her hands.

"She said you needed me," he said, searching Amanda's eyes worriedly.

Sophie Stavros stood in the shadows beside him.

"Good! You found him," Lucas told Sophie, before stepping close enough for their foreheads to briefly touch. "We need to do this quickly."

"Tell me what's going on," Amanda insisted, releasing Mitra's hands and facing Lucas directly.

"I will, I will… Just give me a second."

Lucas massaged his temples with both hands, staring at the ground. Sophie moved closer, gently rubbing his back with one hand as she tried to see his hidden face. After a moment, he stood up and lightly pressed her hand away.

A cold dread spread over Amanda. She'd seen that calculating expression before, during their first meeting on Terra-V.

"I thought I could handle it." he admitted, flashing a self-deprecating smirk. "I had everything under control. All the groups. The stragglers. The delegates. All of them. We were all set for a vote… but revolutions are messy."

"The Vertex?"

"Ah, you've heard of them." Lucas raised an eyebrow. "Rory and Cameron, I suppose. Well, yes, members of the Vertex tend to have their own way of seeing things."

"*The Traveler Times* says they're a hate group," Amanda told him, drawing a dismissive wave. "It says they believe travelers are genetically superior to normals and should rule over them."

"See, that's one of the problems of a shadow society!" Lucas threw his arms in the air and began to pace. "It breeds groups like the Vertex who feel like outsiders in their own world. They become so afraid of being found out—and further ostracized—that they try to get ahead of it by setting themselves up as a higher caste of humans.

"If we weren't secret though… If psychic travelers were a known and accepted part of humanity, we could avoid so much of that…"

"Wait!" Amanda stepped in the way of his pacing. "You want to tell the world about psychic travelers?"

"Well, yes," Lucas admitted easily. "Not all at once, but as a planned effort. Mitra! The Arcadians all know about psychic travel. That some of you can access your mindspace, and some of you can't. And it's fine, right?"

"Yes," Mitra agreed uneasily. "We all have our own abilities and place in society, and each place is important to the good of all people."

Amanda's head began to hurt. She mindlessly rubbed her temples as Lucas had earlier but dropped her hands as soon as she realized what she was doing.

"What are we doing here?" she asked. "Right now?"

Sophie stepped forward.

"You're connecting our mindspaces."

They paused for a beat. Amanda processed Sophie's revelation, realizing she wasn't surprised by it. Lucas studied Amanda's reaction. Mitra watched them all. He'd heard about Amanda's theory but hadn't expected to be woken in the night by the woman they'd seen by the river and brought out to this strange meeting.

"Why now?" Amanda sounded calmer than she felt. "What does this have to do with the Vertex?"

"I may have overplayed my hand there," Lucas admitted lightly. "Protesters from the Vertex were getting antsy about the meeting tomorrow. I know they hold the Arcadians in high regard, and I may have mentioned that you were close to getting them back into psychic travel."

"You what?"

Amanda's mind raced as she considered what that meant. The Vertex had taken the International Council hostage. Were they holding them captive until she delivered on Lucas' promise?

"I was vague on the details," Lucas defended with a flutter of both hands. "And I didn't say you could *definitely* do it, but if you could…"

"Amanda." Mitra stepped in, unable to stay patient any longer. "I don't understand what's happening. Who is this man? Why did this woman say you need my help?"

Amanda looked into his blue eyes, wishing she knew how to explain.

"Amanda." Lucas drew her attention, gesturing toward himself with both hands. "I need you to do this for me. We're so close to having a better system. Imagine if we could combine our worlds, benefit from the Arcadians' knowledge and technology. Imagine if we had intelligent, peace-loving Arcadians taking part in our High Council, being delegates on our International—no, *Interplanetary*—Council. Imagine the positive influence they could have on our world.

"We could have something like this…" He swept one arm toward the gleaming city. "This is the work you are meant to be doing. Not cheerleading and school dances. This is your destiny. To reunite our people and bring about actual peace."

"But…" Amanda's mind swam as she tried to remember Rory's earlier warnings. She'd be *throwing open the gates,* letting the Arcadians in without precautions or a plan. There were PTS guards on most of the worlds they could visit, but with the chaos of the rebellion, what would those guards do if Arcadians began showing up in their realms? They'd let Lucas into Arcadia…

"Amanda?" Mitra caught her hand, and she turned toward him, seeing the gentleness in his face.

"Your people," Amanda began uncertainly, "what would they do if they could suddenly access our mindspace? If I made a door that would let them in?"

"That is not something we are prepared to manage," Mitra faltered, glancing worriedly toward Lucas and Sophie. "Dr. Webb and I discussed it briefly, after your meeting. However, it would take us some time to test the safety of psychic travel for our people and decide the best way for our societies to interact…"

"You, see!" Lucas jumped in, slapping Mitra on the back. "Arcadians aren't invaders rushing in. They're more cautious than we are. We can work out an arrangement—a treaty—once we know the door works. And they would abide by it to the letter."

"Think of me," Sophie pleaded, easing into Amanda's view. "If this works, they could reverse my procedure. I could be a door away from my family, my child, and have real hope for my future. For all of our futures."

"Okay."

Amanda agreed instinctively. Maybe Lucas was right. Maybe this was her destiny. She thought about Drew, her mom, and Trina. All the people who could have a better life if the Arcadians could improve their world.

Rory flashed through her mind, but even she had said it was a good plan, just not the right time for it. Now, things had changed. The delegates were in danger, the revolution was falling apart. This could bring it all back together…

"I already picked a place in our mindspace," Amanda told Lucas in a quivering voice. "For the connection."

"We can have Mitra try to ground you from here, where there's lots of empty space," Lucas suggested. "In case you accidentally create a proximal door to Arcadia instead."

Amanda felt her throat go dry. Her hands shook.

"Good thinking. If I go to the mindspace from here, this will be my origin point. Maybe that will help."

She turned to Mitra and took both of his hands.

"You can help me." She lowered her voice, looking at his face for any sign of resistance or warning, but he easily agreed. "Go into your mindspace and picture me clearly, like in our training sessions. Can you do that?"

"Easily," Mitra whispered. His eyes softened, making Amanda's trembling stomach melt into her toes. She pushed the feeling away.

Back in the mindspace, Amanda was surprised to see daylight in the grassy area beside the houses. She'd traveled through mindspace houses at night before but had never noticed if there was light outside their windows. She made a mental note to ask the engineers about that during their next visit, then remembered that she'd planned to do this with Dorothy and Elaine's help.

She could mentally call for them now, but Mitra and the others were already waiting.

I made a door before without anyone's help, she told herself defiantly. Until the image of an opalescent face reminded her that she'd created the door to Terra-V with Alira by her side.

Amanda looked around the empty lawn feeling more alone than she had ever been before.

Voices argued in her mind. Maybe it was the wrong time. But people were counting on her.

With closed eyes, Amanda took several breaths and shifted her consciousness into the mindspace. When she opened her eyes, she was alone in a hazy black void.

With each breath, she imagined the energy within her growing into an orb of white light. Once the light had grown, she sent it into the darkness in front of her, seeking Mitra's outline as she'd seen it before.

It didn't take long to find him.

The buzz in Amanda's head became louder as she studied Mitra's gray, featureless shape. She mentally drew in his face. His smooth forehead and high cheekbones. His thin chin and angled jawline. His straight nose and blue eyes.

She lingered over his eyes, clearly seeing a web of pale lines swirling through the blue, like a stormy sky. She saw the sparkle in his eyes, their depth, and felt that familiar melting sensation through the core of her being.

In quick succession, her mind flashed to Mitra's lab, sitting by the windows with him—then to the Arcadian street, standing close to him in the quiet zone—then to the open field near the river where they'd last been together. Amanda fought against those images, struggling to keep herself here—in this moment—with Mitra in his mindspace and she in her own.

Mitra! Her mind called out to him and she thought she heard his reply, like a tiny whisper echoing across a great distance. *He's in his space; I'm in mine.* She repeated the phrase over and over.

She saw his face, imposed on a hazy gray shadow, standing behind a sheer veil. The edge of the bubble. She could sense its strength and the beginning of a weakness that frightened her. *Stop! Don't!*

A warning rebounded through her thoughts. Rory's face flashed through her mind. *Not yet,* she heard Rory's voice and tried to pull away from Mitra. Away from the shimmering edge between them.

I can do this! Another voice called out. *It's right here. It would be so easy.* Her eyes narrowed in on the space just around Mitra's shadowy form. *It's just a door,* the voice continued, *nothing more.*

"Amanda!" Rory's shout shattered the darkness.

A blinding light flashed through Amanda's mind, and she dropped to her hands and knees in the grass. Nausea overtook her and she retched, though nothing came up. Gasping for air, she rolled to her back and opened her eyes to see a blanket of stars in a night sky.

She was back on Arcadia.

"You are such a child!"

Rory was shouting, and Amanda cringed at her words.

"You want what you want, and you don't think about the consequences!"

"Rory," Cameron broke in gently, "calm down."

"No!" Rory shouted, her voice shaking with anger. "This was completely irresponsible!"

Amanda squeezed her eyes shut, holding back sudden tears as Rory railed on.

"And to drag Amanda into this? Without any regard to her safety!"

Amanda turned her aching head to see Rory yelling at Lucas while he slouched with his arms crossed and his head down. A moment later, she felt someone kneel by her side and lightly touch her arm.

"Amanda?" Mitra hovered over her, his face a mask of fear. "Are you all right?"

After helping her sit up, Mitra and Amanda watched Cameron pull Rory away from Lucas. She stomped around the grass, shaking both hands, while Sophie kept a wary distance near the parked hover carts. Cameron took Rory's place in front of Lucas, but spoke with an understanding, fatherly tone.

"You have to accept that you aren't on your own anymore. You may have needed these stunts to get attention once, but you don't need them now. You have people who want to help you. If you'll let them."

Lucas lifted his face slowly, then dropped his eyes back to the ground.

"Your heart is in the right place," Cameron continued. "You see things others miss—things I missed for too long—and you want to make them right. But let other people help you—let me help you."

Amanda watched, in awe, as Cameron held out his arms. Lucas stumbled forward. He let Cameron embrace him as he wrapped his own arms around Cameron's strong back. Sitting in the dew-damp grass, Amanda felt Mitra brush a lock of hair away from her face. She turned to face him, seeing a yearning as he leaned close, and she carefully eased away. Their eyes met and he smiled sadly.

Rory tramped across the grass and crouched beside them, forearms on her thighs.

"You okay?" she asked brusquely, without meeting Amanda's eyes.

"I guess," Amanda muttered, feeling another wave of nausea. "Rory, I was only trying to—"

Rory sharply raised one hand to stop her.

"Not now," she snapped, scowling at two hover carts gliding toward them from the city. "It looks like we all have some explaining to do."

Mitra stood and walked toward the hover carts, meeting up with Lucas and Cameron. Rory moved to join them, but Amanda caught her arm to hold her back.

"Are the delegates okay? Back at headquarters?"

Rory exhaled heavily.

"They're fine. We pulled together a strike team and disarmed the Vertex without any casualties. Which Lucas would have known if he hadn't run off on his own."

§

The next morning, the International Council met as scheduled. Their session was held in a customized chamber on the 22nd floor of the headquarters building. Though Amanda knew there would be representatives from all over the world, she hadn't been prepared for the reality of hundreds of delegates gathered in one place.

The council chamber nearly filled the whole floor of the building, with a ceiling that spanned two stories. Three sections of delegate seats were built on auditorium-style risers and arranged in a semi-circle facing a dais where the High Council sat, opposite the International Council. Each seat had a button panel on one armrest, along with earpiece that could connect to simultaneous interpretation in any of the nine official languages used among the delegates.

Above the main floor, balcony seats were available to reporters and guests. There was also a small box of seats off to the right of the main dais. The box was reserved for the Director of PTS, special guests, and non-delegates who would be presenting information during the session.

Amanda, Patty, Judy, Rory, and Cameron were seated in the second and third row of the box seats. Lucas and former Director Alvarsson sat in the first row with two empty seats between them.

During a normal session, the chamber had several empty seats. Nations would frequently send only one or two of their three delegates unless there was an issue of particular importance to their region. The balconies usually had space for anyone who cared to attend in person, and the box seating was often only occupied by the director.

Today, the chamber was packed beyond capacity. Every nation had brought all three of their delegates. Some had brought additional leaders who insisted on being present, even if they did not have a vote.

Without enough seats, some sat in the aisles or stood in clusters near the doorways. The balconies were even more packed with some viewers kneeling by the railing or sitting on someone's lap. Even the main dais was crowded. Guards hovered behind the High Council members, who had been lightly sedated to keep them from traveling if the vote went against them.

The only empty seats were in the special box seating, and Amanda was glad to have some breathing room. From her seat in the second row, between her mom and aunt, she could see the thinning spot on top of the former director's head and a shaving nick on the back of his neck. Lucas had also shaved for the session, leaving a light stubble that played well against his smoothly arranged hair and crisp suit.

Having never been to an International Council session, Amanda wasn't sure if the chaos erupting between speeches was normal or a result of the push to replace the High Council. The end of each speech brought a fresh wave of terror, not knowing when she or her mother might be called to speak.

Amanda used an earpiece to listen to the speeches that weren't given in English but wished she had an Arcadian translator disc instead. The disc changed a speaker's words in her brain, making it a seamless translation. With the earpiece, Amanda could hear both the person speaking in the room and the interpreter talking in her ear.

By the time Lucas rose to speak, her nerves were shot, and she felt ill enough to need to visit the restroom. Patty offered to join her, and a guard led them to the ladies' room out in the hall.

"Are you okay?" Patty asked, as Amanda splashed some cold water on her face.

"Yeah, I just needed a break."

"I understand," Patty said gently, then looked toward the door as if making sure they were still alone. "Amanda, there's something we haven't talked about. About that night…"

Straightening up from the sink, Amanda reached for a paper towel and waited. She didn't have to be told which night her mom meant.

"Those bags in the trunk," Patty continued, looking down at her fingernails.

"Oh, that." Amanda shrugged. "It's okay."

Patty looked up, searching Amanda's face.

"I wasn't taking you away," she insisted. "I just wanted to be prepared…"

"Just in case," Amanda finished for her.

They shared a soft smile.

"Yeah," Patty agreed. "It's good to be prepared because you never know what life will throw at you."

"I get it." Amanda tossed the paper towel in the trash and gave her mom a long hug, being careful of her injured arm. "I'm just glad to have you back."

Patty wrapped her free arm around Amanda and pressed her cheek against her hair. They were still in an embrace when the bathroom door slammed open.

"Well, that's over," Rory announced. "We should get out of here before the crowd."

"It's over?" Amanda asked, trying to read Rory's stony expression. "What happened?"

"The High Council is out," she answered drily. "And Lucas is the new Director of PTS."

CHAPTER 22

THE ARCHITECT'S JOURNEY

"So, it was all about him taking charge."

Amanda eyed Drew skeptically. They were sitting on one of the couches in the party room. Amanda had her back against a couch arm and her legs bent across Drew's lap. Drew had one hand on her legs while the other was slowly twirling a lock of her hair.

With so many changes happening within PTS, Amanda had stayed in Chicago through Friday and flown home with her mom and Cameron this morning. They had been tired from the trip and surprised to find Drew camped outside their apartment door. They were even more surprised when he jumped to his feet and pulled Amanda into his arms.

Recovering his cool, Cameron had calmly suggested Amanda and Drew go catch up downstairs while he helped Patty unpack.

In the party room, they had settled into the couch, carefully not talking about how worried Drew had been or how glad Amanda felt to be home. Catching him up on the week's events had been easier. Until Drew's comment about Lucas.

"He's not exactly taking charge," Amanda responded uneasily. "Lucas organized the whole rebellion. It makes sense that he'd be part of the new leadership."

"I guess." Drew shrugged, seeming to lose interest in the politics of PTS now that he'd heard the whole story.

"He'll report to the High Council."

The members of the new High Council had been elected on Friday, and Cameron was one of them. Amanda was happy for him, but she wondered how much that would change things. For her and her mom, though she wasn't ready to think about that.

"In theory."

Drew hadn't liked hearing about Lucas' push to connect the Arcadians' mindspace. He'd echoed Rory's arguments and Amanda didn't want to rekindle that topic.

"What did I miss at school?"

"Well…" Drew released her hair and let his hand rest behind her back. "There's not a lot of political intrigue, but there is some news…" He paused, eyeing her cautiously before saying, "Trina dumped Trey."

"Really?!" Amanda sat straight up and instinctively clasped both hands over the arm Drew had rested across her legs.

"Yep!" Drew laughed. "Right in the middle of lunch. Called him some choice names, too. I really wished you'd been there."

"Me, too!"

A wave of relief washed over Amanda. She looked at Drew, realizing their faces were inches apart. Their smiles faded, and a questioning gaze passed between them.

Amanda said, "I was only worried about Trina, you know? I don't care what Trey does otherwise."

"I know," Drew said in a voice just above a whisper.

Amanda's heart fluttered as she remembered a moment on the dance floor, just before she'd caught sight of Trina and Trey. She and Drew had been dancing close. His arms had felt safe and warm.

"Can I ask you something?" Drew interrupted her thoughts.

"Yeah, anything," she whispered, nervous but ready to see where this was going.

"When you went back into the school, after tryouts, did you withdraw your name?"

"What?" Amanda blinked, easing back to look at his face more fully.

"I've just been wondering about it."

"Oh." Amanda leaned against the arm of the couch, feeling strangely disappointed. "Well, yeah. But don't tell anyone, okay?"

"I won't." Drew stared off into the distance. "I mean, I'm not surprised. It would have been cool if you'd made it, but I know you have things that are more important than… school and stuff."

Drew's face hardened slightly. Amanda imagined what she'd given up. Cheering from the sidelines with a group of normal students, riding the game bus with Drew, hanging out with the other kids… with Drew.

A surge of regret spread from Amanda's chest into her flushed face. Pushing past her awkward confusion, she could see that Drew was hurting and trying not to show it.

"Drew, I…"

He faced her, and Amanda's mind went completely blank. *Tell him he's important, too!* her mind shouted. But the words were stuck in her throat.

She leaned in closer, seeing Drew's uncertainty before she closed her eyes and pressed her lips against his.

The sensation took them both by surprise. Amanda pulled back before Drew could respond but stayed only inches away, staring deep into his eyes.

"Was that okay?" she whispered nervously, then felt his arms wrap around her.

"More than okay." He smiled softly, before pulling her in for a deeper, longer kiss.

Though his arms stayed around her back, Drew was the first to pull away. He looked into Amanda's eyes, then sighed and loosened his grip, settling her back against the arm of the couch and taking her hands in his.

"Part of me has been wanting to do that for a long time," he said carefully. "Part of me has wanted to tell you that I like you, as more than a friend, as a… well, you know.

"But this other part of me knows you have a lot going on, important stuff. And I don't want to pressure you. You know? Because I'm your friend, even if I hope to be more… I don't want to mess that up or make your life harder."

"Drew…" Amanda felt tears gathering in her eyes and an unbearable warmth filling her chest. Seeing her tears, Drew looked down and shook his head.

"I get it," he said gruffly. "Don't pretend because you feel bad for me."

"Drew!" Amanda said sharply, getting his attention before she laughed lightly. "I liked what you said. It just made me feel…"

She searched for the words, then pointed at her own face in exasperation. "This is me being happy."

"Really?" He gently traced his fingertip over a tear that had spilled down her cheek.

"Yeah, feelings are just kinda… *weird* for me," Amanda admitted. "I mean, you're right. I do have a lot going on, and I don't know what I'm thinking or feeling half the time. I know I like you, more than any other friends—or anyone else—but I don't know what that means, or what you expect, or what I'm ready for…"

"Shh." Drew rested his finger against her lips and smiled. "I don't expect anything. Let's go slow and figure it out together."

They leaned close, lips not touching but hovering close. Amanda studied his familiar dark eyes, noticing how the brown had tiny lines radiating toward the center like creases in velvet. She shifted her eyes, noticing the texture of his dark skin and a tiny black dot below his left eye. He was the same but different at this distance. Her feelings for him were also the same but different.

She was about to tilt her head for another kiss, when the door crashed open, and they startled apart.

"Oh, sorry!" Trina blushed, crossing one arm over her chest to tightly clasp her opposite arm. "I guess you're feeling better then."

"Uh, yeah." Amanda awkwardly swung her legs off of Drew's lap and clambered to her feet.

Trina rocked on her heels, looking between the two of them until Drew stood up more smoothly and gave Amanda a quick kiss on the temple.

"It's okay," he told Trina. "You two should talk. Amanda, text me later, okay?"

Amanda watched him walk out, wishing he would stay.

She and Trina eyed each other warily. Neither knew where to begin.

"I heard about Trey," Amanda said, then backtracked at the sight of Trina's alarmed eyes. "I mean, that you broke up with him. Drew didn't tell me anything else."

Trina nodded, her face relaxing a bit.

"I'm glad you're better," she told Amanda with a timid smile. "On Monday, I kinda thought you were skipping because you didn't want to see me. You know, after the dance. But then Drew said you really were out sick, and when you were out all week… Well, I called, and your mom said you were better, and I could come over…"

Amanda nodded, not knowing what Judy had told Drew, or what Drew had told Trina.

"Drew said you lost your phone, too?"

"Oh, yeah, I did!" Amanda reassured her. "I wasn't avoiding you or anything. I lost it at the, uh, doctor. But I have a new phone now. Same number."

"Cool." Trina nodded. Then, shook her head, saying, "This is stupid. Look, you were right about Trey. He was full of crap, and I caught him kissing Sheila Williams, and I feel like a complete idiot."

Amanda stepped closer to Trina, feeling outraged on her behalf. "What a jerk!"

"He really is," Trina agreed. "But I'm the jerk who believed him."

Amanda shook her head, quickly correcting her.

"You're not a jerk. I was a jerk to you at the dance. I was worried about you, but I blamed you, and I shouldn't have. Sometimes…" Amanda hesitated.

She remembered how Lucas had talked her into trying to connect the Arcadian mindspace. At the dance, she had said Trina was desperate to feel important, but maybe there was more to it than that.

"Sometimes we want to believe something so badly, that we kind of let ourselves believe it, even if we know we shouldn't. You know?"

"And we don't even see that we're doing it," Trina agreed, then shook her head in irritation. "I don't know what I was thinking!"

Neither do I, Amanda thought but didn't say.

§

Later that evening, after having dinner with her mom, Judy, and Cameron, Amanda locked the door to her bedroom and went back to Chicago alone. She wasn't sure what she would find, given the recent turmoil, but the headquarters building was quiet. There was no one else in the entry atrium. The halls were empty. But when Amanda reached the director's office, she found Lucas by the window, looking out at the pinks and purples in the sky as the sun set over the city.

"It's a lot to take in," he said, without turning to see who had entered.

Amanda walked closer, catching sight of her reflection in the glass, and knew he wasn't talking about the sunset.

Thinking about the view from Dr. Webb's office, Amanda wondered what she would think of Chicago. If she were ever able to make the trip.

It was harder to imagine Mitra here. He belonged in Arcadia and she'd rather keep him there.

"What will happen to the High Council?" Amanda asked after some time had passed. "I mean, the old council. Madame Ellis and the others."

"They've been taken to a holding facility for now. Pending an investigation into their undisclosed projects," Lucas answered without concern. "All except our friend, Ben. He was on the High Council for less than a year and didn't know most of what Ellis and the others were up to in private.

"He's on probation and will act in a sort of advisory role for now. Maybe he'll even earn a seat again. If any of the new members don't work out."

He spoke as if the High Council didn't matter to him much anymore.

They moved away from the window. Lucas gestured for Amanda to sit in a wine-red upholstered chair. He poured himself a drink, offered her a soda, and then settled into the plush leather chair behind his mahogany desk.

"Did you mean what you said on Arcadia?" Amanda asked bluntly. "About telling the whole world about psychic travelers."

Lucas set his glass aside and crossed his hands on the desk, eyeing Amanda intently.

"Yes. You think that's a mistake?"

"I don't think it will work here," Amanda told him. "Not like it does on Arcadia. This is a totally different place, and people here don't trust what they don't understand. If they can even believe it."

Lucas held his neutral expression, though Amanda saw a small twitch near his right eye. She remembered seeing him collapse into Cameron's arms and couldn't reconcile that man with the hardened rebel who sat before her now. After a moment, he released his hands and leaned into his chair with a bitter laugh.

"You sound like everyone else."

He picked up his drink and swiveled his chair to one side, throwing his leg over an arm of the chair in the process. Amanda swirled the ice in her soda, guessing Director Alvarsson had never sprawled in his chair like that.

"So, you aren't going to tell the world," she pressed, earning an eye roll and sigh from Lucas.

"No," he confirmed reluctantly before taking a large swallow of his drink.

"But think about it," he went on. "You were afraid to tell your mom—everyone was afraid to tell your mom—and that turned out okay."

"Yeah," Amanda hedged, "but she's just one person…"

"Yeah, okay." Lucas raised a hand to end the subject. "Don't worry, I won't do anything until everyone agrees. But I won't stop pushing for what I think is right either."

"Like Arcadia?"

Lucas kept his sprawled slouch but let his head loll in Amanda's direction. She didn't have to explain what she meant. They both knew she was referring to connecting their mindspaces.

"Rory has some good points about that," Lucas conceded.

"Ye-es," Amanda drew the word out, unsure how to respond.

"But you want to do it anyway?" Lucas asked, already nodding knowingly. "You want to do it just to see if you can, but you don't want the responsibility for whatever happens if it works."

Amanda squirmed in her seat and looked at the ice in her glass. She'd given it a lot of thought over the last few days—ever since Rory had stopped her—and always came back to the same place. Lucas was right.

She wanted to create the door but didn't want to think about the consequences. She'd let Lucas convince her to try because she'd *wanted* to believe it was the right thing to do, even if another part of her had known it wasn't.

The situation reminded her of Tina and Trey, but with one big difference. Lucas hadn't been lying to her.

Lucas believed everything he'd said on that field in Arcadia. He wanted Arcadians and travelers to have an easy connection through the mindspace. He wanted a world where everyone knew about psychic travel and accepted it as a normal part of life.

He believed those things would lead to a better world, and he believed he could make them happen. He was an idealist.

Realizing that, Amanda remembered something Gerald had once told her: *There's nothing more dangerous than an idealist with unlimited power.*

"Dr. Webb sent you a message."

"What?" Amanda was so lost in thought, Lucas had to repeat his statement.

"It's not Edmund's documents," he added before she could ask. "It's just a note."

He opened a drawer, fished around until he pulled out a thin sheet of paper, and slid it across the desk toward Amanda. It was a handwritten note, though given the language barrier Amanda doubted Dr. Webb had written it herself. She would need a traveler to put her words into written English, and Amanda guessed the writing belonged to Sophie.

She ran her fingertips over the clothlike paper before reading the letter.

Amanda,

You are a promising young woman who will one day be a gifted architect and an asset to both of our communities. However, you are not yet ready to begin the architect's journey. I will continue to monitor your progress and gladly bestow Edmund's gift when the time is right.

With sincerity,
Agnes Webb

Amanda lifted her eyes from the letter and saw Lucas watching her over the rim of his glass. He'd sat up in his chair and had his elbows held tight to his chest.

Knowing he would comment on her reaction, Amanda set the letter on the desk casually and hid any trace of disappointment.

"She's probably right. I'll just have to be patient."

Lucas lowered his glass and smiled slyly.

"You may be more ready than Agnes Webb knows, Amanda Jones."

Amanda smiled, unable to resist his praise.

"But what does she mean by the architect's journey?"

Lucas put his drink on the table and planted his feet on the floor.

"I was waiting for you to ask!" He laughed gleefully. "I am not as patient as you, so I have an answer for you. Apparently, the *architect's journey* is what those in the know call a psychic architect's training.

"Remember when Agnes said multiple societies were entrusted with training documents? Part of your training will be a quest to track down all the documents and complete the tasks they describe."

"Dr. Webb told you that?" Amanda felt stunned that no one had mentioned this before.

"Of course not!" Lucas waved off the question. "She says she's already told us too much. I went to Terra-V and convinced Alira to tell me."

"Alira?" The name was enough to calm Amanda's racing mind. Her thoughts echoed in rhythm with an image of tuntum trees lowering for the night. *Tuntum. Tuntum.*

Lucas grinned. "Can you believe she's known all this time but has also been waiting for the *time to be right?*"

A weight draped over Amanda as she processed the idea. Alira and Dr. Webb had been secretly watching her, looking for signs of what? Advanced psychic ability? Or something else completely? Maturity? Wisdom?

She didn't like the idea of being watched and judged. Even worse, she didn't know when the test would be over or what she needed to do to pass.

There was a knock on the door, and a young man entered with a stack of file folders. Amanda recognized him as Director Alvarsson's assistant.

"Amanda, you know Brody, right?" Lucas laughed. "You know how I've mentioned friends in high places? Brody's been my inside man for years. Alvarsson had no idea! He might suspect now, since I'm keeping Brody on, but who cares? Alvarsson's out, right, Brody?"

"Finally!" Brody sounded a little nervous as he eyed Amanda, then quietly explained what papers he was dropping off.

When Brody left, Amanda set down her glass and looked at Lucas suspiciously.

"Maybe I should ask Brody something about Director Alvarsson," she ventured in a carefully neutral tone.

"*Former* Director Alvarsson," Lucas corrected, then waved for her to go on.

"Right, *former* Director Alvarsson," Amanda repeated. "I know I upset him that day at the hospital, but having my mom detained was a really aggressive reaction to that. Doesn't it seem a little… strange?"

"No," Lucas answered with a nonchalant shake of his head. "Alvarsson's a petty man, it wouldn't take much for him to pull something like that."

Amanda considered that perspective.

"I guess. It was lucky timing though."

"How do you mean?"

Lucas leaned back in his chair, gazed at a far wall, and used his foot to swivel his chair in short, lazy arcs.

"Well, it was lucky he ran into me at the hospital. And it was lucky he got upset enough to do that." Amanda spelled it out as Lucas continued to swivel his chair. "I mean, you were hoping people would worry about Gerald enough to protest, but taking my mom away was so much better."

Lucas stopped rocking and faced Amanda, cocking his head to one side.

"You don't seriously think I would tell Alvarsson to have your mother detained? Or that he would even listen to me if I did?"

They stared at each other across the wide table.

"He told the International Council that the whole thing was a big misunderstanding," Amanda reminded, trying to remember Alvarsson's testimony. "He said he'd written out the plan but never ordered it."

"And every member of the High Council said he was lying," Lucas countered. "They had a copy of the order with his signature."

The chair stopped moving. Lucas put both hands flat on his desk, holding Amanda's gaze.

"I've told you before, Amanda, I am not your enemy. I'm the one who has told you the truth from the beginning.

I'm on your side. I might not be perfect, but I am one of the good guys. Okay?"

Looking into his concerned face, Amanda wanted to believe in him. He *had* told her the truth when everyone else was lying.

She nodded and hesitantly returned his smile.

"That's my girl!" Lucas grinned. "We have an exciting future ahead of us, my friend! We're going to find all the guardians of Edmund's precious documents and show them you are ready to be trained. And then we'll go on that architect's journey together. You, me, and Rory. We'll go to Arcadia, Terra-V, and wherever else the path takes us.

"I've been to so many worlds filled with sights you can't even imagine. Crystal mountains, 100-foot carvings, a sea of sugar water that is covered in the most beautiful butterflies. There is so much I can show you!"

The room dimmed as the last traces of pink sky were swallowed by the encroaching night. To their right, amber sconces on either side of a wide cabinet cast a soft glow across the desk and added a gleam to Lucas' eyes.

The idea of the architect's journey both thrilled and terrified Amanda. It was exciting to imagine a quest to other worlds with Lucas and Rory by her side.

"You will master your abilities and build a mindspace house of your own. And then, together, we will make PTS better for all travelers. Maybe even make whole worlds better for everyone!"

Lucas shifted to a more serious tone. "But I need you to believe I am on your side. I need you to know that I would never cause you harm. Do you believe me?"

"I believe you," Amanda answered in a near whisper, still caught up in the images his words had conjured.

Later that night, as she nestled under her covers, Amanda pictured the worlds they would visit and the tasks she would have to master on her path to becoming a full-fledged psychic architect. The visions sent her heart racing and put a smile on her face.

Yet before she drifted off to sleep, Amanda's mind replayed Lucas' words, *I would never cause you harm,* and she remembered something Rory had once said:

Who decides what counts as harm?

The Story Continues...

Amanda Jones discovered her psychic travel abilities in *Healers and Thieves* and formed new alliances in *Family and Foes*. As *The Psychic Traveler Society* continues, Amanda will explore new worlds and face new challenges. But will the architect's journey deepen her training or spark events that could change her own world forever?

Visit SusanQuilty.com for series updates.

Discussion Questions
Spoilers ahead

1. In *Family and Foes,* Amanda regularly visits Arcadia, a highly advanced world that showcases human potential, yet the mystical world of Terra-V has a special place in her heart. If you could visit only one of these worlds, which would you choose? What would you want to do while you were there?

2. Amanda tries out for cheerleading because she wants to be a "normal" high school student. Trina's sister is shown having lots of friends from different social groups. What do you think it means to be "normal" in high school? Do you think it's good to have diverse friend groups?

3. Living in her aunt's apartment caused tension between her mom and aunt. Do you think Patty should have been told about Amanda's psychic travel abilities before they moved in? Do you think Cameron was right to tell Patty when he did? Should he have talked to Amanda first?

4.   Frustrated by the slow pace of her training, Amanda acts out by sneaking off-world, missing classes, and giving Mitra banned books. Do you sympathize with her behavior? Should she have been more patient?

5.   Arcadian society developed through human settlers who wanted to build a better world, avoiding what they saw as the dark side of humanity. People often have similar dreams of colonizing Mars or moving to a deserted island. Do you think a fresh start could lead to a better world? Or does society always breed inequality, crime, and wars?

6.   The psychic engineers are happy to teach Amanda what they know and are honest about what they don't know. They are confident in their own abilities and treat Amanda with respect. Do you think those are good qualities in a teacher? What have you liked about your favorite teachers?

7.   At the school dance, Amanda worries that she should have more interest in dating and romance. She also struggles to define her feelings for Drew. Why do you think she has those thoughts? Where do teenagers hear messages that tell them to act or feel certain ways?

8.   Amanda and Trina have an uneasy friendship, and Trey continues to cause trouble. Are you happy that Amanda and Trina made up in the end? Why do you think Trey acts the way he does?

9.   Lucas' role in the Psychic Traveler Society has changed greatly by the end of the book. Do you think Amanda can trust him?

ACKNOWLEDGMENTS

Writing *Family and Foes* has had its challenges. This is the second book in my first series, which makes it my first experience with writing a sequel. As a reader, I know there is a fine line between referencing events from an earlier book and over-explaining previously established points. Finding that balance with a subject like psychic travel took some effort—and a lot of rewrites!

The Covid-19 pandemic brought its own difficulties. My own health complications delayed the release of Family and Foes by about four months. There were also days when the mental and emotional strain so many of us are feeling took an added toll. It has been hard to cancel book signings and other events. I miss meeting my readers, just as I miss seeing family and friends.

Though we are physically distancing, we need our social connections more than ever. Without the support of my family and friends, this book may have never been finished. Particular thanks go to my husband, Peter Quilty, who shares his support and love in a thousand ways each day.

There are those who helped with this book more directly, by being early readers or helping me talk through logistics and world-building, as well as those who offered support in other ways. While there are too many people to name them all, special thanks go to Jen Pool, Angel Fischer, Michael Cherry, Brian Dunne, Wendy McMullan, Gretchen Schutte, David Fischer, Erika Lundquist, Michael Andrews, Stacy Foster, and Scot Kight.

Thanks to John Baisch, founder of Paladin Martial Arts, who taught me the self-defense techniques that have worked their way into Amanda's repertoire. And, as always, thank you to the owners and staff of Comic Logic Books & Artwork who go above and beyond to support indie authors and artists.

I would also like to acknowledge everyone who has read my books, written reviews, connected with me on social media, or supported me through Patreon.com. Extra special thanks to the generous donations of patrons Stacy Foster and Perry McGrath. Managing my own publishing can be incredibly daunting. All of your support keeps me going!

I hope we can all get back to some form of "normal" soon. In the meantime, I am looking into new ways we can connect on social media, and I hope reading helps you add some more joy to your day. Thank you for sharing in Amanda Jones' adventures!

About the Author

Susan Quilty is an indie author who loves sharing her imaginary worlds with fellow book lovers. *The Psychic Traveler Society* is her first adventure in young adult fiction. The series began with *Healers and Thieves* in 2019. Previous novels include *The Insistence of Memory* (2017) and *To the Left of Death* (2018).

You can learn more about Susan and her upcoming projects by following her on social media or visiting her website: SusanQuilty.com.

Freely Written: A Podcast

Are you ready for a story break?

Join author Susan Quilty as she uses simple prompts to free write her way into strange, silly, or poignant tales. Weekly episodes offer new stories, while bonus episodes share behind-the-scenes commentary. Episodes are short, about 10 minutes each, and suggestions for future writing prompts are always welcome!

Find **Freely Written** on your favorite podcast app.